FISSION
AMONG THE
FANATICS
Tom Bradley

SPUYTEN DUYVIL
NEW YORK CITY

copyright © 2007 Tom Bradley

ISBN 1-933132-33-7

cover art by Brian Strang

Library of Congress Cataloging-in-Publication Data

Bradley, Tom.
Fission among the fanatics / Tom Bradley.
p. cm.
ISBN-13: 978-1-933132-33-4
  1. Bradley, Tom. 2. Authors, American--20th century--Biography. I.
Title.

PS3552.R232Z46 2006
813'.54--dc22
[B]
2006022044

I

In some sort of crude sense which no vulgarity, no humor, no overstatement can quite extinguish, the physicists have known sin; and this is a knowledge which they cannot lose. —J. Robert Oppenheimer

Expatriate novelists are often interrogated about their hometowns. Everyone seems to doubt that it's possible, in exile, to retain that "sense of place" which is supposed to be so essential for writing "anchored" fiction, whatever that is. It sounds like fish stories to me.

I can never respond to this sort of question without sounding morbid, because my particular Bethlehem and its accompanying "sense of place" are bound up with my own premature death, and with the destruction of the human race at large. I was born downwind in Utah in the heat of the aboveground hydrogen bomb test era. There's a projected mass die-off of Utahns my exact age, of thyroid cancer, due to commence any day now. It's not just the poor Uighurs in East Turkestan who get whining rights.

I remember in kindergarten peeking out the lunchroom window and seeing the sky blacker than midnight. It was a flat and unwholesome shade that I've never seen since. Nobody talked about it, including the other kids, which seems pretty odd in retrospect. Large portions of Nevada real estate were passing overhead, and it didn't even make the six o'clock news.

Edward Teller, the famed father of that blackness, showed up several years later with a suspicious lack of fanfare. He gave a couple perfunctory speeches in obscure high school auditoriums—discreetly checking the subject population for mongoloids and harelips, no doubt. He wasn't disappointed.

Answering a question about arms limitation, he said, with a straight face (or at least as straight as that face could ever get), "We had arms limitation from the beginning. It commenced already with the second detonation."

Apparently the first detonation was so huge that it blew a hole right through the stratosphere, and the destructive payload was dissipated in space, quite uneconomically. Teller is famous for betting that "device" would ignite the atmosphere and turn the planet to cinders.

It's not just a simple question of resenting Eddy and Oppy and the boys at the Los Alamos labs, and feeling the victim's comfy sense of moral superiority. I'm not about to hijack the term "Holocaust" for the six-million-and-first time. Those scientists were pursuing a vocation qualitatively identical to the novelist's. And once you've received a vocation, you pursue it or die. If you're not the suicidal type, you don't even have that choice—which makes it as much a part of your metabolic activity as eating or excreting or growing tumors in your neck.

Any serious creative work will reach a certain critical mass, after which it takes off on its own, and you're just hanging on, serving as the amanuensis, your conscious will playing virtually no part at all. It's the most delightful experience imaginable. The word "delight" hardly begins to encompass it. You need to shift upward to the metaphysical lexicon. Anyone who has felt it, or has read an adequate description of the experience, knows that nothing else matters at that particular moment. The world can go up in flames all around your desk, and probably will, if you do the work right, and you don't give a damn.

I'm sure that's what those Poindexters were feeling in the desert outside my hometown fifty years ago. Only in their case the big conflagration wasn't metaphorical. "I am become death, destroyer of worlds," said Oppy on TV (pretending to try, with a more or less recondite reference to the *Bhagavad-Gita*, to rehabilitate himself in the eyes of the liberal intelligentsia, when he knew very well that his perfect face had already done the job for him the moment he went on camera).

It's not just Department of Defense flunkies like him who have access to universally lethal knowledge. In the apocryphal Acts of Thomas, Jesus takes his doubting disciple aside and whispers three esoteric words. When the other apostles crowd around and demand to know what the Master said, Thomas replies, "If I were to reveal even one of those words, you would take up stones to kill me, and those stones would turn to fire and burn you up."

Every writer has just such moments. He looks up from his manuscript, his head reels, and, like Melville, he gasps, "I have written a wicked work." With Coleridge, he says of himself—

> . . . *Beware! Beware!*
> *His flashing eyes, his floating hair!*
> *Weave a circle round him thrice,*
> *And close your eyes with holy dread,*
> *For he on honeydew hath fed,*
> *And drunk the milk of paradise.*

In other words, "Publish this book, big fella, and the world comes to an end." And there's not even a momentary quibble. To Hell with the world, and with me!"

So, indignation is not one of my reactions to those thermonuclear poems of the fifties. Smug victimology isn't part of my "sense of place." But, then again, my thyroid is still intact. Maybe I should hold off publishing this book for a few months, till I've grown twin goiters that can be used as flashlights when the power's out.

Meanwhile, take another look at those gorgeous films of the H-bomb explosions in my back yard. See how the whole sky peels back like a popped blister, and this column rises up into the dilated firmament like a refulgent hard-on. If I could be the first guy to cause that to happen, I doubt I'd be Christly enough to demur. Anybody who's seen or been an adolescent boy with a bag of Wyoming cherry bombs knows the feeling.

Fortunately, almost nobody is approached in the desert by such a great Satan. So it's difficult to get moralistic about those who are buttonholed by the really large temptations, and succumb. It's like feeling holier than a certain president of the previous century because you never ordered up dry fellatio from an underling in your private office—when you have neither underlings nor office, nor indeed that very power which is, as Kissinger reminded Mao (as if Mao needed reminding), the "ultimate aphrodisiac."

*   *   *   *

In the opening weeks of first grade, after the skies had cleared and our mysterious nausea had abated, the teacher told us to go home and write a true story. Somehow instinctively realizing that the recent midnight-at-lunchtime would not be among the allowable topics, I went home and wrote about the time my father and I saved my little brother from the sharks.

The next day when I handed the story in, the teacher got very upset. (This was an unhappy woman, a Mormoness of manic piety, drunk most of the time. Though legally a spinster, she was rumored to have "celestial ties" with the neighborhood "Bishop.") Knowing that I was the youngest child, and that my family had never been out of the landlocked state of my birth, she called my father in for a conference and told him that I was starting out life on the wrong foot with such mendacity. He magnetized the story to the front of our fridge, where it remained until the very crayon faded.

This familiarized me with some of the prerogatives of the writer: to thumb one's nose at authority and lay the lofty low, and simultaneously to enjoy the single experience that Freud considered better than good sex—feeling the superego reach down and pat the ego on the head for a job well done. And all this when you've been having fun lying through your teeth.

And yet, indications are strong that my teacher might have been on to something. I'm not dead yet, so the complete data is unavailable for analysis, but I must have stumbled at some point, for I seem to have gotten nowhere.

Today I languish in a pair of towns no less radioactive and reactionary than the place of my birth. Having received my boyhood's writerly calling among fundamentalist fanatics downwind of nuclear test sites, I now find myself pursuing that vocation in deep exile, surrounded by religious nuts of a familiar stripe. I commute between the two most glamorous nuclear test sites of all: Hiroshima and Naga-*etcetera*. Like a subatomic particle that has yet to split from its nucleus, I've spun full circle.

II

...in the day of atonement shall ye make the trumpet sound throughout all your land. And ye shall hallow the fiftieth year, and proclaim liberty throughout all the land unto all the inhabitants thereof. It shall be a jubilee unto you, and ye shall return every man unto his possession, and ye shall return every man unto his family. —Leviticus 25:9-10

I was privileged to be in "Boom Town" (as it is affectionately known among certain cloddish members of the foreign community) on the Feast of the Transfiguration, 1995. I wore raiment of dazzling white, whiter than any fuller's bleach could make it, in commemoration of this day on the church calendar, when Christ's three best friends watched him chat with Moses and Elijah on the mountaintop. I can't recall what trio of transcendent beings I expected to see through the brownish sulfur and hydrocarbon solids of downtown Hiroshima.

That day also happened to be the fifty-year anniversary of the event that put this town on the map while nearly wiping it off. So I took it into my head to sit in somber reverie on one of the mass graves at the epicenter, at the very minute the bomb went off half a century before. I suppose it was a means of releasing tensions built up during the Cold War or something. And I really should not have been so surprised when it turned out that a number of other people were seeking similar relief.

Not only bicycles, cars, taxis and buses clogged the entrance to world-famous Peace Park, but tens of thousands of multi-colored pedestrians, almost all of them *gaijin* (a.k.a. foreign devils). Compounding the problem were several dozen international media trucks, downright eighteen-wheelers, which bristled like giant sea urchins with cumbersome satellite relay gear.

To skirt this rout, I decided to duck in by way of the Monument to the Korean Bomb Victims, which is segregated in an obscure vacant lot across a back alley. It was the only place within blocks that seemed to have contemplative activity going on, in spite of the well-hyped orgy next door.

Neither the tourists nor the media people were coming anywhere near this monument. Except for a few praying and singing Korean nationals, and me, their fellow unsung nukee, it was deserted. These people were pulverized by the same blast that killed all the thoroughbreds memorialized across the alley, but, having been mere prisoners of war, mere slave laborers with lower-quality fluid in their veins, they didn't deserve admission to the sanctum sanctorum.

Wolf Blitzer was not waiting at the Korean monument to interview me. And why should he care about this particular shrine? It's only the final resting place for a few thousand insignificant lumps of sub-humanity. An unacknowledged target of nuclear weaponry myself (and the "device" that flattened this town was an ant to the elephant that shat in my pre-teen face), I felt solidly in place at this obscure cubbyhole. I hesitated to enter Peace Park proper. Fearing that I lacked the genetic credentials, or wasn't dressed for it or something, I stood on tiptoe on the curbstone and surveyed the chaos before my eyes.

And, as usual in East Asia, I was being surveyed myself. Someone so vastly foreign is forever going to be the cynosure of every eye in this country, even loitering on the sidewalk outside a raging "love hotel" fire, with brunette adulterers, scorched and naked, leaping out windows and splatting left and right.

So, as everyone within eyeshot watches, how does this walking sideshow (let's call him Tom Bradley) celebrate the A-Bomb Golden Jubilee?

Why, he does the—

PEACE PARK PRANCE

As if in preparation for a major overland trek, he shifts his weight from foot to foot, in order to get the blood flowing through his legs—which are as long as entire adults in some parts of the world. Squinting his eyes, which sting in a brief puff of combusted myrrh from the Korean altar behind him, he mutters to himself.

"I offer up my exiled condition on this poisoned and cramped archipelago. I devote my forehead full of the gory imprints of dwarf-level lintels, and my endocrine system exuding bits of decayed nuclei. With my own self, I atone for the greatest sin of my grandpappy's generation. Best foot forward. Two-three-four—"

At this moment, in Tom Bradley's perhaps slightly unbalanced mind, he can hear Max Roach blast out the opening drum riff from the classic recording of "Salt Peanuts" that was cut the same week this town was leveled. In time with the intro, this displaced Utahn shoots his cuffs and tucks in his shirt—which comes untucked again the second he exhales. Then, in time with the imaginary music, he crosses himself incorrectly, a devout expression descending upon his king-sized kisser.

As Charlie Parker and Dizzy Gillespie come in, Tom lurches off, taking two steps to the bar, his foot hitting the petunia bed that announces the boundary of the park in precise time with the downbeat of the tune's A-section.

Tom is incredibly conspicuous, even considering the greater than normal foreign presence in Peace Park this afternoon. The mood of the multitude is self-consciously morose, and it's neutralized by this single scampering Gargantua. He displays amazing agility for such a mammoth creature, for he is sharing in the ecstasy of the resurrected and transfigured Christ. Tom is able to move with all the bashful-eyed, seductive grace of the tutued hippo ballerinas in Disney's *Fantasia*. The effect is like the effortless skateboard-level flying one does in dreams. A shriven conscience seems to have anti-gravitational effects.

To Dizzy Gillespie's explosive trumpet solo, Tom weaves and slides among the international Hiroshimizers: the ivy league humanities professors, the hermeneutic post-modernists, the Navahos and Maoris and Ainus and such like, along with abstract-expressionist painters and surrealist mylar photographers in their uniform beatnik goatees, plus countless wizened potters, folksingers, performance artists and moccasined English language haiku poets, along with an entire universe of post-menopausal flower children in Nehru jackets and medallions—not to mention all the refugees from various other post-World-War-II decades, who show up in Japan on jumbo jets once a year, to invade Tom Bradley's adopted hometown in horrific numbers, to swell a throng around the glitzy epicenter, to hold silent prayer vigils and photo opportunities and strike consternation in the hearts of world leaders who might otherwise be inclined to start a really devastating nuclear war.

On the other hand, somewhat further along the path, representatives of a different world-view have taken up their position: Japan's peculiar version of fissionable fanatics, the local Religious Right. A whole convoy of their sound trucks is double- and triple-parked among barbecued cuttlefish booths under the world-famous Eternal Vigil Clock (selflessly donated by Seiko Industries). Draped with vast posters praising the dead but evidently divine Emperor who brought hell-fire on this city, these sound trucks blare maniacal martial music and racist propaganda at an ear-destroying pitch. The aged fascists wrap their boneless gums around red and white megaphones, and scream paeans to Hitler-mustachioed Hirohito. In their radiating rising-sun headbands, they are like a hot spot on the hypocenter, a carcinogenic meltdown. The multitude weaves a wide circle around them.

Not content to be circumvented, the rightists charge from their vehicles and attack some youthful Japanese Red Army factionists, both male and female, whose identities are concealed under gas masks and crash helmets. The two small phalanxes collide in an explosion of literature, which the reds have been distributing. It is possible to catch a few glimpses of various seditious images printed on the pamphlets: mimeographed hammers and sickles, Che Guevara flashing his armpit curls, cruel caricatures of the dead Emperor spasming and ejaculating ringside at the big Fukuoka sumo tournament, etc. Both the pamphlets and the fighting are unusual for this polite city. But even staid Hiroshimites feel the urge to behave atypically on a day as strange as August sixth. It is, after all, unique but for one other in human history (that is, if you don't count a similar day the Soviets secretly visited upon the people of Eastern Turkestan in the early sixties).

At exactly the same moment that Charlie Parker comes in with his epoch-making alto sax solo, a gigantic figure blasts through the front line of fighting fanatics, cleaving this wall of humanity like a ham actor parting a stage curtain. Easily outstripping everyone by a foot or more, it's none other than you-know-who.

Tom has no political interest in anything that could possibly happen on these islands, and is devoid of civic piety in any country. He sees nothing in the rightists and the leftists but a navel-high stymie in his path. Solely out of mild irritation at the inconvenience they pose, he uses his triple advantage in mass and momentum to bust the scuffle up. Almost offhandedly, he raises both arms and shrieks like Godzilla, scattering both sides in terror. With patronizing affection, he reaches way down and pats a couple of retreating commies on the butt.

Tom whittles a banana-sized forefinger at the funerary

portrait of moldering Hirohito, whom the noodle-Nazis literally worship as a god. Over the music that blasts nowhere but inside his own brain, his mighty voice thunders cheerfully, in fluent Japanese, for the Paraclete has descended like a tongue of flame upon this *gaijin's* head.

"Shame!   Shame on you *Ojii-chan!*   Guilty as charged! The blood of millions oozes between your stubby fingers!   Get thee to a proctology clinic!   Living god, my pink and delightsome ass!"   Tom grabs that body part and waddles like a goose. Four bars later, he turns and wiggles it in the deceased sovereign's face. "Cannibal god!   Buck-fanged Moloch!   Sink your yellowing dentures into this!   Whoo-whoooo!"

Even the Red Army factionists, who feel no surplus affection for the imperial system, are taken aback at this outlander's disrespect. So it's not surprising when a novice storm trooper among the rightists feels the urge to attack. Wisely, he allows himself to be restrained by his older associates, and Tom is left to prance, unmolested, deeper and deeper into the A-Bomb Day Golden Anniversary celebration.

Writing without the intention of publication is a mild form of paranoia.   —John Braine

How does a person wind up in such a remote purgatory? In my case, I can name the entity responsible: Creative Writing. It has expelled me clear across the Pacific. But when did this plague of academic scribbling spin so far out of control that it could generate such centrifugal force?

I think I first noticed it getting truly virulent around the end of the Vietnam era. At that time I had a friend named Streckfuss, a veteran of that very police action, who was intent on transforming himself into a bona-fide Creative Writing Industrialist.

There was a problem, though. He didn't work well with others. In fact, Streckfuss was no fun in groups. He had a tendency to jump up and pin the nearest person to the floor by means of regulation G.I.-style jujitsu. He'd kneel on the kid's chest like a sizzling incubus with razor shinbones, and aim huge eyes deep into each orifice of his or her head. Eventually, Streckfuss would say, "Somebody did something terrible to me as a child... What was it? Who did it? I don't know... Let me check."

Then he would dismount, retire to the corner and get all sulky and pouty. He'd breathe in peculiar ways till the skin that covered the visible parts of his body went corpse-gray and he passed out for indefinite periods. When he came to, he would repeat the process till everyone normal was frightened away.

Streckfuss didn't really fit into my crowd at the time. As a matter of fact, my social standing took a nose-dive during our period of association. But I didn't care because there were Indians at the hotel where he lived. Occupying a semi-circle of folding chairs in the tiny lobby, consulting an ancient television with rabbit ears, they were displaced members of the Shivwit tribe—which meant Streckfuss was never without a big paper bag chock full of the horniest peyote buttons I've ever seen in my life.

Streckfuss and I used to go to various Seven-Eleven stores for a Big Gulp root beer and a cheese dog with extra cheese to ballast his peyote stomach. I, myself, never needed to spend our scarce money on such things, but disdained them as gastric crutches, because my whole, hefty metabolism was made for these little spineless cacti. I was the only person in town, besides the Shivwit braves themselves, who never even got a tiny bit queasy. And that filled Streckfuss with envy, turning him a visible cactus-green. He speculated that I might have the unfair advantage of some aboriginal blood in my veins, despite my physical type, which seems unadulterated Celtic— although that doesn't necessarily inspire any undue feelings of narcissism in me.

I was much larger than my compeer, who, in contradiction of his Germanic given name, was very compact and Italianate. So he never tried pinning me to the floor and kneeling on my chest with questions about repressed infantile traumas. For my part, I found him terrifying as a rabid squirrel with claws bristling from its elbows. In fact, I only just barely learned to endure the elevator-stomach that came from looking into the guy's eyes. So the feelings of respect were mutual.

While waiting to be served at Seven-Eleven, Streckfuss liked to browse through the reading material. Today it's hard for young people to believe me when I tell them that serious literature was once hawked in such places, but it's true. I got my copy of Nabokov's *ADA* off a twirly rack in a grocery store.

One day, as I was watching the clerk go through the recondite process of melting the bricks of quiescently frozen cheese sauce for the dogs, Streckfuss came upon a well-pitched item. It was a classic application of the famous "four P's" in qualitative marketing theory: Product, Place, Promotion, and Price. Many handsome copies of a novel, with embossed and perforated covers, coruscating with foil, were tucked in a special cardboard display stand. Easy to assemble for franchise managers across the nation, this eye-catching promotional device had been ingeniously contrived to resemble a key symbol and central image in the text.

This was intended to give potential buyers, deep in the irrational part of their brains, a sense of what the product had to offer, without their having to read a word. It was a reptilian appeal, zooming through the aperture of the eyeball into those suggestible nodes and nodules of the central nervous system, which, in our case that day, were suffused with the phosphorescent green Eucharist of the southwestern desert.

Streckfuss was enchanted, and already engrossed in page three, when his cheese dog came steaming across the counter, trailing ropes and braids of extra cheese. The better to free his fingers for page ruffling, he balanced his purchase on the top edge of the display stand. It dripped a molten orange on the product, but Streckfuss was too absorbed to notice, and I was somehow incompetent or disinclined to react.

As an example of qualitative marketing strategy, this confection could not have been much better. In order to give customers a sense that they were getting a substantial consumer item in return for their hard-earned cash, it had been printed on thick paper, with wide margins and big type to inflate the page count.

Streckfuss really liked it, because he understood every word and could negotiate each grammatical construction without undue effort. It seemed to be one of those universally appealing works of art that somehow manage to reach both the general public at large and the book-reviewing apparatus of its time. According to the back cover, the author was the recipient of a major critical award, even though his thing was selling like hotcakes all across the continent. So it was with neither a trace of populist chagrin nor elitist guilt that I read over Streckfuss' shoulder as he flipped through the chapters with his permanently discolored fingers.

My little friend washed dishes in a hospital kitchen. He worked all day elbow-deep in that Tyrian purple compound utilized in the food services industry to call drudges' attention to impurities which have not been properly scoured off pots and pans. A former soldier, Streckfuss was hard as a skeleton with the flesh gnawed off, and was able to scorn the rubber gloves that prevented the skin of his co-workers' hands from being boiled away. So he bore permanent stains as of passion among the self-inflicted ritual disfigurements on his knuckles and bony forearms: the BORN TO BE WILD and the ineptly rendered Hakenkreuz with mystic heat radiations slithering around his wrist. He'd dug these tattoos in deep with straight pins and blue ballpoint ink during his former days as a car thief and a minor embarrassment in the more squalid zones of our obscure and blighted far-western community.

"I used to think my skin pictures looked pretty wicked," Streckfuss said when he saw me scrutinizing his fingers at Seven-Eleven that day.

I wasn't trying to be rude, but the juxtaposition on his left thumb of sunset-colored cheddar, purple pot-stainer, and the unnamable hue which the ballpoint ink had assumed after curdling so many years under the sallow layers of his skin, combined with the general shift toward the emerald end of the spectrum which peyote sometimes visits upon the retina, had rendered me briefly stuporous. My eyelids felt like lips, and I was hesitant to speak for fear of weeping bloody tears.

But I snapped out of it quickly when I realized I might be making him feel self-conscious (therefore angry, in his self-alienated case). It was always a good idea to avoid gazing directly at any uncovered part of Streckfuss, especially in public. After almost a minute of looking elsewhere, I was able to moisten my lips and throat ever so slightly, just enough to croak out a noncommittal reply about Third Reich insignia getting a bad press lately.

Streckfuss was unpopular not just because of his wrong-colored limbs and erratic behavior. He was unloved by large numbers of strangers who'd never been exposed to those shortcomings at close quarters. When peeking out his window at the hotel like some eroded gargoyle, all hollow cheeks and residual military buzz-cut, he drew double takes from normal pedestrians passing below on the sidewalk.

"A leaper, a sniper?" they seemed to ask one another, and his notoriety increased.

But, contrary to most people's understandable suspicions, the only time he was predictably dangerous was when someone made fun of his unfortunate name. So, of course, behind his back, there was a regular efflorescence: Strekkie the Trekkie, Streck-Dreck, Stretch-face, Yecchy Strecky, etc. Rumor maintained that the scamp who coined that last one paid for it with her ability to walk unaided.

"This is quite the novel-book," Streckfuss was saying. He took a deep draw on his Big Gulp root beer and examined the black-and-white portrait on the back cover. It revealed a literary man with depths of unfulfilled longing in his eyes, and a dark brown beard, well trimmed.

Amazingly enough, this individual was at that very moment abiding in our miserable townlet. To this day, nobody has ever been able to explain to my satisfaction such a celebrity's presence in our backwater enclave, at the very peak and explosion of his terrestrial fame. My best guess would be that the pressures of maintaining the pace of such an all-out publicity campaign—the acceptance speeches for honorary degrees, the interviews with Bob Cromie on PBS, the black-tie receptions at the White House, and so on, culminating in the shrine to his talent which was spread so appetizingly before us now—had become too much for him, and he had, for the sake of his health, been compelled to escape, to hide out in some provincial no-place, where such vitality-sucking hype remained at low intensities, and his public presence could be cardboard, not incarnate.

Our town couldn't have been a happier choice. Even the most ambitious book tours never scheduled stops within hundreds of miles, the populace being, if not precisely illiterate, then disinclined to spend their money on literature—certainly not hardback editions, the sale of which is the meat and potatoes of signings, authorial appearances and readings. And God knows our Main Street contained no bookstore worthy of accommodating the likes of him and a table full of his mighty works.

I imagined that the creator of Streckfuss' much-admired "novel-book" had come for a salutary sojourn among our staid and, frankly, dull burghers, in order to get back in touch with his deep river of self, so essential to the novelist's silent craft. He was seeking peace and renewal among us simple and subliterate salts of the earth. Like a Hindu pilgrim, he must return to the Ganges to bathe. Our town was his ghat, our homely folk the burnt corpses he stepped over.

On the other hand, he could've been cruising for some sort of primitivistic kick that he imagined to be available here. But an intelligent man like him would have discovered his error in about twenty minutes and cleared out weeks ago. I doubt that an artist of such wide distribution and global sales would be content to waste his leisure time on the sort of thing my neighbors and I did for fun, such as hanging around Seven-Eleven parking lots till the wee hours with the likes of Streckfuss—which is what I did after he shoplifted our illustrious guest's novel.

It had taken a while for us to find a copy that wasn't soaked through with one gastric crutch or the other, both species as it were, because, while I wasn't looking, Streckfuss had a fullbody spasm and spilled his sugary brown drink up and down the length of the handsome display. When the time came to steal one, my accomplice was not very discreet making his selection, slopping the rejects in glutinous piles on the bright Seven-Eleven linoleum.

But we weren't stopped and searched on the way out. Perhaps the clerk didn't think it worthwhile to try, with one of us transcending by several inches the height gauge on the doorjamb, and the other clearly a sociopath with nothing to lose. Or maybe the clerk was a student of the Chinese author Lu Xun, who wrote, "Stealing books is not stealing."

Speaking of the Chinese, earlier that very month when they began to pirate the products of his soul on a gargantuan scale, our visiting author had waxed bitterly eloquent in denouncing such thievery from the pulpit of the electronic broadcast media. He was courageous enough to speak out, despite the protestations of certain lefties in the press who pointed out that the Chinese could never afford his books at the regular price, anyway. They cited Faulkner's words to the effect that the true novelist's sole desire should be to "scratch his name on the door of eternity" without regard to the service charge that could be extracted in return for such scratching. These lefties also claimed that certain writers existed (maybe all dead now) who would be flattered to the point of mania to have members of such a vast and formidable civilization taking an interest in their work, regardless of the financial arrangement, or lack thereof, which had placed the books in their hands.

These more than slightly pink commentators (many of whom were members of our author's charmed circle back east) even got personal. As evidence of what they considered craven hypocrisy, they called attention to the meticulous commie stance he always affected in his published oeuvre—as if storytellers haven't, from the very start of the practice, reserved the right to assume personae and depict Weltanschauungen not necessarily their own. How many readers really think, for example, that Milton the man resembled in any way—

Mammon, the least erected spirit that fell
From heaven; for ev'n in heaven his looks and thoughts
Were always downward bent, admiring more
The riches of heaven's pavement, trodden gold,
Than aught divine or holy else enjoyed
In vision beatific.

It must have been a real crisis of conscience for our best-selling writer, with his chums poking cruel fun like that. But he wrestled with it and came down solidly on the side of the right. He backed himself up with a moving reference to the eighth paragraph of the horned prophet's stone code, intending to shame those Dengists and make them think twice about intellectual property rights as they pertain to international law.

Perhaps, if the clerk on duty at Seven-Eleven had been issued a radio or a television, and given the time to listen to the heartfelt plaints of this victim of robbery—no, of soul-rape outright—on the local PBS and NPR affiliate stations, he would have interposed his pink-jacketed person between Streckfuss and the exit. Had this clerk mustered the courage, if not the conscience, to earn his wage and prevent the author from being deprived of his rightful ten percent royalty on the cover price of what was so palpably stuffed down the front waistband of Streckfuss' funky little underpants—well, I think it's safe to say that the next eighteen hours of American literary history would have turned out quite differently, and I might not be writing this sad memoir today, more than a quarter-century later.

As it was, we were allowed to leave the convenience store with our booty, and to loiter in its parking lot until the setting of Orion in the western sky. (Not that we saw it through the exhaust fumes of peckish insomniacs.)

At one point in the night, Streckfuss edged close to me on the concrete stoop and began to stew even hotter than usual. He was little more than a gristly shrimp on two toothpicks, but, nevertheless, it was impossible to absorb his gaze and simultaneously maintain a settled stomach. I found myself shifting attention elsewhere. Cringing away, I noticed an electric stinger exposed for sale on the other side of the shop window, one of those hot wires used for boiling coffee in kitchenless hovels and prison cells. A bony knee touched mine, and my flesh crawled almost pleasantly.

"You might not believe this," he said, rolling the pilfered volume into an ever-tighter tube, "but there's whole chunks out of my life I can't even remember. My social worker told me that if it wasn't for the draft, I'd still be wherever I was that I can't pin down, all doped up with thorazine and locked in a ward with bent people; or else I'd be running loose, pulling ape-shit stunts like—um, like—"

Streckfuss examined his tiny scribbled-upon doll's hands.

He thought hard.

"Hey!" I cried, in a cheerful honk. With mental fingers I groped my gray matter for something to distract him before he could recollect stunts better left forgotten. "Um, know what? You ought to come along with me to the Creative Writing workshop!"

*   *   *   *

I was a sort of freshman at the non-Mormon university, a barely matriculated back-of-the-classroom lurker, a mere arriviste teeny-bopper, with an undeclared major yet, halfheartedly feeling about for my birthright, my faculty-brat career opportunity as my dad's successor among the tenure-track commies and alcoholics. And I can't imagine how, but I had found myself suddenly a made-member of this glamorous seminar, this symposium, otherwise reserved for MFA candidates in the English department. (Guess who just happened, by coincidence, to be presiding over this weekly dream-salon.)

My classmates (if I'm not presumptuous in using the term) were the future Creative Writing Industrialists of the Intermountain West, and they were working on fictional dissertations and metafictional theses, sans footnotes. These people were right on the verge of finding literary agents, for Christ's sake, and I can only assume that I'd been cast among them, like an earthworm among rainbow trout, through some simple clerical error.

Our registrar still used those computer cards with the rectangular perforations, the sort you were never supposed to fold, spindle or mutilate with straight pins and ink. God knows what miscarriages of enrollment they perpetuated. I'm not sure what levels of technological sophistication had already been achieved by the grand educational institutions back east, where the teacher of our high-tone workshop came from. But it is hard to credit in retrospect that such primitive paper products remained in use, even in our remote and benighted part of the country. Sometimes at night I wonder if I actually did bullshit my way through to a baccalaureate degree, or if it was conferred upon me at random. I suppose it hardly matters in the long run.

Streckfuss looked very excited and flattered at the prospect of going among the intelligentsia. But he hesitated. "In the shop, does this geezer tell you the way to do these kind of novel-books?" He gestured through the darkness with the stolen property. The spine was cracked in many places.

"Syllabus says we'll cover that procedure first thing tomorrow."

I looked to the eastern brink, which seemed to be brightening with rosy fingers and vast dove's wings—but then, so did every other quadrant of the sky I tried to focus my swirling eyes on. So I revised my comment tentatively: "...first thing today?"

Streckfuss, too, was unsure. "Already?" he murmured. "Is it the next day?"

Since it was impossible to go to sleep under the influence of this alkaloid, I figured it would be best if we forewent bed and ate a lot more of the Shivwit people's holy sacrament. I was only eighteen, and green in judgment, as the man says. In fact I was a sort of dusty spineless cactus green in judgment. But spineless in the best sense of the word.

So we spent all night skulking around the wrong parts of town, and trying to empty a big paper bag of peyote into our disparate metabolisms. They were like Swinburne's "green grapes of Proserpine," only smaller, with a hoary topknot, and they tended to banish rather than induce unconsciousness.

During the course of this ordeal of indulgence, Streckfuss

allowed himself to be provisionally persuaded to join the "shop," for, in fact, he was an author, too. He unzipped his habitual one-shoulder backpack and fished out imaginative works, one after another. Squatting on his heels in a lurid alley, ranging the papers between scarlet puddles of transmission fluid from some long-gone truck, he acted as though no particular sequence was required. Streckfuss was simply putting the pages in the order that pleased him most at the moment. He had arrived at an ultra-current, found-poetic technique. It approached Burroughsian paste-ups in sophistication, and was all the more impressive for having been achieved purely by instinct—for my companion that night was virginal of theory, let there be no doubt. Some talent, maybe even some academic potential, was indicated. I found myself already envying his fellowship stipend.

When the real sun actually did come up, Streckfuss began to wonder aloud whether it might not be a shrewd financial move to report to work and punch in, so he could draw his pay while absent. Like many places of employment in our semi-civilized outpost of Christendom, Streckfuss' hospital kitchen was so chaotic, with fruit compote and soap suds flipping in wild arcs all around, that it would be no problem to sneak back out and have his kindly co-workers cover for him.

We approached the greasy loading dock in back and came upon his fellow dish-jockeys having a one last smoke before hitting the sinks. They were gay African-Americans, a down-right gaggle of them, all mothery and fluttery and protective of my little friend, whom they had correctly diagnosed as borderline non compos mentis. Streckfuss' work-mates were the gentle, helpless sort of homosexual, but he jumped on their chests no more frequently than he jumped on mine. Maybe he figured there was no way creatures exotic as they could have the answers to his childhood questions.

He swaggered among them like a bantam rooster and crowed the big news. Today was his big break, his debut. Their honky mascot was about to burst, finally, into the national awareness. There were squeals of congratulations, even tears, as they closed around him like breasts on a wet nurse. These men were accustomed to painting the black part of town red immediately after punching out, so they maintained lockers full of nice things on the hospital premises. They ushered my friend into the employees' locker room and commenced dolling him up, each pitching in from his own gorgeous wardrobe.

I wasn't allowed to follow them in and advise on the makeover because I hadn't been TB-screened, nor had I defecated in a paper cup and submitted my creation to the critical appraisal of the state health department. Streckfuss always swore to god that he knew a transvestite too delicate to do something quite so distasteful with his anus, who had smuggled in a dog turd instead, and was given a job in administration. But there were no dogs around that I was able to see, and no paper cups, at least none in the state of sterility required for lab analysis of the contents. So I loitered on the dock and nervously tried to propitiate with falsetto ditties the aquamarine pumas and coyotes that kept consolidating from deliverymen's cigarette smoke and nipping at my Achilles tendons.

After what seemed like six or seven months, Streckfuss came out, shy as a bride, all primped and preened and ready for his real life finally to begin. Their finery, he promised his dusky godmothers, would be returned by the hands of someone with a literary agent. Origins transcended at last, the skin on those hands would finally have the chance to slough off the purple pot stainer; and the ink, for once, would be supercutaneous. Streckfuss' comrades giggled as they flicked him kisses from the lip of the dock, and "saw li'l ole Streckums off to the varsity ball like Cinderella in his special matrickle-ation suit."

As we headed off down the driveway, he said, "I think they work there because they like to wear aprons."

Streckfuss had on a white silk shirt with puffy Ricky Ricardo sleeves, shiny black hip-hugger bell-bottoms, rolled up at the waist to accommodate some surplus in-seam, and a pair of spit-polished square-toe disco shoes with five-inch platform soles. It was obvious that he could never have afforded such an outfit, not with a facial expression like that. Even now, at the happiest moment of his whole life, his demeanor militated against anything but deep penury and failure. Besides, the various elements in his ensemble didn't fit his reptilian form, each in a different way. To eyes that knew no better, indiscriminate filching would seem indicated. My classmates, my elder brothers and sisters in the craft, were going to assume I'd picked up a shoplifter from some unimaginable haberdashery in a neighborhood that none of them would ever drive through, not even with windows rolled up tight.

He wanted to take a cab and arrive at the English Department in a style befitting his costume. But I pointed out that buying him a fresh pair of gastric crutches would constitute a wiser allocation of resources. It would be best not to have to deal with a psychomimetic reflux of peptic enzymes while having one's life's work subjected to the magnifying glass of informed critical attention. The constant rhythmic cranial shudders so characteristic of excessive peyotism are distracting enough without rumblings from the basement. So we took a bus instead of a cab. With the saved funds we planned to raid the Seven-Eleven near the university bus stop, and also to xerox his Creative Writing.

Streckfuss made a big deal of scraping some anonymous clumps of kleenex off the bus seat. "I can't get any crap on these pants," he said. He fluffed his collar and sleeves in the window, and looked as though he'd rather lose a finger than a fiber of that lugubrious blouse. I had never seen anything like it within twenty blocks of the university. This guy was going to cause the collegiate sensation I had tried and failed to cause on my own.

Sometimes it occurred to me to wonder where Streckie-the-Trekkie could've gotten so incongruous. Our native town was a diseased and inchoate place, it's true, but not some alien planet. But then I recalled his being a vet. So, the recent sensitive movies notwithstanding, I asked him, as we rode uphill to the place of enlightenment, what they'd made him do in the war.

"Helicopter gunner. They had me hanging out the side in a chair and I had a big machine gun and they flew me down next to the ground so I could waste Veecee."

"You wasted a whole bunch of 'em?"

"Yeah. We were eating a lot of Clear Light. I was sort of getting into it. I'm gonna show this one to the shop today."

I was expecting a combat story: *The Red Badge of Courage* with civilian decapitations and lieutenant fraggings. But I was surprised to find something quite different: a peacetime reminiscence of an even earlier period of his immaturity. Streckfuss was following the pattern of a good many writers at the beginning of their careers, who exploit their personal histories like strip mines for narrative material, and proceed chronologically, commencing with infancy narratives, as it were. Later, as my friend ripened artistically, he could be expected to cover the chopper raids on windowpane LSD. But for now it was boyhood. Huck Finn rolling on the asphalt river, if not lake.

He composed in the same Big Daddy Roth script that could be seen under his epidermis, with tiny stylized skulls grinning over the i's and j's. At the feet of the pages were precognitive catchwords, such as those found in incunabular liturgies and medieval Satanist recipe books.

The text read in part as follows:

"*To celebrate me on Sunday my old dad, he put me up inside the window. In the end gate of our Rambler station wagon window. And my butt was on the edge of the window and my arms rest across the auto-top. And the back is full of Basket Balls my old dad, he stealed from his church. The other kids racing on foot all around me. Eggplants, polaks, guinea bastards like myself, rice-negroes, zipper-heads, chinks, harps, papooses, and also young persons of the Jewish purse suasion. All one the same together, Americans. And I bounced them Basket Balls off top their head. My old dad chases a kid down like on TV, he squeals the tires, I bean him with my Basket Balls. My old dad says we are feeling power-full and political. The kids soon had their own ammo of Basket Balls and they some times hit me on the back or my sides. The kids on feet they were less uncordennated than myself. Because they wasn't saddled down with their old dad's Rambler station wagon. Which was faster than them though. Once I fell out, I landed on my side. I had to crawl for cover because both my legs was asleep. Because my butt it was always pressed down on the edge of that Rambler end gate window. The kids they buried me by Basket Balls that time. I was only one big old bruise that time. It was a pleasant uprising. Or so my old dad told it later.*"

"This should do fine," I said.

"I used to kind of worry about not having enough big words in my stuff. But then I saw our shop teacher's novel-book at Seven-Eleven. No problemmo, you know? I bet he won't mind autographing a stolen copy if I gently tear out the pages with the most cheese on them. Except I need one of those computer cards, like yours, to get through the door. Right?"

"What? Oh, you can borrow mine. I'm friends with the, um, ticket-taker."

I reached into his backpack (that's how beside himself he was with feelings of impending personal excellence: under normal conditions, just touching the thing would earn you a dislocated thumb or shoulder), and I pulled out the paper bag of blessed verdure. I indicated my readiness to clean it out once and for all before reporting to class.

"Us college students take 'em all the time prior to matriculating," I explained. "Our teacher won't mind because he's from the east coast, New York even, and so he's sophisticated. Whattaya say?"

I held out a handful: skin-like blobs of chlorophyll coolness to smell and sob over with itchy tears.

Streckfuss lovingly blew some red sand away. He looked famished, and sorely tempted. But he said, "I always get paranoidal and, um, combative if I do it too many days in a row without sleeping."

He was dying to be talked into pushing himself between the lips of the abyss. I could see that he was already having some imaginary brain quakes. And he wasn't the only one. Already I felt traces of the sublimity that would descend when we chastised and houseled ourselves further on the immemorial Shivwit soma, scarfing this gunk by the sweaty armload. Digesting spineless tubercles was the sole reason my DNA was ever braided in the womb in the first place.

I said, "That's what college is for, to be paranoiac and combative in. Don't you remember? Didn't you listen to the American Forces Network when you were over there, face down in the mud in Hoo Dun Poo, or wherever? Come on, they're yours, but I'll be glad to share 'em with you, fifty-fifty. What do you say? Huh?"

My very cerebellum salivates as I recall and record the memory: bulbs full of the concentrated essence of everything potent, grave and reverend yet remaining on the face of this poor depleted earth; the final receptacle for the ghosts of coyote- and iguana-deities, plus Phrygian Cybele and multi-dugged

Demeter; preserver of the souls of prognosticating eunuchs, theriomorphic virgins, and heinous Beelzebub, all chemically wedded within its darling confines, plump and succulent as the buttocks of rareripe babies under your arm—a desert delicacy, an emphatically frontier treat, no city slickers allowed. In fact, I wonder just how far east of rainless country it can be smuggled, before losing its succulent potency. I notice no mention of peyote in novels about growing up in the Bronx.

So perfectly attuned was I, as I trepanned the tufts of icky strychnine from each bulb with my right thumbnail (allowed to go unclipped to a Chinese aristocratic extent for this very purpose, the quick tinged a permanent green), my tongue gradually loosened from its frenum and went into slippery orbit around my cerebral cortex, where it began teasing and butterfly-kissing the outer gray tegument to the point of intra-cranial ejaculation.

"There's no need to fret," I mouthed into the ears of my apprentice, "if I miss a few of these lethal angel-hair filaments woven through-and-through the strawberry-like flesh, the fibrous essence of nux vomica, strung in and out, like systems of unpleasant symbols in an edifying vegetable narrative. Let it stain our tootsies, my boy. Fuck that overpriced Manhattan whore."

Before I could close my mouth on further indiscretion, a pencil-beam of saliva gushed from under my tongue, squirting across the aisle. And we were able to wad up the paper bag and throw it, empty, on the floor just as the bus pulled up to our stop.

"But what if I barf on the homo Negro clothes?" cried Streckfuss in a panicky voice. He'd already gagged the emetic down in quantities, and now the thought occurred to him, too late. He hit himself on the forehead in full-body mortification, and tried, fingernails scraping against the walls, to arrest his descent into the salad-colored tunnel. The atmosphere of that whole end of town suddenly got tense.

But I calmed him down. As far as anybody knew, I was the only one who could do this. It didn't seem to matter what I said, but I could usually cause him to stop vibrating and sizzling. Sometimes no words were necessary, and all I needed to do was take his arm or shoulder and lend him direction, as now. Even while remaining terrified to glance down at the pointy crown of his head, for fear his face would suddenly aim up at mine and start hissing, I steered him to the place where further ballast for peyote tummy could be had, along with the good offices of a xerox machine. Settled and reproduced, Streckfuss went to seek for truth in the groves of Academe.

*   *   *   *

At school there was no talking or moving or breathing, as per usual for this period in world history. The sixties were over, the barricades had evaporated, and almost nobody in this hopelessly reactionary cubbyhole of the continent was prepared, quite yet, to shave his eyebrows and behave like David Bowie. So finding topics of conversation was very difficult. Furthermore, we were located in the Far West, ancestral home of the taciturn type. Papa Hemingway had pinched his tight lips shut for the last time in our general vicinity, and, of course, that only served to exacerbate matters.

This is not to say, however, that all was somnambulism and futility on campus, not by any means. The pair of us scuffed along a corridor lined with sheepish deaf-mutes, it's true, but we were on our way to link elbows with a "community of writers"—for that seeming oxymoron is how they liked to think of themselves.

My schoolmates, most of them—or, at any rate, a solid

majority of the post-structurally inclined—prided themselves on being part of the first major overhaul of the disposition of literature since Dr. Johnson and his compeers sounded the rallying cry: "That man is a blockhead who ever wrote except for money!" Those venerable Londoners, once and for all, had done with patronage, and placed the professional writer at the beck and call of the anonymous arbiter of taste, the "common reader"—a coinage of the Great Cham of Literature himself, and an expression of faith in the book-buying public that had made possible the celebrated presence among us today of an authentic member of the East Coast Liberal Intellectual Establishment, for which we were duly grateful.

But these Creative Writing grad students, particularly the hermeneutic ones, represented a further step in the evolution of the species. With them, there would be no more coffee houses, nor royalties, nor flat kill fees. This new generation would replace such with seminar rooms and stipends and two free contributor's copies. They had a sense of being at the apex of the wake. They were forging, in the smithy of their mimeographed literary magazines, the uncreated conscience of their guild.

These unacknowledged legislators no longer needed to fret about that lack of acknowledgement, because they were on fellowships now, and, if everything went well, would soon be on salaries outright, tenured to boot. And this lifetime support would remain forever unconnected with the reception of their works, if any.

Furthermore, as this was a public institution, they were one rung higher on the evolutionary ladder than their coevals in the private university across town. Their situation was even more consistent with the leftist ideal, which in those days remained yet the default mode of most members of humanities departments, regardless of their opinions about how, or whether, to hawk words. My classmates were pursuing their terminal degrees with state funds. The power structure was reimbursing them to tell the truth, or at least to say nothing recognizably heretical (the path of choice for most of them). They were writers paid by the government.

Streckfuss heard me expound upon this heady prophecy as we approached the venue, and it made him feel intellectually inadequate. He'd been sort of planning on made-for-TV movie deals and cherry-red vintage T-birds full of star-struck groupies. He squeezed his "admission ticket" with nervously perspiring fingers till the perforations got soggy and lost some of their definition, becoming more oval than rectangular. God only knew what class I'd find myself in next semester.

Following an impulse, which, I confess, was not unmixed with gratuitous cruelty, I whispered Keats' words of small comfort into his blushing ear. "We're going among the 'hierophants of unapprehended inspiration, the mirrors of the gigantic shadows which futurity casts upon the present.' I sure as fuck hope they like your stuff, Streckfuss."

So we slunk down the beige-speckled linoleum ("down" is here used idiomatically, for we felt as though we were going uphill, as on one of those ramp-like approaches to the summits of ancient temples; and we were indeed ascending, both of us in a psychoactive, and one of us in a socioeconomic, sense). Suddenly, almost in mid-phrase, and with little enough context, I surprised myself no less than my friend by shrieking, in my most convincing, Emmy Award-winning voice of revulsion, "You were wasting lots of Veecee and *enjoying* it?" I had an idea for the workshop now.

My shriek was calculated to compound with embarrassment whatever other counterproductive emotions he might be feeling—assuming someone like Streckfuss was capable of embarrassment.

His eyes got their trist look and he pressed his little lips together. "Yeah," he said. "Nam'd make a guy like that."

If I shrieked, he whispered self-consciously. And it was the latter, not the former, which caused several hall-lurkers to make emergency dives and ducks into the nearest rooms: wrong-sex toilets, and classes they weren't enrolled in, not even as "audits."

"It got to be sexy, almost. I didn't think it was crazy at the time when it was happening. Now I do, and all I want to do is mellow out."

"Well, you'd better 'mellow out' if you want to live in the real world with regular people, and go to normal places like college classes! Sweet Jesus!"

I hit myself on the forehead twice with my left fist, just as the women in dirty movies do when plying their plastic penises on themselves. I glanced over to make sure Streckfuss was watching.

While I grunted, moaned, grimaced and went "Eeeeew!" at the icky bestiality of it all, he continued with numb momentum, still whispering with a sense of shame that surprised me, and almost made me feel like a horrible fucking bastard.

"I remember the first time I ever shot somebody. It was this lady. She was bringing a tray of Coca-Colas across the paddy. She was talking a blue streak to her girlfriend. I got so nauseous I crawled back in the chopper and barfed all over the navigator's lap. I hallucinated my heart, lying there, beating. And then he said, 'Do you see what I see?' and we both freaked. I just crawled back out to my position and started firing some more. There was nothing else to do. Those guns are so powerful, they make the Veecees' tongues stick out—"

He worked his rosebud mouth a little, as if trying to add something. But no sound came out. He'd rendered himself speechless, aposiopesized himself into a corner.

It was better this silent way. What was needful this morning was a visual prop, some tangible proof that adolescent frosh-boy Tommy was old-fashioned, like our glitzy teacher, and intended to live up to the Johnsonian ideal of serving the book-buying public at large. I wanted to live off royalties, so I shrewdly and bravely surrounded myself with distasteful, even dangerous, but topically promising research subjects, like this poor shell-shocked veteran, who might have a combat flashback any minute and do something rollicking and marketable, and in the meantime could be pumped for ready pathos.

I wasn't, like so many of the other students, a whored-out hireling of the government propaganda machine, a bought and paid-for Big Liar, a la Minister Paul Joseph Goebbels. I was no fellowshipped academic. Royalties and advances against same, and proceeds from the sale of spin-off rights, and movie and mini-series deals, especially—the very sort of thing the Chicoms were totalitarianizing our teacher out of: these were my fondest goals, not a federally-insured pittance and a tenured trammel on my pen. I would never be ashamed to bathe in swimming pools full of filthy lucre, just as our visiting headliner was doing, so long as I could do it without feeling obliged not to write nasty things about anybody I wanted to, such as the Chairman of the English Department and the Dean of Humanities, and whatever tarted-up scribbler they recruited to flaunt his tawdry wares in my face.

I was assuming that the famous novelist, though willing (if not obliged by necessity) to milk provincial universities like cash cows, felt no surplus affection for the parasites he found fastened to their udders. And I was secretly hoping to impress him with my weaned self, and to get a recommendation to his literary agent—though I can't recall if I'd written anything with that untrammeled pen of mine to submit to her. Somehow I doubt it. My eyes were swirling so in those days, I could barely see my feet, much less operate a typewriter. In fact, I now wonder what I produced to justify or at least apologize for my snoring presence in the workshop. Perhaps I felt that, being the result of a random computer glitch, my interloping didn't need justification. I wonder if I even passed.

Whether backed up by any substance or not, this pitching of me would be effective enough if my sidekick said nothing and just sat there looking other-worldly and lower-class in his borrowed Negro clothing. I didn't necessarily want any rib cages squatted upon, or overmuch blood spilled. That's why I'd pretended to almost ralph over those comparatively mild war stories: to shut the little beast up and shut him down. I was very young and callow, even for my tender age, and hadn't yet developed the ethical tone that I enjoy as I sit here and compose my nonfiction memoir today.

As we approached the classroom door, a voice could be heard on the other side. That gave me serious pause. I dragged Streckfuss to a halt, and he froze obediently, as at the signal of the point man on jungle patrol. (Still speechless, he didn't require shooshing.) I cocked both ears at ninety-degree angles to my skull.

On every session before today, the workshop had been just as silent as the rest of the university. This might seem paradoxical for a place where tuition was supposed to be taking place, but wordlessness reigned in that room. A certain garden on the far side of the Wadi Kidron had not been quieter, early on that sleepless Passover night of long ago. And it wasn't just one of our number who wept tears of blood. We all did, watching our teacher, this significant Manhattanite of letters, as he wrestled with his tongue-tied demons, all the while stroking abstractedly his well-trimmed dark-brown beard. His eyelids twitched. I think he wore contact lenses.

One expected orotundities to issue from such august lips.

And they eventually did, a few months later in his career, when he returned to his blessed region of the United States and blossomed personally. He was to become a regular literary lion, and even gained a reputation for having screaming matches with other well-thought-of novelists at PEN meetings. However, at this stage in his career, he was a very quiet type, with pain and sadness in his face. He seemed to have reached a brooding place in his intellectual and artistic development.

My older classmates sometimes wondered in whispers, on those days when he didn't show up on time, or not at all, whether he had arrived at some deep and advanced notion of the utter inutility and inscrutability of words, the inherent oppressiveness of language. Maybe our mentor was registering a silent protest in the face of the Universal Gab. And what more piquant place to express this mute cosmic disgruntlement than within such a haven for unmeasured logorrhea as a seminar, a symposium?

The MFA candidates were content to sit and witness this acclaimed genius bathing in the Ganges that noiselessly flowed inside his own quiet self, for ninety minutes at a stretch, every Thursday morning, when he remembered to show up. It was enough to be in the presence of a man who commanded such admirable sums up front as he was rumored to have gotten in exchange for agreeing to conduct this single workshop.

He was a creature of admirable consistence. In class (and I never saw him elsewhere—I can't imagine how he exited and entered), his nose was forever sunk deep in a book, and always the same one. We never knew the title because he held it flat on his lap, like a monkish missal borrowed from a tradition not his own.

The individual sitting and reading so magisterially before us contained within a single compact human frame so many different types of success that it was a sexual experience for more than one of us to hear him pronounce our names during roll call. He kept strict attendance records, as our grades would be based on class participation. But I feared there was not going to be a disproportion of A-plusses. Nobody was going to accuse this of being a "pud course," subject to grade inflation—for none of us participated any more than he did.

Among my co-adventurers-in-learning were half a dozen hard-boiled detective novelettists, one divorced Ph.D. (ABD) who was working on a divorce novel, plus a "spinner" of 700-page folk tales, along with a quorum of post-structuralists who penned hermeneutic vignettes in the prose-poetic form, I think. But, in spite of all this accumulated talent, I'm forced to admit that much of our reciprocal silence was caused by a kind of regional pudency. Off the page, we all had contempt-ibly hard R's, and nobody wanted to betray a manner of speech identifiable as other than New Yorker—for our teacher was most emphatically that. He had duly contributed to the ven-erable tradition of bildungsromans about growing up in the Bronx in the thirties.

Exactly four, or maybe five, words (not counting our surnames during roll call) had risen from his well-known tra-chea. Early in the term, a non-post-structural type, a naïvely unabashed citizen of an even punier community deeper in the same desert that, like a sponge, sucked the interest out of our own (this person wrote cow-puncher tales, a la Zane Grey, and was soon persuaded to stop attending), had asked our teacher a direct question—not the rhetorical sort, but one requiring an answer in order to avoid the impression of rudeness. The ludicrous question was, "What advice can you give us?" And, to this mere unfellowshipped tuition payer, he replied, with admirable succinctness, "Um, get a different address." ("Um" was a major element in his disarmingly self-effacing idiolect.)

We knew he spoke to all of us, and not just to our country cousin. So we fixed our gazes on our laps, and there they tended to remain. It was an almost genetic chagrin, a deoxyribonucleic mea culpa that, among my fellow rubes, at any rate, tried to compensate for itself with meticulous personal hygiene and religious punctuality.

Unfortunately for me, this was the era before the widespread application of microwave technology in the major nation-wide convenience store chains—at least those franchises that had the bad luck of being located in this unwiped fundament of America, which we miserable half-humans called, with an apologetic yawp, home. And it had taken some time at the Seven-Eleven near the university to render the brick of frozen cheese sauce liquescent enough to bear pouring over Streckfuss' latest dog. And he had, as always, asked for extra, which did not expedite matters one bit. So we were a little late.

Normally, for a teen of my fashionably devil-may-care attitudinizations, tardiness was no problem, and never prevented me from bashing my way into any situation. Such is the headlong vitality of youth. But today the freakish juxtaposition of the classroom door with the sound of a voice coming from the other side made me cautious. Of course, it didn't help that my senses had been systematically deranged for about seventeen hours straight. I could have sworn it was Henry Kissinger talking in there. I thought I heard the words "ultimate aphrodisiac."

Streckfuss hovering hungrily behind me, I cracked the door, ever so slightly. I prayed with success to the Shivwit Mother Bear Spirit for no hinge squeaks as I slipped part of the flange of my teen-oily right nostril through, opening a tiny but serviceable line of sight. I could not make out the possessor of the mysterious voice, but only one or two students (mouths shut, eyes downcast in humility), and, beyond them, the ancient Unabridged Webster's, the departmental dictionary.

This book was the sole indicator (aside from the cushions on the chairs) of the chamber's significance. It was usually the faculty meeting room, and nobody under the rank of assistant professor was allowed. But, in consideration of the sheer significance of our guest teacher, the temple veil of the sanctum sanctorum had been flung open, for the first time in living memory, to the odoriferous likes of Streckfuss and me.

It was like any other land-grant classroom, all pastel-enameled cinder-brick and beige speckled linoleum, rectangular and fluorescent lit, with institutional gray aluminum Venetian blinds (that day, for me, a luminous avocado shade). But on its podium in the corner stood that vast relic from an earlier phase of the campus, a leftover from a frame structure of pioneer times that had once drawn termites and bats on this spot.

This Webster's was a reminder of the continuity of the humanistic tradition, and was kept perpetually turned to the page upon which the word *collegiality* was defined. Certain senior members of the faculty wanted to erect a purple velvet rope corral around the venerable lexicon, strung along knee-high bronze posts, but such a measure had been deemed undemocratic or something.

The publishers—an undying outfit back east—had, as a quaint nineteenth-century promotional ploy, equipped their product with a broad silken bookmark, tasseled and embroidered. It looked like nothing so much as a liturgical stole waiting to be kissed and donned by the celebrant on a day of holy obligation in some papist shrine. Such were the ham-handed attempts at book salesmanship in the era before the formulation of modern qualitative marketing theory and the famous "four P's."

Some of the young Turks on the non-tenured teaching staff wanted in the worst way to clip that bookmark flush with the binding, as it reeked of priestcraft in their view. "We're not Brahmans," they protested (perhaps too much). But, so far, their elder colleagues had prevailed, and the fabric remained flapping from the pages of the doughty tome, dangling in our faces every session.

I only noticed that day, as I peeked in, just how deep and satiny and shimmering the embroidery had remained all these generations, particularly the green threads. I would have affirmed in the presence of a notary public that the bookmark was vibrating like the strop in a barbershop on Saturday morning. I could hear it hum and slap.

The Webster's podium was specially made of some no doubt inferior desert wood, carved in the naively ornate and representational style of our frontier forebears. Needless to say, this hokey antique mortified the Creative Writing students. Even though it was too warm to wear outer clothing this semester, they did, especially the Derrida devotees and the Foucaultians—and the Webster's and its podium became their coat rack, to cover it up and forefend what they feared would be a disdainful glance from the teacher.

Speaking of whom, I was unable to see him within the angle I had allowed myself through my tiny separation of door from jamb. But Streckfuss must have suffered another full-body spasm, or else he was visited by an especially severe access of eagerness to learn, for he pushed me from behind, and made the other flange of my nose pop into the crack, opening a wider view into the enclosure, which included the teacher's special chair.

And, I must confess, at that moment, for the first and last time in my academic career, I regretted my unpunctuality—because the voice that had greeted us through the frosted glass and maple veneer was none other than you-know-who's. Yes, this was the legendary day the legendary author separated those much-photographed jaws and actually said something besides "Um, get another address." He sounded even more like the former secretary of state in person than he did on "Book Beat with Bob Cromie" and "The Dick Cavett Show."

We were bearing aural witness to his sole utterance amounting to more than a partial mouthful of syllables, perhaps only the second or third complete grammatical construction to exit those iconic lips since they'd ventured west of the East River. And it sounded rehearsed. Clearly this statement must signify a home truth dear to the heart and methods of a successful artist.

The air was thick with the sounds of ballpoints and pencils transcribing the pronouncement verbatim. He was propounding his personal creed and artistic manifesto—and the little dishwasher and I had missed the first part. We'd arrived too late to burn the entirety of this revealed gospel onto the walls of our very ventricles.

The collegians were breathing hard, diverse buttocks scooted way forward on seminar chairs. Their idol, their solid-gold calf, was finally starting to open up. Their vocations were on the verge of being endorsed forever.

"—and so, if people are paying for nonfiction these days, you make up a nonfiction, and falsify volumes of spurious documentation to back yourself up, and—"

I chose that moment to come barging in.

And the English Department never treated me the same after that day. It was a public university and bound by regulation; otherwise, as punishment for interrupting their celebrity guest, they would have found a way to make sure, if this Bradley goon ever did get around to declaring a major, it would not be English—because I caused the delivery of the oracle to stop in mid-phrase, never to be taken up again.

What made the famous writer clam up before bringing his

unique pronouncement to full period? Why did he re-bury that heavily televised nose in his customary book, and freeze like a spaniel in the presence of a dead duck? I, myself, was puzzled—till an explanation registered in my nostrils.

Someone in this usurped faculty meeting room carried, on his person, the dioxin-drenched jungle mildew of the former French Indo-China. I just noticed it myself for the first time, even though I'd been inhaling this deliciousness for a long while. It was an olfactible greenness: yet more of the sultry hue that had tinted my whole life over the past year or so, but of a damper, darker shade and saturation, which not only I, but evidently my illustrious teacher could sense, synesthetically.

It took the juxtaposition of the green-reeker and the college-deferred non-combatants to bring it out by contrast. My little Streckfuss was certainly the only person around here who'd ever killed someone, and he exuded the pheromones to prove it.

Toting his unwholesome breakfast of gastric crutches and a sheaf of sinister hieroglyphics, fixing all to their chairs with his huge, dead eyes, Streckfuss was gaunt beyond the point of cadaverousness, but not in any fashionable sense. Even through the opalescent billows of his blouse, cuffs pulled way down over his forelimbs to conceal the inked misjudgments of his youth, he exhibited a malnourishment too genuine to be desirable. There slithered my reptilian sidekick, an "audit," that most problematical campus creature, and he trailed an emerald-colored smog, which caused all commentary to cease.

He broke free of my gravitational influence and very bravely set off on his own orbit. With one of his purple-stained hands this dish jockey was waving his "ticket" in everybody's face, trying to find the person whose job was to tear it in half and hand over the stub for retention.

As his other hand was occupied with the "novel-book" and

cheese dog, one wrapped around the other, Streckfuss held his photocopied imaginative work in his teeth. By some very skilled contortion of lips and tongue, he was dropping one damp copy into each graduate lap he passed in his search for the usher.

It was quite an incredible performance for someone so beset with butterfly tummy, especially with just about everyone staring at him. Here was a man going among his betters, and reaching deep inside himself to find a reservoir of competence. This was his lifetime's sole chance to transcend his origins, and it was all very touching and moving and so forth. I have no idea what he did with his Big Gulp root beer.

Our teacher's nose being textually interred (what title was it, in Christ's name, that had been holding the man so enrapt all semester?), I'm not sure if Streckfuss at first recognized the star, and star-maker, whose autograph and benediction he sought. But he did not single out this averted face for neglect. Streckfuss slid his admission ticket in the narrow space between those eyes-full-of-unfulfilled-longing and their reading material, and scraped it back and forth a few times like a poorly functioning key card in a fancy motel of a somewhat later period of American history.

And he got no reaction whatsoever. Our teacher budged neither face nor book. Like some graven image, he didn't even blink. It was as though these legendary east-coast intellectuals possessed such acute vision that they could read through waggling perforations in a computer card.

But, unlike me, the former army man was reluctant to entertain this astounding possibility. He chose to interpret the guy's behavior (or lack thereof) as simple rudeness. At least the other eggheads were flinching and wincing at Streckfuss, which was a response, an acknowledgement of his tenuous existence. Yet here was this old fart at the head of the table, not even bothering to brush him off like a hovering fly. Anger started to grow in Streckfuss' eyes. Men with a background of selfless service to our country do not like being ignored. Not one bit. It never occurred to him that such a mighty genius might be paralyzed with trouser-soiling horror.

Streckfuss' mouth was full of narration, so he was unable to separate his lips and incisors to snarl. But, rather than simply allow the old fart's copy of the "Basket Balls" memoir to drop, Streckfuss spat it out, with such humid force that it wedged itself, this xerox, impossible to ignore, between the book and the nose buried therein. The recipient was too terrified to flick it onto the floor—which, I can affirm here and now, was much the better for all involved.

"Read that, whiskered possum," my partner sizzled through clenched dentition.

I had assumed those Ricky Ricardo sleeves would be kept rolled down. But now, snubbed, Streckfuss emptied his hands onto the table, in order to mash flat the puffy white clouds and roll them past his depicted wrists, beyond his forearms, clear up to the needle tracks, which I'd never seen before, sunken and swollen in the meatless crotches of his elbows. They put me in the presence of a soldier for the first time. Mars made manifest, red, not green, stood at attention in our midst. Streckfuss had re-upped. Something like pride suffused my awareness, though I was too young at the time to pinpoint the source.

Just about everyone was petrified. But there was one person in the room who witnessed no pagan theophany, who saw no mutilated body parts exposed, who heard no mouths clamming up any tighter than usual, who hadn't even noticed my sidekick follow me in and start building an interpersonal relationship with the famous novelist—because this person was busy grasping the opportunity of the resumed silence to assert her ample presentation self.

She was a local woman called LurLeen, and she made frequent unannounced visitations upon various high-level humanities seminars, today being her first appearance in our workshop. She could seriously talk, this LurLeen, on the phone as well as in the flesh, and had thereby achieved everyone else's dream: a literary agent had recently signed her on as a client. That lent her an air of real authority, which opened doors for her—even ones that would've been better off nailed shut and sealed up with bricks and forgotten for several generations.

But LurLeen wasn't all brass bands and ticker tape parades and gleaming galley proofs and not-so-secretive long distance phone calls to and from the communal TA's office. There was an artistic side to LurLeen as well—her better half, in fact.

She had a lifetime-sharing partner who was quite a remarkable poetess in her own right. This woman's numbers were dredged raw from so deep in her very abdomen that they could only be written in her monthly blood, by means of a genuine horse-hair calligraphy brush which she'd learned to hold just like a real Oriental. Many of her fellow soul-hemophiliacs found it deeply affecting, this literal self-expression. So LurLeen's lifetime-sharing partner kept that brush, the badge of her vocation, poking from the right breast pocket of her woolen plaid logger's shirt, business end bristling out to flick and splatter against you if you ever got close enough by accident. It usually seemed rinsed off well enough. You could tell because it was composed of low-pigmentation fibers borrowed from a local palomino filly's ass.

Billing herself as the Menstrual Minstrel, she had already applied for her first NEA grant, and it looked like it was about to go through. This high success, and the physically felt profundity of her verse, couldn't have contrasted more piquantly with her personal mannerisms, which were those of a nice little boy trying to compensate for shyness and genital meagerness with poorly feigned toughness.

And, of course, at the same time, the Menstrual Minstrel exuded that earnest inarticulateness requisite for masculine creatures in these Far-Western parts. Laconism is all we have to offer, our regional identity, if you will. How many subordinate clauses have you heard from the Marlborough Man lately? Or from Streckfuss, for that matter? Unlike the toughness, the Rocky Mountain inability to employ language was unfeigned in the Menstrual Minstrel's case, paradoxically enough for a poetess.

She should have fit right in with the tongueless crowd of MFA's. But our teacher, for reasons he did not care to specify (some said they were religious in nature), had not granted her admission to the workshop. Today she'd been smuggled in as a claqueur in the service of her same-sex spouse LurLeen—who was by this point in our workshop session well launched into an extended LurLeenian soliloquy.

The Menstrual Minstrel had LurLeen's speechifying mannerisms memorized, her "tee-hees" and her eyebrow archings, and so on. So she knew when something impended which required for its full effect an audience response (never forthcoming from the proper sector), and she laughed uproariously just before the punch lines. Being a physical as well as literary artist (sometimes her creations were brought into this world by means of performance art in one of the few coffee houses that remained straggling among the newly constructed Ziggy Stardust boutiques in the student part of town), the Menstrual Minstrel would gesticulate her appreciation broadly, and often enough jostle and brush up against any people in the vicinity, causing them to spill their drinks and drop whatever snack foods they might be consuming, and sometimes spill stuff, such as molten cheddar, on their clothes.

So Streckfuss wasn't the only "audit" in the room. And,

of course, terrestrial life being what it is, when he did allow himself to be lowered, by me, gingerly, into a chair, it was next to the Menstrual Minstrel he wound up sitting. On her right side.

Looking back, I can now see that I should have interposed myself between this brace of high-potential troublemakers. But I was reluctant to do so, despite forebodings, such as one of my buttocks involuntarily scooting and squinching in the opposite direction, dragging its puzzled mate along the particleboard surface of my seminar chair. If he had been seated on her left, instead of her right, I feel sure that I could have mustered the intestinal wherewithal to wedge both uncooperative halves of my ass between the pair of them, buffer-wise. I have always had the highest confidence in my built-in belly ballast, but not quite that much. I was sure I saw her palomino-tail tampon poking out of that logger shirt pocket. Let the hospital dishwasher, the ungloved scrubber of coughed-up tumor sauce from soup tureens, sit next to her.

And so he was caused to do. At first he hardly noticed his new neighbor. He kept his chopper gunner's sights fixed instead on the guy at the head of the table who wouldn't stop cold-shouldering Streckfuss, in the very climax of his debut, so soon after America's armed forces had saved this stuck-up snob's pudgy butt from communism.

"Shit," said Streckfuss, "he probably is a communist."

"Well," I whispered, "sort of... I guess. Depends on whether you read his books or observe his actions."

"What actions? He's a rich communist."

The only time those eyes unfastened themselves from the balding spot on the author's pricey head was when the Menstrual Minstrel guffawed at something LurLeen said and jostled Streckfuss. It didn't break his concentration so much as bodily disengage his line of sight. She was a wiry little poetess and capable of some seismic nudges with those unpumiced elbows. She only served to stoke whatever source of combustion fired his eyes up. I could feel the heat they radiated, and so, evidently, could our teacher, the rich communist—for new strings of sweat pearls shimmered among the photogenic furrows on that brow each time the searchlights of the Streckfussian chopper re-focused.

As a shoe-in for an NEA grant, Streckfuss' unquiet neighbor was in the government hireling camp. And that couldn't have contrasted her more with her lifetime-sharing partner, her more prosaic opposite, the talkative client of an actual Manhattan-based author's representative, LurLeen. You see, not every reveller at this party wanted to overthrow the Johnsonian ideal. I wasn't the only one motivated by greed. There were very special incentives to remain faithful to the old post-Augustans and their credo about blockheads writing for no money.

In that epoch of American literary history, for serious writers willing to engage the Great Cham's "common reader," there were opportunities to garner good emolument, such as two million dollars as an advance against royalties on copies sold. Such splendid figures often constituted the cornerstone of the publisher's entire ad campaign, which might even, in circumstances of extreme good fortune, include national television spots. Plus these novelists, having been translated whole, like Elijah, to such heights, were guaranteed the chance to see their creations interpreted cinematically by skilled screenwriters and talented directors in the employ of major motion picture studios. It was a flowering of literature.

That "two million" (sufficient, if they were sesterces, to purchase two seats in the Roman Senate) happened to be the magic figure associated famously with our teacher. It had become proverbially part of his name. You could almost see that many zeroes when you looked in his dark brown eyes. At any rate, I could, that day, see a multiplicity of ciphers, green, like artichoke-flavored doughnuts, strung from his lashes. I even saw the digital read-out on his corneas increase a quantum when he stole a glance at the sticky mass-market paperback which Streckfuss, in his fidgeting anxiety to shine today, had wrapped even tighter around his cheese dog as a kind of protective sheath, if not outright armor, against the assaults of the boisterous woman on his left.

I feared the novelist might be offended to see the result of his earnest lucubration, the product of his soul, of his very blood, so misused as a holder for snack food. But I saw nothing—except maybe another shift upward on his corneal display.

"Another price-unit will have to be vended," he seemed to be thinking (in my deranged imagination at any rate). "That copy will be unreadable when the cheddary-looking stuff starts to curdle and rot. We can send that one to the Chinks."

I heard golden chimes clanging in those ears, such as would appetize the least erected spirit that fell from heaven. Or maybe I just heard the tin dingalings of a cash register. For a few seconds I was transported back in time and space to Seven-Eleven. I was standing before the cardboard shrine to his talent, one of several hundred thousand identical promotional setups, from sea to shining sea.

If they'd bothered to fold one up and mail it all the way out here, the things must be half-assedly assembled and lopsidedly displayed in every seedy inbred trailer-trash fuck-hole clear across the Home of the Brave. It was a downright continental blitzkrieg of quality paperbacks.

Theretofore in American literary history, such all-out, hell-bent promotion campaigns had been reserved for what is known in the trade as "formulaic" fiction. But the famous writer's book was not about flying saucers or spies or natural disasters or geishas or vampires or husbands duly outgrown. It was an historical novel, that's true—and, as such, factually edified while it entertained, which appealed to the vast majority of potential customers with only a narrow slot set aside for reading in their busy workaday schedules. This, in fact, was the falsified nonfiction he had invented and backed up with volumes of spurious documentation, because people were paying for such these days.

However, the book made up for this generic concession by conscientiously eschewing the self-indulgent prettiments of rhetorical adornment that deform so many bodice-rippers and period-pieces and other such tawdry lower middle-class romances. It hewed instead with great discipline to the Hemingwayesque line and the simple-declarative monosyllables of the much-esteemed "transparent style," which traces its roots, of course, to the old "Puritan plain style" of our author's native eastern seaboard: the method of those staunch colonials who, though Christians, can be identified as his artistic forbears.

This utter readability, in combination with the author's expertly modulated, leftward-leaning politics (again uncharacteristic of a faux-aristocratic tradition, and calculated to please the upper echelons of the New York book reviewing apparatus), made for an unbeatable package. Therefore, unlike most novels of that particular formulaic sub-category, the thing Streckfuss stole the night before and had wrapped around his cheese dog, our teacher's best-selling *chef-d'oeuvre*, had achieved high critical acclaim. It had won the National Book Award or something equally indicative of literary value.

But, in spite of these and so many other educational opportunities which this college course offered the degree-seeker, Streckfuss was unimpressed. He seemed to hold in utter disregard the hefty curriculum vita of the brainiac who had just ignored him so summarily. Perhaps I had been a bit hasty, or maybe just naive, in thinking such disparate social classes could mix, even in America, the classless society.

After about twenty minutes of life among the intelligentsia, my sidekick was already getting fidgety. Quite methodically, with rodent nibbles all around, he chewed the wax off the rim of his Big Gulp cup. Terrified as I felt, off and on, I could have sworn that some strange part of me was proud to have brought him in, ill-advised though the bringing had probably been.

Through his hardened eyes, I saw my own half-habituated world as for the first time. And I was forced to admit that watching somebody read silently, meanwhile being impinged upon by a poetess as her missus effused in your ear, must be the sort of thing that can get irritating pretty quickly for someone used to a life of headlong action, such as a former car thief and chopper gunner. In fact, this session of our glamorous Creative Writing workshop would have been in danger of flopping altogether for Streckfuss, just as the other sessions had flopped for everybody else, if we hadn't been lucky enough to count the talky LurLeen among our number.

As he never said much more than our surnames and "Um," and remained otherwise inscrutable, I was unable to determine whether the famous writer had asked LurLeen to swoop her large buttery presence down and fill up today's class with sound as a personal favor to him, so he wouldn't be expected to do anything for yet another period, or whether she'd volunteered, in hopes of return favors of the Manhattan kind. She already had an agent. What other sort of favors might she have expected?

I doubt there was any exchange of the fucking and sucking category of favors going on—and not just because of LurLeen's less than nubile physique and her obvious predilections, and the teacher's equally obvious, and peculiar, lack thereof. (He never exhibited the slightest enthusiasm in either direction—or at least none that a crude and inexperienced clodhopper such as I was able to detect through my underdeveloped sense organs.) Rather, I got the sense, from watching LurLeen perform, that she held forth for holding forth's own sake, and that she probably did it even in elective courses taught by those tenured relics who inhabit the more cobwebby reaches of any humanities department, whose favor or disfavor couldn't be less pertinent to the furtherance of anyone's career. I suspect she went on almost verbatim, regardless of academic context, proceeding on sheer nervous energy and the evident bounty of her plush spirit.

I didn't know whether the renowned novelist expected and appreciated, or was surprised and irritated, by the wall of contralto sound. Personally, I found it numbing, in an oddly pleasant way. But then, I was living in a state of habitual and near total nervous exhaustion, like any teenager worth his salt.

This was, after all, a chaotic period of American history, no less than any other, notwithstanding the recent fizzling-out of the sixties, and it was difficult to find a room where you could sit that was not rumbling and rattling. LurLeen's sebaceous syllables coaxed me toward narcosis, a puffy-cheeked stupor of some duration, and I didn't notice whose xerox she was "critiquing" (a transitive verb which had recently become permissible within the walls of the academy).

I could not recall closing my peyotist's eyes in the past seventy-two hours or more, except briefly, if repeatedly, in shrill terror. So I found myself looking forward an hour and a half of humming oblivion, Mommy reading Tommy a bedtime story, something milky from Milne, my brain switched off—well enough aware, at one level, of the untenable admixture of personalities on my left, but still so frazzled as to be soothed by—

Oh Timothy Tim
Has one red head.
And one red head
Has Timothy Tim.
It sleeps with him
In Timothy's bed.
Sleep well red head
Of Timothy Tim.

It half-occurred to me, as my heart and respiration rates began to settle down for the first time in about three weeks, that LurLeen wasn't really reciting from "Now We are Six," and that she must be soliloquizing on someone or other's work, and I dimly wondered whose it might be.

"Your imagination," LurLeen seemed to be saying, "works well enough for the current marketplace, but you use *too many adjectives and adverbs!* You should try counting them some-time and see how many you use. And restrain yourself, because writing is a pure act, and not just wallowing in pleasure like a medieval mass or a gothic cathedral or something like that. Plus you need much, *much*, much shorter sentences and just a whole lot more dialogue, especially in the part where you throw basketballs at the interracial children from the end gate of your father's car."

I sat up straight.

"My agent always tells me that contemporary fiction has to be written in 'real time.' What does *that* mean, this crazy book-biz term? Well, I'll *tell* you. Real time means it takes the same number of minutes to read the story as it would to perform the actions depicted in the story. And that means it's best to just show every-day experiences with every-day people chatting about whatever plops into their minds, and let your modest sincerity, not your invention, hold the reader's interest. Plot only makes people think you're showing off, and we *all* resent a show-off, right? Being manipulated and led around by the nose into places you wouldn't otherwise go, don't you just *hate* it? Well, literary agents do, too!"

My little friend sustained a boyish guffaw and a pointy poetess elbow jammed into the floating ribs on his left side. Internal injuries were indicated: tears of blood traced the convexities of his cheeks.

"This above all: my literary agent said you have to create characters that you, and your reader, aren't intimidated by. As a matter of fact, to be on the safe side, you should only write about people that you can condescend to. I mean, not feel *contempt* for, but gently patronize. Then, for sure, you'll never put any literary agents off, because everybody *likes* to feel superior, right? Except not *too* superior, or else your readers will start feeling snooty and stuck-up, and they'll stop reading.

"I guess it all boils down to *morality*, doesn't it? If you steer clear of any notions of good and evil and things like that, and avoid telling stories where those questions pop up, then nobody will feel like you expect them to feel uncomfortable with life. Make your story like a warm cup of cocoa in a clean, comfortable kitchen, with a few of your calmest friends sitting around and just chatting and being happy about their easy lifestyles. You have to *like* your characters, and that means they shouldn't do anything you're not prepared to do yourself, like take psychedelic drugs and gun down women in cold blood, just to mention just a few of the more obvious examples."

Maybe it was just psychic projection on my part, but I was sure that I could see, on the back of the tattooed hand grasping the arm of the seminar chair next to mine, whitened knuckles underneath hair follicles that bristled like Prince Arjuna's. As the ancient Hindu texts relate again and again, one physical symptom of horror that cannot be faked or deliberately induced, not even by the most skilled yogin, is goose bumps.

"It's a kind of balance, my literary agent said, and she's the expert in the art of fiction. You ought to see the *house* she lives in! On the cool, crisp shores of Montauk Point! My literary agent knows a whole lot more about art than you or I can ever hope to know! And she said that most white males, like you, who try to communicate with something other than their *you-know-whats* (tee-hee!)—"

The Menstrual Minstrel reacted with a preemptive squeal, and almost deprived Streckfuss of his grip on his cheese dog. Both of my buttocks were cooperating now in their flight impulse. I tried to anchor myself to the table. I could see my fingernails leaving ten trails of curly shavings as they scraped along the surface—and it was formica veneer, to the best of my recollection.

"—should just forget some of your macho self-importance and try to *feel*, and you should learn about *relationships*, and also buy and study the novels of—"

LurLeen cited a lot of names which I didn't hear because Streckfuss chose that moment to place something in my bleeding hand.

"Take this cup from me," he whispered.

"—and try, really, really, really *try*, to pay attention to what these women are filling your American sisters' hearts with, year by year, day by day, and, um—what's this say? This isn't your *name*, is it? Hey, that rhymes with breakfast! And I can see you've brought yours. My lifetime-sharing partner's been looking for a word that rhymes with breakfast!"

The hemorrhaging Sappho outdid herself this time. She knocked Streckfuss' cheese dog right out of his swastikaed hand and splatted it into his chest. It slid down and came to rest on the rolled-up waistband of his borrowed trousers.

"Cute!" LurLeen was saying. "Breakfast with—"

My friend rose up from his chair in such a way that even LurLeen took a breather. He dragged the Webster's on its podium from the corner, wedged it in front of the door, and set fire to it. The parched artifact exploded at the first flick of a match, discouraging escape attempts.

Streckfuss hovered in the thickening grayness like a pollinator. He persuaded everyone to remain seated with loud gnashing sounds from the front of his face. Intent on producing an even abrasion pattern on each psyche in the "shop," he harangued the creative writers one by one, and punctuated his criticisms with sharp knees to sides of heads. Lexical smoke filled the room, but if anyone coughed or allowed a tear to slip from under an eyelid, it was as though that person had nodded off in a Zen temple: whacks were dealt, along with judicious karate kicks to vertebrae. Streckfuss was a stern tutor.

I have proof that my friend did indeed climb onto the seminar table and stomp and prance around, contrary to the ameliorating revisionism of the legends that, during the Reagan years, "spontaneously" sprang up in the fern lounges and varsity boutiques of my sedated alma mater. I retain a page from a certain MFA candidate's hermeneutic vignette, bearing the imprint of an African American platform shoe from that period in fashion history, and I'm sure nobody else in the room boasted such footwear that day. I keep this page even still as a souvenir of the passion, as Veronica kept her veil.

The departmental dictionary crackled and raged like a far-western hillside of sagebrush thunderstruck during a mid-August drought. Less than a foot of precipitation per year: you could tell how grotesque the great novelist found this essential fact of our existence. Our air was not good enough for our guest, whose nostrils, even in his current paralytic seizure, sneered with each acrid breath.

As he waited his turn to undergo the Streckfussian saturation treatment, even while wincing at the hollow sounds the
little monster's hobnailed boot made against scholarly tho-
raxes, the famous writer snouted and rooted ever deeper into
his mysterious book—or, rather into the "Basket Balls" memoir
that had been spat upon that book by the young man who had
once saved him from communism. Soldierly saliva was soaked
into the xerox, and it helped filter out airborne toxins, preserving our novelist from asphyxiation, even as he curled back his
nostrils once again and sneered at that very smoke.

He looked as though the only thing he wanted in the whole
world was to go back to his humid home on the northeast
coast of the United States of America. He seemed so little and
exposed there at the head of the table, so full of unfathomable
suffering, so eastern, and out of his element. I could almost
see—no, I did see gills gasping on his neck. He looked a little
green around them. I'd never felt sorry for someone quite that
well-to-do. It was a fresh experience for me.

After all, he was new to our remote region, a guest, something like Oscar Wilde deep in the mineshaft, but without the
ability to hold the local rot-gut so well, and with more than a
touch of claustrophobia. (Were his erotic leanings also diver-
gent from that other great conversationalist's? His extreme
reluctance to be disciplined by Streckfuss did not necessarily
rule out sadomasochistic urges.)

Considering the limited number of times he had looked
up and met people's eyes during the course of the semester
theretofore, and how few of our half-hatched visages, male or
female, he'd bothered to glance at, for all he knew, the maniac
now squatting between LurLeen's ample bosoms and vocalizing like a badger could be a downright mainstream gold-star
Teaching Fellow, student body president, and chairman of the
Headliner's Welcoming Committee. Palpable disappointment

drenched the entire being of our fabulously wealthy National Book Award recipient. He had been hoping for a more collegial reception from our university's Department of English and Creative Writing. (But, honestly, can you expect anything better from these bush-league diploma mills?)

So I scooted next to the unhappy genius and attempted to deliver him succor. I felt like the wretch in "Attic Nights" approaching the lion, as I prepared to murmur certain soothing notions into his ear. It's difficult to explain where I came up with the effrontery to essay such a thing, this bold attempt to leap class boundaries. I suppose the general headlong excitement of my surroundings at that moment must have been contagious: the sense of unbuttoning oneself, just letting go, hurting people and burning things, flinging out one's bosoms and "throwing caution to the wind," as the ladies say in historical novels.

Because I, even I, even someone like me, hailing as I did from a state where the elevation of the settlements exceeds the population by at least three digits; a part of the world infested with white trash who couldn't even claim the distinction of being former slave owners; a mintless urinal of a birthplace located on a wadded-up bit of toilet tissue depending from a smutched hemorrhoid on the anus mundi, where the only parties to go to were the wrong ones, and where your chance of being invited to, or even crashing, the right one, was less than that of a fart offending the nostrils in colostomy ward; yes, I, the scatological rustic, the undeclared freshman, with my hard R's and my obscure name that couldn't reek more ludicrously of peaked-out bloodlines and the exhausted and trite ethnicity which my very frame and coloration so galumphingly exemplified (this was the period of literary history before the Celtic Fringe became a hot item); I, me, cursed at birth with the red hair, white face, and blue-veined tickle-gizzard of Thomas

Jefferson and Paul Bunyan and other such scabrous cancers on the continent; I, that is to say, me, teeny-bop Tommy, the bumpkin Br-r-r-r-radley-boy, the product and embodiment of a rainless region of inbred Neanderthals, hayseeds, the very notion of whose ever, even by accident, getting a literary agent put one sneeringly in mind of Cinderella in a region-wide failure of the pumpkin crop: I somehow managed, in spite of my own undeniable self, to muster the megalomaniacal presumption, the unmitigated cheek, the fathomless gall, to approach the great man.

But first I took pause, in the mayhem. (Streckfuss was knocking chairs out from under people now, and stomping on fingers as they skittered about the floor trying to rescue their typescripts from his flung matches.) I decided to experience fully the above-mentioned ear.

This was such a far-famed organ, with a well-clipped tuft of just-graying and tamed shagginess disposed over it, the then-fashionable fringe skirting the top. I underwent a brief instant of absolute clarity, right then, just there, in the midst of a Streckfussian chaos that might any second penetrate the charmed circle I shared with the owner of this glitzy skull handle. It drew me in so, this ear.

I put my hand on the widely familiar shoulder (he jumped several inches out of the special teacher's chair which the English Department had thoughtfully supplied), and I peered awhile deep into that orifice in the side of his head. In its dilated vulnerability, it was like the auditory meatus of the sweet prince's father.

I took the liberty of reaching out and sliding the "Basket Balls" memoir aside, and prying up the top edge of the mysterious book from the indentation it had dug into his lap during these many weeks. His wrists and fingers seemed taken with a monumental case of rigor mortis, but an insistent, yet gentle, pressure overcame that.

So, it turned out to be *Gilgamesh* that kept the internationally revered author hypnotized for the entirety of my personal association with him. I let the cuneiform epic snap back down flat on his thighs, and read some Babylonian verses over his shoulder, hoping he wouldn't find it irritating, if he even noticed. He was turned to a bit about Enkidu—

Father, there is a man who has come down from the hills.
In all the land he is the most powerful; power belongs to him.
Like a shooting star of the god Anu, he has awesome strength.
He ranges endlessly over the hills,
endlessly feeds on grass with the animals,
endlessly sets his feet in the direction of the watering place.
For terror I cannot go near him.
He fills up the pits I dig;
he tears out the traps I set;
he allows the beasts to slip through my hands,
the hurrying creatures of abandon.
In the wilderness he does not let me work.

Speaking of coming down from the hills, this was one hillbilly's big chance to do just that. It was my break, my whole life's first and only opportunity to have a significant Manhattanite hear my voice—albeit via the half-truth serum of peyote. I would raise that voice over the general discord, and make it glare like the sun bouncing off gritted teeth, greenish. I aimed sky-colored eyeballs into the man's sound-hole a while longer, and elected to remain wordless for a time in the havoc all around. Eventually, I would decant my decoction into Daddy's dark ear.

In the meantime, perhaps a tad impulsively, I ripped the

book from his rigid grasp and tossed it to Streckfuss for pulping. Our author's gaze remained unbudgeably downcast, cataleptic, fixed on the vacancy between his legs. "What are you looking at now?" I said to the stiff. "That's linoleum, not trodden gold. Lift up your eyes for once, like a man. And look at Streckfuss. That's his name: Streckfuss. Do you think somebody falsified Streckfuss? Do you think Streckfuss is a spurious metafiction? Do you suppose there are, or are not, volumes of ersatz documentation to back up his tormented little existence? Does Streckfuss look eager to be up there on that woman's shoulders, whooping like a contemptibly western bronco buster? I suspect that somebody, shall we say, created Streckfuss, and got him all riled up and put him here to do just this, now. So, old man, if people are paying for nonfiction these days, do you think they'll buy my Streckfuss? What, um, advice can you give me, um, Teacher?"

Such was not the succor I had planned to deliver. But such he got. In return for my act of human consideration, I received no recommendation to his literary agent. Not even a phone number. But I feel certain this is only because the man was in such emotional turmoil at that juncture in his personal life, and was unable to unflex his jaw muscles to produce intelligible sounds. His previous languor had caused the same tetanal effect. This artist was paradoxically disinclined to self-expression under any circumstances.

"Damn," observed Streckfuss as he whirled past in mid-atrocity like a desert dust devil. "The old guy must of suffered a stroke."

On the other hand, he might not even have heard me demand a 212 number, any 212 number, depending on how loudly my partner was screaming, and pounding the pastel enameled cinder-brick with his own or someone else's forehead, and sickening everybody with the melony sound it made

Alternatively, his agent's phone number might not have been forthcoming for a much simpler reason. It doesn't seem possible in retrospect, but the flow of communication from that mythical pair of lips was even more constipated than usual. I can only hope that the image in my memory of the final resting place of Streckfuss' cheese dog, along with what remained of its gluey extra cheese, has been distorted by the holy communion of the Great Southwestern Desert.

The Big Gulp root beer cup, drained of its contents, sugary brown residue employed like glue, was affixed, mouth down, to the famous novelist's forehead, like a unicorn horn, or a pink and white suction device, or some other sort of outré apparatus. Somebody primped and preened this dolly.

Some campus cops, too short and fat to realize their pitiable ambition to be real lawmen, finally got to draw their huge revolvers. The forearm-sized barrels twitched in such broad ecstasy that they could have plugged anyone entitled to a seat around that big faculty-meeting table. Unfortunately, most of the future Creative Writing Industrialists of the Intermountain Region were cowering underneath, apostrophizing their mothers, and burying their heads in the spilled contents of scholarly backpacks: pencils, pens, erasers, and charred papers like oversized confetti (an unsettling number of them scalloped with teeth marks).

I'm pretty sure I was the one who caused our Enkidu to become more or less manageable. I said, "You got cheese on your co-workers' clothes, but that can be fixed. I lifted his wallet, and it'll cover the cleaners, but not your bail. I'll pawn his wristwatch for that. It's up to you, in the meantime, to see those threads don't get hurt like you've been. Let Caiaphas' servants load you with chains and take you away, and be meek as a lamb. These would-be police can't dress nearly as well as you, Streckfuss, and they'd love an excuse to yank your Afrosleeves from your shoulders. You cried 'Havoc' and let yourself slip, and God bless your soul for that. Now it's time to calm down."

But still the campus cops manacled him. They wanted a chance to use that equipment, too, for the first time.

As they dragged him out, the bony intruder used both cuffed hands to fluff up the collar of his ludicrous, but silken shirt, lent him by an even more exotic breed of oracular outcast. I tried to fake a proud smile—not very successfully. But nobody was watching anyway.

I caught my last glimpse of Streckfuss as he was driven away in a real cop car. He was not breathing peculiarly, and his skin hadn't turned corpse-gray. He wasn't sulky or pouty at all, and his eyes stared right at me through the mesh of the back seat cage. I heard the little author's voice, very loud, ending on an R hard enough to knock a hole through heaven's pavement: "What they did to me as a child—now I remember."

*   *   *   *

Maybe it's just a coincidence, but to this very day I remain unrepresented in the crystal (and very fragile) canyons of the Big Apple. In whatever afterlife awaits us, I will be raking my anonymous lungs down into my un-bylined bowels, with a two-handed gesture of eternal remorse. Possibly. On the other hand, print-on-demand is working out pretty well for me. If you read classical literature, half of your primary works will have survived the dark ages in one or two or three copies. Maybe four.

For the return on his pinky-ring, I got all five volumes of my *Sam Edwine Pentateuch* between handsome covers (Streckfuss is a major presence in the first book, and his old dad looms large in three of them), and stacked on the virtual shelves of Amazon.com and several other fine on-line book-stores all across the broad bandwidths.

And none of my quints has been remaindered or pulped or burned or mangled or smothered in cheddar, so far as I am aware. My Pentateuch can be sampled by everybody, including any Chinese person in the world with the machinery and the inclination, in return for no charge whatever, at my home page, the piquantly named *tombradley.org*. My sleeves are rolled up way past my elbows, and I am no longer green. My moniker has been scratched on the Faulknerian Door of Eternity, and not a single ass was kissed in the process.

But that doesn't magically lift me off my Pacific Patmos, where I am still paying for the above act of patricide. This remains the memoir of a disruptive member-in-poor-standing of the lumpen-intelligentsia, and his progress, or, rather, regress, from the Far West to the Extreme Orient, skipping everything in between, including Manhattan.

PEACE PARK PRANCE

On the Feast of the Transfiguration-Atom Bomb Golden Jubilee double-header, Tom Bradley, clad all in Christ-white, continues his pilgrimage toward Hiroshima's Ground Zero, to sit in somber reverie on a mass grave or two.

He moves at a brisk, skipping walk, a grin of unaffected joy on his face. He pauses at relatively unpopulated segments of the sidewalk to dance little jigs in time with a hot riff. Nudging everybody aside with his gyrating pelvis, bellying his way through queues, literally knocking the lovers of peace and international harmony flat on their asses, this is one unassimilated barbarian.

Along with the Diz, Bird, Max and Bud inside his head, he shouts the refrain of "Salt peanuts, salt peanuts," while gamboling along, almost floating—for this is the day that Christ, all in white, chatted with Moses and that other guy on the mountaintop.

Small-to-medium-sized school children on a field trip break ranks and scatter in terror at his approach. They try to hide behind their teacher, who tells them to get back in line before the big devil eats them up. Their larger classmates jeer, tug at imagined whiskers on their chins, stick their bellies out, and galumph along behind him.

He suddenly whirls about and roars, "Who has touched the hem of my garment? I felt the healing power go forth from my person! Which one of you little bastards yanked the tassel on my cloak? Was it you? Was it you?"

The kids squeal and retreat, but only an arm's length, leaving the big devil to hyperventilate on his own. At moments like this it suddenly occurs to him that atoning for patricide might be a limp excuse for lingering in such a place.

From his elevated point of vantage, Tom is able to take a moment and scan across Peace Park's grassy knolls, westward, in the direction of the Asian mainland. He has but one solace.

Part of his purgatorial term, here on the wrong side of the International Date Line, has been served over there, across the Japan Sea, in the Flowery Middle Kingdom. Tom can claim that, at least, as a distinction.

IV

The bourgeoisie has, historically, played a most revolutionary role.

—Karl Marx

For years I lived in a seedy provincial city of southern China. I spent a lot of time at this town's only joint venture hotel, a forlorn affair, which rose from among the sooty prole hovels in all four sides like a cathedral to the god of reflective windows.

On the lower floors, where the view through this wobbly glass offered something less than a lordly condescension over the squalor, the rich American and Japanese guests (who never showed up) would've been able to look straight into standard Chinese lives. They would have seen the natives hauling drinking water and sewage to and from a central pit, and slaughtering little black dogs for a month of soups. But these lower windows were discreetly covered on the inside with a kind of plasticky pre-fab tapestry, depicting hybrid Buddhist/pop goddesses dancing flat-chested among pastel mountain streams.

My wife suspected me of taking advantage of the various half-hearted pleasure chambers concealed behind that slick tapestry. But, no, my goal always lay deeper: straight through the kitchen and into the lower intestine of this institution.

I would palm a steamed bun or something off a bamboo rack as I hunched past, to ballast my stomach for the secret greeting ritual with the weird homunculi who hung around the loading dock. Before I could begin to exchange words with these guys—who looked more pussy-whipped than anybody I've ever seen outside an English department—I had to re-impress them with my unsqueamishness, my lack of citified pride.

We shared the spit-off challenge: I voided mucus on their feet, and they did the same for me, like Tom Sawyer or Gilgamesh assaulting the senses of a potential buddy before the all-important male bonding process could begin.

These were model peasants from the only "closed" quadrant of jungle in the district. They produced model tree fruits: lichees, longans, but especially loquats—enormous, aphrodisiac, purgative, deemed worthy of inclusion on the menu of the hotel's hard currency restaurant.

After the spit-off, my pals would wipe their lips and shoes. They would express their customary amazement that, number one, I was still not black-haired or short and, number two, that such a person would deign to speak the Chi-coms' lingo, which they'd only learned in order to do business. They even tried, now and then, to give me a whole crate of their medicinal loquats, gratis.

They had become literally rich off the new Shanghai Stock Exchange. Further embarkations of their collective wealth in the even more corrupt bond market hadn't hurt their bank balance, either. They were embodiments of the normally preposterous myth which most urban Chinese, prole and bourgeois alike, have convinced themselves is true: that the post-Cultural Revolution peasant is a millionaire.

These pals of mine drove brand new 2500-*kuai Zhonghua* sedans. The only private cars manufactured in the People's Republic, and the first privately owned in this entire province, the *Zhonghuas* were made almost entirely of plastic; only the engine, transmission and suspension were adulterated with a little metallic content. They parked these treasures on a rice commune outside town and delivered their loquats on borrowed handcarts, because they got better prices if the manager of the hotel had reason to suspect they weren't quite so fabulously wealthy.

They always came in groups of ten, all men; and no group ever returned until about the thirtieth or fortieth time around. I hadn't hung around long enough to see more than a couple of tens twice, but that didn't prevent me from developing close friendships with the others; for they were one man, in a sense, and all knew everything that had transpired between their brothers-in-law and the big lovable foreign devil, me.

They were honest-to-god aboriginals, and they practiced certain more or less bizarre rituals that gave headaches to local political theorists, who had to reconcile these people's behavior with the Marxist dogma that the first hominids around here had practiced a basic form of communism.

The Lolos (as they called themselves) liked me inordinately, and kept asking me to defy the provincial authorities and come visit them on their closed mountainside. And I was tempted. Judging from the rumors I'd heard about their home life, a visit was something not to be missed.

The men looked like any other millionaire peasants, but their women, an amazon class or something, reputedly went around half-naked and wore extravagant pagan headdresses fashioned from dish towels. But if you wanted to see these exotica, you had to go there—a legal impossibility for a foreigner. According to a strict reactionary reading of the regulations, I could be sent home tomorrow as a spy just for thinking about visiting this forbidden zone.

It was said, though, that even a Maoist couldn't blame a person for stumbling up there and mistaking it for a downright tourist trap. With its tidy paved footpath winding between the men's idealized hovels, this place apparently looked for all the world like the spiffy versions of native villages contrived from cardboard and televised everywhere on National Minority

Day.

Of course, the modernization of their homes would be the work of the prosperous aboriginals themselves. They'd maintained their own immemorial basic design, but had festooned everything with solar panels, television antennae, washing machine hoses and so on, and had even added lean-to style carports for their plastic *Zhonghua* sedans to nestle in. Every structure sported at least one window air conditioner unit.

But the preponderance of domestic goods, as opposed to the flawed but superior Japanese appliances dumped on other rich people and work units, served as a reminder that these people were, after all, not of the "Han" majority, and would forever lack the connections to get their hands on the best.

There was talk of the Lolomen chartering one of the new private Shanghai-based turbojets and going shopping in California after the next loquat harvest. The queen, though eager as anybody else to get her hands on a Frigidaire, was having trouble finding a precedent in their supposedly 15,000 year-long history for such a radical move. But it looked as though she was about ready to loosen up and allocate the funds—which had been earned and nurtured through the burgeoning capitalistic practices of the men, of course, and turned over to Mommy.

In this socialist paradise, these members of "the Great family of the Chinese Nation" had been compelled to pay for and even install their own power lines. No government agency was about to drag giant spools up jagged cliffs for the mere sake of a minority with revolting stone-age customs, whose women showed an unpleasant inclination to roll boulders on top of intruders' vehicles. But electricity these enterprising folks had, and plenty of things to shoot it through.

Nevertheless, my Han friends assured me that the single visual element in the scene that distinguished it from other peasant villages (they were all at least this well-appointed, according to the urbanites) was the conspicuous absence of an infant girl graveyard. This alone set the Lolos off from their mainstream country colleagues as one of the fifty-six national minorities with no birth restrictions.

Even the tax collectors had seen only the men's quarters. The women ostensibly had magnificent secret caves in the igneous side of the mountain, one huge, heartbreaking ballroom per woman, virginal of metal and plastic, and illuminated, as they'd been for more than a dozen millennia, by lit castor beans, strung fragrantly from bamboo rods. I had been privileged enough to see these mansions sketched with loquat stems in crankcase drippings under the hotel's loading docks. That's as close as any barbarian devil had ever been allowed to get to these high-tone jungle-marchionesses.

Having had their class consciousness raised by the early field commissars, who'd paid two quick, nose-holding visits to Lolo Mountain in the very late thirties, the ladies had transformed—some townsfolk would say perverted—Marxist doctrine until it fit comfortably into their own long-established ethos. They referred to themselves as a priestess class, since all females were automatically ordained from the moment of birth (not unlike males in my native Utah, where an adolescent boy can be addressed as "Elder"). They'd picked up on the implicitly hereditary nature of class, but had conveniently forgotten the part about perpetual struggle.

This was a Pleistocene-style matrilineal matriarchy, which meant that everybody knew who his/her mother was, but nobody was sure or gave much of a shit who, among the several candidates (usually ten), might be his/her father. Nobody was supposed to be aware of the modern theory of where babies come from. The assumption was that women produced them in their bellies through an awesome, single-handed act of will and grace. But the men, judging from the off-color jokes they cracked downtown, knew better—or at least, for the sake of ribald conversation, were willing to entertain alternative methods of whelping as possibilities for the propagation of the sub-species called "Han."

This unusual state of sociological affairs resulted from the fact that, for the first eon of their existence as a tribe, until the Chinese had come around with their axes and draft animals and ploughs, the Lolos had never had to think for more than three minutes at a time about food. They'd just stretched out on the warm fruitcake-like rain forest humus and let the loquats fall in their yawning mouths. They'd never let agriculture or animal husbandry seep into their awareness, nor the extended sense of calendar time that comes with sowing and harvesting and foaling.

Thus the gestation period between an innocent act of dorking and the first bursting forth of amniotic fluid was to them, in one sense, an eternity incapable of being stored even fragmentarily in the memory and, in another sense, too infinitesimal a period to be worth troubling themselves about. How were they supposed to associate the transitory boner with the awesome whole-body orgasm of labor?

As a reminder of the half-assed cooperativization of a few decades back, the priestesses allowed their men to pretend to groom a few wild loquat trees in the name of production. Untouched, their formless orchards flourished with a seemingly man-induced fecundity, which was due, according to the tribal witch doctress, to the "magic black shit of our Mother Mountain," i.e., the several feet of rich volcanic ash under the layers of deciduous rot. The men were not exactly hard-pressed to maintain their status as model peasants.

But the women expressed contempt for such labor as man's work, and preferred to feed themselves and the babies they willed into existence by the time-honored methods. They required something of a range, hence their warlike determination to hang on to as much of their mountain as they could. And the remoteness and ruggedness of their habitat, combined with the vast intransigence of the women themselves, might have been the only thing that had kept their children from throwing tantrums, holding their breaths and otherwise extorting permission from their eldresses to perform on Sunday morning national television for the amusement of Han people everywhere. Pandering to a peculiarly communist national philistinism, the poodle-cut producers wanted to dress the kids in a sanitized, sequined version of their ethnic garb, and to coach them to warble the microtonal polyrhythmics of their Neolithic anthems to the accompaniment of an untuned upright piano at the back of the low-budget studio in Beijing. All their beauty and devotion sucked out, the virgin-born Lolo children would be degraded into head-bobbing kewpie dolls—in other words, Hanized.

But, though it had even happened to the proud, outraged Tibetans, it hadn't to the Lolos yet, to their great relief. They sensed that the light of day would dry up the feminized half of Loloism like fungus under a rock.

They were the only minority, in fact, that I have ever heard of without a hefty Han majority living uninvited among them. Even the ideological derelicts and deformed beggars in the remote relocation centers, a faked minority yet, had People's Liberation Army sentries to serve as a nationalistic and stylistic example to them, something to aim for. But the only alien presence in Lololand, as far as I could see, would be me, if I could only muster the guts to accept their invitation.

Perhaps the authorities downtown assumed their own presence was as unnecessary as it would be unwelcome. Since Liberation, almost nobody official had bothered to go up there, and the Lolos had been represented to the outside world by their men only. Henpecked to an individual, and seemingly Hanized to a quintessential degree, with their cars and fairly nice clothes, the men helped keep any military or paramilitary intervention at bay.

As long as the Lolo lady-theocrats stayed under cover in their butterfly-infested caves, their lubricious midriffs invisible, the authorities seemed willing to leave them alone. The totalitarians didn't care what went on in their province as long as nobody had guns (not counting a handful of archaically equipped boar hunters deep in the hinterlands), and as long as no big brothers from overseas saw anything that would contradict the second-world vision of the place imposed by the central authorities in Beijing.

And that was my stated excuse for never being brave enough to accept the Lolos' hospitality. Spontaneous sympathy had sprung up between us, as I, too, come from a line of multi-spoused spelunkers. I would have fit right in with these yellow Flintstones. But still, to this day, I can't decide whether it was the threat of deportation, or the prospect of polyandry, that deterred me.

It's not as though I was unable to find even better reasons for the red pricks to kick me out. I only had to walk a few blocks west from the joint venture hotel's loading docks, ironically into the grotesque Little Moscow district, to find a bunch of other interdicted religious oddballs with whom illicitly to associate.

*   *   *   *

The neighborhood is all square and huge and stony-seeming. They've slopped stucco everywhere and mashed it into beveled shapes to resemble Georgian granite, lending the area a hollow Leninist monumentality. The Parthians did something similar with Euphrates mud to tart up their public buildings in imitation Ionic style. However, since "the opening of the doors," the effect in Little Moscow has been spoiled by coats of turquoise and orange paint, intended to brighten things up for the hordes of moneyed Californians, fellow Pacific Rimmers, expected to arrive any day now.

But the street committee that decreed the paint job is an entity separate from the Maoist-rife chamber of commerce. The xenophobes ensconced in the latter august body deliberately neglected to return the questionnaire that would have caused Eugene Fodor to feel comfortable pretending that his fetch-it boy had dropped by. So the place receives small mention in the Caucasoid traveler's bible, and the candy-colored, mock-Bolshevik monuments go gray with soot and dog-eared with non-maintenance.

The centerpiece of this whole quadrant of town is the giant Mao in Red Flag Square, a chubby man-mountain seemingly composed of some magical alloy, rustproof even here in the land of barely diluted sulfuric acid rain. Warts, dimples, wattles and all, this piece of appallingly vigorous social realism was produced by a committee of nationally recognized sculptors during the climactic years of the Great Proletarian Cultural revolution, after the rustications had already swallowed up everybody of my generation.

If you steel yourself and focus on Mao's bloated face, way up there in the brownish-gray sky, and if you don't trip over something and fall on your own face in the meantime, you might feel as though you're striding across a truly revolutionary city square, in the shadow of the mammoth, outstretched arm of the People's Republic's mighty author, the Great Helmsman. Then again, you might not.

The townsfolk tell tales to rubes who've just stumbled in

from the suburban cash-crop strawberry plantations. With straight faces, the city slickers claim that, while bronze statues in capitalist countries eventually turn green with pigeon shit, corrosion and age, this one has maintained the golden-brown of its first days on Red Flag Square, and no scientist has ever been able to explain why. The rubes, who've never heard of epoxy resin, widen their eyes in patriotic astonishment.

Actually, regardless of its composition, it's pretty astounding that such a thing should still exist in the middle of an otherwise bourgeois roost, that the city fathers or some other such hooligans haven't had their way with Big Boy. (Should he stay, or should he go?) Most of the other Mao's of its scale were erected in cities since Deng Xiaopingized to the extent that their centerpieces have long ago been pulled down and replaced with molded-concrete representations of something innocuous, like orange and turquoise-crested mynahs or stacked female athletes caressing volleyballs. The local progressives have not been powerful enough to revise this square of city space.

I once met a model peasant (Han, not Lolo) who assured me that he was no expert, but he knew the explanation for the fabulous absence of patina on the colossus: the revolution this brassy Mao represented positively did not age, but kept its youthful vigor, even in the worst of times. The sun-reddened sheen maintained itself by perpetually renewing its appeal to each successive generation of China-boys. I asked him to sell me a load of that for my strawberry patch. Then I climbed up on the concrete pedestal, removed one of my shoes, and used it to pound Khrushchev-wise on the toe of Mao's yacht-sized boot. This produced no ringing peals, not even a clank, but a dull thud that the faithful farmer chose not to hear.

What better place to tuck a catacomb full of counterrevolutionary papists than right within spitting distance of the fat bastard's rubbery feet?

In the courtyard of the storefront "ecclesia," (as the tiny removable placard quietly labels this fish shop on Sunday mornings), the ancient sacristan of the underground church can often be found squatting in the shade of a banana tree, clipping wicks. Though the presence of a foreigner is potentially lethal, he doesn't look scared at all, and he's too polite to gawk at you.

The ersatz priest, though not thrilled, takes your presence in stride. "Father" acquired the gift of composure during his thirty-seven years as a prisoner at the Qinghai death camp, way out west. He used his own scant saliva to wash away the original sin of mad, starving political prisoners in the Gobi Desert. But he is not allowed the sacred privilege of serving communion. Only the "Patriotic" priests can do that around here.

Our pseudo-padre may lack the body and blood, but he's got some balls. He and his coreligionists are China's heroic non-schismatics, and they're up against not only Beijing, but Rome itself. Their rivals in the so-called Patriotic Church made a number of doctrinal concessions to gain the imprimatur of the central authorities. Despite his commie-busting reputation, and in blatant disregard of the heretical nature of those concessions, His Holiness the Pope jumped on the bandwagon and upheld the legitimacy of their apostolic succession. The legendary lure of the Chinese market has corrupted far better men than John Paul-John Paul.

Meanwhile, the gallant priests of the underground church all died out. Rather than unspelunk themselves and go begging to the "Patriotics" for fresh consecration, my friends in this fish shop proceeded quietly to starve their spiritual selves. Deprived of the musculature and hemoglobin of Jesus Christ all these decades, they've somehow managed to keep their chins up, even though the Supreme Pontiff anointed his infallible crozier with holy oil and dorked them right up the butt. And I had the gall to claim victimological whining rights back home among the Mormons.

All this can be dismissed as a slightly gaseous form of politics. Physical survival occupies a much more prominent place in the parishioners' minds. Not infrequently, they pause in their undertakings and cock their ears in the direction of the fish-emblazoned storefront. In this police state, sirens can often be heard. It's a sound that never frightens these people to the point of stopping their singing and praying altogether, but it does give them brief pause whenever it echoes into their secret place of worship.

Nobody is especially nervous: not the silent acolyte who floats among the plastic flowers and Christmas tree lights, his face more like a medieval saint's than any you're likely to see on a living body; not the ancient lady with translucent skin, four-inch feet, and the golden eyes that still condescend half a century after her social-climbing warlord husband was smashed by the Reds, and she was liberated and pensioned as a crippled victim of feudalism; and not even the blackened peasant women who pedal incredible distances every week to be here.

Unfazed by the distant shrieks of storm troopers in full charge, they all nevertheless jumped out of their skins the first few times I made an entrance. I have to admit that I bear an uncanny resemblance to the large red-bearded Savior scrawled on the rectangle of shelf paper that is unrolled and tacked on the wall above the card-table altar each week, the icon of the Redeemer due back any day now for true Liberation, once and for all.

To prevent the older mackerel-snappers from suffering heart attacks, I usually tried to soft-pedal as much as possible my relatively awesome barbarian physique. I lurked in the back among the week's unsold fish, as far away as possible from that card table. But there was another reason for my chariness: my whole hefty metabolism has always recoiled like an albino vampire from anything that smacks of the Real Presence.

Dad might have been a god-scoffing atheistic Jack Mormon infidel, but my mom was low-church Episcopalian, and at her liberal knee I learned the very definition of the word "symbolism" by coolly contemplating the poetical nicety of the wine and bread. My otherwise rational wife, on the other hand, is of the Romish persuasion, and kowtows once a week before a wafer-thin slice of the sole material that puts her in divergence with post-seventeenth-century thought. It would be not only disrespectful, but also vaguely terrifying, to approach something that substantial with a head full of attitudes flip as mine. I'm sure I'll see wads of gristle and scab.

So, there I was, my father's son, with my history of brushing past the skirts of Jehovah and staring without a flinch into the chaotic abyss. Having always felt so much more enlightened and sophisticated than my superstitious seagull-worshipping Utahn neighbors, I was now cowering up against a carp tank that doubled as a baptismal font. Even though this was the underground church, famous for its pitiful lack of a goblet full of transubstantial gore, I never did manage to approach the card table, just because of the macabre associations in my mind.

I skulked at the periphery of a foodless and drinkless love feast, attended by, arguably, some of the clearest thinkers in the People's Republic of China: men and women, mostly women, who had the sense to recognize their own history as a perfect illustration of the futility of throwing oneself into the arms of a secular, therefore fallible, savior.

Mao was the creator of the first and only paradise in the history of the oldest, biggest civilization, which is the closest thing to the miraculous ever accomplished by a mortal. (This, at least, is what they tell foreigners like me if the question ever comes up within earshot of a Public Security Bureau man.) After Liberation, Mao gave one out of every four people on earth a sojourn in Eden, the Seven Good Years. The city parks were admission-free, nobody ever shoved on queues, and the party's materialistic idealism served as a fresh moral force among the youth. Millions of flesh-and-blood Lei Fengs strode around in their cloth shoes doing good things as, for the first time in history, a commie economy was on the rise. Western observers were wetting their pants.

But even Nero had his quinquennium. The Great Helmsman slouched duly into his dotage and frightened off poor Khrushchev with his enthusiasm to nuke America. This left the economy on its own to deal with his senile megalomaniacal dream of overnight industrialization. Mao destroyed that problematical paradise just as surely as he'd created it: serpent and God the Father rolled into one chubby little carcass.

The frequenters of this fish shop, most of them peasants and lumpen-types, showed the intuitive sense to put their faith in someone who actually claimed to be God, no pussy-footing, no false modesty about it, who offered them literal perfection, manifest to their eyes at least eventually, who promised that he wouldn't die and go away and leave them in the slimy, bloody hands of a Lu Shaoqi or a Lin Biao.

They believed in someone who didn't require a mausoleum to contain the tissues he left behind, his head lit up bright yellow from within like a latex jack- o'-lantern, but who, on the contrary, even made special, more or less unprecedented arrangements for his body to vanish and go someplace far, far away, so that no matter how bad his executors and successors and administrators fucked up, no matter how many millions of people got burned, tortured, maimed and killed in factional power struggles and other forms of holy and just warfare, you always had the sneaking suspicion that he might return, fresh, moist and fully animated, to fix things up and kick you in the ass.

The Helmsman/Savior whom they bought into cleverly harnesses the power of your own imagination with his claims to perfection, and you do most of the work for him. He's as nearly perfect as your dreamy, faithful brain can make him out to be. And the sky's the limit, because there's no visible competition. You can do the In-Tourist shtick and schlep yourself over to Moscow on the train and see the embalming job they did on Lenin; you can go down to the People's Republic of Vietnam and check out the seams around Ho Chih Minh's hairline: but where can you go to find a rival for somebody who was shrewd enough to outflank the taxidermist altogether, so he can't be seen except in your head?

The guy had class. He never said a single overtly political thing, but just sniffed off the whole question with his "render unto Caesar" line. Yet he carried out a profound coup on the imagination, as indicated by the presence of my pals and the "priest" and the acolyte, all bearing the lumps, bumps and extra holes of past purges.

And, like those doomed Meso-Americans mistaking the whiskered conquistador for Quetzalcoatl, these parishioners thought, at first glance, that I might be Him, with an upper-case aitch, the real Big Boy. Their gasps brought me back to church a few Sundays, at least. I squeezed in and out, every time splintering a couple of the child-sized makeshift pews that were disguised during the week as trestle-supports for fish baskets. Weekly replacements were somehow scrounged in this lumber-poor nation, until the heart-breaking novelty of being mistaken for the Parousia wore thin.

That's a megalomaniacal pleasure unavailable in the

Patriotic Church, which, with the Polish pope's cynical and meretricious blessing, canceled the Second Coming in a display of political canniness. Even market-reformed Marxists can't allow anyone but themselves to end history. So I quit attending mass altogether, and sank comfortably back into my habitual state of irreligion.

But sometimes I walked by the fish store on Sunday, anyway, just to listen to my pals in the tiny congregation wail their caterwauling version of the Kyrie Eleison, set to a microtonal *erhu* melody from deepest dynastic times. They belted it out with more sheer decibels than you'll ever hear from a first-world parish ten times superior in number and bulk, with ten thousand times the reason to praise God. I wish Rome's own Big Boy could have been there to hear them sing.

*   *   *   *

The Chi-coms didn't exactly smile upon my hanging around the subterranean shrine to a god presumptuous enough to usurp their self-claimed privilege of closing the few history books they haven't already banned or burned. But that's not what finally got me kicked out of the country.

In the middle of my second year in China, the dean of the foreign languages department came tapping at my door with an ultimatum from "the leaders." I was to surrender my students' Creative Writing, and be quick about it.

Democracy, or at least the kids' notion of it, was all the rage. The whole country had been jostled the night before by several mild examples of the demonstrations that would eventually climax in the massacre in Tiananmen Square. A lot of people in China were tense, especially my old dean, who'd lived through several political "movements" and bore the lumps and bumps to prove it. The poor guy was on the verge of apoplexy at my vestibule. I was his *waiguoren*, after all: he'd been the one to invite me to this tenth-rate university in the frozen industrial wastes of the remote northeast, and he was supposed to have been keeping an eye on my comportment in the classroom.

Between workshops, a few select graduate students and I had been discussing our pirated offsets of *1984*. Intoxicated by the illusion of freedom that had briefly entered their lives, they'd been writing stories about fat, tyrannous bus conductors, and small-town party hacks lining their pockets in the name of the glorious revolution. These stories, inept as most of them were, had now apparently become objects of intense curiosity for "the leaders."

The previous year I'd taught in the deep south, where the bare mention of "Marxism/ Leninism/ Mao Zedong thought" could be relied upon to brighten a dull lecture with hoots of derision from the back row. My subtropical undergraduates did have a party representative charged with their political and moral nurture, but he hardly ever showed his face. Those two semesters in the sun had made me complacent, and it wasn't until the dean showed up at my door that I realized my seminars here in the north had been infiltrated by party spies, who held mere deans on a short leash.

The old man started moaning up into my face from the blackness of the corridor. "We are colleagues and good friends, are we not? I've told you many times how much I suffered in the so-called Cultural Revolution. The Red Guards made big-character posters about me and placed me under house arrest. They burned all my poems and broke my legs. They forced me to write self-criticisms for a whole year. You are, I suspect, a reasonably intelligent man, and you must understand that you place me once again in a difficult situation. I will be criticized severely for not keeping watch over my foreigners."

I had listened to this at least a thousand times. Till today it had only been on occasions as innocuous as dinner invitations. But this time, though the words were verbatim, the delivery was different: pure terror, like an animal's. More was at stake here than just his apartment on the fifth floor where the rats were a little less dense. The dean knew first-hand what "the leaders" were capable of. The adolescent fury of the Red Guards had merely been a surgical instrument in their hands. (At least that was his paranoid revision of that decade-long incident.)

"I've always dealt honestly with you in all our work together," he was saying. "And I give you my solemn word, as a fellow scholar and teacher and lover of the English language, that none of your pupils will be persecuted in any way for what they have written."

I knew that last bit was an outright lie. The leaders did not want to read the stories for their aesthetic value. But I was nevertheless tempted to comply with the order.

I couldn't afford to be disassociated from the dean and all his editorial connections. He could be a forest-flattening dynamo, despite his dynastic birth date. We may have had our minor differences at the moment, but he and I both preferred collaborating on scholarly articles to doing just about anything else, except maybe attending banquets at the provincial *wai ban*. Back in the good old days, we'd been quite a duo. Of course, that was before the occidental aberration called democracy came along and spoiled everything. That was before the young people's spirits were polluted with thoughts of Pepsi and Rambo and disco marathons on Stalin Square.

And now, if I failed to deliver up the stories and, along with them, in effect, my "pupils," my half of the by-line would be purged from all our pending publications. I'd have to retract the fat vita I'd sent to every university and junior college in the free world, and trim it back down to a page and a half. There'd go any justification for dragging my poor, blameless wife to

China in the first place.

What would become of us? Foreign experts detained in the People's Republic? Interviews on Voice of America, maybe even the BBC World Service? Book contracts? Tenure-track appointments in major first world English departments? Before I knew it, I found myself praying that the communists would pack me off in chains for a brief but grueling stint at the Qinghai forced labor camp. My wife could be re-educated in a stuffed toy factory. Think how svelte and employable we'd be upon release! Our deportation could be a big international incident.

Being a husky male WASP from a prosperous far-western community, and a late baby boomer to boot, I'd never had much experience with this sort of thing. I was still in high school when the draft ended, and only got in on one anti-Nixon demonstration. My experience with police officers was limited to the night I got stuck somewhere outside Provo and a highway patrolman gave me a can full of unleaded and five dollars. So thumbing my nose at totalitarianism—or at least inciting my disciples to thumb theirs—was a new and exciting experience for me.

Occasionally, though, during those cold Manchurian nights, I'd calm down a bit and begin pondering the pedagogical questions that should have been my main concern all along. For example, why had the grad students requested a course in Creative Writing in the first place? China, after all, is a country in which most of the full-time novelists and poets are living on government salaries, and write accordingly.

This is not to say there weren't plenty of opportunities for free-lance fiction translators. One publishing house after another was bringing out series like the highly successful *Contemporary Masterpieces of American Literature*, featuring Arthur Hailey and Sidney Sheldon and other artists of that caliber. On Saturday afternoons my students would track me down for help deciphering lists of "culturally loaded" terms that had stymied their progress through such works as *First Blood, Part II, Iacocca,* and *Nancy and Ronnie, a True-Life Love Story.* Cheap Mandarin versions of Freud's more titillating works were being hawked in street stalls, and Lady Chatterley could be had in Shanghai. There was a corresponding flowering of literary magazines, which were responsive not only to the loosening of censorship but to actual market forces. The formula at that time demanded just a little sex. Some of my students were trying to make a few yuan on the side pitching stories to these magazines, and they needed to be coached in the techniques of the soft pornographer. We devoted one whole class period to that very topic.

But was it possible the kids had somewhat purer motives for asking me to supply them with fiction workshops? Did they actually have something they wanted to say? I considered this possibility with dread, having been indoctrinated alongside the likes of Streckfuss and LurLeen in American Creative Writing programs, where form equals content and preferably replaces it.

And I wasn't the only one reluctant to deal with kids with a message. The same dean who was now twitching at my door had earlier that year asked me to "introduce Derrida to China" by writing an article for the university journal. Nothing would have pleased his tired soul more than to see English majors all across China safely off the streets, wrapped up in fluffy hermeneutic conceits, penning unintelligible, therefore apolitical, vignettes about their tiny navels.

I obliged him with a dozen or so pages of nonsense, just for the vita stuffer. But somehow my article did not generate much interest among the students. The babblings of lit-critters have little pertinence under conditions of actual political oppression. The inscrutability of texts is nothing but a non sequitur to young people whose heart and respiration rates can be visibly quickened by reciting Orwellian mottoes. They scoffed at the notion that all language is inherently repressive. How could something so exhilarating be repressive? They'd laugh in the face of their dorm monitor, and misquote Big Brother loudly in one voice: "Animals and English majors are free!"

They said dangerous things out loud, right in class: a non-revisionist history of the party is impossible to get in China, but, in Hong Kong and America, books as true as Emanuel Goldstein's are openly distributed; the insidious processes of Newspeak are recognizable in Mao's attempts to "de-feudalize" Chinese characters—and a whole catalog of other such oral braveries.

In the halls and the dorms, even in the rest rooms, big-character posters suddenly appeared in English, Chinese, Japanese, Russian—

WAR IS PEACE
FREEDOM IS SLAVERY
IGNORANCE IS STRENGTH

I knew exactly who'd painted and posted these incendiary *da zhi bao*, and I was delighted to have been taken into the confidence of such stout comrades. I felt like one of the boys. So, obviously, I burned their stories in my bathtub and invited the old codger to come in and stir the ashes with the toe of his rubber galosh.

He mourned, without affectation or haste, over the Victory brand porcelain. "These ashes mean nothing to you, Dr. Bradley" he said quietly. "You gorge on Chinese rice and puff up your resume with Chinese publications. And you pray for the personal fame which the declining bourgeoisie crave as a substitute for the self-respect that capitalism fails to provide.

Soon you will return to your country and lay your head down in peace. But we have to stay here and try to keep from smothering each other. This is your forty days in the wilderness. For us it's been forty centuries."

The dean somehow managed to make it out of the apartment on those unlucky old legs of his, but not before quavering, "I can tell you the leaders will consider this an unfriendly act."

But, in this far corner of China, it didn't quite require the People's Liberation Army to put the kibosh on such counterrevolutionary high jinks. Northeasterners might come on strong at first, but they roll over easily, for they're accustomed to being pushed around by bullies. The Soviets, the Japanese and the Guomindang each occupied that very town in living memory. Almost overnight the jackboot came down on my kids' faces, but so subtly that I didn't even notice.

Immediately after the conflagration in my tub, their stories began mysteriously to depoliticize, their expository essays to sink to innocuous topics like child rearing, and to be accepted for publication by the op-ed folks at China Daily, where they'd formerly been rejected with indignation. By the beginning of the second semester, their creative work had completely dried up. To pound the final nail in the coffin, our supplementary reading moved on from twentieth-century dystopias to contemporary novels in verse, as my syllabus had given ample warning it would. Our mimeographs of the equally verboten *Pale Fire* turned out blurry, and the class flopped.

Unfortunately, I wasn't imprisoned or tortured or deported. All that happened was that I served out my appointment, and was unable the next academic year to find another job anyplace in a country where, only two semesters before, department chairmen had been writing me flattering letters and even traveling hundreds of miles by hard-seat to recruit me, as one of the few renegade American Ph.D.'s in the Flowery Middle Kingdom with absolutely nothing to go back to in the States. By the time the tanks rolled out onto Tiananmen Square, I was comfortably ensconced in the suburbs of Hiroshima, gaining weight and teaching Business English Skills to the grandsons of Hirohito's baby-impaling imperial troops.

The magazines that once held out hopes of artistic fulfillment to my students nowadays devote most of their pages to articles on how to pass TOEFL. I hear that English majors have become a rarity, and MBA's are crawling from under every rock. Nobody mentions the D-word anymore, but no matter: the economy is fattening like a pig. They're even developing an illegal alien problem with their unhappily democratized neighbors to the north. For the first time in modern history ice people are waiting table and mopping up and spreading their thighs for sun people.

If the twenty-first is to be the Pacific Rim Century, it will also be a golden opportunity for American Creative Writing programs to justify their existence. Now's the time to send entire regiments of graduates to proselytize the heathen Chinee: metafictionists and Foucaultians marching as to war.

I'm sure that, given an adequate grounding in deconstructionist theory, the future compradors of China can be relied upon to write and think and say nothing to unsettle their deans or incite their classmates to misbehavior. Thanks to Creative Writing, China's MFN status will no longer be jeopardized by unsightly videotapes of students squashed on the cobblestones, and our economic wagon will remain guiltlessly hitched to the red star that rises from the far shore of the only ocean that matters anymore.

Besides, with all the new MFA's and Ph.D.'s gone among the heathen, their professors back home will no longer be troubled in restaurants and taxis by that embarrassing question: exactly how much do you tip someone whose graduate committee you served on?

*   *   *   *

I sometimes wonder if maybe it wasn't such a bright idea to burn my kids' papers after all. The fire only aroused suspicion where, almost certainly, none was warranted. How stupid did I think those graduate students were? How likely was it that they would commit counterrevolutionary notions to paper and place them in the hands of a typically blabber-mouthed American barbarian?

I have no doubt their papers were politically meticulous. In fact, looking back, I now seem to recall, among the ashes in my tub, fragments of ideas framed in curiously tight hands:

We are finished with the ten years' chaos. We are modernizing now, and the people don't need to hear bad news...

The workers are not involved in the marches, and the students are nothing without them. So foreign experts need not write home saying that our society is unstable...

A foreigner, especially an American, can never understand what Lu Xun meant when he said, "In China, men eat each other." If we take a look at the way men are behaving today in the new free markets, we will see why we must move more slowly, why we are still unfit for democracy...

The younger students are just bored. They think that democracy is disco dancing and brawls in the lunch lines. This is nothing...

*   *   *   *

Considering what happened soon after I hightailed it off the Asian mainland, I suppose it is unfortunate that I wasn't imprisoned or tortured or deported for this particular act of shit-stirring. Unlike certain other parties involved, I was always able to rest secure in the knowledge that nothing worse would be done to me—which leads us to the inevitable topic.

Now, before you get all riled up at the things I'm going to say about certain goings-on in China, remember that they're happening within the borders of a sovereign nation whose people have, for four thousand uninterrupted years, placed a different value on human life than Americans do.

Try to get a typical Red Chinese lumpen-prole to sit down with you and share a few minutes of pleasantly goose-bumped thermonuclear war paranoia. He'll first look puzzled, then think about it for half a second. And then he'll say there are so many of his people around that lots of them are bound to survive even the biggest holocaust Bush can provoke—so, no need to fret. And his lack of a silly grin when he says this cannot be ascribed to the legendary inscrutability of the yellow face. He's not joking.

This is Asia, remember? Do you think the Greeks were just goofing around when they took up their spears and pushed the Persians back across the Hellespont? They were doing nothing less than inventing the West. This was no arbitrary line drawn in the mud, despite the Turks' recent grotesque attempts to graft Asia Minor onto the European Union.

We live in the incessantly touted Age of Globalization, but the East remains the East, and the absence of a humanistic tradition is one of its defining characteristics. The individual counts for nothing except in the context of the group. A single Chinese existence, unless it belongs to someone of the ruling class, or to someone in your immediate circle, is unimportant.

Human rights are a non sequitur, democracy an impossibility. Both are regarded as bits of barbarian fatuousness by most comrades who haven't been overexposed to American professors.

I did my damage there during the years leading up to the most recent massacre in Tiananmen Square. There were student demonstrations in those days as well, particularly during 1988. Most of them took place in provincial cities, so they were suppressed more subtly, and did not receive much attention in the outside world. But plenty of students did cease to exist.

For example, my teaching assistant Wei FuLiao was quietly put on trial for his life, which means he was dead before too long, because, in this socialist country, people aren't tried unless they're guilty.

He and his fellow scholars were political prisoners, even though they were arrested without fanfare in a supposedly non-political "anti-crime campaign" on charges ludicrous as they were trumped-up. These arbitrary police orgies have always been famous for spawning novel offenses: "The aggravated saying of lascivious things to girls in the city park" is but one example—the one they pinned on shy, virginal Wei FuLiao.

There was another consideration that hastened the boy's dispatch, once he was in custody. Regardless of the circumstances of their arrest, imprisoned students have historically shown the tendency to say and write counterrevolutionary things, and to attract embarrassing international attention, as certain enterprising veterans of Tiananmen Square '89 have been doing lately. So Wei FuLiao and the other hapless degree-seekers were silenced quickly, rather than being kept on ice, as it were, in the Public Security Bureau lockup.

Then, as now, an indefinite period of what our own proportionately more numerous prisoners call "dead time" was prescribed for the students' proletarian cellmates: those mute, illiterate, almost pre-lingual, certainly apolitical rapists, house-breakers and bike thieves who comprise the steak and potatoes, or rather pork and noodles, of any robust Chinese anti-crime campaign.

There's no danger in letting the uneducated ones hang around. "Foreign experts" such as I have not had the chance to expose those humble boys to the seductive lies of bourgeois individualism. I flatter myself that only Masters Degree candidates in British and American literature enjoy a few hours of useful consciousness among the zombies. And it is precisely this consciousness that poses the greatest danger to the power structure, hence the speedy carrying out of their sentence. Education has its benefits. Parents tell your children.

On the other hand, when society condemned the poor unlettered townies, they effectively died on the spot. Never having been taught to distinguish themselves from their lost "face," they became tongueless as corpses that vultures have gnawed on. That's why there is so little mugging and wisecracking at your typical Chinese bloodbath. The People's Republic has not produced many self-composed martyrs like Saint Lawrence, the fricasseed deacon, who quipped, "I'm done on this side. You can turn me over now." And I doubt many Chinese look sarcastically up to heaven and say, "Let's do it," as my glamorous fellow Utahan Gary Gilmore did—assuming Norman Mailer didn't pull that deadpan one-liner out of his ass, like so much else.

Their personalities may be less than fresh and dewy, but this is not to say there is anything lacking in the non-matriculants' physiques. A strapping young hooligan will tend to be better nourished than your typical varsity boy, and probably healthier in other respects as well, here in the land of forty percent hepatitis-B infection among the general populace. Even in the Chinese context, student dormitories and college cafeterias tend to be exceptionally squalid, with rats and roaches of Jurassic proportions.

And that's the other reason for the swift application of "justice" in the students' case, regardless of fluctuations in the heart, liver and kidney trade. Their produce is less marketable. The working-class stiffs are not put out of their numb misery till demand for the saleable bits of their bodies generates a price worth the bother of causing them to be dead.

And it is a bother, after all. This is not just some spontaneous lark. Two or three People's Liberation Army trucks have to be gassed and loaded up. Patients in the hospitals have to be notified that their transplant operations are scheduled for the morrow—and this is complicated by the fact that most of them are foreigners and don't understand the language of the Mandarins. The utility poles in town must be pasted over with posters bearing the condemned's names (mass invitations to a beheading) —and do you think it's easy coming up with the correct hieroglyphs to render these kids' monikers, when half of them have never even been taught how to hold a pen properly?

Like his more famous classmates crushed by tanks a year later in Beijing, Wei FuLiao was sacrificed in the name of the man who was called "Doctor of Mimeography" in his Parisian student days; who should have recalled how he and his betters came to power as idealistic youths; who, in the infinite cynicism of extreme old age, proclaimed the national anti-crime campaign that was my T.A.'s undoing.

It was, of course, like most proclamations by Comrade Deng, something else in disguise. It was an opportunity for enterprising civic officials to thin out the ranks of dissidents while they were still too insignificant to warrant outright political persecution, while they could still be simply disposed of without calling attention to the hellishness of this society. If the fundamental militarism of China hade been revealed only in part, it would have cut into the tourist dollars that Americans were scheduled to sprinkle from their airplanes that summer, in those early days of troll-cute Deng's "Four Modernizations," when the PBS and NPR were sedulously making the place look and sound like Shangri-La East.

Way back in 1980, one of these anti-crime campaigns was inspired by warring teenaged gangs hindering the progress of Deng's limousine through the streets of the nation's capital. By the time I came stumbling through, the preposterousness of the excuses for his temper tantrums reflected the little prick's intellectual disintegration in the meanwhile.

According to one of Wei FuLiao's dormitory mates, who had just returned from a visit to Beijing, some idealistic youths somehow managed to sneak into the garage where Old Deng's limo-of-doom was resting between not-to-be-hindered prom-enades through the imperial city. They soaped the following dangerous slogan on its bulletproof windshield:

RAT PISS AND PIG SHIT
IN THE MOUTH OF
THE MALIGNANT PEPPER-FARTING DWARF

Clearly, a ballet of death was overdue.

The last time we honorable foreign experts saw our little Sydney Cartons, they were rumbling across the cobblestones of Stalin Square, standing in the back of an open-bed army truck with not a few of their former classmates, their heads shaved. They were unable to wave at us, for their hands were tied behind their backs.

Everyone in my particular town watched them take that last spin. They were paraded a long time, disguised as hoo-ligans. But it was a poor disguise, for only underfed students could have so many ribs showing. If the authorities wanted the locals to mistake them for members of the criminal class, instead of beating them in the lockup, they should have fattened them on noodles and pork lard, the diet of thieves in China's newly rich age. Everybody knew exactly who the students were, it was clear, for the staid burghers were not as pleased as usual—though not particularly displeased—to observe these troublemakers' exit.

Sentimentality has never been a popular vice in the land of jasmine tea and porcelain. By way of illustration, let's say that, for some surreal reason, regulations suddenly required these folks to embalm and bury, rather than efficiently to cremate, their dead. It can be safely assumed that the Chinese would never have caused a scandalous ruckus like the one in Britain lately, over the stripping of baby carcasses in hospitals. All it would take would be for someone wearing glasses to go on television (as someone did on the BBC, to no effect), and point out that precisely the same process takes place, at a hefty price, in mortuaries, in preparing defunct tykes for tasteful, scentless, display. In China there would be no supernumerary funerals, no parents grieving after the fact, no modern versions of gruesome canopic jars, and no parasite priests pocketing the proceeds.

As for those youngsters who haven't quite reached the stage of being profitably strippable, yet retain a certain holistic worth—I would be willing to bet forty or fifty dollars that the rumors I've heard lately in this regard are untrue. It's whispered breathlessly in the Free World that condemned Chinese prisoners who happen to be pregnant are being deprived of their soon-to-be-ex-spawn beforehand, which are then sold as health food, and also as the active ingredient in high-tone American society matrons' hand creams. This is probably mere nonsense. If there are half as many Palestinian medical students chained to the conveyor belts at municipal abortion mills today as there were a few years ago, the not-quite-children of well-behaved citizens are in plentiful supply, and extraordinary measures to garner felons' fetuses would create a redundancy in the larder. (Swift suggested ragout, but in this case I think it's stir-fry.)

Masochistic religiosity is another shortcoming which is not typically Chinese. If Japan's famous child-dismembering serial killer, Miyazaki-san, had spent a working holiday on the mainland, they would never have gratified him with bushels of tearful petitions begging him to reveal the whereabouts of his victims' legs, so they could be cremated and wafted up to third-hand Buddhist heaven, there to be magically reattached to the rightful owners, who could then run and play among the pink clouds and keep in lock-step with all the other dead kids. (Japanese are inclined to bully anyone of their number who happens to be handicapped.)

In China, executions serve two purposes, at least one of which is arguably nefarious. But enhancing the fame of non-governmental egomaniacs is not among them. Even the most whorish of China's famous novelists could never be expected to attend the execution of a particular criminal as preparation for belching the "true life story" into a dictaphone—unless, for some bizarre reason, the party, which keeps writers on salary, assigned this famous novelist to engage in such behavior.

As for that other group of citizens of the People's Republic who are lately having a disproportionate number of their skulls perforated and vitals harvested, the *Fu Long Gong*—it does occur even to my educated, enlightened, "westernized" Chinese friends that an organization which encourages its prepubescent female members to set themselves on fire should, perhaps, be subjected to a certain amount of discouragement, with judicious numbers of its followers put down as an example. China has to be a hideously difficult place to govern, and the uneducated masses do tend toward a certain extravagant faddishness, particularly the youth. Large numbers of teen self-immolations in public squares can only have a destabilizing effect.

However, the carrying out of legal sentences on convicted criminals, and the recycling of viscera they have no further use for, in order to liberate law-abiders from coronary disease and the living hell of dialysis—this somehow sits well enough with most Chinese I've shot the breeze with. They may not cherish each member of their nation in the same heartfelt way that an enlightened Occidental such as George "the Reaper" Bush does, but they are not heartless. Neither are they brainless. That's apparent on execution day.

A single round fired point-blank into the occipital lobe is preferred to our kinder, gentler lethal injection, as the latter chemically taints innards and renders them unsuitable for sale. This back-of-the-attic approach also leaves precious hearts and kidneys unpunctured, which makes them more attractive to the people-giblet mongers who cater to rich sick people, including Americans. So greed does enter into it.

But, in my day, before there was so much saturated fat in the Chinese diet, causing heart disease and gout to flourish and the giblet market to boom, these preservative effects were considered merely incidental benefits of inducing fatal brain trauma. There used to be, and probably still is, a much deeper reason than greed for the "head shot," to use the phrase made famous by G. Gordon Liddy.

In spite of their typically Asian lack of a concept of the individual, the people of the Flowery Middle Kingdom have contrived an eerily individualistic method of execution. Personalized service, if you will. For purposes of rapport, each boy is held from behind by the boy who is about to shoot him. The killings are as much for the benefit of the soldiers as they are for the ones about to die. And it's easy to understand why they refrain from stepping back in a squad and putting a dozen bullets into the front of a torso tied firmly to a post or chair, as they used to do in my beloved home state of Utah, most glamorously to Gary Gilmore.

Kneeling down, flopping forward with the blast, the condemned undergoes a split second of total subjugation and repentance. Before his head scrubs into the ground, there is a moment when it seems that, not the bullet, but the shocking realization of his own culpability makes his body thrash out of control. And the solitary soldier standing straight above and behind, is filled with a reaction to that action, an equally overwhelming sense of his own righteousness, and that of his superiors.

Many of the executioners' pectorals swell, their chests ballooning, at the moment their cousins' split faces slop into the cobbles—though their disciplined mouths remain inscrutable, unsplit by grin or gape.

This way of liquidating undesirables in China could not contrast more ironically with the anonymous gang-bangs that only a few years ago were choreographed in my native Utah, in order to obey the Mormon prophet Brigham Young's injunction that "He who spills man's blood, so shall his blood be spilt." (Not only the hangman, but the electrician and the pharmacist were cheated in the Latter-Day-Saint Zion.) A dozen unnamed volunteer Mormon farmers and drugstore cowboys were selected by lot and handed high-powered rifles at random, one of which was supposedly loaded with a blank shell, so they could each go home after the brave feat was accomplished and tuck in their eight or nine blond children at bedtime with the news that Daddy maybe wasn't instrumental in granulating a person's torso that day.

Multiple killers, working as a team, a small robotic mob of them, in which each can lose his identity; the refinement of the problematical blank cartridge, affording at least the technical possibility of anonymity even within the executioners' own minds—this is the sort of procedure one would expect an Oriental civilization to devise. Meanwhile, China invents precisely the personalized method of state-sanctioned murder, the hands-on, man-to-man delectation of gunpowder-driven sadism, that could come straight from Dubya's brain (which seems to function well enough on this vicious level).

It was said in my Chinese town that from among the ranks of these one-on-one death-ushers would come a disproportionate number of the lieutenants which the revisionists were introducing into the formerly rankless People's Liberation Army. But maybe one particular student's executioner wasn't destined to receive his commission as soon as his comrades, for he wasn't allowed his full measure of warrior-making exhilaration. It was reported on the streets of the city afterwards that my own Wei FuLiao, alone among his death-mates, had refused to yield to the full measure of degradation.

Though frailer and lighter than the others, and though his milkless skull had disintegrated more completely than anybody else's that day, or on any other festival of public homicide anyone had ever witnessed, Wei FuLiao's small body resisted the final insult with enormous insolence. Refusing to go limp, my teaching assistant's spine knelt straight up for almost ten full seconds, minus two-thirds of its crown. Then it thrashed as if in moral, or at least electrical outrage. It stomped on two knees, then one knee, and only fell to the ground because it slipped in a puddle of spit.

But even then Wei FuLiao did not fall forward, exposing his buttocks and anus in a ritual offering of the penultimate submission, but actually fell backwards, into the blast, facing the soldier in bright-red faceless scorn, snagging the smoking muzzle among his ragged membranes, wrenching the rifle from the soldier's hands and thrashing some more until not one, but two men had to use their bayonets to carve out his cardio-pulmonary system—which used to be the regulation response to this rare circumstance, before cardiopulmonary systems became worth their weight in foreign exchange currency.

In those days they hadn't yet dreamed up the cynical measure of deliberately placing the bullet in such a way that the body could stay alive long enough to keep its saleable bits fresh for surgical removal. No, they still had a certain level of squeamishness under cuddly little Deng Xiaoping, and shot to kill every time. And when an executee failed to cooperate, as Wei FuLiao did, they said, "Fuck the harvest," and put him out of his misery. They cheated the audience out of its spasms of delight by rolling him over and performing their own soldierly style of surgery with their bayonets. Presumably, in this bright new millennium, the recent boom in the market for hearts, brought about in part by the opening of the doors to America, has put paid to that remnant of what we big dumb cowboys used to call compassion, and the victims are left alive, even strapped down so their thrashing won't bruise the goods.

Sometimes I wonder if the warden at the Utah State Penitentiary during Gary Gilmore's glitzy stay had already dreamed up the notorious Chi-Com refinement of shooting a few of the brighter-eyed wretches someplace far away from the head, to preserve their corneas for harvesting, as is done once in a while today, now that market forces have rendered P.L.A. officer training less important than before. Gary had some lustrous peepers, as you'll recall. There could be a rich Salt Lake City polygamist ogling his newest twelve-year-old bride through that sage's lenses at this very moment.

Wei Fuliao wore Coke bottle glasses—but not to the execution he so selfishly disrupted with his obduracy. As it happened, one of the bayonets snapped off between his ribs, those early stages of modernization being incompetent to produce steel resilient as my favorite pupil. It's said that a mysterious female derelict took advantage of the chaos to run up and pluck the broken bayonet out of the carnage. She vanished into the cheering crowd, thirteen centimeters of serrated death, red and bristling with bone slivers, concealed in her crawling rags.

This was not good, because, like most sane countries in the world, even ones which place a low value on a lone human being, China has not only gun control, but knife control, and unregistered blades over a certain length are illegal. The piece of stolen government equipment had to be located and secured. Impetus was provided for yet another anti-crime campaign, on the local level. The bamboo-and-rag doors of many suburban prole hovels were booted down in the following days and nights.

If every municipal government in the country had acted so swiftly and decisively in 1988, a lot of fuel for army tanks could have been saved a year later on Tiananmen Square.

PEACE PARK PRANCE

By this point in Tom's pilgrim-progress among the heathens and Hiroshimizers, the expression on his face has intensified into one of bona-fide religious ecstasy. Tears of joy flow from his eyes, as he periodically raises them to the heavens in beatific reverence and gratitude. On this Feast of the Transfiguration, his raiment has begun to glow like a really clean undershirt in a black light tavern. Meanwhile, the Bud Powell inside Tom's head has already torn into his unbelievable piano solo, so it's time to prance on.

He comes upon a huddle of wheelchair-confined prepubescent hemophiliac AIDS patients, hand-picked from the deep rural institutions where they will be hidden away for the rest of their brief lives. Video crews from everywhere except America are interviewing them for the wisdom that might tumble from their translucent lips regarding man's inhumanity to man. This is as close to being mainstreamed as they'll ever get in such a proud nation; so Tom drags a CNN man over, to catch them with a creepie-peepie before they're sent back to the dungeons.

To the rubber-gloved, surgical-masked wheelchair wrangler, Tom explains, in flawless Pentecostal Japanese, "These kids ought to make my president really nervous. Don't worry about a thing. We'll send him a copy of the videotape, and he'll think twice before pushing the button."

Having accomplished that, Tom continues his ministry, bearing glad tidings of great comfort and joy to the benighted.

V

As if you could kill time without injuring eternity.

—Thoreau, *Walden*

I n certain moods, it's difficult not to wonder whether it's my own fault, this expatriated condition of mine. Has my exile been imposed by my own lack of discipline? It's true that I received my writer's vocation at a promisingly precocious age. But that doesn't mean I neglected the electronic media. And maybe I wasted altogether too much vitality on this sidetrack, when I should have been honing my low-tech craft. Is it possible that I could have scribbled myself a niche in my own country, after all?

But the small screen, and the silver screen, can be so seductive to a little kid. And I will never forget one early morning, in the latter half of my elementary school career, when the local Mormon TV station made a mistake and actually broadcast something stimulating.

It was a silent short subject, one of those ancient slapstick orgies, the first I'd ever seen. The proper frame-rate to run such movies hadn't yet been recollected from the misty past. Everyone thought they were supposed to be fast-motion and jerky. That false quality caught my eye, and I asked my dad what in the hell I was looking at.

"Watch the language," he said. (For a second, I thought he was referring to the titles.) "It's an example of primitive movie making."

Dad's antepenultimate was one of my buzzwords. The other

was *heuristic*. I was in a serious do-it-yourself phase. It was the pre-rental video era, yet I had managed to see *The Swiss Family Robinson* seven times. That's how many different grownups I'd pestered into driving me all the way downtown. (This was also the pre-suburban mall era.)

"Like how primitive? Could I make a movie like that by myself?"

"Well..."

"I mean with just stuff in the backyard."

Dad was holstering his slide rule and heading toward the door on his way to support the family. But he paused a couple dutiful seconds and rubbed his freshly scraped chin. "Backyard stuff, eh?" he said. "Are you including the old Bridgestone tires and the jugs of lawn chemicals? And that broken Frigidaire the neighbor kids like to play house in? Or just *Swiss Family Robinson*-type stuff?"

He knew where I was headed.

I had read Defoe's contribution to this genre of prepubescent male fantasy, probably the kiddy version, as well as *Lord of the Flies*. At such an early point in our father/son heart-to-heart, I wasn't thinking of much more than twigs and tendrils in various combinations. In that halcyon period before the eighth grade and excessive LSD, educators tended to tell me I was "borderline-precocious." But I needed a nudge from novels and movies into the anchored empiricism of physical substances and processes. I would oblige Dad to give me my nudge, even if it doomed him to miss his usual jump on the morning rush hour.

"Interesting question," he said, and sat down, his briefcase poised on his knees for a speedy exit. And he murmured it once again, more vaguely. "Interesting question." (Was he trying to convince himself?) "Hollywood on a shoestring. Minus the plastic ferrule."

He winked at me. But I didn't know what a ferrule was, so I didn't wink back or chuckle or anything like that. I probably should have.

"Well," he said, sitting up a tad straighter, "we moderns have a considerable technological history behind us. To be fair, you'd have to give yourself a sort of racial amnesia, and start with no prior knowledge of the properties of materials. Or that they even had 'properties.' You'd need to do an awful lot of research very quickly. In your shoes, my boy, I would fail immediately." Without quite standing up, he reached out his extraordinarily long arm and groped for the knob on the door.

I wonder, in hindsight, as they say, if such a ready admission of fallibility on the part of my lifetime default role model shocked little Tommy, me. I don't recall any emotional reaction to that paternal caving-in, except maybe impatience.

I detained the old man and somehow, with my boy-level locutions, got this general idea across to him: the way I saw it, there was no obligation to "be fair" and "start with no prior knowledge of the properties of materials." I could remain the modern youngster that I was, with a more-or-less clever pre-teen layman's knowledge of technological history—but with an admittedly peculiar need to make art from absolute scratch.

"Obviously," I piped (or words roughly to this effect), "poetry and painting and song and dance are simple to arrange. A movie is more of a challenge."

"'Challenge' is putting it mildly."

"And I'm giving myself the maximum believable luck."

"Which you'll need. Especially with regard to the animals, vegetables and so forth that we could scrape—or, rather, *you* could scrape—?"

Dad looked at me in an odd sort of way. Was he offering to pitch in, or trying to be gentle about begging off? He and I always did have a rough time communicating our basic desires and motivations to one another.

"—that *one* could scrape from the trees or dig from the dirt."

Maybe he was just hoping to scare me off in time to get to his classroom before his beloved disciples wandered off. It was impossible to tell. I followed my father's glance as he averted it from my face to the tube.

It was turning out to be a downright Mack Sennet festival. Some Latter-Day-Saint at the TV station must have had a nervous breakdown and become non compos mentis. Here it was, kiddy-narcotizing hour, yet "Augie Doggy and Doggy Daddy" were nowhere to be seen. I could swear, in retrospect, that they were even forgetting to insert the breakfast confection commercials. But that's impossible.

In apparent dismay, Dad watched five or six rickety Model-T's barreling down a Los Angeles back street. They wove in and out among themselves in fast motion, like a squad of basketball players on drill.

His voice took on a slightly pleading tone when he said, "How about if you just did the screenplay? Your big brother and I laid some nice flat flagstones around the sort-of patio, and I could show you how to make a nice Cub Scout fire for charcoal, and you could scribble—I mean, write—"

He knew it was no go. I may have received a calling for it, but no red-blooded American boy wants to be seen, out of doors, frittering away his vitality on the wimpy alphabet, to go around with people snickering cruelly behind his back, "There goes a print man," and applying to him that most contemptuous of modifiers: *bookish.* Far better to be called a Nancy-boy. Whatever reading and writing I did was a death secret outside the house.

Without acknowledging his suggestion, I told him what I

wanted. For example, tearing branches off the trees and ornamental pyracantha bushes for fuel, melting the contents of the sandbox to manufacture camera lenses—

"—and, also, I guess, I'll need to siphon off some glass to make insulation for my generator and electrical components, since rubber trees will not be available, and I've declared the old tires off-limits—"

I was trying to stick to Thoreau's ideal, yet couldn't picture the operation without electricity. A generator seemed requisite.

But Dad said, "Whoa back, Trigger." (He thought I was still on Roy Rogers.) "I can tell you right off the bat, kid, that home-made electricity will not be plausible."

Thus, with that single flat and unqualified pronouncement, my dream was shattered to shivers, like substandard glass. Throttled at birth. I couldn't believe such summary betrayal was possible within the nuclear family. What was this, Attic tragedy?

Just from the way he enunciated the words *home-made electricity*, Dad made my whole idea sound so unworthy of consideration. Building a generator involved too much. Everyone should know that, should have it pre-wired in his brain at birth, if not braided in his DNA at the moment of conception, for Christ's sake, as a basic rudiment of the common sense God gave a newt. My ambition of from-the-ground-up electronics was so infantile and preposterous, evidently, that I decided not to bother to ask him why.

But, I asked my sullen self, what was so insuperable? Dig up a little iron for the magnets, some copper for the coils, insulate where necessary with home-made glass—I wasn't planning on mega-watts here. I assumed that the old man was just getting, shall we say, *mature* and unambitious. Or, even more unforgivable, he was withholding permission for fear of my electrocuting myself. I elected to pout like a teenager in a movie.

That pout brought forth a weary sigh. "How sharper than a serpent's tooth," he groaned in body language. He took his briefcase off his knees, set it down on the linoleum, and plugged the distant percolator in, barely unbending his phenomenal arm.

"Do you really think," he said, "that you, or we, or anybody, confined to the backyard, without the aid of shovels and picks—"

I decided that Dad was being defeatist. Or else he was just coming on like the typical absent American father, unconcerned with his own spawn's intellectual development. This guy was not heuristic.

"—and, even if you dug deep enough, straight down to bedrock, and somehow hacked through that, using your fingernails presumably, and scritched and scratched and nibbled and bothered your way clear down to the Mohorovicic Discontinuity, do you honestly reckon, son, that you could come up with the ingredients for this generator? And collect enough of the various metals for your electronics? I don't mind telling you that it's highly unlikely—"

My face fell. I was not quite past that stage of development where tantrums are effective. Large as I was for my age, I could throw some elemental doozies. The whole block lived in dread of my hissy fits.

"Careerist," I hissed under my breath as Dad stole a furtive glance at his watch.

"—but not altogether impossible," he hastened to add, in a higher pitched voice, yanking his cuff down over the crystal. "I mean, if we're talking theoretically now."

"Theoretical is good," I said, in a soft but intense voice. I looked ominously down at my feet.

"After all," said Dad, sounding like a slightly depressed shoe salesman, "our backyard is situated within coughing distance of the world's largest open-pit copper mine, right?"

"And all I want is a little buzz," I moaned.

"And you're probably right about glass insulation—"

He gave me a "there's my bright boy" cuff on the side of the head, as a sort of consolation prize, mussing my imitation Beatle haircut with patronizing affection.

"But," said Dad (and he accompanied himself with stealthy motions of the shoulders, trying to ease the following notion into my little brain without chafing against any raw edges), "the result will be such a big cumbersome thing, won't it? Such an inefficient generator will need a giant crank, don't you think? No, a treadmill. Some animate creatures will be required to provide traction. I don't see any oxen grazing out there." He waved his arms in what he obviously hoped would be a gesture of broad preposterousness. "What would you do? Enslave a few dozen of the neighborhood children?"

Now, I am sure that his conscious reason, at any rate, for saying the above was to discourage me further. As the official report card signer, he knew I was bringing home C-pluses and even an occasional B-minus in civics class. This was one American lad tolerably well indoctrinated in human equality and human dignity and human freedom and that shit. But Dad's voice had placed altogether too much emphasis on the key word not to introduce at least a few complications.

"That's fine," I said. "I can enslave."

I was still just normal enough, in those pre-Purple Haze and Orange Sunshine days, to have friends. They visited our backyard frequently enough to be considered natural constituents thereof, and thus comprised an exploitable resource, if one were willing to stretch a point. So, Father's helpful suggestion posed no special difficulty at all. It was but an afterthought, especially compared to the technical questions we had yet to grapple with. Not to mention the cosmological puzzles that would soon envelop the Bradley household.

Nor would press-ganging enough warm bodies to rotate the treadmill pose any particular physical challenge for the likes of young Tommy. I was busily expanding to my present six feet, nine inches, three hundred and twenty pounds. (Can't help it: basketball family, you know. My father holds a plausible claim to having invented the hook shot when he was a pro in a cage in Chicago, way back in the olden days; my second-cousin Bill Bradley played for the Toledo Twats or whoever, and then went on to become one of the next presidents of our nation; and my Mormon nephew Shawn Bradley is currently the NBA's premier shot blocker or something. I have no idea what team he plays for, but he's seven-foot-six, so he gets to be in Bugs Bunny movies. It's not fair).

I chose to be no less systematic with the problem of human bondage than with my more scientific quandaries. An economy was being built here, as well as a motion picture studio. Introducing slaves into that economy required, of course, a source of calories for those slaves to burn. I informed my dad (his face blanching the while—he was a Kennedy Democrat and a card-carrying member of the American Civil Liberties Union, Utah chapter) that I would feed my livestock on the crab apples that casually fell on our side of the redwood fence from the laden boughs of the neighbors' tree, which esculents we Bradleys rightfully owned, according to something like Anglo Saxon common law, probably.

This was getting serious for Dad. I could tell by the various colors his face was turning. Babies in bondage in the backyard, Simon Legree for an heir: it was time to wax seriously dissuasive. "Turn back, oh man, forswear thy foolish ways" is what they sang in the non-Mormon church we were supposed to be members of but never went near. But he knew better than to appeal to my higher nature and impulses. Any alert parent who understands the sheer contrariness of little boys' minds will choose indirection in a situation like this.

"Tommy, hang on. I mean, it's very good that you've provided for your, er, employees' dietary needs. But why don't we back up a tad, shall we? Just for a moment. Don't you think a fellow might run out of fuel pretty quick making all these fires, lots of huffing and puffing, to prepare the copper? And especially the iron? There's only two trees out there."

Two and a half, actually. They were black locusts, and they filled the whole block with seminiferous things every year that caused the Mormons to resent us. Popularly known as a "trash tree," the black locust is a loosely organized being, the farthest thing from hardwood, and couldn't be a more inefficient source of fuel for very hot fires. Dad was right. The sorry organisms would be cakes of dead carbon in no time. If I was a scribbling poofter we might have something to talk about here. But I most emphatically was not.

So even something as simplistic as a blast furnace was proving no less impermissible than the generator itself. My dreams and ambitions of artistic self-expression, still sparkling with the moisture of youth, were popping like spit bubbles. I said nothing. Instead I just let my little face fall, once more, to tummy-button level, with that disappointment, that disenchantment, so chilling to a parent of future teens.

"This is not heuristic," I whispered.

Father yet again backed off from his dismissal. He was turning out to be one of those modern American parents who have difficulty saying no and sticking with it. Instead he tried gently to persuade his impulsive boy from such a dead-end path.

"You may tear down and set fire to the redwood fence—"

"Thanks, Dad."

"—if it's not too adulterative for your program."

"What's that supposed to mean? Thou shalt not—?"

"No, no. Outside stuff, you see. Not occurring naturally within your topographical perimeter. Violates your own ground rules. That fence has been creosoted and varnished and painted god knows how many times, with the devil only knows how many different store-bought compounds. For Hell's sake, creosote comes from the destructive distillation of coal. And do you think, if coal was anywhere near our backyard, Brigham Young wouldn't have caused this whole neck of the woods to be gutted long ago?"

He paused and looked at me with a peculiar sort of intensity. I couldn't tell if his question was rhetorical.

"Um," I said, "well—"

"But, let's say you loosen up a tad on your no-outside-stuff requirement (your big brother would say 'cop out'), and go ahead and consume the fence. Even still, depending on how many sequels and prequels the entertainment market will bear, you may wind up needing to grow more trees. And you know what that takes."

"Time?"

"You said it." With the finality of a coffin maker driving home his ultimate fastener, he intoned, "Time, my boy, is one commodity that can't be stretched out, or fudged on, or substituted for, or snuck past. Time's unlike creosote. You can't cop out on that."

"Time's unlike creosote? Can I quote you?"

"You have only so much. And I have almost none."

Dad looked at the clock. Pavlovian class bells would be ringing now at his place of employment. He visibly fought the conditioned reflex to reach into his briefcase and fetch his roll book.

"Time is no problem," I said—and learned that fact only as I uttered it. I didn't know why it was true, nor why I'd been assuming it so deeply that I hadn't bothered to verbalize that requirement (or lack thereof) before now. It gave us both pause, this odd little utterance of mine.

My father heard it well enough, and nodded in agreement, with a similar lack of consideration. We didn't even glance at the television.

I said it again: "Time's no problem."

Not forgetting to feign another sigh of resignation, Dad looked at me with unmaskable pleasure in his eyes. He took pains to restate my notion, his boy's new insight, so that it would sound as nearly rational as possible—for now. This was still supposed to be merely a scientific discussion.

"Of course," he said slowly, "time's no consideration. I mean, not for someone your age, right?"

"Right, Dad. Us kids have no sense of—"

"Time. Right."

His roll book, for the moment at least, was forgotten.

"Especially," I added, "since, unlike you, Dad, I've got nowhere in particular to go today." I beamed a proud grin at him, which his own face reflected like a convex mirror.

I was undergoing my most recent suspension from school, a regular thing for me. I am fortunate to have undergone brat-hood in the days before Ritalin and Prozac and Luvox. Otherwise I would have been doped into submission instead of banished. Not a bad boy, exactly, I was just following parental orders when I refused to stop arguing the origin of species with a certain sacerdotal functionary who spent his weekdays posing as a public school teacher. (This guy, incidentally, was never one of the educators who told me I was "borderline precocious.")

It was this crew-cut crypto-proselytizer's "Utah history"

class from which I was continually being ejected, because my fourth- or fifth-generation excommunicated Jack-Mormon atheist dad sent me there each morning with a bad attitude and a head full of amino acids, primordial soup and other evolutionary decoctions, and a directive to challenge the "Elder" on the doctrines of Creationism.

This was just one of the several ways in which Dad, in his own words, "systematically corrupted" me, his priceless boy. He had started the process early on, trying to subvert my socialization already in kindergarten, about the time Teller launched all that lethal Nevada sand in our faces. Filling my head with locally heretical doctrines would help ensure my never backsliding into some "hare-brained throwback Latter-Day-Saint crapola" as my nephew Shawn Bradley did. Bugs Bunny's co-star hawked the faith of Brigham Young in Australia for two years when he could have been earning about sixteen million bucks getting his nose and collarbones broken by ebony elbows in the NBA. The fans throw bottles at him and call him The Great White Ope because he looks and acts and sounds like an elongated version of Andy of Mayberry's fair-haired boy.

Rather than allow anyone in our branch of the clan to be sucked into such a downward spiral, Father was bent on getting me officially and publicly expelled from the second most potent disseminator of Mormon "culture," the Utah public school system. He would cite my permanent record to embarrass me into relenting if I ever, by some freakish twist of circumstance or some gross overdose of mind-bending drugs, decided to get baptized by full-immersion, and convert, like my seven-foot-six clown cousin, to the sect that had spilled and nearly expunged our very Bradley blood in one of the many episodes of savage tyranny that have since been deleted from the pages of early Utah State history.

So I cut my rhetorical teeth facing down the "Elder." He was a textbook paranoid-schizophrenic who had ninety-eight percent of the *Book of Mormon* memorized, and who, in order to be able to keep his own animalistic self contained in his polygamist pants, simply had to believe that he bore no relation whatever to the naked chimps that hung their private parts between the bars at the zoo and flung excrement at people.

So far, my limited debating skills had only managed to get the lunatic to kick me out for brief periods. But I intended to be an obedient child, and to continue rubbing the rock salt of natural selection into the open sore that was the "Elder's" psyche, until I got an outright parole from formal education (every real boy's dream).

When and if I ever succeeded, I wasn't sure if Dad was planning on coughing up the exorbitant tuition for Episcopalian parochial school, or on home-educating me, as our polygamist friend Mr. Singer did with his own children before the state authorities came and shot him to death on his front porch for such lawless presumption.

Speaking of which, the ancient comedy flickering in front of us now jerked in a very big way, right off the reel. It stopped altogether, browned, and started to bubble, as it got stuck in whatever hot contrivance TV stations utilize to put film on the air. Someone at the station downtown, presumably the mad Mormon who'd started this sepia jamboree in the first place, acted fast, gave the thing a good thump, and got it going again, after only five or six seconds of the televisual equivalent of dead air.

"Still and all," said Dad, shaking his head slightly, like someone who's just been nudged awake in an auditorium, "um, as you said, time's no problem... yet, be that as it may... yes, even with the, er, scheduling restraints loosened up a tad..." He cleared his throat. "Even taking your, let's say, boyishly inchoate sense of time into consideration, there's still one bugaboo, one utter perplexity."

"A bugaboo?"

"The sheer size of the *energy* requirement here. You could place the entire student body of your elementary school under the yoke, for Christ's sake. Stake out a space as big as the whole block for them to twirl your treadmill—and that last bit's by far the most implausible: Brigham Young wouldn't allow your great-great-great-grandparents enough dry dirt to die on, in blatant violation of the Federal Homestead Act of 1862—"

He was back on track, and pouring coffee, oddly, into two cups.

"—but I still doubt you'd be able to get the amounts of energy, of *light*, you'd need for a movie. Tommy, I'll have to go with my previous statement that no dynamo would be practicable—"

Again, my face fell. I was starting to feel stretchy around the hairline. But, before I could throw myself on the floor and start howling, he quickly said, "—or *necessary.*"

But I didn't hear that promising qualification, because I was holding back tears (or maybe pretending to), and very obviously grasping for means to salvage not only the project, but my budding sense of self-esteem. I hiccoughed, bravely, "Well, gee-whiz, Dad. What about a wet cell?"

The "Elder" had shown us how to build one in pseudo-science class the previous year. (Such tinkering was devoid of overt cosmological implications and hence permissible.) I knew the salt requirement for a wet cell could be easily met. All I had to do was glance out the window at the blighted landscape of my birthplace. Neighbors of Scandinavian and Anglo-Saxon descent, but with the faces and hands of Essenes, squeaked past in brand new cars, undercarriages already rotted away. Salt was no problem. I could maintain an ample supply just knocking deposits off the rain gutters after the briefest of April showers.

"Well," my father replied, with monumental amounts of patience in his voice, "let's talk about that, okay?" He felt obliged, like the competent nurturer he was, to tell me what was good about my fancies before giving them the thorough trashing they deserved.

"It's true—and I am so proud of you for learning this at school, Tommy—that a saline solution is needed for a wet cell. But it would have to be even bigger than the generator. It would have to be a continental wet cell. Did I hear you wrong, or did you not say *just the backyard*? I thought this backyard thing was a spatial restriction, too. Was I wrong? Are you going to spread the contents of our god-damn garden clear across the—"

He was getting a bit frustrated and starting to treat me like another grownup. That was no good. So I said, "Teacher says the Great Salt Lake is a wet cell battery. That's not continent-sized. They bisected it into halves of unequal salinity with the causeway, and—"

"And it generates about one thirty-thousandth of a volt every year." Father fanned his arm toward the window, at the dead sea on the horizon, which suppurated under its customary shroud of sulfur dioxide. "You're really going to get great picture quality with that. Talk about *film noir*. Your teacher has his head up his sea gull-worshipping ass."

Dad got serious now. It was time to light up a cigarette. Being the most emphatically non-Utahn of all mainstream tobacco products (designed and marketed, as they were, to appeal to African Americans, whom the Mormon scriptures describe as "black and loathsome"), Kools were what he smoked, in those days before experts decided all that extra menthol crystallized the lining of the lungs to no wholesome effect.

"Tommy," he huffed secondhandedly in my face. "Son. My boy. Think of a movie. Think of all of the brightness coming from a movie. That's a reflection of what the projector is sending to the screen. Today's screens are efficient reflectors. Your screen would be the backs of large pieces of bark or mold. How would you go about getting light to pass through the image with enough power so that you could actually see it? That would be about two intensities of a typical overhead projector. Just a whole damn bunch of light, Tommy. Bags and bags of light. Powered by proportional amounts of electricity. And it must follow, as the night the day, and all that crap, that your wet cell is an even dumber idea than—"

"We could use magnesium," I countered. "I bet there's some out there. Teacher says it's the eighth most abundant element in the earth's crust. Or else I could derive it from the chlorophyll in the plants."

Even though he must've known, as a full-time professional educator, that sarcasm rarely works on the young, and certainly never twice in rapid succession, he couldn't curb the irony.

"Magnesium? That would be a very strange and short movie."

"Fuck it," I said. Little Tommy commenced skulking off to his bedroom to assemble model airplanes with that seductive-smelling glue.

Dad was on the verge of losing his son, a nation-wide malaise in that epoch. His tardiest beatnik grad-students would have been accumulating among the rows of desks about then, yet he felt constrained to reach out and buttonhole me. To all appearances, he started warming to the task. But that was deceptive, a desperate job of play-acting. He began talking fast, trying to haul his boy in and fasten him to his side with ropes of words. Dad had a counterproposal.

"No, no, no, no, no. Don't fuck it, son. Not just yet. Watch the language," he remembered to add. "Electricity is not necessary. I'm thinking solar. You know, Save the Trees. Your big brother and all the other cool college kids eat this stuff up. Sunshine, not that dark subterranean shit from Hell that you have to melt just to get it to behave. I'm thinking of the nice easy things ol' Sol helps to grow every day."

"Twigs?"

"Tendrils as well. Like that. Like our little plywood playhouse we built together in an earlier and less, um, complex period of your youth. Fond memory, right? Let's do that again. We'd build a small hut, like our playhouse, but with light seals all around, fashioned from tree sap and mud, and a small hole in a wall or two. If we could get a good beam of sunshine through this Latter-Day-Saint smog, that would project nicely. Oh, and we need bearings for the hut, because it's set on a rotational device so it can follow the sun, while the mice are turning the twig-and-tendril cage wheel to run the images through. This is going to look more like Jacquard's loom than Edison's Kinetoscope."

I decided that I liked the sound of that. The idea of a clickety-clack affair appealed to me. It was better than some hot sputtering thing, truer to my Flintstone roots, more like *The Swiss Family Robinson*. It had taken some doing, but this little representative of the newest generation of Bradleys was successfully weaned from directed drifts of electrons.

"A hut *cinematique!*" I hooted.

Father saw the habitual tension leave my face, and felt emboldened to say, "Now, son, by this time you will have manumitted the neighborhood kids from generator detail, as in free the slaves."

Hearing that, however, made me petulant again. I should have known there was a social program lurking behind this. "You never want me to have any fun," I whined.

"You know that's not true!" he cried, desperate to swap his social conscience and political convictions for some filial affection. But he failed to demur quickly or ardently enough to prevent my retiring, like Achilles, to sulk in my figurative tent.

I consulted the television in silence. It continued to serve an uninterrupted stream of pre-Depression slapstick, from a time when the majority of rank-and-file Hollywooders were bumpkins—like my extended family, come to think of it—and had thick-skulled notions of what was amusing, and what was permitted.

I only just consciously noticed something that my eyes had been registering for several minutes about these silent short subjects: most of the interest lay around the edges of the frame, where palm trees blew mournfully in an odd gray haze. It was an opportunity to see what southern Californian vacant lots looked like, back in the days when most (instead of today's mere many) members of the Bradley tribe were still living like the Flintstones, deep in the Utah mountains.

One of my buzzwords, as I said, was *primitive*, and I came by it honestly. It wasn't just *The Swiss Family Robinson* that piqued me. It was the Deracinated Family Bradley as well.

In the 1850's Mormon missionaries had enticed us all the way across the Atlantic from the coal mines of Sheffield, England (I don't know how we could have fit in the tunnels; maybe we worked behind the counter in the company store, fetching hardtack off high shelves), only to kick us almost immediately out of their territorially omnipotent church, and drive us naked into the wilderness. We howled at the moon and subsisted like Neanderthals and interbred for two generations, or maybe three (amid such genealogical chaos, spouses and spawn are difficult to differentiate), self-creating in a literal sense.

Unlike Mr. Thoreau, who was back east at the time having

his camp-out, we did not hear "the rattle of railroad cars, now dying away and then reviving like the beat of a partridge." We heard grizzlies and timber wolves beating the hell out of each other just outside the glow of our campfire. And there were no trains within eight hundred miles.

It was only in the past sixty years or so that we Bradleys had begun to shamble back down from the federally designated Primitive Area, high and deep in the Rockies, where it's still legal to kill anything not worshipped by the aboriginals as long as you eat it. We'd stealthily settled among the very folks who had, for reasons still in dispute, chased us off like flatulent pets so long ago. Keeping a low profile, not receiving the benefit of the Mormon welfare system, the Bradleys were socially ostracized (thank Christ almighty: I'd have made a horrifying missionary). The only career opportunities open to the likes of us were sordid positions among the communists and alcoholics and other deviants at the non-Mormon university. If my boyhood's backyard was to be a self-contained unit, it would be modeled on my clan.

Only that summer we'd planted a great-grandma (or great-great-auntie—nobody knew) who, before senility claimed her, could sputter a few spasmodic syllables of the private language her cousins (siblings?) had invented among the stalagmites, Brontes without the basic literacy skills. Ours was one family that had not forgotten its victimological heritage.

Primitive was the buzzword, even like my father, still, in the most important parts of himself. He was a professor at that time, but remained a troglodyte under that thin tenure-track veneer. And it was starting to come out this morning, I could tell. Waylay the old man long enough, get him sufficiently bored and irritated with some insoluble problem, and the sagebrush lycanthrope would poke its damp snout through. Briefly bring out the Bradley, and then the instruction would start in earnest.

"Someone will have to be outside, rotating the hut *cine-matique*, won't they?" asked Dad, not removing half-closed eyes from the screen. A little man with a big black hat and beard was being dunked headfirst in a rain barrel. "'Manumit *most* of the neighborhood kids' is what I should have said."

"Yeah," I grinned. "We'll need hut rotators."

"You can withhold freedom from two or three children," Dad sort of leered. "Selected for tractability more than strength, as this hut won't be all that difficult to move, if we get the bearings smooth and nice. I see a sort of pivoted roller system, using logs from the two and a half black locust trees. But they will need patience, these kiddy-chattels, to follow the sun, and steady little personalities. Real bourgeois types."

On television, raunchy mayhem was being perpetrated upon minor characters, recruited by the casting director and enticed with alcohol from Los Angeles skid rows. Their con-genitally abnormal faces had been enhanced with pancake makeup and mascara to haunt you like details from a repressed childhood trauma. I couldn't have been more enchanted. We were looking at a division of our tribe who'd stumbled a little further west than the rest of us.

"I suggest," said Dad, "that little Latter-Day-Saint next door who wears glasses."

"LaMar Jacobsen?"

"And his plump sister. The one whose kitty-cat uses your sandbox as a latrine."

"Tiffany."

At the mention of that lugubrious name, Dad regressed even deeper into an atavistic back-tunnel accent. His upper canines began to chaw at his lower lip. "Named after the famous maker of *favrile* glass. Later we'll have a special use for her."

"How do you mean?"

He failed, or refused, to acknowledge my request for clarification.

"We build the hut for, say, seven people. Six customers and the exhibitor (you, I assume). I think we should also install a pedal device as a backup so that you, the exhibitor, can rotate the hut, just in case the wretches toiling outside die from sunstroke or malnutrition, or organize a strike, or burrow under the redwood fence while you're at the movies with your—um, where's the audience coming from?"

"Fishing for an invitation to the world premiere?"

"Not necessarily. But, if you plan on selling tickets, or, rather, bartering them off (as there'll be no currency that I've been informed of), shouldn't the population pool from which these patrons are drawn be a natural occurrence of the backyard?"

He was driving at something I was too young to cotton on to readily. I didn't pursue it, and neither did he, for the time being. As usual with such subjects, it was very tantalizing, but somehow better left alone.

He did appear to be genuinely warming to the task this time. As the pre-World War Two inhumanity escalated further on the television, Father was unable to avoid injecting himself a bit more assertively into the scheme: *"You'll* do all this?" he said with his eyes and arms. *"We'll* do it?"

He was ready to get this pesky pronoun question out on the table, finally. It was time to firm up the duty roster. He was prepared, maybe eager, to jump in. But he seemed willing to concede that this production might be qualitatively different from the playhouse we'd knocked together. It was little Tommy's individuality being produced from the ground here. Father himself was an already finished product, for better or worse, and now must act only in an advisory capacity, and as chief financial backer.

Also caterer. Since I wasn't planning to live like my human

cattle on crab apples, I assumed I'd be coming indoors on a regular basis for a sandwich or so, maybe some macaroni and cheese, composed of ingredients bought with the salary earned on the job from which my demand for parental attention was keeping my father. Kindly, indulgent, he didn't trouble me with this obvious fact, which had so conveniently slipped my boyish mind. He would remain my victualler, steadfastly and without comment, for the eons required to grow my fuel trees and produce my equipment and make my masterpiece from scratch—because, as he always said, he was immortal.

Whenever the big question came up (and it often did, with a morbid tyke like me underfoot), he pleaded deathlessness. And it wasn't just the untarnished posthumous reputation guaranteed the inventor of a major advance in human culture, such as the hook shot. Dad was talking corporeal permanence.

Not a really deep thinker, my old dad: denying the basic fact of everything, the prime condition of organic existence, from whose pondering comes all serious and headlong action; ignoring when not explicitly contradicting this most obvious of all obviousnesses, up until his sixty-fifth or seventieth birthday, when his own experience finally started making it undeniable, even to himself. I got my cockamamie ideas about time's unimportance from him.

Just to check and see whether it was a generational thing, I've since asked several friends and acquaintances of my approximate age if their own fathers staked this mightily wrong-headed claim for themselves. Nobody said yes. It seems to have been a peculiarity all my dad's own, this notion of a personal earthbound incorruption. But still I suspect it was more offhanded than hubristic, more Far Western, somehow, than megalomaniacal.

So, the Bradley lad's nourishment was indefinitely provided for, and he had settled on an alternative energy source, and was actually quite content to allow the nearest yellow main-sequence star to project his movie. But, project it via what medium? It was no longer possible to put off dealing with a certain indestructible synthetic compound, as undying in fact as my father fantasized himself to be in person. This needed subtlety.

"All right, we're set," I said, enunciating with pursed precision the first-person plural for the first time today, deliberately roping Dad into it. (I knew that, with the sinister shit I was about to moot for consideration, adult supervision was recommended.) "We have just about everything we need," I chirped. "We have manpower and some fashionable, vitamin D-enriched sunshine. Oh, and, also, Dad, not to forget—we'd better get ourselves a supply of something transparent to put the pictures on, to shine the sun through. Right? Um, Dad? What's the name of that plasticky stuff real movie guys use for—"

But before I could go any further, or recollect the name, he jumped to his feet, spilling both cups of coffee, and blurted, "Do you know what the earliest photographs were made on?"

"Huh?"

"Plates of *glass*, Tommy!"

"Blades of—?"

"Plates. Of beautiful, clear, biodegradable glass."

He was being a bit too emphatic in contradistinguishing glass' relative purity and simplicity from the toxic convolutions of the material that had just been on the tip of my tongue. For unknown reasons Father suffered from a violent and unreasoning prejudice against the plasticky stuff. This animadversion evidently overrode his need to go to work and his responsibility to discourage me from time-wasting enterprises. I found myself wondering what sort of childhood trauma he could possibly have suffered in the ancestral cavern, involving the dreadful concoction.

"Yes, and," he panted, supportive parent that he remained even under duress, "we can use your smart sandbox idea. For this *glass*, you know? You'll have to comb out the shit of Tiffany Jacobsen's cat. Tidy little beast."

"'—comb the shit out of—'?"

"No, no. From the sand. Comb out. Remove the feline excrement. As in impurities."

"Clean the latrine. Gross."

"Nobody said science was fun. Unleash her brother from the hut bearings and have him do it—oh, damn."

"What? What?"

"Niter."

For a moment I was delighted. Was this a new secret dirty word from the universe of grownups? Perhaps an epithet? "Niter?" I said, eagerly.

"I suppose it's not impossible that our small backyard might yield niter to supplement the sand for primitive glass manufacture. Although I'm not sure of this at all. I guess," he said, vaguely looking toward the room where we threw most of the books, "we could look it up..."

"... Naw-w-w," we said in unison, after no undue pause. This was just a casual dad-son conversation between two amateurs with no particular scientific bent. Dad was a professor of economics. The slide rule was for figuring out goods and services, inputs and outputs, greed and need, human stuff, not the physical universe.

"Anyway," he said, "you'll have to round those slaves back up to dig for niter. Maybe, while they're at it, you could ask your youngsters to scratch up a little manganese, too, if it's not too much bother, like the Phoenicians did. They invented the process by accident. A ship laden with niter wrecked on their shore, and the gentle Mediterranean surf blended the spilled cargo with the sand, which later, at low tide, was subjected to heat when the sailors set their cauldrons on the beach for a cookout. Or something like that. I don't know if they always had cookouts after shipwrecks, but there you have it."

"Subjected to heat? I thought you said—"

"I changed my mind. We'll have to get your smelting operation back on line. Since you insist that we are blessed with the history of materials and ability to use them, we'll have to invent the blast furnace, just as you suggested earlier. My bright boy," he beamed, giving credit where credit was due, and mussing my fair hair again.

So, just like that, by arbitrary adult fiat, my dad declared my blast furnace permissible after all. Little Tommy, who had barely adjusted himself to less flammable techniques, complained that he was being taken on an emotional roller coaster ride.

"Speaking of rollers," said Dad, "you will recall that the bearings for the hut are logs, which leaves you that much less fuel. We'd probably only need one batch of glass if we did a good job. Nevertheless, son, I'm afraid that our beloved little playhouse, which we worked so hard together to build, will have to be razed. For the plywood."

"I don't want to be sickeningly sentimental or anything, Dad. But wouldn't it be easier to just whip up some of that plasticky stuff real movie guys use for—"

"Silver!"

"Huh?"

"We need some."

"But I thought this was a barter economy."

"Primitive photographs were silver halides prepared in the dark and exposed to light on glass plates. Do you have fillings in your teeth?"

"You know I do. You pay for them."

"I mean silver fillings. We need them for the halides. Do dentists still use silver these days? My head's packed with the stuff. How about yours? The sadistic pederast down the street charges like he's using platinum."

It was not mere oral hygiene being bandied about here. The removal of dentition in dreams, says you-know-who's much maligned book on the interpretation of same, always signifies patriarchal castration: the Father attempting (not consciously, but as an involuntary function of his very biology) to subsume and absorb, which is to say emasculate the son, according to basic psychoanalytic theory. I was not enthusiastic about this proposition. Unsure as to what alloys had been tamped into my own reamed-out molars, I crossed my little legs and said, "Hey, Dad! I know. How about if, while my slaves are digging for the niter and the magnesium—"

"Manganese."

"Whatever—"

"Not 'whatever.' You'd better get that one right."

"—what if the kids come upon a hoard of old silver Mormon pioneer-type coins, and we use them instead of my—"

A shudder, stemming not necessarily from either of my yet unshaven jaws, shook the last word off.

Desperate to avoid, or at least postpone, the ultimate Oedipal showdown, I was willing to stretch yet another point. I reckoned its having been buried in our backyard for more than a hundred years would somehow render this bullion permissible—unlike the old Bridgestone tires and the broken Frigidaire, which had only lain there rotting for about a decade. I was prepared to disregard any treasure trove statutes that might exist on the Utah law books.

"A hoard of Mormon specie?" scoffed my dad. "Untithed? Left unpillaged by Brigham Young, the greedy son of a bitch who nearly had us all killed over a couple acres of scrub oak?"

"But Gr'auntie said it was because we—"

And the phrase recurred: "Very unlikely, but not entirely impossible. Yes, I suppose you could get sufficient silver halides off this sad pittance left by the voracious cult. We're assuming a single-take operation, anyway. Due to paucity of fuel, we're only going to have one chance at our blast furnace. But, these few coins would be seriously defaced, I think, by the process. What about the archaeological interest?"

We both got a chuckle out of that. They weren't exactly owl drachmas.

"So," said Dad, appearing nearly tension-free for the first time all day (that shared chuckle must have been therapeutic), "if we were to be satisfied with a negative image movie run on glass plates, we could stop now, and I could go to work and get there just in time for lunch."

My little ears perked up, like a doggy's. Did this process end in a negative image? Why was I the last to know? That struck me as superb. It would look like death, which, as our morning confabulation progressed ever closer to lunchtime, asserted itself more and more as the theme of my production—though I wouldn't at that point have been able to say why. It does seem to me now that I was a little young to have death on the brain.

"Oh, boy! A negative image would be swell, Dad! Real avant-garde, and like that!"

"Remember," he said, confidently gathering up his briefcase, "we're looking at some really lousy picture quality here. You'll probably wind up with just vague gray shadows hulking around on the wall. Plato's cave-type stuff."

"I don't care."

I wasn't aiming for a sequel to *Cleopatra* with Burton and Taylor. Something more along the lines of very early *Little*

Rascals before Farina grew testicles. Cinema naivete.

"And, it's all very, very unlikely—though not altogether impossible."

"That goes without saying."

"Good," said Father, "it's settled then." He lunged for the door on his first-string center legs. And here I thought we'd just been talking in principle.

I said, in a firm enough voice to arrest his progress, "One eensy-weensy question. About the silver—um, things."

"Halides. Silver halides."

"How do we get them to stick on the glass?"

"Oh, they're suspended—"

He caught himself up short, and shoved another Kool in his mouth to impede the flow of indiscretion. I'm sure my ears did another cocker spaniel twitch.

"Suspended from what? In what?"

"Nothing."

"Even I'm suspended *from* something. Today, at least. Or is it suspended *in* nothing? That doesn't sound heuristic. What the fuck are you talking about, old man?"

He was cornered. Once again the doorknob left his giant fist, and the chair received his buttocks. He sent his briefcase sailing across the room. Hook shot. The pleasant look left his old face, the enthusiasm seeped from his voice, and he murmured, just audibly, "Gelatin."

"Yeah? So? What's the big heart attack? Wait till the Momos have a picnic, slide a twig through the fence slats, latch onto a plateful, suck out the tiny marshmallows, and it's show time."

"That's jello. What we need is gelatin, not just any old colloidal guck. It's animal jelly."

Dad paused, in the forlorn hope that such a notion would elicit an "Eeeew, for *ick*," and put his child off the cinema altogether. But it was no sissy-pants he was raising. Every regular boy loves mucus, in all its incarnations.

"Heuristic!" I crowed. "Earthworms are animals. We could use earthworms. It's easy to grow masses of earthworms if you know how. You would just stick your hand into the mass and withdraw it slowly, like when you're about to go fishing. Then you could harvest maybe enough animal snot for mixing with the tooth decay filling crap."

Dad spoke quietly. "You honestly don't care about picture quality. Do you?"

"Maybe I should go into TV."

"No! Gelatin is derived from the connective tissue of vertebrates. Not the secretions of annelids, you little—"

"Oh, I do beg your pardon if you please. And this nectar can be had by? From? How?"

"Not every man is blessed with a job he really enjoys," said Dad, his face filled with longing.

"Yeah, but don't you want your favorite son to do heuristics?"

"Hooves are the best source, pound for pound. I imagine most is cow now. Used to be horse. The glue factory. We'd have to skip just a whole bunch of work and sit around on our butts and wait for a herd of one or the other to stampede across the street and down our driveway. Or listen for large numbers of some sort of wild ungulate to clatter by and make inroads, migrations, establish habitual trails. A hole of appropriate size would have to be kicked in the redwood fence. I feel like doing that now."

"I thought we burned it down already."

"Figures. I doubt many hoofed creatures were wandering past before Big 'n Hung and his ninety-seven wives showed up with their ox carts. Just lizards and Utes and pumas and hantavirus rodents. It was desert the Mormons made bloom, not green pastures. And it's not exactly dromedary country, is it? Are camels hoofed, anyway?" (The poor old guy was showing signs of exhaustion: he asked himself questions out loud.)

I tried to bring him back on topic, or at least to the right continent. "I guess buffalo are out these days."

"Since time is not of the essence, Tommy, maybe you could wait for a giant asteroid to come along and knock our planet out of kilter, just enough to adjust our backyard into a clime and latitude more appropriate for the harvesting of animal jelly. Such as Brazil. I always thought tapirs would make nice gelatin. Kind of amber-colored."

Dad got dreamy for a second. He was getting mature on me. It was downright foreboding. The day would come when I'd have to say goodbye to this old soul.

"Dad? Hey, Dad, how about small inoffensive animals? Would the feet of small inoffensive animals yield this dreck? Like, could I render appreciable amounts from Tiffany's cat? What if I were to be conscientious about pulling out its claws by the roots every time it comes to defile our glass works?"

"Assuming cat claws can produce gelatin, which they most definitely cannot, sure, why not?" he said, ambiguously enough.

After a brief, silent moment of shared puzzlement, Dad decided it might be better to clarify the question a bit further. It was decided that I could cause Tiffany Jacobsen to have a birthday party with a rental Shetland pony, whose little feet I could mutilate, then dole out the residue, pickled or jerked, to my niter miners and hut rotators as a treat to forefend that general strike. I'd entice the creature to the redwood fence with a fistful of velvety, fragrant clover, or whatever constituted our lawn.

On TV was a violent silent, eyes poked out and heads cracked open with billiard balls. The star did some authentic juggling and instigated a revolting mud fight, which metastasized gradually to encompass a whole neighborhood and scores of strange-looking people, including a dozen Bradleyesque pituitary cases.

"And grab a pygmy pony foot or two—"

"With a snare—"

"Contrived of plaited tendrils—"

"Of course."

"—and tear the hooves off."

"With one's teeth—"

"None left. Sacrificed for the emulsion."

"My father and I are one," says Jesus in the gospel of his beloved disciple. Mine and I were getting carried away—no, galloping off together, united under a yoke of hereditary lawlessness.

"Hack the hoofs free from pinto ankles with a crude stone implement."

"Dislodge a flagstone from the patio. Crudely bonk it against the foundation till you get a jaggedy edge for sawing."

"Yeah. Dislodge all the flagstones. Scatter them. Grind the Nancy-boy charcoal underfoot. Fuck the screenplay."

"Language!" cried Dad.

Frowning dutifully, he made a two-handed move like a symphonic conductor urging a diminuendo. The television cooperated, quite coincidentally. After the messy orgasm of the mud fight, the on-screen activities were getting a little calmer. The Bradley grizzlies were coaxed off-screen with chunks of raw pork. Some crude exposition was being laid down, in preparation for the next access of post-Gold Rush bestiality.

"That pony," Dad reminded us both, "comes all the way from the Shetland Islands."

"Damn. That's right."

"I mean, the Shets, or whoever, speak English. I guess. But that's still way, way out. Ultima Thule. Long way from the old backyard you know so well."

"Adulterative," I agreed, and cast about desperately some more. I was on the verge of wondering out loud whether LaMar Jacobsen's fingernails might be in any useful way similar to the homologous bits on horses and cows, when our eyes met, and I knew Dad was having the same thought, or one equally impermissible, even for a Bradley.

Well, it should come as no surprise that my father and I came very close that morning, on moral grounds, to an outright rejection of gelatin as a recourse. Animal products carried too many implications. And glass itself wound up faring not much better.

"Hold on, son. Let's just say, for argument's sake, that you and I somehow managed to cough up copious amounts of primo animal jelly. And we got the images onto glass. It would have to be a pretty remarkable glass, wouldn't it? Not just bubbly, cat-shitty melted sand. And the frame rate would be ridiculously low, about one and a half per second. Say we were able to sneak a pinch or two of manganese in there. Still, any glass the likes of us could fabricate in such a place as our backyard would probably show a fatal tendency to shatter, even at that snail's pace. So we're talking really jerky picture quality here. Make old Harold Lloyd look like little Miss Seen Yer Hynie, or whatever that curly-headed skater's name was. We'd provide our audience with barely the illusion of the motion that gives motion pictures that certain moving quality from which movies take their mobile name, if you take the hint. It would be more like 'Pictures at an Exposition' for easily bored people."

"Glass pretty much sucks, doesn't it, Dad?"

"That it does."

He was primed and ready. I would try again with the unhallowed preparation. It was getting too late in the day for emotional blackmail to be necessary. I remained cheerful and spoke frankly. For the third time (and you know how often things have to happen in fairy tales and dirty jokes), I asked him, "So what's the name of that plasticky—"

"Hey, I thought kids these days were supposed to be lazy. Why are you making everything so difficult? Why do you need to produce and direct and shoot your own? Don't I drive you downtown whenever some Walt Disney pig-and-rat show comes around?"

"—stuff they use for film?"

Theretofore he'd succeeded in distracting me. But now I'd gone and said the F-word. Supportive, kind and gentle, and liberal, he didn't want to nip a young person's dream in the bud. He didn't want to pee on my parade. But—

"Celluloid?" he gasped. He sighed. Or did my father moan? I hope he didn't whimper; in any case, I refuse to depict him doing so.

"We need something see-through, and we're agreed that glass bites, right, Dad?"

"Are you sure you've received a true vocation for the cinema? Is this going to be like the bass clarinet and the ham radio? You don't really like movies that much, do you?"

He knew very well what my future slaves must never find out (particularly the males among them): that I secretly preferred reading—-with the exception of The Swiss Family Robinson, which is a genuinely vile book in every respect.

But, in prosperous countries, youngsters must be given, must be force-fed, if necessary, the opportunity and the wherewithal to pursue even their most fleeting and halfhearted interests. These are little human beings forming themselves, after all. Just that year I'd already gone through astronomy, cartooning, sandal making, ventriloquism (lessons mail-ordered from the back pages of a Sergeant Rock funny book) and the cello. If such an institution had existed back then, Father would have offered to mortgage the house and send me to film school after I got myself expelled from the publicly funded Mormon seminary-in-disguise, if I'd only let him go to work in the meantime.

"For celluloid I'll need, obviously, cellulose."

"Obtainable from trees or little boys' cotton underpants," came Dad's muffled words. In dejection he had folded his leg-long arms into an ostrich-sized nest and buried his head. He moaned, "And you've just got to have some alcohol, I suppose. There's something fermentable out there, don't you fret, Tommy. But no drinky-winky."

Even without being able to see his face, I could tell there was something else. Those mammoth shoulders shuddered at the very idea of the unnamed stuff. He tried to tuck it deep as a hemorrhoid pad, presumably for later, in case he hadn't succeeded in putting his son off creativity altogether in the interim. Dad unburied his head, for there was an announcement to be made.

"Coming by the third ingredient for primitive plastics manufacture is going to be a problem, kid. The third ingredient, I'm afraid, given the perimeters and parameters you've established for yourself—"

"Who said I established them for myself?"

"—is flat-ass impossible. It doesn't grow here."

"Oh, so it's a plant. Wow, old man, you really tipped your hand there. Blabbermouth."

"It's plant-derived. And, as far as I can see, the only absolutely insurmountable obstacle to your directorial debut would be the irremediable absence of this particular type of vegetation from our backyard. Not in a thousand years could you grow that here in our Rocky Mountain enclave."

"Why not? What about a million or two?"

"Well, boy, given that sort of time frame, our backyard

has been under ice, under sea water, and is sort of half-assed desert now. But I really doubt it was ever sufficiently like those locales in the Far East where the camphor tree grows. There, I said it: the camphor tree. And it is by no means a cosmopolitan organism... at least I don't think it is." He glanced toward the book room.

My reluctance to resort to that place heartened Father, and supplied him with confidence in the accuracy of his point. In fact, he felt triumph coming on, and the sensation made him wax a tad grandiloquent. The ostrich nest was dismantled, and he began to beat the air with vast wings.

"Yes, think of the unfathomably intricate combinations and permutations of pollinators and predators and so forth required to nurture even a normal type of tree—"

"And how much more so," I reluctantly concurred, "a weird-ass one that you can sniff and clear the snot out of your nose."

"It also chases moths away. Do you reckon, young Tommy, the necessary far-eastern camphor tree-friendly things could occur, all at once, in perfect concert, here in the Far West? Old Mother Earth wobbles on her axis, but not that much."

Dad went even further and pointed out the historical unavailability of camphor in the entire western hemisphere. "That, no doubt, explains why the Greeks never discovered plastic. They harnessed steam, for toys, and invented the notion of coin-op. But not celluloid." He paused, looked at the bakelite clock cellophane-taped to the polyvinyl-chloride wallpaper, and muttered, as an aside—certainly not to me, and maybe not even to himself (did he hear himself say it?), "Thank God Almighty."

Was he, or was he not, capitalizing the substantive? Was he thinking of the implications, in the context of our confab that morning? Almost definitely not. It's too late to ask him now.

"Turn the old Greeks loose with a source of camphor wood," he mused, "and we'd be sitting on two and a half millennia's worth of brightly-colored, incorruptible shit, instead of just a century's."

"Hey, that's right!" I was even more eager to proceed now that I understood my efforts might remain everlasting. "Maybe something close enough to camphor grew here at one time, in the New World, right where our backyard is now. The Utes couldn't be expected to—well, you know."

Dad looked at the clock again, but with a different sort of expression this time. "Would have to be millions and zillions, positive Sagans of years ago," he anachronized.

"If then."

And we looked at each other and said, in unison, "But, so what?"

"Time's no problem. Like that Eternal Thingamabob you were teaching me."

"Recurrence," said Dad. "Eternal Recurrence."

We were now officially no longer even pretending to be scientific. This shift in mode of discourse was certainly heralded or accompanied by a parallel escalation in Mack Sennet's special effects. But I don't recall what that might've involved, dream images being hard to keep in your head over time.

Suppertime had rolled around, followed by a discolored sunset over the dead sea, and the madman at the Mormon TV station was still displaying his sepia shorts, sans commercial interruption. Dad and I had not only forgotten about his job, but about nourishing our bodies, as we continued this duel literally to the death. Now it was just a matter, also literally, of materials, finite, and a question of the spatial boundaries of my system, self-imposed, self-circumscribed—for we had dispensed with temporal restraints once and for all, and entered the realm of the Eternal Recurrence.

This was a further step in the program of my "corruption" at Father's hands. He had given me Eternal Recurrence as ammunition, to stow in my arsenal alongside Darwinism, for salvos against the "Elder," that bristly indoctrinator of the Latter-Day-Saints' world-view and faith, who, salaried with state tax money, thinly masqueraded as my homeroom teacher at the neighborhood public school. I was equipped with Eternal Recurrence for use as a further prod, a second prick, as it were, to torment the Mormon educator, just in case I ever succeeded in getting him to engage me on even more cosmological questions than the origin of species. I hadn't, yet, gotten him to engage me, but had retained this peculiar doctrine in the back of my head, where, evidently, it had been percolating and depositing layers of something or other in the fatty synaptic clefts of my central nervous system.

The idea, bluntly, is as follows: the way God, or the Demiurge, or whoever, would build, say, a car would be to take the components and throw them against a wall again and again, over and over, for however long it took for those nuts and bolts to fall accidentally into the right places to produce a car. He's got time. No efficient assembly lines for him. Henry Ford was no child of this unhurried crapshooter deity.

Dad would always drawl it out, "Gaw-w-wd the Faw-w-w-wther," in such a way that I could feel the quotation marks like fishhooks. This was definitely not the guy the "Elder" groveled to and praised so piously in pseudo-science class. Not a regular sort of guy at all. For example, he didn't appear to have a whole lot of personality. In this way, Dad's god resembled LaMar Jacobsen.

Along with atoms crapped sans surcease against the wall, came irrefutably the concomitant notion that the backyard, and Dad, and Tiffany's cat, and even (unlikely as it may sound) little Tommy, right along with everything else, would eventually happen not just once, but again and again, infinite numbers of times, over the course of eternity—-for, if the atoms fell in these particular configurations once, what's to stop them doing so again? Dad assured me this was an idea tailor-made to irk the ire of any mainstream Utahn with the basic intellect to grasp it.

Only later in life did I learn this doctrine was the self-same Eternal Recurrence that tortured Nietzsche and tickled Schiller. I suspect cheerful Schiller was Dad's source, assuming he had a source, and didn't independently arrive at this conclusion—which seems so obvious and inevitable and common-sensical, once your brain's been exposed to it.

We were both assuming, like those two fine old Krauts of yore, that the process was restricted to currently available matter, such stuff budgeted from day one, shuffled and jumbled but undestroyed if not uncreated. God was grounded in a backyard, too, with a fence.

"But," asked Tommy, "how do we know matter is finite?"—and answered his own idiotic question with another question before the former completely exited his mouth. Do you see a density as of lead between the surface of your corneas and Alpha Centauri? Matter is palpably finite.

I was too young, and my father was too late for work, to broach the horrible subject of the identity of energy and matter, and the recent theories of time, which limit and bend its duration in very messy ways. But it wasn't as though the "Elder" would be prepared to throw these in my face by way of refutation. My homeroom was a nineteenth-century time capsule, and there was no need to hit the book room and arm myself with the latest conceits—which tend to be no fun, anyway.

Eternal Recurrence would be just the thing, my father evidently thought, to drive the Latter-Day-Saints wacky all the way and get me expelled altogether. Darwin was only good for suspensions—but this was dynamite. I, on the other hand, doubted the idea could be introduced into my homeroom teacher's clouded mind with sufficient clarity and completeness to raise so much as a half a hackle. Besides, I didn't think explosive results were guaranteed. I still don't.

It's no weirder than what they're already taught to believe. With a little bit of tinkering here and there, you could probably adjust Eternal Recurrence to jibe more tightly with the Mormon world-view than the Catholic or Protestant (neither of which they share, being an unChristian outfit, despite the posturings of a certain failed presidential candidate).

If you are a Mormon male, and if you discreetly marry and fecundate as many females as you can without going to jail, meanwhile tithing faithfully off the top every month "without stint or surcease," and if, via the conduit of your plural spouses, you bring down to earth a grotesquely large contingent of the finite number of pre-created souls from heaven, or whatever repository they are stored in (my nephew Shawn never clarified this point for me), and if you baptize them into the Utah church and teach them to tithe—then, upon death, you will become a Mormon god yourself, and be furnished with, not merely your own backyard, but your own planet, and a harem of secret, eternal, nameless wives, upon whom to get souls with which to populate that planet, who will tithe, and tithe, and continue to tithe still more, and so on ad infinitum.

It seems to me that the metaphor of a perpetual crapshoot could be substituted with a semen shoot of comparable duration, and the rest of Mormonism would fall right into place.

Considering his modus operandi, it's unlikely that Gaw-w-w-wd himself, even with the full recruitment and cooperation of the Church of Jesus Christ of Latter-Day-Saints, could make a movie in my backyard without starting all over again, shooting that stuff against the wall, constituting and reconstituting the universe until some really big asteroid congeals in a previously unoccupied cranny of our solar system, and swings along and busts the fuck out of earth, knocking us entirely out of kilter, so that, as my father said—

"Up becomes down, this becomes that, the first shall be the last, and so on. Except this time you'll have to make arrangements for it to clobber us even harder than it did when sending us to animal jelly latitudes. It'll have to whack us silly until our backyard gets relocated all the way over to the Orient, where the snot-zapper tree grows. But I wouldn't count on that happening real soon. It's very unlikely. It's not the sort of thing a good manager is eager to factor into his timetable. And I assume we want to bring this project in under budget. Jesus Christ, kid. Instead of waiting around for this rogue heavenly body to tumble us ass-over-tea-kettle behind the Bamboo Curtain, wouldn't it be a skosh more efficient to just get on your bike and go down to the drug store and get a box of fucking camphor? I'll front you the bread, man."

(He frequently used beatnik lingo when trying to persuade me, thinking it sounded youthful and hip enough to get through. Not even my big brother fell for it any more.)

I said, "Nope, fuck that," or the little-boy equivalent thereof, and stopped listening.

My unconsidered, hardly verbalized, congenitally prewired instinct told me, if you're going to bother to get off your lackadaisical Bradley ass and actually do something (which by no means was a requirement in those prosperous days of my boyhood's America, where white folks like me, even non-Mormons stuck in "Zion," were owed a living on account of our external characteristics), then you should make it something you can do yourself, alone, from scratch, no shopkeepers or midwives or pimps or pinsetters involved. Collaboration dilutes, renders maculate. It's not the American way.

And why throw yourself and your budget of non-renewable energy/matter into something that requires a whole military-industrial complex, backed up by a world-wide distribution network, just to gather the basic materials to bring it into existence? My great-great auntie managed to invent her private language eight hundred miles away from the nearest railroad track.

One of the requisites for making a movie came from elsewhere, down the block at the drug store. The asteroid that might bring it closer was not exactly sizzling on the horizon. And the whole point was that no ingredient must be alien or extraneous to our perimeters; each constituent must stay within certain redwood boundaries. This strange process had to be topographically circumscribed, as part of the discipline, the decorum. On that day—though neither Bradley was more than dimly aware of it—our backyard was nothing less than the self. Whole and individuated, quadrilateral and topiaried, it was the archetypal walled garden of the soul.

So, rather than allow his virginal soul to be sullied, rendered maculate, was little Tommy finally ready to throw in the directorial towel? Did he really mean it when he said that other F-word a minute ago? It's not as though he would be alone in acquiescing. Even Dad seemed to think the time for fucking it had finally arrived.

"You've got problems, kid. Glass plates would shatter, and there can be none of the proverbial celluloid, probably, and your world premiere is permanently postponed—if you can talk of permanence, which you can't. I'm afraid your production has hit a wall, and it's never going to bounce back in one piece, no matter how many times you ram your little head into the bricks. No silver screen magic, not even moldy bark magic, in suburban Salt Lake City, at least not this time around in the cycle of Eternal Etcetera. This sort of thing happened to Orson

Welles all the time. He learned some card tricks and just got on with his life. And he has been hailed as an authentic American genius. Can I go to work now? It's almost time for me to start heading home—that is, if I want to get my usual jump on the return rush hour and make it back here in time to spend some quality time with you before beddy-bye, as a good daddy ought. Goom-bye please?"

In the elemental face of all this, with the Father and the Universe both refusing to cooperate, did little Tommy dig deep into himself and somehow muster the wherewithal to persevere? Don't you know he did? This is what they mean when they talk about the tenacity of youth.

I buttonholed my dad just as he stooped to make it through the door and, this time, with nothing but a plucky little facial expression, blocked the former basketball pro. My feat was all the more impressive because it was dark now and neither of us had switched on the lights. The flicker of primitive celluloid transmogrified into rudimentary pixels was all we had to see each other by.

The congenital subnormals had been allowed back into the picture, and were getting vaguely organized. A contingent of the Bradleyesque pituitary goons was on the verge of gaining the upper hand. They restarted the mud fight and escalated immediately to rocks.

"The asteroid belt," I whispered, "is a flying Rocky Mountain range. It's only a matter of time."

Dad looked at me for an indeterminate while. Then he sighed with all the reluctance of a general who's decided to go nuclear. He sat back down.

"Okay, okay," he said. "We've loitered out there for a hefty segment of geologic time, and the blackjack of Jehovah has come along and given us a planetary subcranial concussion. And east has met west, up has become down, this that, first last. Wonder of wonders, camphor is growing in the backyard. We have a whole fucking forest of nasal decongestant, and bags and bags of celluloid, more than enough to make about eighteen sequels to *Lawrence of Arabia.* Now, boy, are you ready for the hardest question of all?"

"Does a fat dog fart?"

I sat up straight and flipped my Beatle bangs out of my eyes, ready. In the silent short subject, a two-story frame house was being razed to the ground by the bare hands of a gigantic man with a lopsided face.

"What about your actors, son?"

I don't recall if he'd already given me the embarrassing speech about the Birds and the Bees and the Condoms (sturdy latex—none of this farm critter intestine tripe). I don't think he had. The received wisdom in those days was to hold that speech off till your child started smelling bad. That malodorous moment was also the signal for parents to start allowing dates with the opposite sex. I hadn't started smelling bad yet, I'm sure of that—though my olfactory memory can't claim the sharpness of Proust's gustatory. In any case, I was not prepared for Dad's question at all. I thought Lassie was a boy and Bambi the opposite. Little Tommy, while "borderline precocious" in certain ways, was a perfect latency-period sexual cipher, like a 'droid in some cheap sci-fi flick of a slightly later time.

Yes, in this respect, I was a typical doomed preadolescent, deep in the pre-genital phase, if you want to get all psychoanalytical. In other words (not to sugar-coat it or anything), I hadn't quite started "beating the brains out of Charles the Bald," as the French intellectuals like Derrida and Foucalt like to say and do in print. But I'd reluctantly heard naughty talk at school, and wasn't eager to be subjected to more at home, from my own dad, yet. It was far too icky.

"What about my actors?" I said in an innocent-sounding

tone, trying to deflect the paternal will and impulse. "Well, I'll feed them on crab apples just like my slaves."

"You know I'm not talking about commissary privileges now. I assume you want full artistic control of this flick as well as every other kind of control. You want to decide absolutely everything, right down to the genetic makeup of your performers, right?"

"Gee-whiz, Dad. I honestly never—"

Tongue-tied, I looked to the TV for moral support, and saw great aunties and second cousins-once-removed, all botched. Control should have been exerted over their coming into being.

"Given, Tommy, a nice little twig-and-tendril lean-to for privacy back there, and the proper, shall we say, management techniques, you could probably come up with just those characteristics your little heart desires: the cheekbones and the precise shade of turquoise irises, the vocal cords and muscles, or lack thereof, and even, depending on where you stand on Nature versus Nurture, the personality traits dramatically called for in your script. You are using a script—?"

"Charcoal on the flagstones. Like you said."

"I thought we scattered the flagstones."

"I just gathered them back up."

"And didn't we grind the charcoal underfoot?"

"I gathered that back up, too."

This was getting altogether too heuristic, even for little Tommy. It was little Tommy's turn to demur, to put the brakes on, to introduce restraints. Maybe step back a bit and scribble out a preliminary scenario, to see where we're headed before we get in too deep. Engage the alphabet, effeminate though it may be, before we start churning out the bodily fluids. Little Tommy cleared his throat and asked, "How much time are we talking about here, Dad?"

"Time? What does time matter? We're in Mormon heaven now, and you're the boss. It's your planet we're peopling."

Unfortunately, this was in the days before human genetic engineering oozed off the pages of the trash novels and into actual labs. In any case, I'm sure we didn't have the time, that dwindling day, to determine whether I could scratch and scrounge up the necessary pyrex and agar (which comes from seaweed, a definite no-have in the Mormon "Zion"). We were stuck, in that dim epoch, with old-fashioned, messy selective breeding. Now I understood his earlier cryptic comment about a special use for Tiffany Jacobsen. She was too chubby. The thought was very off-putting.

So little Tommy, all by himself, came up with what he considered the only truly insuperable stymie to his homespun Hollywood hopes. And what would that stymie be? It would be Dad's sick-making idea of doing it in the backyard, people dorking behind twig-and-tendril lean-to's, with girls. Gross. Cooties.

It only occurred to me later, in adulthood (about three seconds ago, as a matter of fact), to wonder if Dad was thinking about asking me to film the kiddies doing it. Forget that, you sick old prick.

He did, however, have an excellent point, which was not to be ignored. My actors would be my screen personae, the various aspects and attributes of *me* that I presented to the world in my art. Was I going to let their lineaments be determined by god knew what Utah-style miscegenation, what unconsidered polygamist inbreeding, these very creatures whose images the foregoing rigmarole had been essayed to capture? I should say not. Besides, I didn't want Dad to think I was a homo, an invert-sugar. He wasn't getting my gonads that easily.

So, no turd-burglar, I managed to swallow the nausea of my own first sexual flusterment, and choke out a tiny, "Okay," to which Dad replied with a double take and an audible gasp. He'd thought he had me by the bicuspids this time. He'd been counting the fillings, like a concentration camp commandant.

"We're talking about many, many generations here," he reminded me. I detected an edge of desperation in his manner. He'd already lost a day's work, so that wasn't what made him twitch now with an evident urge to dive out the front door.

His present discomfiture notwithstanding, he knew better than to ask me outright if I had a problem with the multi-generational thing. A question of personal immortality is the wrong one to ask a full-blooded American elementary school boy with no special needs or professionally diagnosed learning disabilities or alternate sexual orientations to speak of, as yet. The answer you're going to get is, "Forever. Just like you, Dad. I'm immortal. It runs in the Bradley family. Must be a recessive gene. Time's no problem."

And yet, of course, in spite of my brave affirmation (and I only imitated my father), it was the point of death I was unconsciously considering this whole time, even at that tender age. Maybe Father was, also, at his no less tender age, despite his own asseverations to the contrary, pondering that ultimate moment, when the things you can't take with you when you go, are gone, and you're on your own for real, rattling and gasping away in a doomed declaration of independence, with hardly any help, then no help at all, then outright hindrance, from your heart and lungs and so forth.

What I was ready to dig so deep for in the backyard dirt was that self-sustaining system which we all wind up embodying so briefly at the end-time. I was looking forward, in the back of my prepubescent, self-absorbed brain, to demise and disengagement, when girls and the icky cooties they bring couldn't be more irrelevant. The child is father to the man, and the pre-teen forebear to the corpse.

I scrounged back there for utter autonomy, which (for a non-Mormon at any rate) can only come with the precise arrival of death: the sole moment of pure freedom, mortal coil successfully shuffled off at last, after a lifetime of squirming. And this freedom continues—who knows how long? Probably about the duration of a short subject illuminated by a pinch of magnesium. And it feels, no doubt, a lot like nitrous oxide recreationally administered to excess.

My father, the self-proclaimed "immortal," achieved that fleeting liberty eight months ago, as I'm sure you knew he was going to do—we all must kill our fathers eventually. I kept my teeth, not to mention my balls, which means his life had to cease. This is how it's supposed to be.

Just a means of bumping off Dad, this section of the book, I'm making it very explicit. I did it, and you watched. Over the course of this thing I've driven the poor old fart crazy, actually rendered him a dithering maniac at the end, sitting at the kitchen table in the dark, snickering incoherently about a backyard jail-bait stud service, his work torn away from him—that is to say, I murdered my father in the only way that matters. And, up until the paragraph just before this one, most of the Aristotelian unities have been preserved.

"We're talking real primitive here," he says to me at night, sometimes, after I've fallen asleep in front of the television. "You might wind up with shadows hulking on the wall, just ghosts disembodied. Doomed for a certain term to walk the night, and all that sort of thing."

Every month or so they tell us a bit more about what's in outer space, and so far it just sounds like one big hazardous chemical dump. The multitudinous Mormon gods up there are committing the sin of Onan on a very large scale, perpetually spilling their seed on the most barren ground. If the rest of our solar system is any indication, the extra-terrestrial universe must comprise mere worlds with sulfuric acid rain and nitrous oxide atmospheres, maybe a squalid wretch of a microscopic worm here and there, more mud than life—but mostly this toxic idiocy, repeated over and over in the context of billions and quadrillions of galaxies and so on.

That sounds to me like just about the right number of trial runs and abortive attempts and false starts it would take, throwing a limited number of atoms against the wall for an unlimited period, to produce, this time around, what's coiled and tucked so neatly behind my personal eyeballs and between my Bradley ear-holes.

And no matter how bored this crapshooting Jupiter got trying to toss up the next version of me, he couldn't very well get on his bicycle and go down to the drug store and get a box of Bradley molecules to help him fudge a bit, speed things up a skosh, not any more than I could have fetched that box of imported camphor, now could he? Not very likely, I'd say.

However, just a few hours ago, with the aid of the internet, I discovered that camphor trees from China and Japan do indeed grow in the western hemisphere. They were imported to the U.S.A. about a hundred years ago, not too long after a certain clan of hyperextended coal miners arrived from Sheffield, England. And they (the trees, not us) are multiplying like weeds, to the detriment of native life forms. The *cinnamomum camphora* is choking out whole forests in Florida, where it is subject to no natural predators. Introduced as a garden ornament, it's now registered among the Category One pest species.

There was a camphor tree, in fact, unbeknownst to the Bradleys (neither being a botanist), rankly sprouting a few feet beyond Tiffany Jacobsen's mom's crab apple tree, just out of reach. The asteroid would've only had to nudge us about ten yards in that direction. I might have made my contribution to world cinema after all, but for that groundless, ill-informed, careless, facile parental discouragement. A waste irrecoverable, a loss immeasurable for human culture. Besides, I'm told that turpentine would have worked almost as well.

But, on that day of my early youth, which won't come again (at least not this time around), the unavailability of celluloid's third ingredient was presented to me as an insurmountable stymie, and rubbed in my little face, right along with the simple fact of my constitutional inability to do what it took to exert deoxyribonucleic control over my performers. So I said, "Fuck it," and became a novelist instead.

I immersed myself in the sissy-pants alphabet, and, with that single stroke of fearless will, obviated most of the problems discussed in this section of the book. I confess I have no idea where the graphite in my pencil comes from, but it could, with extra effort, instead be charcoal from my dad's unpopular black locust—if that trash tree hadn't died of aphids or something and rotted to nothing about twenty-five years ago.

Now I'm writing one, not about a boy and his old pappy in a backyard, but about a pair of stumblers across the length and breadth of the entire world as known and unknown at a certain circumscribed epoch in the relatively distant past. It involves a lot of research, and the books I'm using come from everywhere, and are made from every bookish substance.

Dad's last words were actually crooned: "I'm checkin' out, goom-bye." And, before he did that, I borrowed his library card and did some checkin'-out and goom-byeing myself: nearly 200 books taken far away across the Pacific Ocean in suitcases, to the lands of the camphor tree, where I now languish in economic exile, having long ago been deemed too unsocialized even for the non-Mormon university back home. Father's program of son-corruption succeeded beyond his dreams.

Yes, I confess that I put a hideous number of items on his

account, and he croaked in the meantime. My big brother goes around telling everybody back home that the first overdue notice killed him with shock.

God knows what glues, what gelatins, what larval wormlets, what inorganic compounds and artificial dyes I've introduced into the ecosystem of my far-oriental hovel. Books from places like Bombay and Holland and Oklahoma State University, some from another century, and now a new millennium (if you're prepared to overlook Dennis the Lesser's miscalculation).

Even though the Chinese say "Stealing books is not stealing," I would not want any astronomical overdue fines tallied against his reverend name in the Golden Register Up Yonder. So I renew these babies' checkout status every two months, by transoceanic fax, with his immemorial name and social security number ball-pointed, immutable, at the top of the sheet.

But the date is buried a half-dozen times per year under another layer of liquid paper, progressively thicker and thicker, composed of lamp black and mustard oil, which would have been easy to manage in my backyard, but also methylcyclohexane, vinyl toluene-butadiene copolymer, dioctyl sodium, titanium dioxide sulfosuccinate, not to mention vinyl toluene-butadiene copolymer, plus isobutyl methacrylate and—hard as it may be to believe—n-butyl methacrylate.

See how far I am now from that boyish fantasy? See what remains of my ambition to build a natural economy to parallel that of my outcast pioneer ancestors in their Rocky Mountain caves? I have to employ all these outré essences and quintessences just to get my novels written.

Every two months I personally account for a quantum rise in the world-wide consumption of polymeric fatty ester, alkyds, cyclohexa-nedimethanol (I feel particularly guilty about that one), pentaerythritol, phthalate, certain coumarone-indene resins sold under the trade-name Neville, and, most mortifying of all, dioctyl sodium sulfosuccinate as well as bistridecyl sodium sulfosuccinate.

My closed system is falling apart with a vengeance here, as I sink deeper into material promiscuity, substance abuse, layer by layer, until my check-out renewal form can barely be crammed into the fax machine anymore. A technology, already dated and idiotically simple in principle (snot, available by the quart in any red-blooded American boy's backyard, would do almost the same thing), reveals my multiple chemical dependence, my adulterous nature. We don't remain for long unsustained from without.

We have (or need to believe we have) an undying dad, our perpetual victualler. And, for the purposes of this piece of non-fiction, I had to quell my grief long enough to adjust my own victualler's passing into non-perpetuity. I knew I would have either to kill Father off much longer ago than the actual half-month that marks the short-term anniversary of his death today, or else cause the Salt Lake City Public Library circulation department to require renewal faxes at the unreasonable rate of every day or so, in order for the accumulation of liquid paper to get egregious enough to warrant such an elaborate image in a nonfiction book of this particular length.

I can encompass and re-schedule the death of a minor sports figure, but am impotent to arrest my own descent into technological whoredom. Liquid paper is only the flaky epidermis of my Karloffian organism of corruption. I shudder to think what was required to bring this book to your eyes, simply pencil-scrawled though it might have been in the original: the interlinkage of contrivances that no single person could build from scratch, no matter how borderline-precocious his brain, how big his backyard, or indulgent his father.

Account has been taken of Einstein's temporal relativism. The signals of the email message to which these words were attached traveled so far at the speed of light that the new-fangled wishy-washy time was obliged to slow down for them. After bouncing off whatever communications satellite hovers over the Pacific between here and there, they arrived on the surface of America too late, even though the whole transaction was instantaneous. (Figure that one out with a prepubescent brain full of *The Swiss Family Robinson*.) The receiving dish in Kansas or wherever was necessarily nudged just the right distance toward my modem in East Asia, to compensate for the earth's rotation that we, but not my ideas, lived through in the meantime. Thanks to the account taken of this newly enfeebled fourth dimension, my words were prevented from swishing right past you—and thus is illegitimized the very basic assumption of all: the immutability (and hence purely unproblematical nature) of time. Time, it turns out, is indeed a problem.

My ultimate act of unfiliality, of Dad-betrayal, is not his murder, but rather the practical negation of the doctrine he taught me for my self-preservation. How can you have Eternal Recurrence when time is compressed and stretched like poorly rendered animal jelly? Eternity itself becomes a non-sequitur, "recurrence" an oxymoron, the moment you blur the distinction between then and now.

So I'm left with no secret weapon against the "Elders" of this world. I might as well kiss ten percent of my income good-bye, undo my belt, and just let go, backslide. I should sign up for baptism into the faith that nearly wiped us Bradleys out long ago.

Until that ultimate succumbing, I whittle my Ticonderoga 2.5 to what may be a compulsive degree, so the point where my enthusiasms scrape the paper will remain almost geometrically circumscribed, a contact that will be easiest to disengage when the time for disengagement comes.

But, before I can be allowed to disengage altogether, I must live out my Oedipal exile in the Land of Camphor, where working off one's metempsychotic debt is more than just a poetic image. And there's no better place in which to atone for double patricide than the Lands of Mao Zedong and General Tojo.

PEACE PARK PRANCE

As he penetrates deeper and deeper into Boom Town's blighted hypocenter, the be-bop inside Tom's ecstatic head is suddenly drowned out by a hideous racket.

Dominating an entire quadrant of this hootenanny is a twenty-foot-high memorial portrait of Yoko Ono-san's croaked squeeze. It's being adored by a multinational coven of ecofeminists, who sway back and forth, their hands held high in peace signs. They try to harmonize in simple thirds, but can't manage it, and do their best to drone each other, and everybody else, into a Za-Zennish stupor.

Whenever there's a lull in the rants and chants from the rightists' sound trucks, Tom reluctantly hears them singing, or maybe moaning, over and over and over again—

"All we are say-y-y-ying, is give peace a cha-a-a-a-a-a-a-a-ance... ".

VI

Baptism enslaved me. —Rimbaud, *Night in Hell*

God knows there are plenty of Mormon proselytizers here in Boom Towns I and II. Just like every other population center in the known world, we play host to whole platoons of callow Latter-Day-Saint males who'd just love to lave us in the Water of Righteousness. They congregate at my place on Saturdays to watch *Little House on the Prairie* reruns on the bilingual television. They urge me to ogle polaroids of their big soft moms back in Provo.

And, during commercial breaks, what do these "Elders" teach me about this cosmos which I share with them? Well, for starters, were you aware that Our Heavenly Father did not get around to making the heaven and earth and Adam and Eve until approximately the end of the Ubaid Period in southern Mesopotamia, in spite of all the green pottery those uncooperative folks left behind?

The word "approximately" appears above only because the dates of the Ubaid people are usually preceded by a "circa." The date of creation, on the other hand, is an absolute certainty. Pretty much.

Fundamentalists calculate the precise year by tallying up all the "begats" in Genesis: "Cainan lived seventy years and begat Mahalaleel... Arphaxad lived five and thirty years and begat Salah... Peleg lived two and thirty years and begat Serug," etc. This hard data is then dovetailed with the family trees of Jesus Christ in the Gospels of Mathew and Luke—which are divinely inspired, just like the rest of the Bible, and are therefore literally factual right down to the smallest syllable, except they contradict each other. But you sort of split the difference, and continue doing your ciphers till you arrive at the birth of Our Redeemer at the dawn of the so-called Common Era.

Christ was actually born four or five years Before Christ, due to an honest boo-boo made by a lovable but ditzy monk named Dionysius (a.k.a. "Dennis") the Little. But, never mind. Crunching the numbers just so, and maybe playing the odds here and there, you come up with precisely 4004 B.C., anno mirabilis, and how: the year everything—space, time, matter, anti-matter, us, etc. —came into being.

Lovable and sad as their missionaries can be, Mormons are not Christian by any means. But they also choose to disregard Mesopotamian archaeology. They accept 4004 B.C., or a date pretty near it, for the beginning of our world. Those green Ubaid pots, right along with fossils of trilobites and pterodactyls and Lucy the glitzy hominid, and so forth, were deliberately placed on earth to test our faith. Which are you going to buy into, the comforting and manageable truth of the scriptures, or the disorienting lies that secular humanists and communists and anarchists try to feed us?

Mormons also believe that, at the time of creation, six thousand and some-odd years ago, God whipped up a batch of souls, a finite number of them, all at once, and one time only, and tucked them in cold storage amongst the clouds. With an ever-accelerating rate of attrition, these souls wait patiently to be embodied. Whenever a baby is conceived on earth, one of them flutters down and squeezes itself into the embryo. Imagine squeaky sounds, as when someone in the back seat of your car is desperately trying to pull on a wet rubber swimsuit before the Highway Patrolman can come to the window.

(I'm not altogether sure about this, but I think that, in the case of clomiphene-induced sextuplets, each fetal sibling winds up with one-sixth of a soul. A good way to test my hypothesis would be to look up a set, invite yourself over to lunch, and look deeply into their eyes. Maybe strangle one or two slowly and watch any cats that happen to be in the room.)

Now, if an embodied soul joins the Mormon Church during its terrestrial tenure, at death it can bounce right back to its cozy pigeonhole in Heaven, and that's the very best thing that can happen to anybody. Therefore, it is the humanitarian duty of every right-minded Mormon to fetch down as many souls as possible and initiate them. This is the practical purpose of polygamy. As America's inner city demographers have noted, one man, given the proper motivation and a sturdy brace of gonads, can maintain any number of women in a state of fecundation.

Another reason for this frenetic coughing-up of new members is that Mormons have been instructed by their leaders, the unassumingly designated "General Authorities," to pay ten percent of their yearly income to the organization. This is the tithe, as prescribed in the Book of Deuteronomy. (Mormons have their own scriptures, which serve their spiritual needs better than the Old and New Testaments ever could. But, as we will see shortly, the General Authorities are not averse to lifting whatever's useful from the Holy Bible and bending it to their purposes).

In a denomination that makes tithing compulsory, it's only good business sense for the leadership to encourage grotesque levels of procreation. The coffers swell exponentially with each generation. In Utah, the birth rate is the same as that of the Indian subcontinent, while the rest of Caucasoid USA wimps oxymoronically out with a "negative population growth." There is no graying of Utah society. Dying nations such as Japan gaze in envy at Salt Lake City's omnipresent dumpsters brimming with fulfilled Huggies.

In my hometown's suburbs, the sidewalks and crew-cut lawns are barely visible under teeming throngs of semi-feral youngsters. As Mommy is confined in perpetual parturition, and Daddy's every free moment is occupied with sacred volunteer work, these skittering, screeching mobs wax no less numerous when the sun goes down and the boogey-man comes out trolling. And, as the majority of the tiny Mormons are blond-haired and blue-eyed, perfectly fitting most infertile couples' profile for adoption fodder, these neighborhoods have become a professional kidnapper's paradise. Vanishings of tykes usually have to be aggravated by gutters full of blood and bone fragments, or multiple UFO sightings, to make it beyond page two of the local newspaper's ho-hum B-Section. No matter, plenty more where they came from. The mini-Mo-mos just keep on sliding inexhaustibly down the old wazoo.

You can see that it is no exaggeration to call this suburb a Utopia, though in the original Rabelaisian rather than borrowed Morian sense:

"...the Utopian men had so rank and fruitful genitories, and the Utopian women carried matrixes so ample, so gluttonous, so tenaciously retentive, and so architectonically cellulated, that at the end of every ninth month seven children at the least, what male what female, were brought forth by every married woman..."

—*Gargantua and Pantagruel*, Book 3, Chapter 1

It's astounding, the level of cooperation the General Authorities can command over the very reproductive organs of their flock. But there's something in it for the rank and file as well—or at least for a good fifty percent of them.

Remember, it's the man who gets to become God. All he has to do is to tithe and tithe, and tithe still more, meanwhile keeping as many pregnancies percolating as humanly possible inside numerous bellies, aged twelve to fifty (the ideal Mormoness never touches a Tampax in her whole terrestrial life). And, when the time comes, he must persuade his vast armies of spawn to join the church. Then, upon death, he gets divinity and an infinite harem of conveniently faceless "spirit wives." (It's easy for a full-fledged god to ignore the words of a mere Son of God, as recorded in Matthew 22:30, where Jesus says unto the Sadducees, "For in the resurrection, they neither marry, nor are given in marriage.") And, being God, the transfigured Mormon man is free to knock up his cosmic broads wholesale, getting Carl Sagan-type numbers of souls to populate his planet, who will pay ten percent of their income to his very own hand-picked General Authorities, and so on forever and ever. It's an endless gushing forth of carcasses and cash-money.

I guess that sounds like big fun to certain categories of postmodern personality. And this is why Mormons think their Heaven is such a good place to be, and why they feel a responsibility to make sure that as many souls as possible wind up there, whether they desire an afterlife of ceaseless porking, or not.

The notion that a man can become God removes this wacky bunch far from the realm of Christianity. There are many types of Christian, with all sorts of conflicting doctrines, but one belief they all have in common, by definition, is that only one man was God, and that man was Jesus Christ. And he was unique in history, to the extent that his eventual return to earth will constitute the end of history. Any deviation from that basic assumption ends up somewhere in the category of heathenism.

This particular Mormon deviation bounces us all the way back to pre-Sumerian times. One of the three advances (the others being agriculture and bureaucracy) that distinguished the first civilization from everything that went before, was the fundamental insight that man is not even potentially divine (present sovereign excluded). This is the subject of the world's oldest epic. It's the whole lesson Gilgamesh learns on his quest.

But the notion of Orders of Being is alien to Utah theologians, blinkered as they've been by the most naive American populist democracy. In the Mormon cosmos, Jesus was merely one of many sons of one of many gods, whose peer any man can become through correct practice and a high sperm count with good motility. If each of us is potentially the first person of his own trinity, it follows that Jesus is nothing more than a kind of paradigmatic super-nephew.

By now you will have noticed a certain wrong-headedness, if not outright sloppy-mindedness, underlying this whole deal: beneath the tastelessness and exaggerated horniness lies a telling kind of mythopoeic ineptitude. It smacks not of long-lived tradition motivating hearts and minds across the generations, but of deliberate contrivance on the part of a less than inspired, or even sincere individual. You could be forgiven for suspecting that one of those so-called "charismatics" is behind such a scam: one of those cynically manipulative Sunday morning demagogues who seem to flourish only in North America, since the Enlightenment drove them from Europe. And, in fact, Joseph Smith, the founder of the church and its first "Prophet, Seer and Revelator," to whom the golden tablets of the BOOK OF MORMON were delivered by the angel Moroni, started out life as a part-time dowser of buried treasure in gullible farmers' fields, and a full-time hymen demolisher. Examine the black velvet paintings of him for sale in Salt Lake City souvenir shops, and you will see the fathomless, yet vacant eyes of the born seducer-con man.

In a politically motivated attempt to appear to be part of

mainstream American culture, Joseph Smith's successors have named their heresy The Church of Jesus Christ of Latter Day Saints (lately they've even started putting the fourth and fifth words in larger type). And, by way of camouflage, they superficially ape the outward appearances of a few legitimate Christian practices. One of these is baptism. Perhaps not surprisingly, the General Authorities have taken this rite and tweaked it to their own worldly advantage, unearthing a whole new (rather, old) customer base. They are the only denomination in existence that baptizes dead people.

This grotesque idea derives, albeit indirectly, from no less venerable an authority than the Apostle Paul. In the early years of Christianity, that human dynamo went around the Roman Empire organizing cells of the new faith, and advising them on doctrine and procedure. He wrote a lot of letters to these communities, several of which made it past various editorial board meetings and into the New Testament. In Paul's first letter to the faithful who were abiding at the northern Greek port of Corinth, the following problematical line can be found:

> *Else what shall they do*
> *which are baptized for the dead,*
> *if the dead rise not at all?*
> *Why are they then baptized for the dead?*
> —1 Corinthians 15:29

These words were the source of much confusion when Christianity was just getting started. Nobody really knows exactly what Paul was talking about. But it is generally assumed that he was referring to some strange rite performed by a fringe group who have long since died out. It is known that at least one second-century cult developed the habit of digging up and washing corpses based on a misunderstanding of this verse.

But they also died out (probably of diarrhea from all the gross germs), and the whole question raised by Paul's words has long since been forgotten by everyone—except the canny modern-day cult presently under consideration.

It occurred to the General Authorities that many of the finite number of souls arrived on this planet and departed before Joseph Smith began his hustle in the eighteen-twenties, A.D. Those poor wraiths never had the chance to be properly baptized while incarnate, and so they are out there, floating around in limbo, with no means of getting into Paradise.

So the Mormon theologians dug up that almost forgotten line from First Corinthians and decided to build a huge industry around it. The goal is to proxy-baptize the ghost of every personality ever to visit the planet—be he righteous philanthropist, depraved cannibalistic pederast, or middlebrow nebbish (runners of pyramid schemes are never interested in making such fine distinctions). The earth's ever-renewable reserves of worm bait are to be nudged awake and suddenly teleported to the lower floor of Heaven, there to dance attendance on Mormons properly christened while alive. (Talk about enslavement by baptism. It's enough to make Rimbaud soil his pants and forget to write a poem on the table with it.)

To promote this celestial slave trade, Mormons have compiled the biggest genealogical library in the world. They gather disembodied names from the archives of nearly every parish church in Christendom and pagan shrine in the rest of the world. Otherwise completely forgotten dead people, more than a billion of them, wait on microfilm and hard copy, presumably with bated breath, to be scanned and burnt onto CDs and eventually baptized by proxy. The librarians are all unpaid "volunteers," forced by threat of damnation to spend their weekends wrestling with gigantic bales of smudgy xeroxes.

Much of the collection is kept in a hydrogen bomb-proof

vault bored straight into the solid granite side of a mountain on the outskirts of the Mornons' plagiarized "Zion," a.k.a Salt Lake City. It's a nightmarish hole in the rock, a place devoted to drudgery, devoid of decor but for a non-sequitur accumulation of Oriental shadow puppets that line the shaft down to Hell.

It's difficult not to suspect that this entire subterranean enterprise was actually undertaken for a reason which couldn't be less eschatological: to serve as a monument to the administrative talents of a handful of men. If you are susceptible to another recent bit of pseudo-historical flummery known as the bicameral mind theory, the Genealogical Library of the Church of Jesus Christ of Latter Day Saints might remind you of the Great Pyramid of Cheops at Gizeh, or the Hanging Gardens of Babylon, any of the other labor-intensive Seven Wonders of that historical epoch which supposedly ended, in the rest of the occident at least, with the awakening of the side of the brain that permits individual volition, as opposed to slavish, social insect-like devotion to hubris-bloated tyrants and their megalomaniacal whims.

Fair enough: the old Ozymandias syndrome. But modern economics, i.e., big bucks, enter into this equation as well. You may take a moment for your astonishment to subside.

Every Mormon is urged to spend his vacation time in Salt Lake City, burrowing like a self-referential termite into his family tree, filling in the blanks with as many of his forbears as possible, that he might wash their past-perfect sins away and "carry their souls to Heaven on his back." To facilitate the accomplishment of this purpose, he must purchase pricey research materials direct from his neighborhood "bishop": attractive leatherette loose-leaf binders, and high-rag-content ledgers with a sky-blue angel motif embossed along the margins. The celestial honor roll can't be scrawled on the backs of doughnut wrappers, after all.

Their "research" accomplished, Latter Day Saints make further pilgrimages to the temples, to undergo as many baptisms as there are monikers on their lists. They must shell out for overpriced sacramental paraphernalia and official gauzy garments to wear in the sacred font, which are mass-produced by Mormon laborers in consecrated factories. And these damp pilgrims must stay in motels and eat in restaurants run by Mormons, who pay ten percent of their money to the church.

By this point their wallets barely raise a bulge on their buttocks, but they report to the fonts with a smile. Otherwise, without the watery consummation, all those hours giving themselves terminal asthenopia over the microfilm machines would be pointless, and they would end up looking like idiotic dupes—something like devotees of Philip Morris with their nicotine delivery systems stuck in their faces, but no benzene in their Zippos. At this late date, could they be expected to admit to themselves that poring over blurry reproductions of centuries-old obituaries in one of the world's nastiest and most boring cities is a ludicrous waste of their own particular souls' scant sojourn inside a skin?

It all adds up to a very profitable, self-sustaining supplement to the tithes that are piling up in the General Authorities' shiny brass collection plates. And you'd think the poor marks would by now be sapped of all their wealth and enthusiasm. But, miraculously enough, on top of it all, they somehow manage to come up with the wherewithal to mount the most active and successful proselytizing program of any faith in history. And this worldwide high-pressure promotional campaign is financed not by the church, but by the families of the missionaries themselves.

As a result, Mormons are the fastest growing denomination in the world, with as many members as Hitler killed Jews already—and I'm talking non-Holocaust denial numbers here. (Maybe now would be a good time to...well, on second thought, never mind. Forget I said anything.)

Youthful proselytizers are sent everywhere, two by two, in three-piece suits, on one-speed bikes. (They are almost always male: it's the ultimate failure for a young Mormoness to be sent on a mission, as she's supposed to be perpetually in a family way, unfit to scent a bike seat). Their task is not only to recruit living souls and to encourage the grunting-up of more, but also to gather birth, death and copulation records. When two handsome, tall white boys come to your door and want to talk to you about the Kingdom of Heavenly Father being established on earth, pay close attention to them. If you don't pay close attention, they might sidle up to your mantelpiece, snag onto the family Bible, and quietly tear out that page where your sweet old Episcopalian godmother wrote her name in purple ink.

But do let these pillaging marauders into your living room, by all means. They may be able to help you place yourself in the grand scheme of things, especially if you happen to have Charlemagne for an ancestor, or one of the other historical notables whose line has been traced back to Adam. With the help of the Mormons, it just might be possible for you to know who begat the begetter of your begetter, and so on, all the way back to the beginning of time.

Then you can be moistened on behalf of each name on the catalog, and rest secure in the knowledge that, when you die, you'll go to Paradise and embrace every single one of your relatives, including either Cain or Abel, whichever side you came from. Finally you will know where your people got those close-set eyes, buckteeth, and that pesky predisposition to every learning disability in the book.

Actually, this prospect doesn't appeal to me, personally—but then, I'm probably a special case: I've got great-great-great uncles who make Timothy McVeigh look like Oskar Schindler, (you'll meet one of them shortly; brace yourself), and at least one cousin who died sharing a cell block in the Nevada State Penitentiary with five of her twelve children. George Pickett, the Confederate general responsible for the biggest and most pointless massacre of the War Between the States, would be waiting at the Pearly Gates to shake my hand. A rugby scrum of Liverpool's worst yobs would be more fun than a trans-temporal Bradley family group hug.

But not everyone is sprung from the seed of Cain, like me. The General Authorities meet with little difficulty persuading plenty of people to bend every effort to achieve such a desirable end.

The faithful file obediently into a secret chamber in the temple, which has a big tub full of magical water, set upon the backs of four giant bronze oxen, also magic. By definition, magic intends to coerce a gullible deity, so gymnastics are everything. If the smallest detail does not go perfectly, the whole rigmarole must be repeated from the top. They baptize by full immersion of the body, and if so much as half a pube detaches from the root of your tickle-gizzard and floats to the surface, you have to take a deep breath and start all over again. I have no idea how long the mouth and nose must be submerged in order for the metaphysical graft to take. There's no way to judge by scrutinizing the rank and file for symptoms of oxygen deprivation to the brain, as no control group exists.

But, even with all the difficulties and dangers, this is no impossible chore. Remember, the world is only 6000 years old. You can figure between forty and fifty generations for every thousand years—until you get back to old boys like Methuselah, who lived nine hundred and sixty-nine years all by himself, at which point the inconvenience to yourself has decreased considerably. So you wind up with probably fewer than a couple hundred guys in your direct line, and that's only if you were industrious and stupid enough back in the old library to trace yourself all the way back to the Garden of Eden. A couple hundred baths in the Water of Righteousness—a good Mormon can encompass that in less than a month, with diligence inspired by a fervid desire to sit for eternity upon the right hand of Our Heavenly Father, and a good blow dryer.

I have no doubt there are convenience store managers and gas station attendants who've been proxy-baptized for the immortal souls of Abraham Lincoln and Albert Schweitzer and Johann Sebastian Bach and Mother Teresa. (Admittedly, that last one is going to need all the help she can get. Charles Keating's main squeeze, indeed. How did those people in the Calcutta stadium know it was really her in the open casket? I, for one, hope to die before gravity has enough time to make the whole shape of my head transmogrify whenever I lie down on my back. But, come to think of it, that very bloodhound quality of Mama T's face makes her ideal for conversion to the sect: didn't Mark Twain say that Mormon women were so ugly that polygamy was an act of charity?)

After a hard day's work redeeming the dearly departed and dealing out salvation in the preterit tense to faceless strangers who otherwise might as well have never existed, Latter-Day-Saints like to slap on the old feedbag in restaurants near the temple. Their favorite places are all-you-can-eat smorgasbords, as they tend to be big-eating Nordic types on a budget (don't forget that pesky tithe). It's humbling to hang around the tables and watch their massive hands as they reach for the prime rib and pimento loaf and green jello with tiny marshmallows. Their fingerprints are wrinkly from spending all day underwater.

Strange dogma, to be sure, and weird group activities. But this is not just an ephemeral oddball cult, like Heaven's Gate. Remember, they pretty much own and operate one of the fifty United States of America. And the financial arm of their church, the Bonneville Corporation, is one of the biggest corporate entities in the country. Calling themselves a religion, they needn't trouble with taxes.

Their ambition, of course, is to get a Mormon into the White House. And since America is still mostly a Christian nation, the Mormons are trying to push their strange unchristian doctrines and practices into the background, hoping the rest of us saps will mistake them for regular vanilla Protestants. One of the perennial candidates in Republican primaries is Utah senator Orrin Hatch. He keeps saying, "It's not a cult, it's not a cult," but the majority so far haven't chosen to believe him.

As the European cultural traditions that formed America decay and are gradually forgotten, and our education system somehow manages to decline even further, and people become more and more ignorant and sink into the pit of cultural relativism, it's very likely that the time will come when Americans no longer find it strange or distasteful to have many wives, or to believe that men can become God, or that dead people should be rousted from their eternal repose and forced to do bizarre things without their consent—or, indeed, that dunking oneself on behalf of the long-defunct owner of some syllables on a chart is any stranger than sprinkling a little water on a brand-new baby's forehead. And I have no doubt that a Mormon will one day be president of our country.

A president who believes the universe is only a couple hundred generations old will have no problem starting a nuclear war and allowing pollution to destroy our planet. It can always be rebuilt and repopulated in a week by God, or some other Mormon.

PEACE PARK PRANCE

Two strapping young men, clean-cut, flossed with a vengeance, straddling identical one-speed bikes, have taken their position aslant the path, barring Tom's way to Boom Town's glamorous bull's-eye. The pockets of their conservative suits bulge with Holy Writ.

"Ah, Dr. Bradley, neighbor, it's so nice to behold your radiant countenance among us."

"Fuck off."

"You'd better treat us nicely or we'll be forced to have recourse to the LDS missionary's secret weapon."

"Oh? And what weapon is that?" lisps Tom, sweetly.

"Heh-heh, we actually don't take it too seriously," says one of them, squatting down on his heels among the Jap-brand cigarette butts and rice-ball wrappers, warming for a chat. "But it's been used a few times to great effect. Not too many decades ago, in fact. A pair of our boys were run out of a certain town on a rail and beaten by the accursed pagans."

"Now," intersperses the other, "these were two good and dutiful brothers of the faith. So they just got up off the ground, dusted their shoes off, and uttered a few esoteric words. Less than a week later the whole community was feeling poorly."

"At least those who hadn't been vaporized instantly by the blast."

Tom's fellow displaced Utahns dig out their good books and commence reciting in unison the magical procedure, as prescribed by Christ himself on this very day of his transfiguration:

If anyone will not welcome you or listen to your words, shake the dust off your feet when you leave that town. I tell you the truth, it will be more bearable for Sodom and Gomorrah on the day of judgment than for that town.

"Matthew, chapter ten–"
"Verses fourteen and fifteen," interrupts "Doctor" Bradley. He leaves the two youngsters awash in the unbaptized heathen horde, gaping with heartfelt admiration for their townsman. And he continues his progress toward the blasted hypocenter.

VII

Back in Nagasaki
Where the fellers chew tobaccy
And the women wicky-wacky-woooo.
—Harry Warren

Having lived among, and even been partially descended from, such pious folk, I'm in a better position than most American mongrels to be aware of my antecedents, my "blood." And, in addition to General George Pickett and the usual yobs and cons, there happens to be an outright vampire in my genealogy. He has stalked me all my life, but he failed to fix his fangs in my jugular until, like an idiot, I blundered into his tomb and offered up my throat. Now I'm stuck.

My mother is an opera enthusiast, but (for understandable reasons) no particular fan of libretti. She played *Madame Butterfly* for me on her phonograph when I was little, without much comment other than to say it was about a sad lady over in Asia. "Your imagination can make a better story," she said, "so just listen to the music. That's what I do."

So, the Bloodsucker of Nagasaki missed that particular chance to invade my awareness. But then the Mormon branch of our clan scraped the clods from his face and started him up from the dead.

A couple of my grampa's cousin's eighty-year-old plural wives got bored because the old man had contracted some fresher sofa fodder, so they spent an entire summer fidgeting around in the behemoth genealogical library of the Church of Jesus Christ of Latter-Day-Saints. These sweet old ladies supplied my reluctant but polite mother with information about her bloodlines gleaned from miles and miles of microfilm. You can see how difficult it is, in Utah, to keep skeletons firmly buried in the family closet.

Apart from being disgusted by the whole notion of human pedigree, my mother felt guilty about accepting the smudgy xeroxes. She didn't want to encourage this sort of thing. Like someone heating the house too much in coal mining country, she couldn't help thinking of those "volunteers" sweltering in the vast genealogical crypt, their pre-bicameral ant-like minds placed at the service of the modern-day Cheops who decreed this Eighth Wonder of the Ancient World. (But then, who am I to sit in judgment, when my will is no longer my own, but belongs to the Bloodsucker, the living-dead Ozymandias who founded modern Japan?)

In any case, my plural gr'aunties were not miffed in the slightest by anything that a hopelessly unsaved heathen like their distant nephew could say about these mighty works. They had only to point to the then-current "Roots" phenomenon and the craze for personal pedigrees among far-western nouveaux riches, to demonstrate the usefulness of compiling and preserving birth, death and copulation records from every parish church in Christendom and every pagan shrine in the rest of the world (including, unfortunately, the Land of the Rising Sun).

My plural gr'aunties remained unembarrassed in the face of my jeering. They continued to spend most of their waking hours burrowed deep in that nightmarish hole in the rock. There, surrounded by the bizarre (yet hideously apropos) Oriental shadow puppets, my personal Vlad the Impaler was waiting to be awakened. I suspect the baptismal water scalded whatever poor Mormon tried to carry his sick soul to Heaven.

Mom saw me off at the airport when, without knowing why, I moved to Nagasaki. (Somehow, it seemed to me that the sit-down job I had gotten there was an inadequate explanation for such a grotesque relocation—and I was right.) While I was waiting to be scanned for concealed ordnance, she briefly mentioned that, "according to the Mormon stuff," one of her great-great-or-whatever uncles seemed to have been a shipping magnate or something in the neighborhood of my new home, about a hundred, hundred-twenty years ago.

I had no historical context in which to place this bit of trivia. So the Bloodsucker's name should have leaked out of my brain thirty-five thousand feet in the air and fallen into the ocean somewhere over the international dateline. But it didn't. I couldn't even remember the name of my place of employment when I got into the taxi at the Nagasaki airport, but this bastard's moniker was wedged like a worm inside my gray matter, waiting to slither to the surface.

*   *   *   *

Anyone who rides elevators or avails himself of the sit-down toilets in pricey hotel lobbies in my newly adopted town cannot get away from Puccini's sad heroine. The Muzak around here always plays a synthesized disco version of the famous arias to which this matchless prose was set—

They outcasting me. Aeverybody thing me mos' bes'
wicked in all Japan. Nobody speak to me no more
they all outcast me aexcep' jus' you; tha' 's why
I ought be sawry...But tha' 's ezag' why I am not!
Wha' 's use lie? It is not inside me that sawry.
Me ? I 'm mos' bes' happy female woman in Japan
mebby in that whole worl'. What you thing?

The story from which the above quaint dialog is excerpted,

and upon which Puccini's libretto is based, was written more than a hundred years ago by a lawyer named John Luther Long, whose sister was an acquaintance of the son of my mother's great-great-great (and maybe one or two more) uncle.

This uncle was a thoroughgoing son-of-a-bitch who killed everything he glanced at. A Scotch gunrunner without any of Rimbaud's redeeming characteristics, he helped restore the vicious emperors to the Japanese throne (making possible the blood-bloated reign of Hirohito). He single-handedly industrialized this once gorgeous country, turning it into the toxic wasteland it currently is, by introducing the first railway locomotive and the first mechanized coal mine. And he climaxed this series of signal achievements by founding the dark satanic mill called Mitsubishi Heavy Industries, the unfortunately missed target of our second A-bomb in 1945.

Not content with raping the place, my dear old unker bought himself a sex slave from the impoverished natives, doubtlessly dickering till he got a rock-bottom price. It wasn't necessary to lie to the girl about his intentions—everybody knew the score. But he sadistically promised her holy wedlock, anyway, probably to get more sincere hip action on the old futon. He first made her a proper respectable Christian, of course, thus permanently alienating her from her family and culture. Only when she was dependent on him for everything did he leave the poor wretch (who liked to wear butterfly appliques on her kimono) with the mixed-race baby (also named Tom) whose cries were the only thing that stopped her from hacking herself to death with a samurai knife (just a short one—not one of the glamorous long ones used to impale women and skewer babies later in China, after my uncle supplied them with the steamship technology and the imperial impetus to get them over there).

My unker left behind not only a half-caste bastard and a

discarded sex slave whose belly never quite recovered from self-inflicted slashes, but also a grotesquely bloated Raj-style estate on Nagasaki Bay, with gardens that would've been big enough to provide living space for several working families. These digs were also unfortunately missed by our Big Boy in '45.

And instead of razing this blight on the landscape and turning it into, say, a hospice for the pubescent native girls who are raped and torn to shreds and infected with AIDS and hepatitis C every year by brave soldiers from America's nearby military installations, the Nagasaki Chamber of Commerce turned the place into western Japan's number-one tourist destination. They mispronounce it "Grubber Gardens," and suppress any connection between this source of revenue and Puccini's greatest hit. They instruct the American collaborators who write their tourist pamphlets to insist that the story of Madame Butterfly is "probably fiction."

Rather than declaring my Uncle Tom "Grubber" a national anathema and erasing him from the public awareness, chipping his name from the monuments and milestones, as the Romans did with their dead nauseating powerful people, the Japanese have posthumously dubbed him "the Scottish Samurai." They have enshrined the memory this ravenous monster, who destroyed one of their own women in return for a few orgasms, and poisoned their archipelago in the meantime. They call him the Founder of Modern Japan.

Fresh off the plane, I knew none of this, except for the melodies of the opera which, if it had a conventional happy ending, might be called *Madame Glover*. I was dimly aware that my mother's maiden name is identical by no mere coincidence. But that was an arbitrary bit of data floating in my short-term memory, and might have evaporated in a day or two, had I not mentioned it, in passing, during a lull in a boring but compulsory orgy of watered-down Suntory whisky guzzling in a hand-job hostess bar.

My new colleagues' eyes got wider than when you quote them greens fees in an Arizona country club. They choked up and said, "You uncle be Scottish Samurai, yes, no? You name Tom, too, jus' like you mos' bes' famous uncle, yes, no? Ah, werr-come home, Bladderly-sensei! Werr-come home!"

Now I am expected to publish paeans to my esteemed forbear, and to hold forth about him on demand at parties and faculty meetings. Having barely escaped polygamists who dunk themselves in water to save their dead grannies, I'm obliged to join my unbaptized hosts in heathenish ancestor worship. I've been urged to set up a sandalwood-reeking shrine to Thomas Glover in my apartment.

My place of employment has offered to fly in a famous calligrapher all the way from Kyoto to render my matrilineal family tree on exquisite rice paper, to be mounted under glass and hung on the wall in my office. I have only to phone my mother and somehow persuade her to dig up the Mormons' smudgy xeroxes and mail them to me.

They want me to be Grubber II, an honorary *Nipponjin*, like my Uncle Tom. There have been exquisitely subtle hints that I'll be given tenure in return for this disinterment of leering evil, and enough of a raise in salary to get a house with a garden and a view of Nagasaki Bay. No more bullet-train commuting from Hiroshima.

Do you think that someone of my exhausted bloodlines has anything like the gumption to turn down lifetime employment at a sit-down gig, especially now that my children are fluent in the local dialect and can phone in pizza orders for me? The gerontocrats are planning to invite Grubber, Jr., to stay on till his prostate implodes and his teeth and hair fall all the way out, and he becomes one of them. The vampire Grub is leeched onto my neck and sucking steadily.

*   *   *   *

On top of a modest eminence, in a tiny one-room apartment, the various members of the Nagasaki literary scene squat on rice-straw floor mats, pens in hands.

The hill on which they hunker is surrounded by a raging torrent, like one of those Punjabi villages which Alexander the Great besieged—only in this case the torrent is composed not of lush Himalayan drainage in summer spate, but of Mazdas and Toyotas, unhampered by emission standards, in a bumper-to-bumper, two-lane, sixty-mile-per-hour traffic jam that screams all day and most of the night through the volcanic gorges.

Particles of lead and unburnt diesel fuel, compounded with dioxins from Japan's omnipresent styrofoam bonfires, waft up between the puckering bamboos and slither almost audibly through corroded window screens, to accumulate on the smooth upper lips and the rough drafts of the various members of the Nagasaki literary scene. Meanwhile they hack away at their cycles of piquant haiku like forsaken women trying to disembowel themselves.

The bamboos straggling around the apartment are shrouded in a mist reminiscent of those depicted in Ukiyoe prints, so inspirational to the post-impressionists. It's strange how bamboo can make lung-lacerating fumes look pretty. There's something about the feathery textures of the fronds, and the languid way they sway and turn brown and pucker in the sulfuric acid that falls from the Nagasaki sky instead of rain. Alexander, also, had to contend with grotesque Asiatic atmospheric conditions, during the monsoons.

And these members of the Nagasaki literary scene resemble

that soggy Macedonian in a further sense. They are Occidentals making a significant noise in the East—or trying to, anyway. They tend to ignore Matthew Arnold's lines on the subject:

> The East bowed low before the blast
> In patient, deep disdain;
> She let the legions thunder past
> And plunged in thought again.

Of course, Arnold was referring to the India of Chandragupta, not the Japan of Hirohito's Beatle-banged grandson. So perhaps the comparison is a tad shaky (especially the reference to "thought"). At any rate, this particular lost generation of expatriate writers are Oedipusses more than Alexanders, for they have fathers to kill.

There is a pantheon of in-print forbears whom these Nagasaki writers, in order to be worthy of that epithet, must come to grips with, must overcome and assimilate, must avoid being overwhelmed by and subsumed under, so as not to lose their artistic individuality in the established greatness of their adopted city's formidable literary heritage. And, like James Baldwin doing away with Richard Wright, or Camille Paglia liquidating Susan Sontag, the Nagasaki writers have to encompass their patricide-by-pen before they can solidify their own sense of place (so essential to writing "anchored" poetry and prose). Only then can they stake their claim on this seismic terrain, and buckle down on their rice-straw floor mats to produce something truly substantial. Before their daddies can castrate them, they have to kill their daddies, if you want to get all psychoanalytical about it.

I'll be glad to pitch in. First on the Oedipal hit list is the local boy who wrote that butler novel they turned into a movie starring Hannibal the Cannibal. In a subsequent book, which was not made into a movie, he has provided our town with its reply to that most far-famed of fictional last lines—

I go to encounter for the millionth time
the reality of experience, and to forge in the
smithy of my soul the uncreated conscience of my race.

It's said that four generations of Dublin writers were blocked by that final sentence from Joyce. Well, here's the daunting prose gauntlet the butler novel guy has cast down before us. I'll allow you to experience for yourself this clincher. Like Joyce's, this one also depicts the outset of a voyage—

I stood in the doorway as she walked down to
the end of the drive... I smiled and waved to her.

Just imagine that followed by the piquant words, "The End." This gem, in its unaffected purity, has blocked a couple of our haiku writers, I think.

They embarrass even themselves by their hero worship of this Booker Prize-winning Nagasakian, and dream of his triumphal return to his hometown, with a public reading and a reception afterwards, which they will be invited to. I fear they won't bring fangs and vitriol to that reception, but puckered lips and unction.

Another illustrious native occupies second place on our list of local deities overdue for a Gotterdammerung. This guy wrote a memoir that has become the Bible of the Nagasaki literary scene, or at least of those members who don't swear by the butler novel. (It's a downright schism, of you want the truth, sky-clad vs. white-clad.)

This memoir is about the author's attempts to gain an international outlook by seeking out and sharing global perspectives with servicemen from a certain nearby U.S. military installation. Unlike the guy who wrote the butler novel, whose name I seem to have forgotten, this memoirist has an easily remembered name. At any rate, I can recall it, because it's mentioned in the following representative quotation from his book, along with certain other identifying characteristics—

Bob's huge cock was stuffed all the way into Kei's mouth... Ah'm jes' gonna see who's got the biggest. She crawled around on the rug like a dog and did the same for everyone... Hey, Ryu, his is twice the size of the one ya got...The penises of the black men were so long they looked slender...That's jes' awful, she said, slapped Reiko's butt and laughed shrilly. Moving about the room, twisting our bodies, we took into ourselves the tongues and fingers and pricks of who[m]ever we wanted.

Once a year certain members of the Nagasaki literary scene pool their aluminum yen and make a pilgrimage by highway bus to Open Base Day at the nearby American military installation, to ogle the black servicemen and try to imagine which might be the sons of those mentioned in the book. And they also dream of a visitation by the author, and a public performance which they can attend, just as other members of the Nagasaki literary scene dream of such a manifestation of the butler novel guy.

Like the recent catastrophic pyroclastic flows in the neighborhood, this literary heritage, so firmly established in the local consciousness as almost to be part of the ground underfoot, periodically oozes up and coats everything with hot stickiness. Particularly Ryu's stuff. At every meeting, or salon, or soiree, two or three of the younger members of the Nagasaki literary scene will always insist on reciting from memory choice passages of the aforementioned memoir, seeming always to select those paragraphs where lots of inverted rim jobs are given specifically to African Americans. They seem to be stimulated by the older members' visceral reactions to this moving prose. Here's another representative quotation:

> *I felt as if my insides were oozing out through every pore, and other people's sweat and breath were flowing in... Especially the lower half of my body felt heavy and sore, as if sunk into thick mud, and my mouth itched to hold somebody's prick and drain it.*

Japan is on its way out. The place is dissolving before our very eyes, like one of their paper doors in a typhoon. The supply of eighteen year olds is in sharp decline, due to infertility brought on by post-economic-bubble existential despair. So the universities are in deep trouble, and are hiring fewer and fewer fulltime foreign professors.

There are almost no more actual grownups with tenured time to read and write, and the discipline to reread and rewrite, and even the maturity and taste to discard stuff that stinks like unwashed sailor crotches. They all cleared out when the Japanese economy took its ludicrous pratfall in the eighties. So the Nagasaki Community of Writers languishes, but hangs on with heartbreaking tenacity.

Only youngsters remain, itinerant TEFL trash, who are here just to stockpile money between heroin-soaked trips to the Golden Triangle. Almost every sentence that comes out of these kids' mouths turns up at the end, like a question, and most of their vowel sounds are schwas. It's very strange to imagine them at the helms of English conversation classes. But it's reassuring to remember that they're only working in storefront language schools where tuition is but a secondary, or even tertiary concern, if that. The owners don't seem to care, or notice, if their youthful Caucasoid instructors have speech impediments, but are satisfied if they agree to brighten their hair with bleach and their eyes with turquoise contact lenses, and fornicate with the students on demand, as it's good for business.

Handsome Chip (surname suppressed by earnest request) is your average member of the Nagasaki literary scene. When not abusing the green grapes of Proserpine in Southeast Asia, he's a part-time job subsister, teaching twenty-five ninety-minute classes per week in fifteen different storefront language schools. In a good month he makes a million yen (eight thousand dollars). Chip keeps body if not mind together by smoking clean-burning Yakuza methedrine in public squatty toilets, and does his eating and haiku writing, on those rare occasions when his appetite and frontal lobes are up to the tasks, while wandering up and down the aisles of the supermarket. He scribbles and scarfs the free samples of spiced picked cabbage and toothpicked wads of deep-fried pork, and washes it all down with little paper cups of chemical beer.

But lately there's no peace in those aisles for literary endeavor. Suddenly, touts scream everywhere, some even using megaphones, which they wedge up against the side of your head while trying to persuade you to buy more and more packets of freeze-dried ramen noodles. It has become nearly impossible for Chip to calculate his clutches of five and seven syllables.

Once again I say it: Japan is on its way out. People's fundaments have gotten as tight as their grip on their flimsy aluminum yen. More and more employees must scream in the aisles of the stores, under orders to destroy their voice boxes in a frenzied effort to move the merch, move the merch, move the merch. Their efforts only bear fruit late in the day, when blood gurgles satisfactorily inside their necks.

It's the *gambatte* spirit: when the chips are down, throw

yourself into a frenzied mania, exhibit brainless nervous energy, preferably the sort that causes pain and tissue damage. Above all, look and sound busy. It's a Tennessee Valley Authority of the soul.

Gambatte translates as follows: pulverize your personality with hysterical activity; incur a metabolic debt gross as it is pointless; twitch, simper, grow duodenal tumors, tailgate the speeding Toyota in front of you like a suicidal maniac—do anything, in fact, but reflect on the gerontocrats who misgovern your life, and the empty hole inside you, the ragged wound, where a self should have been allowed to grow beyond the earliest stages of adolescence. Didn't old big-butted MacArthur mention something about a race of twelve year olds?

Nagasaki is not Paris in the twenties. Japan is a nation in its death throes, vocalizing its terminal agony, not going quietly. There are more screams today in this city—and, with the plague of cellphones (a means of extending screams), more carcinogenic radiation—than at any time in the past fifty-six years.

And it's not the lethal rain or the lousy jobs and the lousier company, but the screaming, which will finally drive the members of the Nagasaki literary scene away. They will leave this twice-doomed town with nothing to mull over but its own native literary produce: tales of Afro-phalli and verbally challenged gentlemen's gentlemen.

Till the decibels accumulate to the point that bags must be packed, the members of the Nagasaki literary scene, these suffering souls, will continue steadfastly to squat on their rice straw floor mats like forsaken Mesdames Butterflies. And, if by chance one good evening soiree happens to roll along, when the Nagasaki air isn't scrubbing too viciously down their esophagi, for just a few moments, they might allow themselves to lay aside their desiccated poetic forms and fantasize, in complete sentences and paragraphs, about a triumphal return home, to America. Maybe, one fine day, the powers in control of their own civilization will decree their literary output worthy of grants and creative writing fellowships, and the services of literary agents.

At night we dream of leaving our gracious hosts to deafen and poison only each other. With our small pinches of seventeen syllables, in the meantime, we try to whisper away, rather than shout down, the madness, the degenerative nervous disorder, that is Nagasaki, Japan.

PEACE PARK PRANCE

A cross the grassy knolls, on top of a modest but serviceable rise, a codger in a Hirohito-Hitler mustache can be seen. Resplendent in white gloves, a silk ribbon sash, and a blood-colored carnation which obscures almost the entire front of his boy-sized morning coat, this is Tom Bradley's transfigured Christ. But where have Moses and Elijah shambled off to?

The geezer's somberly releasing clouds of diseased doves from chrome-plated cages. Directly upon release, the poor animals, which have plastic olive branches stapled symbolically to their upper beaks and ankles, belly straight into the gravel like overloaded sailplanes, to be trampled to grease spots by stampeding Hiroshimizers.

The pigeon fancier is none other than Hiroshima's much-regretted mayor, old What's-his-name, a Liberal Democratic Party boy all the way. He has come with bells on: all dressed up in a clown suit, a deluxe boutonniere stuffed in his buttonhole. You'd never catch his Catholic counterpart down south doing that routine.

The mayor of Nagasaki is a coreligionist of Tom's Papist wife, and a heroic man. Those aged rightists in the sound trucks, armed with ordnance provided by the Yakuza, periodically try to assassinate the mayor of Nagasaki. They've put at least one bullet in him already, because he says incorrect things about the Holy Family in Tokyo. And yet he stands firm as an eighteen-year-old's hard-on. That's how much heroicity of virtue this old mackerel-snapper possesses. The mayor of Nagasaki is definite beatification material, a man of genuine spirituality.

And it makes sense that Tom didn't wind up pissing away

his middle years as a legal resident of the latter scenic city. (He only commutes back and forth: mere coincidence, not unwholesome obsession). As a fulltime Nagasaki "expat," Tom could never make the claim around which this whole book has been organized. He could not boast, or lament, of coming full circle in his life, of winding up in a mirror image of his hometown, suffering a poignant recapitulation of his boyhood, in yet another irradiated city overrun by religious naifs and nuts.

In Boom Town II, Tom would have no cause to compose such jeremiads in the first place. He would be obliged to serve as mouthpiece for the philosopher king—which is no way to write nonfiction with the hard biting edge that today's tough marketplace demands of a memoirist, or whatever.

VIII

> I have not seen the walls at Babylon...
> nor have I heard the account of any eye-witness.
> —Pausanias

Nagasaki boasts not just one memoirist, or whatever. There's a whole literary scene lousy with us. And write we do, and submit our stuff to electronic lit-mags, and proudly answer to the name of e-literati, in defiance of the ossified and incestuous cabals who've controlled literature ever since Pisistratus the Athenian tyrant caused the Iliad and the Odyssey to be "put into order."

You remember Pisistratus. He's the same enterprising soul who grabbed a husky country girl, cleaned her up, dressed her in full body armor, and went riding his chariot into town with her at the reins, telling everybody that she was his personal chum, the goddess Athena. Today he'd be at the helm of a major communications corporation.

Literature, to people like this, is a means to a usually nefarious end. Pisistratus decided that it would be useful to regulate the public performances of poetry, maybe do a little manipulation of the poems themselves, in order to achieve certain propagandistic effects that would shore up his authority and enhance the credibility of his cronies. So he descended upon the humble Homeridae, a clan of jobbing reciters said to be sprung agnatically from the loins of the blind bard himself. These "Sons of Homer" had long pursued their hereditary trade of doling out memorized bits to live audiences, meanwhile preserving the hodge-podge of written transcripts on their island.

Drawing on slave-generated proceeds from the local silver mine, our sacrilegious tyrant caused the scrolls, which contained all the wisdom and knowledge under the sun, to be corrected and collated. No doubt, from that point forward (at least till Pisistratus' son and successor was run out of Athens) there were Iliad and Odyssey police standing ready at the festivals to drag off any performer who dared deviate from the municipal text. So much for oral improvised verse. No more slams on the old Acropolis.

Fast-forward 400 years, and the Official and Definitive Pisistratid Homer, Deluxe Critical Edition, is chief among the volumes being copied and stockpiled at Pergamum on the Anatolian mainland. The local king, Eumenes, has a hankering to adorn his reign with a proper library. But the powers that be in Egypt get wind of this project, which threatens to give their own Alexandrian stacks a run for their money. So, what do they do? They slap an embargo on papyrus. They pinch off the western world's supply of non-monumental writing material. And you thought Bill Gates was a pharaonic little prick. Egypt had become the Microsoft of antiquity: whoever craves knowledge can come crawling to us, and we'll see what can be arranged.

And what is the best weapon against Bill Gates, besides urging clever youngsters to hack in and crash his system? (Julius Caesar will do just that to Egypt soon enough, burning big parts of the Alexandrian library during Cleopatra's watch; and the ancestors of Bin Laden will come along seven and a half centuries after that, and finish the job neatly.) While we wait for the hackers to work their magic, what recourse do we have? Ask Linux and Apple, and ask King Eumenes of Pergamum: innovation.

Did the king let a little problem like the sudden unavailability of a data storage medium stifle his big plans? Hell no. He put his clever Greeks to work on the problem. Since their local riverbanks, unlike those of the Nile, had no suitable weeds, they turned their attention to a completely different category of substance that happened to be lying around in abundance: the inedible leftovers from banquets and sacrifices. They scraped the hair and fat off goat- and cow- and sheepskins, and soaked the split hides in a special brew whose active ingredient was dog shit. A few more or less elaborate physical manipulations were performed, and *voila*. The result was called "parchment," a new word derived from the name of the city. It was slightly less dear than the vegetable product for which it was the sole competitor, but still pricey enough: one drachma per page—a week's wage for many.

This same basic recipe for parchment will accompany the Pharisees in about 250 years when, Herod's temple destroyed, they retire to "Babylonia," carrying in their heads the Second Sinai, which Yahweh whispered esoterically into Moses' ear just after slipping him the old Decalogue. The scribes will commit to parchment scrolls these Traditions of the Elders (so under-appreciated by a certain young rabbi from Galilee). However, in the tanning process, the famed fruit of the Mesopotamian date palm—a commodity sweet enough to be worth its weight in medium-grade copper—will be substituted for dog shit. (Something to do with kosher legislation, perhaps.)

And, for the next half-millennium, until the Arabs take a Chinese POW in future Taliban territory who will finally teach us to make actual paper, Western and Near-Eastern Literature will continue to be a tale of two competing media—at least from the book-hawker's point of view.

In an age like ours, when editors and agents have abolished the slush pile to give themselves time to "author" best-selling memoirs, it may be hard for apparently growing numbers of people to believe, but the book-hawker's point of view is not the only one worthy of consideration here. For example, it might occur to some to wonder where the writer himself figured in all this scheming and market manipulation and tugs-o'-war between venture capitalists and potentates.

The writer? He's tucked snugly under the wing of aristocratic patronage, and there he will remain until the storming of the Bastille. I know the armpit of a marquis sounds like an awfully stifling place to be tucked for such a long time, but that's just because we are products of the degenerate modern age. As Kenneth Rexroth reminds us in his introduction to the second issue of the Evergreen Review, "...only our industrial and commercial civilization has produced an [artistic and intellectual] elite which has consistently rejected all the reigning values of society."

Up until that jarring discontinuity in world history which saw the shutting down of the Paris Sorbonne (I mean the time before 1968), artists and writers served as "moral vates to the ruling classes." Rexroth says we were "ultimately the creators of all primary values" in the pre-modern world. (I suppose that having to drink and fornicate on demand with blue-bloods was a small enough price to pay for such an honor.) He sums it up in a very memorable phrase: "There were no Baudelaires in Babylon."

The best poets, in other words, were not driven underground in the long, long ago. Even Catullus, hero of Bukowski (our very own American Baudelaire), was cuddly with generals and senators. His father was tight with Julius Caesar and had him over to dinner often. Of infinitely greater importance, Catullus was in a position to be invited to the soirees and salons of the fabulously wealthy Atticus, who had several cohorts of his slaves trained to copy and bind manuscripts, both vegetable and animal. This Atticus took it upon himself to promote and circulate the work of the greatest writers of his day—or at least those we are aware of. Christ knows how many he buried, either deliberately or through neglect. A god-maker generates his own self-fulfilling prophecies. The ship of state in the pre-modern world may have derived its keel and ballast from the minds of poets, as Rexroth suggests, but I refuse to believe that the moneyed types, according to whose whim select writers were allowed to die leaving behind some trace of their existence on earth, were any better than their modern counterparts.

How do we know there were no Baudelaires in Babylon? It's not as if there was a net where they could post their stuff. They could have been squashed under giant piles of approved texts, as we Baudelaires tend to be in today's world of print. We are aware of Catullus only because he happened to please a mover of merchandise who was squeamish enough to deal in books instead of job lots of angelic British catamites, who controlled access to large amounts of papyrus and/or parchment and had the connections to import oak gall ink of good enough quality to contain the iron sulfate that would withstand the wet rags of palimpsest makers, who wielded the knout over stables of Greekling copyist slaves in their harried hundreds, and thereby supplied the pigeonholes of bookstalls throughout the Latin-speaking world. Atticus, by virtue of being the sort of half-hatched personality who devotes his brief stay on this planet to manipulating matter instead of ideas, allowed Catullus' cerebrations to see the light of day.

That's why the canny poet hobnobbed with the literary dictator of Republican Rome as well as the political dictator, and addressed poems to them. And if we e-literati had been born, or somehow managed to weasel our way, into the correspondingly celestial stratum of our own society, wouldn't we be doing the same thing right now, instead of casting our pearls gratis before the stingy swine of the internet? That's a loaded question, of course, as circumstances have been drastically altered since Roman times.

Between then and now, the man known as the Great Cham of Literature came into existence, in a very big way. A dozen years before Jean Paul Marat climbed out of Paris' glamorous sewers, Samuel Johnson had already caused the decidedly unglamorous gutters of London's Grub Street to re-echo with his rallying cry about blockheads. The great lexicologist placed us at the beck and call of the book buying public at large. And the goodness of that news is unadulterated only if you insist on looking at it, once again, strictly from the book-hawker's point-of-view. Businessmen have taken the place of dukes and duchesses. Now, thanks to Dr. Johnson, if we want our stuff to see print, we have to kiss Si Newhouse's parvenu ass, instead of Atticus' equestrian buttocks.

The question remains on the table: would you versify for the postmodern Atticus? How about for the Caesar of the New World Order? (Forget, for the moment, the truest words ever spoken: "All money is dirty money.") If they gave you a high six-figure advance against royalties on one of your novels, could they purchase your soul to the extent that you'd write Senator Bob Dole's acceptance speech at the 1996 Republican National Convention? That was the $800,000 question for Mark Helprin, America's closest moral (but not artistic) equivalent to Catullus. Guggenheim fellow, National Book Award nominee, recipient of the Penn-Faulkner Award and the Prix de Rome, Wall Street Journal contributing editor, senior fellow of a reactionary think tank in Indiana, Mark Helprin is responsible for such narcissistic abortions as *Refiner's Fire*, *Winter's Tale*, and *A Soldier of the Great War*. He answered the eight hundred-grand question in the affirmative. Again, Rexroth's words come to mind: "No literature of the past 200 years is of the slightest importance unless it is disaffiliated."

Now, as my fellow e-literati will affirm, being disaffiliated is not all Cadillac convertibles and brimming bushels of hothouse sinsemilla buds. Disaffiliation has a tendency to be, shall we say, less than remunerative. And the alternative has been made to appear so delicious (not the least by Helprin himself, who takes care during his interviews to mention that his office has genuine rosewood paneling). Since Dr. Johnson's time, when they usurped the nobility's power to corrupt us, the merchandisers have had plenty of opportunity to hone their seductive wiles. They have gotten very good at breathing their perfume deep into our nostrils, and sloshing their cup of abominations ever so close to our sorely tempted lips.

As for our well-affiliated Guggenheimer, our Wall Street Journal man, we have to remember that the hawkers and mongers first draped their purple tissues and scarlet textures over that poor zhlub way back in the pre-web era, when their charm was even more potent. These days, if a writer is going to sell out, he has to be more of an asshole than Mark Helprin, whose early stories, unlike our glorious, universally available electronic texts, would have languished as typescripts in his underpants drawer had he not rolled over and said "Please," and "Thank you, Sir." We net authors have no excuse but greed to act that way.

Thanks to e-lit, our own universe-upending revolution, the center of literary power has shifted, suddenly, and for only the second time in history. To the extent that it's humanly possible, moneyed types have become irrelevant. As Barney Rosset, editor of the aforementioned Evergreen Review, has said, "For once the technology is in the hands of the relatively impoverished." The web has made it possible for a writer to develop a more or less gigantic international following without the patriarchal blessing of rich bastards. With our submissions pasted into the bodies of email messages and our virtual galley proofs, we are not forced to make the Manichean compromise of getting into bed with manipulators of matter and movers of merchandise.

Hence the existence, no doubt eventually fatal, of a powerful cadre of internet haters. To play Saint Peter at the Pearly Gates, to hold the keys to the only form of immortality available in a godless age: is there any prouder accomplishment for an untalented person of the merchant caste? And do you think they are going to sit back and let those keys be wrested from their pinching little claws by a bunch of literary lumpen-proles like us, who don't even use paper when we move our mental bowels? They're closing ranks now. Have you noticed how many books coming out of New York these days are dedicated not to the long-suffering spouses and children of the authors, but to their agents and editors? These dedications tend to be more succinct but no less nauseating than Colley Cibber's 600-word grovel to the inbred aristocrat who urged him to do Shakespeare a big posthumous favor and rewrite Richard III.

Now I've gone and done it. I've resurrected the proverbial Lousy Writer himself, Dullness personified, the one contemporary of Dr. Johnson who doesn't seem to have heard the line about blockheads, George II's lapdog and pet poet laureate, the clown prince of ludicrous hacks. I have invoked the name of Colley Cibber—and in the same breath as a certain contributing editor for the Wall Street Journal. I wish I could say it was by random free association.

It's way too late for the former, but maybe we should give the latter a break. Perhaps we ought to refrain from eviscerating Mark Helprin and draping his entrails like a feather boa around his neck for all the ages to snicker at, as Alexander Pope did to Cibber. Restraint on our part might be called for—and not just because the poor man is reputed to have sustained a small amount of brain damage while patrolling the Lebanese border in a combat unit of the Israeli armed forces.

Why single him out for disdain and mockery? After all, even Shakespeare knew what side his crumpet was buttered on. And Aristophanes may have enjoyed drinking with Socrates, but it cost money to mount comedies, and the playwright did not hesitate to parade the philosopher's quirks in order to tickle the funny bones, and rouse the ire, of the latter's wealthy enemies, with fatal results.

On the other hand, for every Shakespeare, how many Kit Marlowes? And while Virgil obediently churns out occasional verse to help the self-proclaimed First Citizen kick-start one of the most oppressive regimes in history, I can't help thinking of Ovid languishing all alone on the Black Sea, dodging those arrows which the barbarous Skythians shot at random over the town walls to amuse themselves.

And when Chuck-Buk fondly hallucinates our well-connected young Catullus at the race track, I always remember another poet from the same city, several generations later, when Rome was no longer the valiant and amiable new ally depicted in the first book of Maccabees, but had become the imperialistic oppressor which slithers off the pages of a certain well-known sleeper of that particular publishing season: "... the Harlot, arrayed in purple and scarlet color, and decked with gold and precious stones and pearls, having a golden cup in her hand full of abominations and filthiness of her fornication... drunken with the blood of the saints, and with the blood of the martyrs of Jesus."

Atticus was no longer around, but his moral descendants were, only more so. The Harlot's reach had extended to the point that Martial, the first world-wide best-selling author, could brag that his books of epigrams were being hawked to Rome-worshiping provincial middlebrows everywhere, from the tin mines of Britain to Zeugma on the Euphrates (no doubt in parchment as well as papyrus editions). Such was the level of acclaim this poet enjoyed even while serving as moral vates to the vicious Emperor Domitian, the Hitler of classical antiquity—whom Martial's ditties often enough slavishly identify with the god Jupiter.

For some odd reason, Senator Bob Dole's gag writer just sprang back into my mind. (He won't stay down for the count.) Mark Helprin may have sold as many books, but in the talent department he's less of a Baudelaire than Martial, and infinitely less than Catullus, of course. It's not as though his corruption constitutes any loss to the sublime trans-temporal conversation called World Literature. And, on some at least semi-conscious level, the Cibbers and Helprins of this world must be aware of their own ephemerality. So why shouldn't they allow themselves to succumb to the lurid type of temptation that the likes of us will never know? It takes a Son of Thunder to stare down the purple and scarlet Whore. And it takes a son of something much bigger than that to say "Get thee behind me, Satan."

Luckily for us, we are mere web writers, insubstantial blips on the broadcast spectrum, and we can only dream about the Great Satan buttonholing us in our virtual wilderness. We white trash from that trailer park in the ionosphere would tip over like a round-heeled flat-backer if we found ourselves in Helprin's Gucci's. Every writer is a potential toady, or "fart-catcher," as the Great Cham's contemporaries put it. It's been that way since the "Sons of Homer" grabbed their ankles for Pisistratus. Our egos are open sores. Otherwise, why would we be scribbling instead of climbing the corporate ladder or getting laid or something normal like that? Mark Helprin, that dutiful secretor of Senatorial oratory, with all the standard cretinous diction and mongoloid parallelism, is more disgusting than us only by degree.

But there have been exceptions to the law I just promulgated about all writers being potential fart-catchers. I have been thinking of the greatest exception of all. Pace Rexroth, I do know of at least one Baudelaire in Babylon. This particular poet was such a Baudelaire, in fact, that he got booted out of Babylon and sent to a place almost as remote and unreal as cyberspace itself.

As a personal acquaintance of the bestselling epigrammatist we've been discussing, this guy had the chance to kiss some really big ass, the biggest in the known world. In these latter days, when any ambitious young writer spends more time with his fingers soaking in a manicure trough than wrapped around a pen, his head immobile under the unctuous mitts of a pricey hair technician than sailing in the breezy firmament of letters, and his two most strenuous mental disciplines are rehearsing his Hollywood-style elevator pitch and learning how to order wine, just in case he gets to "do lunch" with a currently hot author's representative—it's hard to imagine someone deliberately blowing his big chance.

But blow it this particular poet did. (His name, incidentally, was Decimus Junius Juvenalis—Juvenal, for short.) He had an "in," and was but a simper away from gaining entree into the midst of the glitterati of the richest empire on earth. And not only did he neglect to deploy the appropriate interpersonal skills, not only did he refuse to pucker up his ass-kissing muscles, but he threw away the dream-opportunity of a careerist's lifetime by insulting a favorite sexual plaything of the empress.

How can this behavior be explicable? We can only throw up our hands and assume that Juvenal was some kind of historical sport, a freak ahead of his time, for he fits Rexroth's description of today's poets to a tee: "...they can only vomit in the faces of the despots who offer them places in the ministries of the talents, or at least they are nauseated in proportion to their integrity."

Imagine how smarmy Mark Helprin had to be in order to nuzzle his way into Senator Bob Dole's inner circle, where anyone even tangentially connected to books other than the cookable kind was looked upon as a commie atheist, or worse. Then ponder soberly upon this undistractable seer and teller of truth, this Decimus Junius Juvenalis, who was so desirous of tearing down all privileged idiocy no matter where it reared its puffy face, that he couldn't even hold his tongue in the presence of the autocrat of the world.

The mighty have always flattered themselves with the presence of show people. And occupying a prominent position in the Palatine inner circle was a certain high-strung pantomime dancer named Paris, who was the Marilyn Monroe of Silver Age Rome. (He was no female, strictly speaking, but you know how the Greco-Romans were.) He was a fixture of the court: not the best choice of person to make fun of—at least not before he, himself, fell out of the ruling family's favor, and was murdered by them in cold blood, as Marilyn Monroes tend to be.

We don't know what Juvenal said to Paris, but it must have been as savagely indignant as his poetry, because it got him smacked from Italy, from Europe, clear out of the ballpark known today as the temperate zone. While circumspect Martial was allowed to stick around and take pleasure cruises down to Naples, to be seen affecting Grecian attire and angling for sardines off the porticoes of rich patrons' bayside vacation villas, our impolitic Juvenal was exiled among the beast-worshipping fellaheen of Upper Egypt, from which inhospitable outpost even the hardiest centurion returned prematurely decrepit, if at all. He was damned to Syene, the driest city in the world, previously known to the prophet Ezekiel as Seveneh, the absolute southernmost limit of Egypt, after which came the no-man's land of Ethiopia. The natives so far upriver were not habitual cannibals—just when they got drunk. Talk about a hardship post. It was definitely not Alexandria with its generous colonnades and cool marble porticoes. The coiners of the famous phrase "Bum-Fuck Egypt" surely had Juvenal's place of banishment in mind. Broiling there on the cancerous tropic, Syene was the second grimmest frontier outpost known in those days before the unfortunate discovery of Japan (where I languish now).

The grimmest frontier outpost known in those days was the island of Patmos, which is where, at the same time, and for a not entirely dissimilar crime, Emperor Domitian stranded another literary man (of sorts): an excitable old fellow with the colorful moniker "Son o' Thunder," who'd quaked at the foot of his best friend Jesus' gallows sixty years earlier and never quite gotten over the emotional trauma. John (his real name) beguiled his perhaps too ample leisure time on Patmos by scribbling away at the Apocalypse which I quoted a couple of seconds ago, and which I quote again: "...lo, the sun became black as sackcloth of hair, and the moon became as blood. And the stars of heaven fell unto the earth, even as a fig tree casteth her untimely figs, when she is shaken of a mighty wind..."

I think you will agree that, while it does possess a certain epileptoid charm if couched in Elizabethan English, John's Revelation cannot exactly be described as a work of the highest art, any more than can the Gospel or Epistles of John, which were also composed, traditionally at least, by the same person. Unlike Juvenal, their contemporary and fellow disaffiliated person (whose literary fate, as we shall see, was strangely hitched to theirs), this John, or these Johns, and the other members of their literary set, or sect, were pretty crappy writers—as Saint Augustine later couldn't help but notice, to the mortification of his soul. So, in this case, Rexroth's thesis is secure: the followers of the "disgraced magician" (as the

Second Person of the Holy Trinity was known back then) were no Baudelaires in Babylon, or even out of it. Nietzsche put it best: "To have glued this rococo New Testament... to the Old Testament... is the greatest sin that literary Europe has on its conscience." But I don't need to tell you guys that, in the great demographical scheme of things, almost nobody can appreciate, or even dimly recognize, uncrappy writing. As this good news was intended for everyone, not just Baudelaires like us, a certain Hemingwayesque dumbing-down was necessary.

But let your souls be reassured when I say this to you: what those crappy writers were doing is jam-packed with significance for us e-literati: spiritually, of course (because even the unsmutched souls of us non-Cibbers need saving), but technically as well. Starting in Juvenal and John's day, the first century after Christ, at the beginning of the first millennium AD, just as now at the outset of the third, a revolution in publishing—or at least in alphabet-based communication—was taking place. It was a revolution almost as wrenching as the one we are fomenting right now on the web.

Take yourself back in time a couple thousand years. Imagine yourself to be a pagan or Jew walking around a good-sized Mediterranean city in the moonlight of a balmy March night. The first ominous indication of the coming revolution which you will see is a cheap traveler's edition of the notoriously pornographic Milesian Tales, clutched in the left hand of a guy jacking himself off on a public portico, where he's camped among other unkempt wayfarers who couldn't afford proper lodging for the night.

The second harbinger of the coming upheaval of the whole world's literary and spiritual life will be in the hands, or, rather hand, of a follower of the aforementioned disgraced magician. This meek saint has also staked a modest pitch on the public portico, and is trying to ignore the embarrassing wanker on the next pallet by burying his nose in a collection of epistles from someone called the Evangelist. Naturally you'll assume, from the configuration of his reading material, that he is a self-lover as well, and his ilk also, by association. And you will add that to the list of their demerits, right after baby sacrifice, blood drinking, random urban incendiarism, and general unclubbability.

What they have done, as far as you can tell from the distance you wisely maintain between yourself and these vagabonds, masturbators and Christians, is to steal and vandalize real books. These barbarians have sliced a proper scroll into its constituent parts, and stuck them together along one edge, all in a pile, like the grimy working copy of a ship's manifest or some debased sausage retailer's account book, only larger, so as to be suited to serve as a palimpsest for—well, you wouldn't want to call it literature, this bent stuff which disaffiliated types and perverts and weird cultists like to salivate on and snickeringly pass among their socially corrosive selves. In other words, as you took your evening constitutional through the streets two thousand years ago, you would be harboring the same not necessarily unjust suspicions about the users of the codex as people unweaned from print today harbor about us habitués of the web.

It's hard to overemphasize the utter discontinuity that was developing. The immemorial primacy of the non-Christian majority's favorite knowledge delivery system (enshrined on the very capitals of the Ionic order) was being challenged. The hegemony of the wound-up book would eventually unravel altogether at the hands of these tent-makers and itinerant sawbones and unpopular smalltime tax farmers. The followers of the disgraced magician were immersed up to their wrists in the first copies of not only The Book, but also the book, as we know and revere it.

And none too soon. Despite the 2.4 million-dollar price tag on that 120-foot spool of onion skin covered specifically in "typing" (to quote catty Capote) which ultra-glamorous Christie's auctioned off recently, this involved format was already a dinosaur 2000 years ago. A Bill Gates-like spirit of enmity toward innovation and the free flow of knowledge had overtaken the mainstream communications industry of antiquity, and technical improvements could only be effected on the fringes, in semi-secret, by the Pauls, Tituses, Timothys, Lukes and Linuxes of the day.

The scroll was unwieldy as a wooly mammoth's trunk tangled in its tusks. Like Bill Gates' Internet Explorer, it was a chore to use, constantly tearing or crashing, as the case may be. It was an impediment outright to close reading. What passed under your eyeballs was immediately spun into a coil at one side, and could only be recalled by a laborious process of backtracking, during which you must relinquish and most likely lose your present place. It needed both hands, and etiquette required its being rewound after use, like today's rental videos. Uncooperative volumes were a favorite subject of vase painters. The scroll couldn't be better designed for the purposes of a tyrant like Pisistratos or a prideful monarch like Eumenes of Pergamum, who consider books as a means of buttressing authority, to be perused gingerly, under strict supervision, in the marble confines of the royal library, not objects of pleasure to be carried on picnics or stained purple in wine shops. It was suited particularly to the rich, most of whose reading was done out loud, to them, by Greekling slaves, whose lives were meant to be largely composed of inconvenience.

The codex, on the other hand, was ideal for the scrambling existence so many of the early saints were forced to lead. The rest of the volume didn't strain constantly on either side of the bit you happened to be trying to read at the moment, so it could be made of much cheaper stuff than a scroll, yet would still last longer, even if you bled profusely on it. When the soldiers came smashing down your door with their hobnail boots and dragged you off to be in tag-team matches with hungry mastiffs in the arena, you didn't have time to rewind. You could, however, slam shut your little rectangular solid and tuck it under your tunic. In America, I'm sure palm pilots will come in similarly handy when the Ministry of Homeland Security hits its stride.

The physical qualities of the codex lend themselves to individual study on the part of someone who requires the mediation of neither Greekling slave nor priest between himself and his reading material, whose relationship with God is as personal as it can only be during those unimaginably privileged epochs when that particular entity has, in living memory, walked among us. God's word is there, conforming to the shape of your lap, the very best news of all time. Easy to read, simple to understand, effortless to consult, spread generously on pages that can be turned backwards or forwards at will, written on both sides with all the natural economy of universal truth itself, the codex provides reference readily as any non-electronic medium can. And—marvel of marvels—the dog ear suddenly becomes an option.

Nevertheless, the proper pagan literati scorned the new way of packaging literature, much as their moral descendants would later turn up their noses at the first paperbacks, and now sneer at e-lit. The intelligentsia of late antiquity clung to their cachet-dripping rolls of papyrus and parchment, the coffee table books of a coffeeless time and place—and these were coffee table books par excellence because, to be used, they required a table and a floor upon which to set that table. That substantial numbers of the new codex folk had no dependable access to such luxuries surely added to the appeal.

The Roman elite insisted on deluxe pumiced ends, chamois covers and ribbons of genuine Tyrian purple to tie the whole cylinder together. This forced poets to seek out the richest patrons who could afford to underwrite such lavish production values. Thus, patronage remained firmly in the hands of the same sort of people who today coo in appreciation of the smell and feel of paper and ink and embossed covers, and moan that literature simply cannot speak to them through that inhuman screen—as if the alphabet were intended to engage any sense-organ but the eyeball. Pretension and conspicuous consumption flourished among the pagan literati, even as the quality of what they read took a nose dive. Juvenal, who they were still ignoring and would continue to ignore till their Weltanschauung had unwound itself all the way to the bitter end of the final reel, was the last Latin poet worthy of being called a Baudelaire. There's nobody worth mentioning after him.

Can it be a surprise that, in his lifetime, far from being distributed by a major communications empire from one end of the known world to the other, Juvenal's works languished in utter obscurity, and continued to do so till the fourth century of our era, by which time it was necessary to provide scholia to aid comprehension? During the centuries it took to establish itself in the public mind, how did Juvenal's poetry survive? A manuscript or two in the back reaches of some curio collector's private stock room?

It's likely that his stuff never saw the inside of a scroll. By the time he finally reached the public awareness (a couple of centuries too late to do him any good—as far as we are able to ascertain without consulting revealed religion), the humble codex had been declared undisputed king of books, and the disgraced magician, whose followers had pioneered its use, held a comparable position in heaven. The works of

Juvenal's equally marginalized contemporaries, the Johns and the various committees of faux-Matthews, theoretical Lukes, a.k.a.-Marks, et al., had become, to put it mildly, quite well established—inelegantly composed as they were. (So much for polishing and rewriting; perhaps it's better that the great satirist was never in a position to review the New Testament.)

Juvenal's works gained a toehold in the public awareness at about the same time that Constantine the Great hallucinated the gallows of Christ superimposed on the sun, a bit of graffiti scrawled underneath. (We don't know if it was scrawled on airborne parchment or asbestos-treated papyrus, or if the molten surface of the star itself took the letters, or if our own ionosphere was being literarily engaged for the first time.) By this interesting coincidence, our poet-hero finally got his big break, and got to do the Big Lunch, even as Constantine gave the Christians theirs: granting them total freedom of religion, and founding the Empire of Christ, to be administered from the new imperial residence at Byzantium, which he renamed after himself and reconsecrated to God's mom.

The codex had ascended to a sovereignty that would remain undisputed outside the synagogue till less than ten years ago, when we baby-sacrificers and blood-drinkers, we unclubbable burners of buildings and practitioners of other alternative lifestyles, came skulking along with our own upstart medium. Now our forbears' mode of transmitting texts is poised to make way—assuming the web doesn't collapse in the meantime.

What an enormous assumption. I don't know about you, but if I were America's Minister of Homeland Security, capturing and interrogating Muslims and detaining them in secret for extended periods of time without benefit of counsel would be second on my list of Things to Do Today, just after killing the web. How could I ever maintain a robust Ministry of Homeland Security when subversive cybernauts like you keep bouncing ideas and information off each other, not to mention poems and stories, in a "free and unfettered manner," like the saint and the wanker we left camping on the portico?

The time will soon arrive when today's New York-London publishing axis will almost look like a free press in retrospect. Say the Bush administration hires a highly efficient Minister of Homeland Security, and he suborns and recruits every clever white teen boy in the country, and they set up a world-wide system of firewalls that makes the Chi-coms' look like a corroded fly screen by comparison, and nothing gets through to our monitors ever again but Islamophobic propaganda, Mark Helprin's cloying schmaltz, and Microsoft come-ons.

It might not even require the intervention of the coming totalitarian regime to bring an end to our world. Bill Gates, in his own apolitical, amoral, anal-oriented way, will probably do it all by himself, in the name of free enterprise. We exist at his whim, and he knows it. The web as it presently exists makes him petulant and fretful, because he's not making a big enough killing off it to satisfy his mutant gluttony. He has every intention of destroying our plane of existence.

Say he manages to realize his heart's ambition, and he chokes every browser but his own out of existence. That will leave him free to cause every unpaid-for link on the net to refer back to an advertisement for one of his inferior products (virus sponges all). And suppose he cuts our lines of communications as well. He buys up every email service, just as he did hotmail. com, and deep in the fine print buries the interesting bit of news that that he now owns the copyright to everything we send, therefore controls the fate of all our stories and poems and essays and novels, our letters to the world, as Emily Dickinson called them. You can imagine what will become of the ones that don't directly redound to the benefit of Microsoft. To continue to exist as e-literati, we'd all have to become worse than Mark Helprin: we wouldn't just be speechwriters for the new Domitian, we'd be ad writers for the silicon Antichrist. The whole web edifice, too good to be true in the first place, will collapse under the weight of Bill Gates' sociopathic greed. But what can you expect from a guy who named his company after his dick?

Will the destruction of the net destroy us as writers? Any medium is ephemeral. The twin towers of papyrus and parchment, those prideful pinnacles, were brought down by Arabs, who acted as deliverymen for the Chinese invention of paper, which itself, in turn, is a house of cards, a Babylonian skyscraper, tumbling even now before our electronic one-two punch. And we web writers are just waiting our turn. We are not even as secure as Keats. His name was at least written on water, which is a tangible substance—more than can be said for our directed drifts of electrons. Words written on water don't depend for their existence on an elaborate and vulnerable infrastructure of fiber-optic lines and telecommunications satellites and nuclear power plants and so forth.

But we writers have always found a Patmos or a Bum-Fuck Egypt in which to strand ourselves and flourish in all our agony, while we wait for another Constantine to come along and set us up as first-class citizens, finally, where we belong and have never yet been: at the very top of the pecking order, instead of just underneath it, catching farts and serving as moral vates. Give it time. Soon we will all drink champagne in the new Constantinople. We'll be the "hierophants of unapprehended inspiration, the mirrors of gigantic shadows which futurity casts upon the present," and our legislation will at last be acknowledged.

While we're waiting for that to happen, we can turn our disaffection inside out and into a privilege. No money or literary groupies to distract us: what a stroke of luck! We have nothing to stop us from digging in and making like Decimus Junius Juvenalis. While his more successful and presumably happier friend, Martial, lounged in the presence of quality and sipped their fine vintages, leaving behind nothing to represent himself to the ages but brief epigrams designed not to tax the attention spans of preoccupied magistrates and silk gauze-swathed Patrician pathics, our hero Juvenal, isolated and broiling in the glare and grit that blew off the Wadi Hammamat, produced complete long poems, fully developed works that you can sink your whole consciousness into again and again without losing the sensations of sheer novelty and delight.

Unless the cosmos is disposed in such a way that there's an afterlife (and I heartily doubt it—but your guess is as good as mine; the original wielders of the codex had certain notions on the subject), and unless this afterlife includes an element of personal omniscience, or at least a burst of trans-temporal awareness—then Juvenal never, or has never, stopped thinking he failed. He never learned any better than to consider all his poems a waste of time and ink and expensive papyrus, doomed to crumble to dust not long after his body did. He "fouled his life up," in the words of T. S. Eliot, describing the pursuit of the poetic vocation.

Meanwhile his "failure" has earned him nothing less than adjectival status. He is in Websters and the O.E.D., not just in citations, but as an entire entry, all to his glorious and unforgotten self. He has joined the select group of authors whose names have become grammatical constructions modifying something besides their own specific work. This unsmutched, incorruptible man, who wrote so beautifully and died in such utter loneliness, has left us with the word Juvenalian, which denotes corrosive satire—just the thing that got him uninvited to Domitian's soirees on the Palatine Hill. It also has earned him, in subsequent ages, a reputation as the undisputed king of

Silver Latin authors, and the emperor of all satirists, regardless of language or time or place. By actual readers, as opposed to book-mongers (who, thanks to Fellini, make more money off Petronius), he is considered to be the greatest Latin poet after Virgil—some would say including Virgil. Catullus and Martial are not even in the running.

Proverbially, "the net has changed everything." What has it changed? Nothing, for the writer. Nothing of importance, at any rate. He's still alone, like Juvenal, with nobody to converse and contend with but himself and his worthier forbears: Kenneth Rexroth, Keats, Kit Marlowe and the rest. It doesn't matter if a king or a merchant or nobody at all is breathing over his shoulder. Whenever and wherever the writing is going well, nobody exists but the person doing it. And when a story or poem is well written, it has a way of surviving (although there is no way to test that hypothesis, obviously). The Iliad and the Odyssey toughed it out clear through the dark ages of the Dorian invasion, when writing itself was forgotten. The codex is a great invention, as is the net, but both are completely devoid of interest except as delivery systems for the greatest invention of all: the alphabet—which itself can readily enough take a back seat to human memory. The poet may need to revert to formulaic oral verse, he may need to shut his reading and writing eyes, as Homer did, and go on the road and begin to chant. But he will be no worse off, and no better off, than he is in now, and always has been.

We're scribbling hostages to fortune, and there is no guarantee that anything will refrain from drying up and fluttering away. Our stuff might not even stick around long enough to prove our efforts more than vain to our own nephews. Traces remain of neither Nero's Fall of Ilium nor Claudius' histories of Carthage and Etruria, and these men were better placed even than Mark Helprin, if that can be imagined. I have a great uncle whose novels were made into Clark Gable and Alan Ladd movies, who lived like a king on the Riviera, and even abebooks. com can't locate his titles or his name. And, remember, unlike us, these guys used to be in hard copy in a big way.

In his excellent essay, "Adoption of the Codex Book: Parable of a New Reading Mode," which I read on the web at booknotes.com, Gary Frost says, "The adoption of the codex among early Christians is as explainable as the attraction of modern sectarians to cyberspace. With both groups there has been a need for a reading and communication mode suited to construct a society of odd, dispersed and beleaguered individuals."

Odd, dispersed and beleaguered...well, I don't know about you, but he's certainly got my number. Here I languish in my place of apparently permanent exile on a remote and sulfurous island that bears the barbarous name Kyushu. *Kyoo-shoooo...* You can't get much more dispersed than that, or disaffiliated.

But, for the moment, we e-literati can pretend that we have a secure supply of our own glowing species of papyrus, and nobody's threatening to slap an embargo on it. Let's just pretend that the hackers and the Arabs are going to keep a certain pharaonic little prick away from our gates for a good long while.

We are all Juvenals, and the web is our Bum-Fuck Egypt. The web's our Patmos, and we share it with the ranting epileptoid Sons o' Thunder of our time, our beloved fellow deportees, who dare to write the truth about, for example, America's 9-11 Reichstag fire. We're saints producing and propagating the apocalypses of the day, but also the good news of the future. We're Baudelaires kicked, safely and gratefully, out of Babylon.

PEACE PARK PRANCE

Tom goes among a platoon of Hiroshima city cops in full dress regalia: white gloves and gaiters, silken shoulder braids, golden epaulets, and so on. With fastidiously curled fifth fingers, they roust the barefoot transients who quietly reside every other day of the year in washing machine cartons picturesquely tucked among the azalea bushes.

A few of these bums break away and hobble over to greet Tom, their new pal, and he allows them to come into contact with his person. They gape in toothless wonder as they run blackened fingers over the red hairs on the backs of his orangutan hands. They stand on tiptoe, stroke his orange beard, and babble like pleased babies. Their dirt-crusty bodies begin to glow, ever so faintly, as some of our protagonist's newly acquired holiness rubs off on them.

Miraculously enough, the bums can hear "Salt Peanuts" too; so they all link arms and dance a group-jitterbug. Tom leads them by the hand in complex figure eights and cha-cha-cha patterns on the sidewalk, interposing his body between theirs and the clutching claws of the police. He yells the most exquisite Hiroshima gutter dialect down on the cops' heads, his words just audible over the raucous jazz.

"Why not let them join the party? This is their home! These cats are Ground Zero's regular and rightful denizens!" He pauses to slap a white gloved hand away from a grimy Adam's apple. "Why are you doing this? To prettify this dump? For the benefit of today's visitors? Are you kidding? Have you even bothered to look at your international guests?"

He calls the cops' attention to the plague of Hiroshimizers. In other words, on this summer day, exactly the wrong people are being ejected from the festivities. The normally soporific municipal park is under occupation by the western world's sole surviving class of people who would feel obliged to tolerate homeless types. It would tickle them pink to be spare-changed by authentic Oriental hoboes. It's the megaphoned Moloch-worshipers, the Hirohito-worshipping fanatics, whom the police should be giving the bum's rush to. They're the ones jeopardizing municipal tourist revenue.

By this time, the transients are filled to the brim with Tom's communicable grace, and the oppressors have their chance to regroup and overcome their trepidation of the Caucasoid who looms and preaches in their faces. So Tom is magnanimous enough to permit the cops to do their job. Render unto Caesar, and all that.

As nobody at the precinct has consulted Tom's superior reading of the crowd's mood, the cops go charging into the cardboard shantytowns in the bushes and, with their spotless ivory dress-truncheons, bust several greasy heads. They stuff a miniaturized Toyota paddy wagon with raggedy bodies, and speed off at full siren about twelve yards down the street, where they get stuck in the same traffic jam that Tom skirted via the Monument to the Korean Bomb Victims.

He starts to wonder, as he scans this Cecil Blount DeMille circus for familiar faces, whether he's the only reasonably sane resident of Boom Town within five blocks of this weird shindig.

Meanwhile, the holy-of holies heaves soberingly into view.

IX

The real foundations of contemporary Japanese life are the achievements of the Aryan peoples.

—*Mein Kampf*

The formerly "borderline precocious" Bradley boy has wound up teaching conversational skills to freshman dentistry majors in the Japanese "imperial university" where they used to vivisect our bomber pilots and serve their livers raw at festive banquets.

Ever since I first reluctantly mounted the bamboo podium, back in the days when this was the richest country in the world, my campus has been under occupation by platoons of boys who call themselves "cheerleaders." Seeming to grow like bunions out of the karate and judo teams, they're too bristly to get laid, so they scream and march a lot, and flail their arms around. They're seminarians of a sort, practicing to be full-blown Hirohito worshipers like those I saw officiating at the Feast of the Transfiguration in A-Bomb Park.

I can understand a few guys with halitosis, low-average IQ's and overbearing personalities getting involved with this. Their American counterparts would be frat rats. But this is an entire army. At my place of employment they recruit underclassmen by literal arm-twisting, to the silence of the dean of students. I think he approves secretly of this return to militarism among the otherwise politically flaccid youth of Nippon.

The cheerleaders spend their time frenziedly rallied under giant rising-sun flags and blood-colored banners emblazoned with reversed and righted swastikas. To the accompaniment of a mammoth bass drum, which is beaten to death like an evil seductress, they march outside my classroom windows and chant jingoistic songs from the thirties and forties—or rather howl them, so loudly as to damage their throats. It always sounds as though several have grapefruit-sized nodules hemorrhaging on their voice boxes already, but still they never let up. In this fundamentally sadomasochistic sodality, tumors are an inducement to strain even harder. The impression is of an orgiastic sexuality, just barely sublimated.

Christ knows I'm not the best judge of this sort of thing, but it seems to me that these unhappy kids aren't the only ones here who come down a bit off-center in the orgasm department. Or am I just belaboring the obvious? If all was erotically foursquare in this country, would there be such a thriving market for the flesh of anonymous sex slaves from the former member nations of General Tojo's Greater East Asia Co-Prosperity Sphere? As it is, a whole gate at the Tokyo airport is devoted to offloading jumbo jets full of "foreign entertainers." A certain amount of whoremongering is universal, of course. But, in Japan, matters pertaining to horniness and its alleviation get a lot more peculiar.

For example, there's no such thing as a urinal without a full view of the user and his unit, through strategically placed doors or windows or both. And every tourist who stumbles off the beaten path has been subjected to their exclusively male exhibitionism: those bare-buttocked lunar festivals, which the inverted genius Yukio Mishima found so inspiring; and the naked scramble for the amulet in the local temple, with thousands of sleek young men howling lesions into their larynxes, under banners whose meticulous calligraphy reads, not KNOW THYSELF, but LOSE THYSELF.

I have a slightly homophobic, but lovable old colleague, a permanently exiled Brit, who recognizes certain parallels to a well-known ancient culture. Classical Greece, with its select corps of geisha-like hetaerae, also did not allow the majority of its women to become fully human for fear of their multiorgasmic power. So the men were forced to rely on each other for stimulation, and shared their most intense moments naked in the gymnasium, with all the anality and, therefore, sadomasochism such a situation engenders. My grumpy old colleague rides this train of associations further, to the point of claiming that, "like all members of essentially homoerotic cultures," my honorable hosts are narcissists.

I am forced report that is true of the immigration officials, at least. They preen themselves on their racial purity, to the point of denying the sanctified privilege of permanent residency to such a splendid hominoid specimen as me. After nearly a decade and a half, I'm still on a one-year visa. Yet, if you steel yourself and look around in the omnipresent communal bathhouses, you will see legs almost as hairy as mine, and pubic bushes such as are simply not found on the Asian mainland. Except for the lovely golden-brown Filipinas, whom they find attractive enough to force wholesale into indentured prostitution, the Japanese are the extreme Orient's most "miscegenated" people (to use the cheerleaders' own pet term in translation—impermissible in polite Western society for at least three generations).

When the sun goes down, my furry little pupils repair to their reinforced-concrete dormitory and wrench from their throats an orgy of screaming. They're supposedly rehearsing the venerable school song in preparation for a visitation of old and distinguished alumni. But it's just formless retching, convulsive and inarticulate. It's nightly throughout the first two weeks of each semester, this aberration, and lasts without respite till three in the morning, and takes the place of studying or talking or drinking or, certainly, anything most Occidentals would define as non-metaphorical sex. In the morning, the boys, fortified with caffeine and nicotine, always have square knots yanked in their vocal cords, suppurating thickly enough to preclude participation in my conversation class. The dean of students urges me to respect this, because all night they've been "doing their best and trying hard and displaying enthusiasm." When I ask, "Trying their best to accomplish what?" all I get is an inscrutably averted gaze.

As if this wasn't enough (enough of *what*, for Christ's sake?), the cheerleaders impose still other forms of domination and submission, of mindless austerities and chastisements. The thinner recruits are always shirtless as they tromp and stomp outside my classroom, and are forced to go barefoot, even in the dead of winter, because it tickles the sadistic glee of their revered ancestors in the spirit world to see their toes turn black with frostbite—or something approximately metaphysical like that. The upperclassmen are shod with traditional wooden platform sandals, the only footwear in the world more uncomfortable than bare feet, and they wrap themselves in strange, early Showa-period military uniforms of dark-blue wool, stifling on the bleakest November day.

They are nothing less than apprentice Shinto-fascists, well-scrubbed super-patriots, directly descended from the infant-eviscerating imperial troops whose antics brought a couple of atomic bombs crashing down on everybody's head sixty years ago. If any of my colleagues or neighbors have made that ominous connection, they're too polite to mention it.

Sometimes the boys seem to be auditioning for their elders. A journeyman rightist will trot and waddle on Jiminy Cricket legs alongside them, holding up a decibel meter and shaking his head in critical disgust at the cheerleaders' paltry vocal performance (just paltry enough to neutralize my lecture through the window). The full-fledged master maniacs discreetly follow in their city block-long sound truck, which is occasionally draped with a squinty-eyed, bunny-toothed, Hitler-mustachioed portrait of the dead emperor—though their more mainstream counterparts in sophisticated places like Tokyo and Osaka consider this public flaunting and flapping of God's image to be gross sacrilege.

Two of the lower-ranked cheerleaders will struggle to keep aloft a vast banner. Strung on bamboo poles fifteen feet high, clearly visible from my vantage point at the professorial pulpit, it howls some such measured lyrical strain as follows:

BIG-NOSES OUT!
MISCEGENATION FOR AMERICA, PURITY FOR DAI NIPPON!
HAIR GROWS ON DOGS' LEGS, NOT PEOPLE'S!
DAI NIPPON IS A TINY RICE PADDY, AMERICA A TREELESS PEAK:
FLOOD CONTROL IS PARAMOUNT!
A MYRIAD OF YEARS! A MYRIAD OF YEARS! A MYRIAD OF YEARS!

They always climax with a bit of wisdom received directly from the loose lips of the current prime minister—

WE ARE A DIVINE NATION WITH THE EMPEROR AT OUR CENTER!

The poets who paint and sing and shove these lines in my face never meet any difficulty penetrating the university's front gate. The old porter genuflects them in, bowing so deeply that his brow ridge audibly bops the rim of the open sewer which moats the place where I've been condemned to waste my remaining days. To uninitiated eyes, the rightists appear to be little more than lecture-disrupting noodle-Nazis. But they are treated with all the fear and deference due to a sacerdotal caste—which, of course, is exactly what they are: celebrants of an autophagous Eucharist.

Speaking of priestcraft infiltrating places of public education, it occurs to me now to wonder what might happen if the "Elder" of my boyhood, the man who suspended me so regularly from elementary school, could be persuaded to leave the holy land of Utah and come here to engage these rightists in cosmological dispute. Which side of the red-hot evolutionism/ creationism controversy might they come down on? Their revealed scripture, the *Kojiki*, speaks of the royal line descending directly from the Sun Goddess. That puts a kink in natural selection. Maybe there would be no dispute at all.

Lately there are signs that the rightists' eager acolytes, the cheerleaders, are dying out as a phenomenon at my school. I've always been one to hail the withering of clergy in any form. But, considering who is replacing them, I think I might sort of miss the weird little pricks.

Now their big bass drum is not beleaguered quite so vigorously or often. Instead, unmuffled motorcycles idle everywhere, making it even more unpleasant to breathe than usual. Working-class punks from the neighborhood vocational high school, the so-called *bosozoku*, or teen bikers, have been admitted—no, seduced and sucked—into the higher education system. And their wholesomely nihilistic presence makes all religio-patriotic display seem quaint, even cute.

With their spiked tangerine-flake hair, tattoos, nose- and nipple- and navel-rings, and all the other courage-boosting mutilations of tribal warriors, these arriviste "bozos" lend the collegiate scene a hellish quality, reminiscent of genuine varsity bashes at Heidelberg and other centers of learning on the European continent. Sneaking behind a styrofoam incinerator now and then to mainline their methedrine, these honest, burping degenerates are the only people on campus, besides my curmudgeonly old colleague and me, who know how to behave like scholars in real countries. They speak quietly to one another, and do not even look twice as I lurch past on my way to the language laboratory. I hear no genocidal slogans or nationalistic sentiments from their brown-painted lips. They have more mature, or at least cooler mannerisms than the dwindling leaders of cheers, who watch them from a safe distance with unconscious admiration and metaphorical penis envy.

How can the complexion of the Japanese matriculator be changing so drastically in such a short time? If this wasn't the proverbially hyperfecundant yellow race, one might almost wonder if there has been a sudden decline in the supply of eighteen year olds. Is the bottom of the demographic barrel being desperately scraped? Well, as a matter of fact, I have been told that my school hands out admission certificates in the railroad stations, stapled to free packets of mini-kleenex to persuade people to take them. A lot of the incoming freshmen would have been better advised to use the latter and discard the former for the sad joke it is.

With the graying of this society (potential baby-makers would rather window-shop), college entrance requirements are steadily being lowered. The two classes of youngster become less distinguishable, as buzz-cut kamikaze nerds with red polka-dotted megaphones morph into gutter punks toting contraband Italian stilettos. By this time next academic year I will be confiscating paint thinner and zip guns from the customary knot of blackness that tends to form against the back wall of any classroom, Japanese or foreign.

Unlike my native colleagues, I do not dread this development. It will be my professional apotheosis: my jackbooted teaching style will finally come into its own. Besides, if I'm still here when it happens, that will mean my position hasn't been rendered redundant in the meantime for lack of interest, and old Bradley-*sensei* hasn't been sent home to manage a convenience store in the middle of the Salt Flats, there to dodge the semiautomatic fire of New World *bosozoku*.

These scooter-trash dope-fiends are not so much taking over Japanese academe as seeping up from below, and supplying by default a vacuum left by the infertility of their betters. As it is, the top two floors of our classroom building have been sealed off and allowed to sink into cobwebbed desuetude, and the remaining desks barely have a thirty-percent occupancy. To walk down the corridor is creepy even for a former desert dweller like me. I miss the Caucasoidophobic rants as the shuffling sound of my regulation slippers rebounds off the vacated linoleum.

To grasp the sheer apocalypse I'm prophesying here, you must understand what blood lines have always meant in "this backwater called *Dai Nippon*, this lightless cranny of the modern world," as my politically incorrect limey colleague calls our adopted home. The natives' spiritual development has been arrested at a point similar to that of the very early Jews and Greeks. They cannot imagine the deathlessness of the individual soul, which suffers or rejoices eternally according to its own deserts. Instead, like the rank-and-file members of the Troy and Canaan expeditions, they've always cherished hopes of blood immortality, of descendants countless as the stars of the sky and the sands of the seashore, even unto the umpteenth generation, and so on and so forth, with no shortage of great-great-great-, etc., grandchildren to maintain your effigy in the household shrine and feed your numb ghost with the smell of burnt sandalwood. Hence the adulation of their own well-chlorinated gene pool, and the rabid chauvinism that actuated the cheerleaders back in the days when my university, and Japan itself, seemed to be flourishing.

The old chestnut, "Blood is thicker than water," translates directly into their idiom, and seems to have been coined independently. If pressed, a habitué of Christendom, whether pious or not, will at least feel obliged to allow that the blood under consideration should ideally be that of humanity at large. But in this country it is invariably taken in the much more circumscribed sense. And what strikes our ears as a stale cliché has, until recently, lost none of its piquancy here.

But now they appear even to have lost faith in that pitiable and dangerous deoxyribonucleic delusion. Their own uniqueness and superiority have evidently become matters of indifference, unworthy of perpetuation. Japan's current "negative population growth," according to my disgruntled old colleague, is the expression of an unexampled moral degeneracy. "Here is a people so exhausted and shortsighted," he sputters, "they've sold what little dangling scab of a soul they had for a shopping spree."

In amelioration of that perhaps borderline-racist statement, we must glance at our surroundings. The geography of this archipelago is so cozy, the mountains so tiny and green. Rivulets of sweet water trickle gently from feathery bamboo groves. Hornets are the most dangerous animals. Maybe we can excuse the natives for never developing a spirituality beyond the gutless Zen. The only reminders of Providence's down-side are occasional typhoons, volcanic eruptions and earthquakes, as impersonal as nature gets, and just random enough to encourage mindless totemism.

I find myself forced to agree with my crusty colleague on this point. The level of spiritual attainment on these islands is as low as any I've encountered in my random stumblings from the Far West to the Extreme Orient, including the white-slum Sugar House district of Salt Lake City. But what right have I to be surprised to find them just as theologically inchoate as the polygamist cultists who founded my hometown? What should I expect other than yet more anemic religiosity on this side of the Pacific?

Read your Second Book of Kings, where the Israelites' backslide into degenerate Canaanite cultism is disdainfully described: "On top of every high place and under every big tree, shrines appeared." Then take a drive through the Japanese countryside and see if you can begin to count the shrines. And visit some of them. With their thatched roofs and splintery altars stacked high with citrus, are they not merely modified tiki-huts? These children of the Mikado should not be classed among the major Asian civilizations. They're island-hopping Polynesians who paddled their canoes a little too far north, and wound up over-financed by us.

If you unshade yourself from under the big tree, and traverse the high place, you will probably come to a temple outright, which is to say a fane dedicated to the local third-hand style of Buddhism. If this temple happens to be located in my depopulated and depressed neighborhood, it might very well look at first glance like an abandoned garden, poinsettias drooping over everything. It will be enclosed by four nostril-high walls, wattle and daub, topped by rotting pine bas-reliefs of fox demons scarfing fried tofu.

A greenish carp pond will send small belches of airborne murk to sink in around the graven lineaments of pagan idols, called *jizos*, nearly featureless under the granite pudge, looking like neonate Buddhas, or Gary Bauer. Stacked at their toeless feet will be baby toys, canned food offerings, and mandarin oranges caved in like bottled fetus-heads in high school biology labs.

A dozen questions will pop into your mind about the pink bibs on those *jizos*: where do they come from, what do they signify, what invisible hands mend and replace them, and why are they the only elements of this scene that receive any kind of maintenance? This temple yard is such an obscure place of devotion that the food offerings have long ago been carted off by crows and mountain-roaming derelicts. But, even so, someone has been by to replace the bibs. They're pink as the bolt in the fabric store.

In answer to your questions, hear now the time-honored words of Japanese grannies preparing their granddaughters for womanhood: "Once you've contrived that he should cease to be, all you need to do is place a little piece of fish, or perhaps a dab of pork gristle, between the lips of the youngster after you expel him, before you burn him. He will not become a buddha as a result of this dietary indiscretion. He will return to the cycle of metempsychosis, his tiny soul and penis 'recycled,' as your mother says of milk cartons and plastic bags. Perhaps, with any luck at all, he and not some other youngster will return to your household when the time for parenthood is riper. And if you're inclined to feel sentimental, stitch a few cozy pink bibs for the baby-sized *jizo* figurines in the temple yard."

I don't want to come on like the above-mentioned Mr. Bauer (heaven forefend I should get such a licking), but I need to point a few things out here, purely for the sake of cultural context: there is not enough demand to persuade Nipponese pharmacists to shelve the latest oral contraceptives; rubbers are unwrapped less often than miscarriage is procured (retroactively in no rare instances); far more bouncing bundles of joy get liquidated than are permitted to feel the smoggy sunshine on their sweet little cheeks.

Meanwhile, another wing of classrooms at my place of employment is scheduled to be surrendered to the spiders. And guess whose job it is to mop up after the few howling sons of Tojo who manage to dodge and duck down the birth canal more-or-less intact.

*   *   *   *

Picture, if you will (as Rod Serling used to say), seventy-five to a hundred narcoleptic zombies. Packed on plywood benches in a room big enough for half that many bodies, they congregate once a week, for ninety un-air conditioned minutes—for an English conversation class.

Maybe Jesus Christ could feed them lunch with half a bag of potato chips and a can of Pepsi. But I don't know any mere mortal teacher—regardless of how many mail-order Master's Degrees he has earned in TEFL and TOOFL and TAWFUL—who could accomplish anything in that situation beyond simpering and adjusting his tie.

Even under optimum conditions these particular narcoleptic zombies would be ineducable, as they're Japanese college students. That means their inner beings have been previously reamed out in junior high and high school. Haitian voodoo is not more effective than Japanese secondary education in producing the Living Dead. Needless to say, the joy of learning is nothing but a one-liner in the universities.

I used to be the only blue-eyed redhead in the room. But far-Eastern motorcycle-punks and their molls love to alter their appearance with bleach and henna and contact lenses of bizarre coloration. When the class bell rings, it looks like the Saint Patrick's Day Parade—or maybe the morning after.

These are kids from so deep in the underclass, they have tuberculosis with symptoms. I'm living the national health crisis. I stay hunkered behind the teacher's desk, next to an open window. I don't circulate, and I accept no papers. It's impossible to get homework out of them, anyway.

You're not supposed to ask for homework, or any other

kind of work, from these zombies. College is the only period of repose they get between the cradle and the crematorium. They're not expected to learn anything. It's considered inhumane to ask them to do more than sleep or chat on their walkie-talkies with coevals across the corridor.

They wind up in colleges not because of academic interest or specific talents, but strictly according to entrance exam rankings. If, for example, a technological institute happens to be the second-best school in the region, kids whose national exam scores fall in that range enroll there, regardless of technical inclination or lack thereof. I once had a roomful of seniors majoring in physics who were unable to effect the conversion from Celsius to Fahrenheit, even after I wrote the formula on the board for them.

The companies that will enslave them upon graduation pay attention only to the numerical standing of the universities that churn them out. The employers assume, correctly, that their new recruits know absolutely nothing, and simply train them from the ground up, starting with proper groveling techniques.

And that's if they're lucky. In some of the lower-ranked Junior Colleges, the most the kids can aspire to after graduation is a lifetime of pumping gas, or selling methamphetamine for the Yakuza, or continuing for as long as possible the so-called "compensated dating" practices that got them their Gucci bags in high school.

Now you know why there has never been any world-class Japanese historiography or philosophy or literature, and why I haven't, after abiding nearly twenty years here, bothered to learn the language. If not for Lafcadio Hearn, I would be in the Guinness Book of World Records as the guy who lived the longest in the Land of General Toe-Jam without absorbing a syllable of Hirohito's lingo.

So why do I feel so comfy here? Why do I brag to everybody that I have a cool job? Is it because I only have to "teach" (which is to say, baby-sit) three to five "conversation classes" a week, with six months vacation, and no administrative duties, and no faculty meetings?

Well, that has something to do with it. This is one Anglo-American who has grown beyond his Puritan heritage, especially the "work ethic" bit.

At a tender age I fell into an anomalous way of life. I became a novelist the day my dad magnetized my first act of crayoned mendacity to the front of our fridge. Throughout my adulthood, I've been forced to arrange my existence accordingly, to search for ways of eking out a livelihood that conserve each calorie of mental heat for writing. And I begrudge every minute spent doing anything else.

So I'm lucky to have landed more or less randomly in Japan, which, for my special purposes, has the finest system of higher education in the world. If someone were to hold a gun to my head, or a samurai sword to my good kidney, and say that I must be gainfully employed in order to continue existing inside my body, I couldn't invent a more suitable workplace.

Here's an anecdote that shows how Japanese universities foster literary endeavor. This short parable will shed some light on perhaps the saddest country in the world—but a happy place for a confirmed scribbler, who craves time to write about other, less pointless places.

You'll recall, a few years back, a pair of eggheads at the University of Utah announced that they'd effected cold fusion on a tabletop. (I think they were trying to make up for all those poor atoms that underwent the opposite process in the neighborhood when I was a tyke.) For a couple of days, even respectable members of the scientific community were suspending disbelief. Cold fusion was touted globally, to the maximum, during those couple of days. We were told that the energy needs of the human race had been permanently satisfied by the most important technological breakthrough since Prometheus showed us how to harness fire. The Kingdom of Heaven had finally been established on Earth. And it was to be fueled by Cold Fusion, and centered at the University of Utah.

Now, as it happened, on the very days when those tidings of comfort and joy were being trumpeted everywhere, I was preparing a group of college students here in Hiroshima to go to a Study Abroad Program at—-you guessed it—the University of Utah. My pupils were to stay at a dormitory located coincidentally within spitting distance of the laboratory where the miracle was bubbling and simmering away on its famous tabletop. And I, as a native who presumably knew the ropes, was to chaperone them.

I had only just arrived from being kicked out of the People's Republic of China on charges of pedagogical hooliganism. There, the students consider their education the most fabulous privilege of their lives, and are fond of reminding themselves and each other that it takes the sweat of four peasant families to support one college kid. My Chinese charges were real, honest-to-God university scholars, the type who can be engaged on a roughly equal footing as fellow adults, who give as much as they take from their professors.

Naive as I was, coming straight from the genuine higher education system of the Asian mainland, I assumed that my new Japanese students would have similar attitudes and capabilities, and that Cold Fusion in particular was something they would be excited by. Unlike my beloved disciples who I left behind to die on Tiananmen Square, these Japanese kids had cars and motorcycles, which they cherished and polished. And I figured the radical transformation of the world's energy supply would be of personal interest to them.

So I mounted the professorial podium with a big grin on my face, and began to talk about all the important and exciting things that lay in store on the other side of the Pacific Ocean. I was brief as possible, because I fully expected to be mobbed at any moment by grateful and thrilled and adoring little people.

But I couldn't seem to get a rise out of them. They only sat there, passive. I was puzzled. Were Japanese as inscrutable as the old stereotype claimed?

I had been emphasizing the scientific and economic angles of Cold Fusion. Maybe that was a little too tough for them at first. So I tried a different approach. I said (or perhaps I shrieked), "Think of it, kids! You'll be at the nerve center! Electronic broadcast media types from all over the world will be camped right under your dormitory windows!"

And not so much as a single eyelid fluttered. It was as if I'd just informed them that the cafeteria was serving fish and rice for lunch.

For maybe the first or second time in my life, I was stunned into speechlessness. They took advantage of that moment of silence to ask a couple of questions: would MTV be available in the rooms, and was there a shopping mall near?

And the scales fell from my eyes. I suddenly understood this whole archipelago. I had a downright Joycean epiphany, and grasped an essential fact—probably the essential fact—about the Land of Pokey Mon and Carry-Okie. All at once I knew the answer to the question that plagues every foreigner who comes here.

How does Japan turn its people into—well, into Japanese? How do you drain a whole people of psychic vigor? How do you render them incurious and intellectually languid, with only nervous energy and shallow greed to fill the mental vacuum?

I already knew why this was done. Everybody knows why.

Such people are easy to govern. They're made-to-order dupes for contemptuous plutocracies, such as the one that runs this country so badly.

The answer to the question of how this is done lies, of course, in the secondary schools. The educational system is deliberately and cynically designed to serve this end.

Starting in junior high, through sadistic amounts of homework and relentless cramming of the short term memory with arbitrary data, young souls are reamed out like melon pulp, and young minds are robbed of curiosity, which we Homo sapiens are supposed to share with the higher, and even mid-level mammals. Once you've killed curiosity, you've killed the cat—to turn the proverb upside-down.

The proudest boast that a Japanese junior high teacher can utter is that he knows exactly which words his students have learned. Most occidental teachers would be ashamed to admit that their charges hadn't set off on their own to master more.

By the time the poor saps get to college, they are ineducable. Their professors couldn't have an easier job. It's like being the night-shift nurse on a narcoleptic ward. So I can pursue the novelist's silent, solitary vocation in perfect peace, because my classroom is filled with solid Japanese citizens. Solid as rock, and equally impervious.

Yes, my roll book is full of the grandsons and -daughters of Nakasone—which is to say, people conditioned to be content to live in second-world conditions in the middle of one of the world's richest economies, looking forward to an adulthood of working sixty-hour weeks and scrimping so they can afford the insane college tuition (much more than Harvard), to send their own zero-point-five children through the same absurd cycle of waste, to be exposed to barbarian pedagogues like me, and watch us write in silence.

Like so many other middle-aged guys, I have become the

father I killed. If I thought my students would understand, I might open my mouth just long enough to say, "Um, get a different address."

The very term "Japanese University" is an oxymoron, in the sense that, properly speaking, universities exist to stimulate independent thought and lifelong curiosity—the very qualities which, if unloosed on this nation, would cause the whole edifice to crumble. Scrutiny is one thing Asian oligarchies have never been able to stand. An ignorant and incurious populace is a basic requirement for Japanese society, and the educational system couldn't be better designed to serve such ends.

The return to my alma mater was less than triumphal. I was not embraced by white arms and invited to claim my tenure-track birthright among the non-Mormons. That Study Abroad Program at the University of Utah flopped as badly as Cold Fusion flopped, right there on the same campus. (Fission seems to be the specialty in my home state.) I was sent back across the ocean, to continue the aging process in the Land of the Camphor Tree.

And nobody on this left rim of the Pacific cared, or even noticed. It was just another somnambulistic gesture, a pointless utterance, a riddle with no answer, signifying the regulation Zen emptiness. My job security wasn't threatened in the least by that burlesque of an international student exchange.

All this may sound like an elaborately indirect way of pissing and moaning. But it's not. Here in the Land of Hirohito I never meet with that fatal conflict of interests that plagued me in the Land of Mao Zedong, where I had real pupils and an actual subject matter (literature, not EFL), and I came to know what real teaching is, how walking into class is a pleasure you anticipate all week, and walking out you feel shot full of methedrine (and your students are likely to be shot full of lead).

That's why the Land of the Futon and Stocking Feet is perfect for me. The puerility and sloth of the so-called students, the pure nothingness of the curriculum: it's all sham and mummery, gutless as a Haiku poem.

But I had plenty of time to write this book.

My father's systematic program of son-corruption may have succeeded in rendering me too unsocialized for a professorship back home, but no matter. I've found a niche in these languid institutions, which the natives call, with hardly a smirk, *daigaku*. "Big schools."

"Parasite" is such an unpleasant term. I prefer "opportunistic organism." Where dead things are, there will be happy worms.

Yes, I have spent years with my head buried deep in the umbilicus of post-modernism, glamorous Boom Town. Once a year in the summer, in pathetically named Peace Park, I listen to liberalism's last gasp. My fellow North American exiles assure me that I fail to grasp the significance of the oddly warmish soil upon which we waste what's left of our lives.

This is it, they tell me. This is where the contemporary age began. This is where we all became existentialists, consciously or un-, where all of us—not just the philosophy grad students and the black bop musicians in the Big Apple, but each and every single mother's son of us—were finally taught to grasp Universal Absurdity.

I'll buy a big load of that.

PEACE PARK PRANCE

In feudal days, traveling Japanese left dispensable parts of themselves at home with their families so that, in case they fell prey to the swords of bored *ronin* and were minced beyond recognition, or they just disappeared altogether in the usual pyroclastic flows, earthquakes or typhoons, there'd be something to bury at the funeral. In certain conservative communities, this quaint custom survived well into the industrial age. The Hair Monument, a hollow granite monolith not fifty meters from Ground Zero, contains the sole mementoes of several thousand such itchy-footed and unlucky non-Hiroshimites. It's a tonsorial mass grave, with bushels of straight black hair spilling from a vent in the base of the stone. Talk about blow-dry.

This is the only one of the many mass graves in Peace Park that seems to inspire a contemplative response in everybody who passes by, resident and tourist alike, joggers and picnickers, commies and fascists, as well as Hiroshimizers, amateur and professional.

A small distributary of the Ohtagawa River dribbles along the edge of the Hair Monument. On the levee, a Picassoesque statue depicts an anguished local mother holding her scorched baby out to the viewer in mute protest. Greenish tears as big as basketballs flop down her cheeks and breasts.

Impiously lassoed around the baby's left testicle (the other is undescended—an effect of gamma rays), there is a frayed and ratty rope. It straggles and droops over the azalea-crowned embankment that shields park-goers from the sight and smell of the filthy fluid bordering this end of the enclosure. This questionable rope slithers down through the mud, and terminates in a droopy bow tied by unskilled fingers around a small outcrop of rock, which marks a secret spot on the bank that only the riverine hoboes and the street urchins, and I, and now you, know about.

If, when the river is feeling stingy with its substance, you steel yourself and crash through the azaleas and use the ratty rope to rappel down the concrete incline, and if you go down into that toxic mud, and squat on your heels and reach out your thumb to scratch away at the exposed river bed, you will see, where the currents and eddies peculiar to this spot have kept them covered with a thin cold-cream layer of protective sewage, fragments of the original bed stones. The Daimyo Mohri himself, founder of Hiroshima, author of the local way of life, laid them down four centuries ago, long before post-World War II land reclamations transformed this distributary into something more than a castle-master's ornamental garden trickle.

Your thumb will be scratching the filth away from these flat stones to reveal definite tweed-like patterns: nothing less than the scorched silhouettes of carp skeletons in various attitudes of terminal agony. This is where the blasted river abandoned its course, shutter-wise, for a brief exposure to Harry Truman's gift of hell.

Flaming people, Hiroshimites, Korean slaves and American POW's alike, scrambled down here to bathe their effervescing epidermises, only to find that the blast had parted the water from its bed and left nothing behind but a vast mud-poultice. Many of these folks were overwhelmed and washed away when the boiling liquid flushed back. They fell for the old Red Sea ruse.

And if you look up from the fishy X-rays and train your eyes across the ruined face of the water, clear to the opposite bank, you can believe the stories the old-timers tell, of a brief period, right after Hirohito undeified himself on the radio, when this town was just impoverished enough for the river to be pristine. Children could swim and put their faces underwater and open their eyes without permanent chemical burns or cyanide poisoning, and see that the entire course is a downright gallery of marine perdition, mirroring the one of terrestrial perdition memorialized in granite on the other side of the azaleas.

It's the Lethe of the Far East, a waterway to induce lassitude of a depth few Americans over fifty have imagined, especially if you get on a boat and cruise the tony neighborhoods of the *nouveaux riches*. It feels natural to relax your conscious mind, to acquiesce, as you float through these plush quadrants of the City of Peace. Gape at the landscape bobbing soporifically before your eyes. Today, in this still-rich nation, on this shallow inland stream, the levees are pillowed with topiary. Every twenty meters a patined plaque suggests which nearby architectural confection was released into the atmosphere back in 1945.

This is a whole city of vaporizations, solidity itself relaxed into its constituent particles and blown off as easily as powder from a moth's wing. It's a perfect excuse to secure a professorship and settle into expatriated middle age. Your father grows feeble and dies without you back stateside, as you pursue the most nihilistic burlesque of all academic careers. You wait for numb, self-alienated death to overtake you, while you repeat, over and over and over again, into deaf matriculated ears, "This is a pen. This is a pen. This is a pen. This is a pen."

CRITICAL APPENDIX

"Tom Bradley and the *Sam Edwine Pentateuch*"
by Cye Johan, *Exquisite Corpse* [14]

> *And he arose, and did eat and drink,*
> *and went in the strength of that meat*
> *forty days and forty nights unto Horeb*
> *the mount of God.*
> —1 Kings 19: 8

How do you go about reviewing a novel that, in the present tense, takes exactly twenty-seven minutes (a taxi's waiting with the meter running the whole time), yet, before publication, occupied the same number of reams of typing paper as the monstrosity by that other nearly seven-foot-tall Tom, which legendarily required a pickup truck to lug it to Scribner's, so Maxwell Perkins could nibble and scratch and worry its balls off?

And how do you (critical descendant of that mincing deballocker you'll never admit to being) even start to sketch out the rough draft of an essay about the so-called "Pentateuch," the new and lawless Torah, of which the abovementioned volume is but the Genesis? How even formulate intelligent questions about a splintering shelf-load of books, amounting to more than a million words—a frightening sport of nature, like all sets of quints?

You steel yourself, is what you do: you buck up your courage, fling out your bosom, throw antiquated "New Critical" theory to the wind, and seek out the lawgiver himself. You try to catch the new Moses on top of his personal Horeb, before he hikes down and trips on the golden calf, after which point you'll never be able to get near him again, except for three seconds every few years at mob-scene book signings.

But how physically to locate this mountain of God? According to the promo-copy, *The Sam Edwine Pentateuch* "follows a disruptive Gargantua from the Far West to the Extreme Orient." Finding myself adrift in the latter region of our planet, I thought it might be possible to use the words of the great recluse himself as clues in a kind of scavenger hunt, Tom Bradley as the grand prize. In a recent essay published in London's magisterial nthposition Magazine (shortlisted for the European Online Journalism Award) Dr. Bradley speaks of being surrounded by—

"...itinerant TEFL trash, who are here just to stockpile money between heroin-soaked trips to the Golden Triangle."

Now there's a solid hint. It sounds as though he's been stranded, or exiled, in some East Asian hell-hole that happens to be prosperous enough, at the moment (thanks, no doubt, to America's noblesse oblige), to support a troop of those white monkeys who feign "the Teaching of the English as the Foreign Language." This couldn't be more fortuitous, because that's exactly what I am (stranded in East Asia, that is—though I guess I might qualify, in Dr. Bradley's book, as a piece of TEFL trash, too).

It occurred to me that my author and I might be within tangible reach. So I went, not bar-hopping (not just yet) but language school-hopping. I tiptoed and cringed through the dockside alleys of a certain port town on an obscure island in the East China Sea where he seems to have been marooned—at least the most recent Bradley sightings have occurred in the sordid vicinity. In dive after pedagogical dive, I kept my auditory meati reluctantly dilated for sounds fitting the following description (from the same nthposition essay):

"Almost every sentence that comes out of these kids' mouths turns up at the end, like a question, and most of their vowel sounds are schwas."

I came upon one clip-joint in particular whose closet-sized "classrooms" exuded such muffled moans. So far so good. After standing on the sidewalk outside and listening awhile, I had to agree with Dr. Bradley that—

"It's very strange to imagine them at the helms of English conversation classes. But it's reassuring to remember that they're only working in storefront language schools where instruction is but a secondary, or even tertiary concern, if that..."

"Storefront" is right. A member of the faculty was lying on the stoop at my feet in a puddle of chemical beer, tousled braids of pork-sauce ramen swirling from the side of his mouth. Shitzu dogs serviced him like Lazarus, causing me to recall the remainder of Dr. Bradley's paragraph:

"The managers don't seem to care, or notice, if their youthful Caucasoid instructors have speech impediments, but are satisfied if they agree to brighten their hair with bleach and their eyes with turquoise contact lenses, and fornicate with the students on demand, as it's good for business..."

Hardly any dark roots were showing under the educator's regulation platinum dye job, and one of his corneal suction cups remained firmly in place (the other had slipped from between flaccid eyelids and was glistening like a sapphire zit on his chin). His adherence to the dress code notwithstanding, it was hard to imagine this comatose stud drumming up much business. This clearly was not the institution my author had described. So I decided to hit the bars and collect my thoughts. If you're going to step on drunks, anyway, you might as well get in on the action.

I stumbled onto the right track. In a seawall tavern that offered the services of a sad gaggle of early-teenaged hand-job hostesses, some young and youngish American alcoholics said things like, "You mean that really, really, um, huge-ungus-type dude? With the sort of, like, orange beard? He never comes to drink here? But newspaper delivery guys and milk, um, men? You know? They, kind of, whisper about someone? Like on top of that, um, sort of mountain?"

A thumb was aimed over a shoulder at the largest of several dark entities that lifted their cloudy masses from among hovels in a muggy-looking suburb a few blocks inland: not quite the "backside of the desert" mentioned in that other Pentateuch, but wilderness enough for me.

Between rib-splitting coughs, a certain Englishman chimed in. (I didn't see his face because he was slouched in a dark booth and receiving a lap-job from a tiny Filipina white slave who seemed, strangely, at first glance, to have fastened her fingernails deep into his bony chest.) "If this is going to be one of those literary blowjobs, Mate, best be ready to grin and swallow when that 'orrible old cunt squirts spunk."

A subject of Elizabeth II in these special circumstances is allowed to express his thoughts in more developed periods than our own countrymen because, after all, his ancestors invented the lingo. It also helps if he happens to be the manager of the educational institution which furnishes this dive with the bulk of its clientele. I left this Brit drilling his little lap-dancer on today's lesson, which she was obliged to recite to the accompaniment of his agonizing, chronic lung seizures:

You taught me language, an my profit on't
Is I know how to curse. The red plague rid you
For learning me your language.

I'm already tired of reporting the dialog of Tom Bradley's fellow ejectees, with whom he never deigns to associate, but who seem to have made him the main subject of their amphetamined and opiated gossip. So let me just paraphrase the remainder: stomping around on top of that geological formation in the blackest hours before each dawn, someone fitting his description (and who else in this whole hemisphere comes close?) has been glimpsed. I can't imagine how he's been glimpsed. Maybe a pair of those infra-red night-vision binocks the Syrians pilfered from our stalwarts in Iraq have made it here on the black market to please insomniac voyeurs. I doubt many people would sneak up and try verifying his puzzling presence with naked eyes. It would take a foolhardy weirdo or an obsessed stalker type, or a hybrid of both.

All that remained for me was to dig in on a bus bench and wait for the first subtle insinuations of sunrise. This did not require the *patienza* of Mother Teresa because, around here, it comes at four o'clock. The natives, who are mostly middle-class office-workers (though that's about to change, as their country relaxes deeper and deeper into the trance called penury) are not allowed to go home until the boss does, and it's easier to make the old rooster feel guilty if it's pitch dark outside; therefore Daylight Savings Time is a taboo subject among elected officials.

There. That's all you know, and all you need to know, about the setting of this encounter. (Incidentally it's Nippon we're talking about—Nagasaki, if you insist on pinching and puckering it down even further.) Now you understand why this brush with genius has to happen on top of Horeb East, in the wee hours, elevated in space and insulated in time from the inscrutability, the misdirection, the willful uncommunicativeness, the suffocating group-pressure brought to bear with exquisite obliquity even on the slave masters themselves. So, the boss won't close up at a decent hour? Instead of rising up like other prisoners of major industrialized economies and demanding a contract with set work-hours, let's just quietly cause the sun to go down and come up again with unnatural prematurity, and meantime huddle together, sullen at our desks in the gathering gloom. Land of the Rising Sun, and how.

Why in God's name is our author here? Though craving an immediate solution to this and countless other Bradleyan perplexities, I decided for the time being to tuck them all away, to empty my head as far as possible for a non-zen master or an American over the age of twenty-five, and just start climbing blindly.

*   *   *   *

Through near-pitch blackness my way spiraled up and up, switching back and forth in the foreign air. The track's soggy surface seemed always to bank in the direction opposite to what any sane surveyor would choose, assuming his purpose was to discourage vehicles and beings from falling off the outer edge. Below, in blackish-greenness, fanged with fronds, a bamboo maw gaped and groaned with the breeze, as if some exotic category of the damned were lodged in its throat-thick stalks. And beyond that weedy perdition, steadily sinking from my point of view, our author's adopted city moaned out its own continuo to the chorus. The further each of my steps lifted me above it, the more definitely I could hear Nagasaki's song—and it wasn't Puccini's greatest hit.

Dr. Bradley's mainland neighbors have, for thousands of years, recognized the Root Tone of Nature. A city of any time or nation, if situated far enough away to be apprehended as a whole, produces this note, the same sung by a river in full springtime spate, or a vast deciduous forest when the wind rushes through its boughs. It is said to share the wavelength of F above middle-C on a piano well-tempered and tuned precisely to A at 440 hertz, of which there are precious few in China—and small wonder: imagine the interlocking layers of high civilization required to bring such a marvel into existence. Back in the dynastic days when this notion was formulated the Celestials were using guitar-like contraptions.

"Hast thou attuned thy heart and mind to the great mind and heart of all mankind? For as all Nature-sounds are echoed back by the sacred River's roaring voice, so the heart of him who in the stream would enter must thrill in response to every sigh and thought of all that lives and breathes." Thus says the *Book of Golden Precepts*, as translated by the mighty Pythoness of Dnepropetrovsk—whom I've long suspected of being Tom Bradley's spiritual guide. (And if it seems strange to you that the author of such works as "Squirting Chubbies" and "Baptizing Dead People for Fun and Profit" should have one of those, imagine how it strikes me, his disciple.)

Did I hear the Root Tone of Nature on this dwindling night? Elijah was privy to nothing less than the "still small voice" when he hiked Horeb; but what about simple Cye Johan? Was he worthy of even a single sigh or thought from anything that lives and breathes? Or perhaps just a whispering hint of the "eternal note of sadness"? I can't say. But I can identify what did get my poor unenlightened timpanic membranes quivering in their merely mechanical way—and dare I admit that the Bradley-possessed "heart of me" did indeed "thrill in response" to it?

I heard "...the dogs and delivery trucks of the distant East Asiatic metropolis; the screams of prepubescent Filipina sex slaves waking chained in attics; the rhythmic sucks of police helicopters circling over some famished housebreaker; a psychotic voice bellowing into a megaphone as the rabble yawns in the face of yet another day's wage slavery; displacements, varied and numerous, of styrofoam smoke and stale fish-breath at overpopulated bus stops—everything, at a grateful distance, blends into a single sigh that strains softly like a half-dead fly against a greasy windowpane..." Thus goes *Black Class Cur*, which constitutes the reluctant Exodus of our one-man diaspora, Sam Edwine.

Gradually, on black reptile wings, this made-in-Japan counterfeit of the Big F rose up to the same small number of meters above sea level that I had already attained on foot. There it separated into its constituent frequencies, several of the higher and more piercing overtones grinding together to form a jagged decibel wedge, the narrow end of which drove straight into the hole on the downhill side of my head. I could hear a noisy herd or gaggle or pack or gang approaching—from which of the many directions they were capable of swooping, creeping, burrowing or sidling, I couldn't say; but it threatened to surround me, the wall of cacophony upon which hell's unquiet denizens advertise their regrettable existence and trumpet their approach. And it was played not in the Daoist key of F, but something closer to deteriorated Bud Powell's key of S.

Like the foxes that have overrun the ruins of Jerusalem more than once, these hellions make many different kinds of weird noises at those times when the sun has selfishly forsaken the sky—so they stand accused, at any rate. To make that accusation plausible, their vocabulary would have to exceed any other inhuman creature's—at least those apprehensible by the usual five human senses. Some people claim the deviated beings, whatever their nature may be, took up local tenure on a certain August morning in 1945; others say they were here first, hovering in the foam even before the magma destined to coagulate into Nippon oozed up from between mismatched rocks that grind like the molars of hateful spouses at the bottom of the East China Sea. In either case, hills like this one become particularly noisy right about now, toward dawn, much to the perturbation of superstitious native Shinto animists, as well as secular-humanist violators of the foreigner curfew, such as me.

The rationalist minority in these parts comfort themselves by positing the vociferous presence of Rikki Tikki's cousins—you know, "rather like a little cat in his fur and his tail, but quite like a weasel in his head and his habits...and his war-cry, as he scuttles through the long grass, is 'Rik-tikk-tikki-tikki-tchk!'" The assumption is that the noises must come from the throats of certain sundry razor-clawed but reassuringly material mongooses whose ancestors, ostensibly, time gone by, were introduced into Nagasaki's environs from someplace even more purulent than Kipling's Segowlee cantonment in Gujarat. Tom Bradley decrees it to have been Sumatra, probably because he likes the sound of the name—and therefore Sumatra it is.

All this can be gotten, passim, from *The Sam Edwine Pentateuch*'s Asiatic volumes. And nobody who has been transported into the upper crannies and convolutions of his own frontal lobes by the prose in which these claims are expressed will feel the faintest inclination to check the accuracy or thoroughness of Dr. Bradley's research, if any, into this land and its lore. If the natives want mongooses—more to the point, if he thinks that we, his readers, should be given mongooses—then rest assured that he will supply the most serviceable members of that tribe, and plenty of them, with his usual furious noblesse oblige. The spatial and temporal entirety of Nippon itself puckers to less than nothingness in the presence of the consonants, vowels, syllables, words, phrases, sentences, paragraphs, chapters and books in which it has been couched, or rather entombed, by my author. We, his fans, just lie back in the volcanic quicksand and enjoy the sensation of being raped with such doctrine, and are pleased to assimilate it as gospel, secure in the knowledge that nobody with a much bigger readership (at least among our sort) will contradict our man to the particular notice of anyone whose opinion we'll ever value to the extent of bothering to make ourselves aware of it. As he is fond of saying in interviews, "I'll libel a whole race, religion, ethnicity, tribal affiliation—I'll sink a fucking continent—if it makes for a nice transition between paragraphs."

So he makes with the Rikki Tikkis. The notion of such an infestation might not sit too badly with the world-view of a bourgeois homeowner with four more or less solid, if paper, walls to cringe behind (his flesh crawling from the rodent revulsion that seems to cross the broadest racial boundaries with no loss of intensity). But it offered small comfort to a nocturnal pedestrian like me. The frisky Sumatrans, or some entity capable of doing a fair impression of them, began shrieking and dry-heaving in the nipple-deep grass on the slope below. They kept close harmony with the internal combustions of what sounded like several oriental-style motorbikes revving and rolling in concert somewhere in the distance, in definite crescendo, which I chose to ignore for the moment. Then, invisibly crossing my path, they occupied the slope above me, bringing their stridulations with them like cicadas stirring at the close of a clammy night, or blood-sport fans doing The Wave across a stadium overgrown with vines and underbrush. I was surrounded. This prompted me to ask, out loud, the question which, in the unlikely event that the story might be true, addresses the most implausible part of all: "Who was dumb enough to come up with the bright idea to import such skittering horrors?" (I mean the mongooses, not the motorcycles.) As with all such questions, the intelligent hiker will consult the pertinent book of the new Torah, specifically *Flip-kun*, our Leviticus.

As it turns out, this being the Extreme Orient, nobody, not even sage Dr. Bradley, is able to name a specific mortal human on whom the irruption can be blamed; but credit is taken, just as the date is defined, by the living god who happened to occupy the Chrysanthemum Throne at the moment when the shipload of miniature carnivores supposedly arrived from the abovementioned booger of geography in the Indian Ocean: in this case, the emperor's sneezy-sounding moniker was Taisho. It was "his" idea. In other words, the blunder, if it was performed at all, was performed under his administration, and he wound up personally symbolizing it—very aptly, in this case, as that divine and august personage was inbred to a vicious degree, and behaved like a mongoose himself, once again according to Tom Bradley, the World's Greatest Old Japan Hand. (I'm proud to say I helped bury the former holder of that title in my Exquisite Corpse review of *The Curved Jewels*.)

Therefore, as far as you and I know and care, it is a fact, established solidly as if it were engraved three fingers deep in black diorite, that, in the Taisho era, Rikki Tikki's cousins were brought in for rat control, but wound up being much better at beating the shit out of grannies' lap-poodles instead, so were chased up into suburban hills, like this Horeb, where their kind yet thrives on the steaming contents of stray pets' jugulars. And their liberation is all the more ironic because mad Emperor Taisho himself, their rabid personification, was "kept in a cage...and let out only to get mooncalf princes on his few fecund nieces."

Furthermore, it is a Bradleyan given that the most egregious specimen of imperial mooncalf was Taisho's heir, "... blood-bloated Hirohito, of Nanking-rape fame, whose nibbly buck-teeth and rapacious character suggest that his cousin-mother must have entered upon parturition in the middle of a royal progress into the countryside and been frightened at the key moment by a gang of the helpful little verminators. By the time the nipping godlet hunched on his homunculus-sized coat of skin, the patterns for his physical build and moral makeup had already been driven from the rat- and poodle-rich downtown and were probably occupying the rice terraces with their third or fourth generation."

One can see (or, at any rate, the good doctor, and therefore we, can see) how the mythos of the mongoose was generated and encouraged on several levels by the persons and manners of the sovereigns themselves, just as the Chakravarti kings of India were consecrated by the blood of white horses, and the emperors of China were harbingered by dragons and phoe-nixes. The bestiarial bathos is deliberate and couldn't be more apropos.

But, even though these living symbols of His Divine Imperial Nipponese Majesty are capable of several scalp-cor-rugating cries, such as the one cited above, "Rik-tikk-tikki-tikki-tchk" (at fifty paces the sound can nibble the hairs off the nape of your neck), it seemed more and more likely to me, as I labored uphill to keep my appointment with the redoubtable novelist who put all this in my head, that Nagasaki's enormous variety of nighttime snarls and cackles might be attributed a bit too readily to the feral descendants of these strangers from conveniently demon-rife subequatorial regions. If you have spent at least one night in this haggard land, you will know all to well the racket I was hearing now, and will scoff at any-one who attributes it to mere woodland creatures, rapacious though they may be.

Like an audible and perverted version of Proust's cookie, it filled my body with dismay, from the collarbones down to the callus ridges in the soles of my feet, in the instant before my brain had time to put a name to its source. On this night the local damned had chosen to coat themselves not in sleek fur, but in pocked and pitted skins which usually belong to another species of tiny monster, known, in the quaint lingo of the country, as bosozokus: "...those unemployable highway virtuosos, bringers of insomnia to an already sleep-disordered land, teen bikers who spend each night trying to play Marilyn Manson riffs on the throttles of their unmuffled rice-burners," to quote *Hustling the East*, Tom Bradley's Dai Nippon Trilogy.

Such a presence on his mountain in the wee hours was no easier to explain than the mongooses'. There was an overcrowded stomach cancer hospice lodged in a kind of duodenal kink in the foothills; and, one of their few stated functions in life being gleefully to increase the misery of the dying, this particular contingent of bozos (or however you care to abbreviate their name) had probably gotten lost on their way to or from making sure that no in-patients were able to sleep away a few moments of the impending day's agony. The marginally less cretinous bozos, who tend to ride somewhere near the front of the pack, would justify buzzing that sad place with eugenic theories inherited from General Tojo: one must speed the way of weaklings incapable of survival; mouths unworthy of food should be closed sooner than later (timely conceits, ripe for revival, now that this society is graying even faster than Caucasian America). The rank and file bozos, on the other hand, like all gnomes of subhuman rank, require no theory, but just do what they do for sheer dharmic spite. Possibly they derive a sort of superficial annelid stimulation from such pursuits, but this must remain a matter of speculation, as they are inarticulate and unable to account for themselves and their behavior.

I knew, yet again from careful perusals of my favorite author's novels, that it would be best to shield myself somehow, not so much from their noise and knives as their adulation and halitosis. In emulation of their colleagues in more sophisticated places such as Tokyo and Osaka, these troubled teens tend to halt their motorcades and gather around any non-doddering occidental in sight, chatting him up for fashion tips, and also for practical advice on what to eat to make themselves seven feet tall, or pretty near, like a white man—"maple syrup" is what they want to hear, as trees don't lack height (an example of Asiatic thinking). But what they want most are solid LSD connections—ghastly as it is to imagine what might go on in their minds, or any mind at all, while trying to trip on these islands.

I was new around here, and in the Controlled Substances Department was only aware of the Israelis who everyone stumbles over when arriving in town. They stake out their gutterside pitches in front of the train station after shelling out for protection from the Yakuza, who permit them to occupy rectangles of sidewalk precisely circumscribed, not to say quarantined, among steaming-fresh street pizzas of bibulous native "salary men." Exactly as they do in the Bradley books, these sons o' Jacob spread out their quaint tasseled rugs, hunker down in a picturesque manner, and set to work hawking generic middle eastern-style ormolu trinkets, which, you might be surprised to learn, are actually not hand-crafted by quizzical old Hassidic craftsmen in the little town of Bethlehem, but rather churned out by babies in purgatorial Indonesian sweat shops.

Bric-a-brac flogging is the Israelis' stated purpose for being in Cherry Blossom Land, according to their official work permits (purchased no less dearly than their barf-puddled parcels of pavement). But, true to the entrepreneurial instincts for which the Levantine peoples are anciently famed, they also brave Nippon's draconian dope laws in order to part, more or less discreetly, with dog-shit blotter acid, for which they are willing to accept the equivalent of seventy-five American dollars per hit, or maybe sixty, if you are capable of dickering in the noble tongue of King David and Isaiah and Jeremiah and Ezekiel. This earns them the contempt of otherwise knee-jerk philosemites, such as Tom Bradley, who (unlike the present scribbler) is old enough to recall the days when legendary

What'hisname, also Jewish, but American and upper-middle-class all the way, used to ramble through the Home of the Brave in his VW van with the portable chem lab in the back, broadcasting little tabs of the purest and most beautiful Orange Sunshine as liberally as Johnny did apple seeds, with a profit margin of comparable dimensions.

Though Orientals themselves, Nagasaki's strychnine peddlers are, after all, Tom Bradley's fellow exiles, and mine as well, and one's heart is prepared, by reflex as well as by Hollywood, to go out to them—especially when, to attract business, they break out their battered clarinets and little violins with the hairline cracks in the varnish, and render simple traditional happy Hebrew sodbuster tunes from Norman Jewison's heart-warming "Fiddler on the Roof." (I'm particularly susceptible to "Matchmaker, Matchmaker, Make Me a Match," which is what they were playing about eight or ten hours ago when I squeezed my love-handles, one by one, through the turnstile.)

But, charming as they are, this particular branch of whichever tribe they belong to hardly warrants the sort of special consideration granted, say, to the gypsies in Europe, which persuades all right-thinkers to turn a blind eye upon what small depredations upon society-at-large their unhappy condition necessitates. Nagasaki's pseudo-psychedelic vomit-squatters may not be comfortable as their cousins the Rothschilds, but they're not particularly to be pitied. I just demonstrated that they have achieved at least one out of the total of three ambitions cherished by so many of their youthful countrymen, as expressed in the famous proverb, "Get high, get laid, get the fuck out." (Of Zion, that is.) One out of three is more than most of us are granted in a single incarnation.

So I felt no liberal guilt in taking upon my shoulders the civic as well as consumerist responsibility to foil these pushers of dangerous narcotics. Proudly as it would have done my heart to watch them burn the noisy bozos almost as badly as my own tribe of intrusive foreigners burned the noisy bozos' grandparents fifty-eight years ago—and as famously as I was sure they'd get along with the night-raiding, misery-sowing, sadistic bully-biker storm-troopers—I deemed it best to steer no custom in the direction of the train station kibbutzniks today. Therefore, self-concealment, at the moment, became a priority, before the acid-starved convoy could overtake me, whether from uphill or down.

Now, when you clamber up a hill in the suburbs of the burg which our author has famously and cruelly renamed "Boom Town II," you cannot but remain aware, at the epidermal level, of the vast pyroclastic vulcanism writhing a few inches beneath the soles of your feet. Besides engendering the temblors and tsunamis for which this quadrant of the North Pacific is notorious, this buried ferment sends up a tenacious mineral vapor that seems almost consciously to clutch and suck at your Achilles tendons. It retards not only forward progress but the sort of sideward mobility required when diving for cover—which, as the stuck-pig Suzuki squeals grew louder, was what I considered doing, on feet enmeshed in translucent tar. But something I recalled reading in *Black Class Cur*, the China volume of Dr. Bradley's planet-girdling Pentateuch, or maybe dreaming the night after reading it, told me that struggle was pointless under such mucous conditions, and would only make things worse, as in quicksand.

So, barely aware of doing so, and unable in any case to explain how it was done, I calmly willed the earthly bonds on my feet to loosen, just a skosh, just enough to strain credulity to a degree acceptable in a literary work of this genre (whatever that may turn out to be); and, like my hero Sam Edwine in his rollicking, psilocybin-fueled Oaxacan jungle adventure (see *Acting Alone*, our blessed Deuteronomy), I allowed the perverse gradient of the road to settle me into the downhill shadows of the soft shoulder, like a surfer shooting the curl.

There, deep in mongoose territory, I waited for the kamikaze punks to whine past from whichever direction their scale-model plastic Harley knockoffs were dragging them. Meanwhile, my hold on gravity evaporating as quickly as an adrenalin spike, I found myself sinking deeper and deeper into pulsating jungle mulch, getting moistened up to the crotch, then pits, then beard, by rivulets of cloying dew that filtered and drained like saccharine tea between acid rain-dwarfed banana trees, up-slope.

And on they came, the salamanders—not from below, which would have been odd enough, but from above, rolling in procession down the incline ahead of me. At that point I could hardly imagine what business these beings could possibly have had on Horeb's sacred summit. Huddling there in the writhing mire, I was just on the verge of persuading my mind's eye to picture my author and them in the same frame. I hadn't yet begun extrapolating a cause for their association (was he sending them on infernal errands? Under what compulsion?), when, suddenly, as if in reaction to the sheer incongruity of that attempted mental juxtaposition—and as a psychosomatic manifestation, no doubt, of the violent jealousy it caused me (I, his Boswell, had traveled this far only to be preempted by un-Englished scum)—a nearly complete disorientation slammed like a leaden lid over my head.

It hovered and buzzed in particular around my inner ear on one side—I couldn't have specified right or left even at the time: something like a whole-body, planet-upending, universe-encompassing dose of Jonathan Swift's own Meuniere's Syndrome, vertigo and tinnitus in precise proportions, exacerbated in no small degree by what I can only call visitations from the other world—I mean the one on paper that parallels and surpasses this one, and must forever be closed to juvenile delinquents of any category. Like the "snot green sea" that inundates tourists' awareness when they visit a certain stone tower on a sandy cove near Dublin, imagery from the Bradleyan oeuvre obtruded upon and usurped what I used fondly to call "my own thoughts."

The acne brigade hadn't yet completely passed. Peeking between puckered bamboo shoots at nostril level, I could see the derriere garde, the inferior bozos, if such can be imagined, who hadn't managed, or bothered, to complete the transformation. They appeared to be compounded of unformed stools and styrofoam smoke, in spite of obvious labors to camouflage their semi-solid state under hair and lips dyed the color of old earwax on a Q-tip. Their exhaust stuck out behind them in furry swirls, like cat tails, and, rather than rolling, their wheels half crept, something like weasel paws. I couldn't see the avant garde, but I could hear strange splashes way down at sea level, and squeals.

Conscious that the unwheeled noisemakers, the ones with fur, would at any minute descend on me like piranhas on a dog-paddling tapir and set to work defleshing my skeleton, I decided that I really ought to run screaming out into the middle of the road, even if it meant giving a group-heart attack to these straggler-bozos.

To that end, I fought with the mud-vacuum that encased my lower self. As soon as one foot was freed, another problem struck close to home. Indigo-bellied lizards, also eager to avoid nourishing the ravening Rikki Tikkis, crawled off specific Bradleyan pages, assumed scaly skin, scrambled up inside my trouser leg, and fixed themselves to my poor perineum by means of crusty suction-cup toes—or, at any event, I had been led to anticipate such treatment by reading certain maniacally despairing fiction which gnaws at its author's exiled condition like a rat at connective tissue, and teems with as many tiny bloodsuckers as Grunewald's Temptation of Saint Anthony (a horrifying detail of which serves as the cover of *Killing Bryce*, the abovementioned Genesis of our new Torah).

I think I ran the rest of the way. Or maybe the shudders with which my sympathetic nervous system obliged me were violent enough to bounce me to the summit like a basketball in reverse. "Nature," to mangle once again you-know-who's words, "is too evident in this town. They need an even bigger lake of asphalt."

*   *   *   *

As if in an attempt to fulfill that request, the very top of his mountain has been blasted off to make room for something unnatural. The trauma is rectilinear, but only in the vaguest way, as the edges have been blurred by volunteer vegetation. It's hard to give it a name in the moisture-thickened darkness, but the project obviously went bust, time gone by, or was aborted due to tired tribal blood. Meanwhile, giant tiger-striped spiders have grabbed the opportunity offered by rioting plant life. Hoping to profit from mongoose-horror in vulnerable ground-dwelling creatures like me, they shit high-tensile webs everywhere, thick as deep-sea fishing line, which pluck and ping like koto strings against my marauding shins, raising an alarm, announcing my approach to the author of all this crawling damnation. Enter Cye Johan, to a flourish of untuned ukuleles.

I've been hoping to sneak up on him instead of vice-versa, as that would leave me the option of changing my mind and fleeing in terror, or maybe just shambling off in embarrassment. Instead I dive into the blackness and resign myself to dying of old age while hiding behind something very odd. At first grope, it can only be described as the improvisation of a plumber with a few dozen cast-iron pipes, a monkey wrench, some time off, and an easily satisfied creative urge. No mammoth Prospero yet in evidence, I use the dead time to consider this clanking skeleton. At my touch, various layers of enamel slough off the pipes in lead-rich chips, a different shade of pastel for each receding year of the strangely familiar assemblage's existence, till the bare metal shows through, tortured and orangish-brown among the weeds. My hiding place turns out to be an antique set of tricky bars, or a jungle gym, or whatever kiddies call these places of social resort. Little Cye just got here, and has already been put in his place.

Here's a context that clarifies and shapes the shadows beyond, and I can now situate myself, by the light of a moon that's making one final effort to look alive before the bully looms up and laughs her to nothingness. I've come to rest at the edge of the faintest recollection of a schoolyard, an abandoned country kindergarten just recognizable in ruins hanging off the opposite cliff. The tiny hillbilly matriculators meant to chatter and brachiate upon my sad tricky bars must have been carried off by malignant nature spirits during recess. Or maybe they've just grown up and begun, if not completed, the process of dying off unspawned. Even during the Pax Japonica, suki-yaki-deluxe heyday of the eighties, it's likely this whole RFD route boasted nary a pre-menopausal wife that hadn't been mail-ordered from the Philippines, and precious few of them. Here's a people long gutted. (And I'm not referring to the extra span of small intestine their senile physiologists have bizarrely hallucinated inside them, a proud peculiarity of the race, to supply the void.)

A ring of pulverized grass and atomized gravel is tromped around this flattened peak. Something enormous has been making an habitual, if not compulsive, circuit of the ragged rim. A rogue water buffalo, surely, has taken possession of this poor mountain, which can't be responding well to such rough treatment. Like the humans who failed to homestead it, Horeb East verges on dissolution even at the best of times. Loosely compounded of wild banana rot and pyroclastic sludge, softened by typhoons, undermined by its own constant seismicity, this hill is prone, like all its neighbors, to the geomorphological equivalent of a nervous breakdown: the catastrophic mudslides which several times each year deform the profile of this whole quadrant of the Pacific Rim. An even briefly definitive topographical map of apocalyptic Boom Town II has never been drawn up, before or after the summer of 1945, as far as my most assiduous researches in that area have revealed.

Suspended like a mini-marshmallow on top of a poorly-set jello mold, I'm scared to breathe, move, blink, or think jostling thoughts—unlike the creature which approaches now. I can hear it huff through the pre-dawn inkiness, fart and mumble, spit strangely numerous times, also snort through nostrils "the glory of which is terrible as he paws and rejoices in his strength." Inexorable as a Mack truck in low gear, it's circling around to the point nearest to where I cower behind baby-blue and pink playtime equipment. He's about to heave into my physical sight, finally, for the first time.

I can't help it. After what seems like eighteen lifetimes lugging around a heart and guts crammed with thousands of Bradleyan sentences, I can only find in my head two paltry phrases, and they don't even belong to him: paired prissinesses, a matched set, worthy of Scribner's nanciest scrote-nibbler, which "the present reviewer" once published in Exquisite Corpse.

I was discussing the fictional portrait of Japan's Crown Princess in his roman-a-clef, *The Curved Jewels*. I had particularly in mind the poor woman's puzzled appraisal, in the moving eleventh chapter, of Hirohito's grandson's procreative member (which is this Divine Nation's spiritual *fons et origo*, the current incarnation thereof, and strictly speaking shouldn't be treated any more flippantly than, say, Jesus' flaccid corpus is bandied about within Christendom). The passage runs as follows:

"That part of the Prince had looked, to this virgin, like a formaldehyded specimen of the backwater vermin which her in-laws constantly fondled and talked about and identified themselves with in the world's eyes. Such bloodless things, spineless, pale and soggy, were all they knew, for marine biology was the field of endeavor the Imperial Family had fastened onto, in a halfhearted effort to justify their existence. She was dying to know if Caucasoid equipment also looked like something you wouldn't want to step on at low tide..."

With reference to the author's choosing to reside in the land which has deified that "formaldehyded specimen," and in consideration of his occasional but legendary run-ins with extreme rightists eager to defend that divinity with violence, I felt emboldened, on those famous electronic pages of Exquisite Corpse, to suggest that Dr. Bradley might suffer from a "megalomaniacal urge for public self-annihilation" and an "unwholesome Christ complex...which the present reviewer finds a bit unsettling."

"...megalomaniacal"? "...unwholesome"? Can anyone blame "the present reviewer" if he finds his own pedantry "a bit unsettling" at the moment? If you were "unsettled" as "the present reviewer," wouldn't you prefer to stay put among the tricky bars, sheepish as a porpoise drowning in a tuna net, idiot grin fixed on your bottlenose kisser?

Now's the moment he chooses to blast out of the (for him) knee-deep mist—on hooves, from the feel of it. My intellect has been forewarned about his dimensions—behemoth Sam

Edwine is obviously a self-portrait. But nothing could prepare an autonomic nervous system, nothing could steel the reptilian subcortex of a mere human brain, for Tom Bradley's elemental appearance on a dark and deserted mountaintop. This is a huge biped, and hairy. I've seen hairier, but never a huger, not in person, neither horizontally nor vertically.

He's a regular one-man Hell's Angels Motorcycle Club, Boom Town II Chapter, and he rolls right past me, oblivious as a legion of bosozokus. Even while assuring myself that I'll nail my author next time around with a tough set of proper interview questions, I know very well that it will take more than one lap before I can persuade myself not to choke. Instead of acting like a man, or even a journalist, I dig in and play the voyeur. Have I climbed this far only to let Tom Bradley get away?

Clockwise, counterclockwise, I am unable to say in which direction he forsakes me, because the leaden lid of disorientation has slammed down on my head once again and twisted everything. I've caught an extra-literary dose of dyslexia. When the clouds part briefly overhead I try to read the constellations, but Ursa Major and, it seems, Orion, too, appear as in a mirror, reversed. Two of the only unchanging items in the whole catalog of mankind's visual experience are catty-whompus. It's as unlikely a sight as even a dyslexic could expect see in several hundred million lifetimes, and inspires small confidence in my own state of mind. I do see some planets, of course, just about where you'd expect most of them to be; but Mars hangs down way too close, like a bare light bulb in a shitty Japanese one-room apartment. My giant author has to duck to get under it, and even so bumps his red head. The two of them melt together into one inflamed bilobular pumpkin.

I see this happen, and have small trouble believing it. Compared to his other accomplishments, merging his head with Mars is trivial. He is, after all, Tom Bradley, the novelist who, according to rumor, has imposed himself on this Mount of God for nearly twenty years, whom the diminutive natives have no doubt been ogling from afar like a circus freak during that endless period, yet whose own attention they've distracted to a preternaturally slight degree. (My textual analysis reveals that he knows fewer than five words of their language, and three of those are hairy-carey, okie-dokie and hunky-dory.) Meanwhile, in an award-winning feature-length screenplay, in scarcely believable numbers of stories and essays (more than seventy have appeared under his name in the past four years: see the Media Page of tombradley.org), and in the final novels of *The Sam Edwine Pentateuch*, where he exhausted the subject once and for all, Tom Bradley, the walking, stomping paradox, wrote with more perception and truth about this country than anybody in existence, now or formerly.

So, if it's no longer a fit subject for a real writer, why does he stick around this bleak archipelago, especially now that it's plummeting into race extinction, that terminal withering of the will to press on which has always signaled a nation's utter moral exhaustion? Even mighty Greek Thebes wound up with cattle lowing and grazing on its citadel; so what pitiable weasel-squeaks can our author expect to hear from the gutters of a twice-doomed toy-town like this? Assuming he hasn't died of earlyish old age himself by that time, will Dr. Bradley yet be lingering here in another ten or fifteen years, when his honorable hosts are flat on their bellies, gazing enviously up the asshole of the Philippines and sending their own dwindling granddaughters to Manila as sex slaves instead of vice-versa? In loitering like a crow on this carcass, is our author "indulging his intellectual masochism"? (Such was the accusation leveled at him during a wild online debate at David Horowitz's fanatical neo-con/Zionist Front Page Magazine, after they were gutsy enough to publish the eviscerating essay, "Ethnic Narcissism and Infertility in Japan"—excerpted from the ninth chapter of the present volume, and featured, like so much of Dr. Bradley's astonishing nonfiction, in the million-hit-per-month, Webby Award-winning Arts and Letters Daily.)

I'm not the only one hanging around here who's intimidated by the double threat of such a reputation and physique. Also hesitating self-consciously, holding back with craven diffidence worthy of me, is our local yellow main sequence star. That particular wimp fidgets behind a nearby peak, pinching his dick and sending on ahead a couple of expendable junior beams, pale and wan (respectively). So far, peeking between bamboo stalks, they have only been bold enough to scout out the atmosphere several yards over our heads. That's how intimidatingly phosphorescent-orange my author's patriarch-whiskers are, even in shadow, and how glaring the flushed Celtic skin stretched across his balding dome. (Why do I feel on shakier ground referring to his head and mine in the same paragraph than perpetrating a pathetic fallacy on a couple of defenseless sunbeams?)

The good doctor and I remain twilit under a low ceiling of day. Hawks sailing almost within reach (for him) are now pointed out in light. Each of their complex markings looks sharp as a hieroglyph on a freshly excavated graven image. One swoops down upon the inferior plane of existence that I, at any rate, am forced to call home, and latches onto a bit of breakfast among things that mongooses consider beneath eating. Before he's able to resume cruising altitude, huge obsidian ravens consolidate from the residual nighttime and harass this hawk, three against one, recapitulating their rascally behavior in *Kara-kun*: "...flapping and pecking alongside until the hawk drops its football-sized rat... [the ravens] are more than aerodynamically capable of retrieving the tidbit in mid-air, but prefer to let it fall down and mature awhile in the languishing stinkweeds."

While my attention is diverted, less by nature than the mirror he has held up to it, Dr. Bradley completes a second orbit without incident—of the physical sort, at any rate. But does he peer, for a nanosecond, into the vapors that still encase me? And does he nail an affectless but sociopathically intense glance right into the pit of my left eyeball, as though in acknowledgement of something that, if it possessed even a single atom's worth of significance, could almost be called my presence? It's clear that he attaches no particular importance to what he sees, if I can be said to have registered on his retina at all. It feels like being appraised by a hawk's lidless orb, and dismissed as unappetizing, therefore non-existent. Have I just been neutralized by a more-than, or other-than, human consciousness? Not a question calculated to settle the nerves. It's best just to pretend the glance never happened, like so much that ostensibly takes place here on the more inscrutable side of the International Date Line. Maybe Dr. Bradley has no idea anyone waits in ambush on this defunct playground.

Flitting about on the hilltop next door, clearly incapable of registering anything like my own pudency, is a colossal Sakyamuni, exoteric adipose edition. Its jadedness has been gussied up with molded-concrete blobs of representational flesh and sluttish silk, and accessorized by the broadest affectation of a tranny-style headdress I've ever seen, with iron reinforcing rods poking through at the worst possible places. The whole cetacean abortion is spray-painted metallic yellow and sprinkled with tasteless Kandy-Kolored tangerine flakes straight out of another scintillating Tom. This god (as I suppose it must be called) touts for a stupa, an off-white dome with a well-placed cowlick, which Sakyamuni straddles primly enough. Like thousands of others throughout Hirohito Land, this stupa is stuffed with the third-hand and shopworn residue of a certain Nepalese, who, we are asked to believe, was dragged across the waterless Tarim Basin, then shunted mongoose-wise across the Tsushima Strait, yet could still muster enough sheerly incarnated testosterone to shed many thousands of bushels of reliquary-quality facial hair.

That's a whole bunch more than the greatest and butchest of American novelists ever could manage, even the extra-fuzzy one presently under consideration. But, even though he's bested in quantity, I prefer the quality of my own guru's whiskers. I haven't yet gotten a good up-close look at them through this lingering steam; but his authorial portraits, online and on paper, explode in all directions with fibers of an angel color hardly approximable by any subcontinental type, pure Aryan warrior-caste or not.

A creature hovers and tickles and flitters in the hollow of our enlightened neighbor's Chunnel-sized left nostril, flirting with a Buddha sneeze that could blow Nagasaki to hell again. It's a tiny bird, much littler than the dog-fighting scavenger-hawks and carrion-ravens that squawk and screech over our mountain, but it's easy to hear his voice clear across the gorge that separates saggy Sakyamuni from Dr. Bradley. The little frizzy-feathered birdy does his morning air-gargle, a sunshine-welcoming warble routine hundreds of times more complex and eloquent than anything I've yet heard from a moonlit mongoose. The tweets and chirps are prestissimo, a series of split-second phrases lasting without rest or repeat, for three whole minutes that could perhaps have been more profitably allocated among the day's first crop of earthworms. It's like listening to a sylph with Olympic lung capacity discourse idly on Heisenberg's uncertainty principle and laugh hysterically at the same time, by means of Rahsaan Roland Kirk's circular breathing technique. Birds of this sort (which have an English name, I'll bet) are said by unsentimental native ornithologists to have a Darwinistic purpose for making such beauty way up there: they are supposed to be cruising for prospective fuck-buddies, i.e., mounting a formalized mating display in the name of species propagation—which is the only other permissible behavior for organisms in a rational universe besides procuring food by whatever undignified means necessary, such as skyjacking half-dead rats. If that's so, their tribe has gone out of its way to select for suppler throat muscles and sharper ears than any loved or unloved soprano saxophonist's I'm aware of.

But who's to say a tidy nest lined with a dozen buckshot-sized eggs is necessarily the end towards which this particular miniature brown Sidney Bechet is working? Why does everything have to be done to impress the broads? Certain old pilgrims have worked off tribal debt, and have shed those unsightly metempsychotic pounds through regular exercise. Do we require the heavy-handed burlesque of a morbidly obese Buddha to remind us that not every spirit is encased in karmic pudge? Some have earned the choice of fending for themselves, if they happen to feel like it.

Not to overextend the avian pathetic fallacy, but what if that ecstatic warbler is choosing to come on like, say, for example, an unfeathered biped who consecrates his life to expressing himself beautifully, when, for all the red-hot action he gets in return, he can do no more than posit an audience—maybe not even hoping, but just willfully hallucinating them, huddled unseen and mute in the mist around his ankles, dazzled to paralysis by his song, consumed from afar with chaste adoration for him, and only him, as opposed to some prospective new and improved junior version of him that can be parturated, possessed and duly pussy-whipped?

Without having come across this notion in any of his works, and therefore confident, as the World's Foremost Bradley Expert, that he has never published it, I am nevertheless positive, one hundred percent doubt-free, that it constitutes one of the reasons why our author behaves so much like the songbirds with whom he exchanges mutual greetings each morning. Furthermore, I can somehow intuit, just from pondering the expression on his face, grinning or glowering, in those authorial portraits, that he himself is unaware of this reason, except as a persistent, life-informing physical sensation of near-perpetual, intense and almost perfect delight, for which I will envy him till the day I curl up and rot and die.

I tell you that Dr. Bradley has devoted his existence to writing, number one, because it's fun (I mean the big complicated fun that none of us can ever hope to imagine, except during infinitesimally brief and rare moments in nature), and, number two, because he intends for every center of consciousness, everywhere, in all planes and conditions (not just terrestrial female Homo sapiens in breeding prime) to love him, forever, starting as soon as possible, though he's prepared to wait thousands of centuries after he's dead, or even longer if it turns out to be necessary. That's the ambition he cherishes. Talk about an ability to defer gratification.

I may not be able to answer the most basic questions about his quotidian love- and work-life (e.g., is Dr. Bradley married? Is he bisexual? Is he sexual? How does he get food? Does he eat food? Is he aware that the laundromat formerly connected to the stomach cancer hospice at the base of his hill is now open to the public and would love to serve his personal grooming and hygiene needs?); but I've been clear to the bottom of all his books and back several times, and am as sure of these two motivations as I am of my own artistic sterility and terminal uxoriousness.

Then again, I could be mistaken, couldn't I? For all I know, he might not be self-expressing at all, but rather selflessly working off some kind of tribal karmic sludge—though, like most ethnic Europeans, my own spiritual intuitions remain as yet too church-blunted even to hazard a guess as to how his solitary behavior could serve such an esoteric function. The big question, for me in any case, remains unanswered: what in the name of God is he doing here? If his soul be untrammeled as that little warbling birdy's, why doesn't he fly off this mound of semi-soft shit, and put an end to the too-long exile which rankles him so?

(Our occasionally inhuman writer is humanized by his homesickness. I find this muted but constant anguish evoked most affectingly in the Harper Collins/3am Award-winning story, "Even the Dog Won't Touch Me." Sam Edwine and his saintly wife Polly—an exclaustrated nun of the Popish confession who "divorced Christ to join him" in what The Journal of Evolutionary Psychology has called "their glorious and tender hierogamy"—are shown to be the New Adam and the New Eve. Though expelled, they "carry the garden with them," Eden being, in this case, a battered Samsonite that stays perpetually half-packed as the couple takes its solitary way through the Far East Asiatic wilderness.)

Speaking of the East, my fellow shy Bradley fan-boy over there seems to be just as befuddled by all this as I am. He still hasn't waxed any braver, the wussy. Now he's starting to twitch behind his nearby peak. He bounces on one leg while continuing to pinch his dick with increasing urgency. One spastic yellow dribble spills down to sea level, staining the dockside stoops of the storefront language schools and the teenage hand-job hostess bars—as if any amount of UV radiation could disinfect those wallows of corruption. A stronger wavelength, tried and true, is indicated.

Nagasaki Bay heaves into view, out there beyond the cliff-edge Dr. Bradley is now skirting. This deepwater inlet of the East China Sea has always been the back door to

Nippon, through which undesirables have slunk in an uninterrupted string, like mucus supped from a cuspidor. Today it's TEFL trash; yesteryear it was droves of pound cake-pushing Portuguese and Papist proselytizers. We have the latter to thank for the glamorous Twenty-Six Nagasaki Martyrs, townies all, who got spiritually colonized to that grotesque degree guaranteed to earn the veneration of the diseased Romish mentality. Consecrated beings, they self-consciously allowed themselves and their children to be impaled on spears rather than place their feet briefly on a pair of shellacked laths with a diapered manikin thumb-tacked on. In the blood of these slavering masochists, Tom Bradley's adopted town was christened the "Catholic nerve center of Japan." (Guess which other Japanese town called "Boom" serves the same purpose for protestants, just by random coincidence, of course—unless ecumenical Ialdabaoth was in a particularly vicious mood one summer week almost sixty years ago.)

You could trade that whole gaggle of Nagasaki martyrs for one Tom Bradley and be much safer up here. You could throw a regular weenie roast with all twenty-six lightweights mincing and milling about, so particular about where they place their dainty tootsies, traumatizing no tremulous mud membrane. By contrast, consider my ponderous hero. Only a miracle prevents him from bringing this whole edifice down like hairy Samson. Any other pair of human feet would be cracking under the stress of his trot, arches falling, toes curling backwards in ultimate rigors. But he's my road-surfing instructor, my guru in the skill of loosening gravity's shackles, and appears to be functioning under no special stress. He floats along, legs, torso and head registering no reaction to the violent action of his feet. You could say that, from the anklebones down, Dr. Bradley is coming on like the twenty-seventh Nagasaki martyr, the one they never tell you about, who did the Frug, the Watusi, the

Mashed Potato and the Cool Jerk up and down a whole trunk-load of Papist gewgaws, till they had to shove a spear up his ass just to calm him down.

Daylight creeps up from the greasy surface of Nagasaki Bay. It sidles along the docks like a Turkish merchant seaman with unparaphrasable B.O. and offputting mannerisms that you can't quite put a name to. It heads uphill to Japan's second most popular tourist destination. Raised a bit higher than the sloughs of despond I visited in the first section of this essay, overlooking the bay from a terrace covered in cherry trees, world-famous Glover Garden is one fabulously pricey piece of real estate, whose rightful inheritance my author just might not altogether inconceivably have been "butt-fucked out of," as he says, with a modicum of indelicacy, whenever the question comes up in interviews. (Who's the last guy in town you'd ever suspect of being old blood?)

It happens to be the former palatial Raj-style digs of his maternal great-great-great-great-etc. uncle, Tom Glover: none other than the "Scottish Samurai," the gun-running, ecosystem-destroying, sex-slave-disemboweling, emperor-enthroning asshole whom Giacomo Puccini honeyed over in the three-hankie opera, "Madame Butterfly." The natives call him the "Founder of Modern Japan," echoing Der Fuhrer's pronouncement in *Mein Kampf*, volume I, chapter II: "The real foundations of contemporary Japanese life are the achievements of the Aryan peoples—" except Tom Glover, like his present namesake (not to say incarnation) was rubicund carrot-topped Celt, all the way back to the Druids, without a doubt.

If Dr. Bradley is pleased to say something is so, and if the notion yields him some nice transitions between paragraphs, then by all means, so be it. Who's going to check, anyway, besides some pedantic local historian, probably ex-TEFL trash himself, who managed to wangle a neighborhood junior college gig by flattering the locals' self-importance with half-assed "research" into their past? It is, therefore, a solid, indisputable historical fact that a cabal of grasping half-caste rival cousins ganged up and butt-fucked our favorite novelist out of a proper cherry blossom-carpeted veranda from which imperiously to sip the finest green breakfast tea and survey his domains on a bay so rich in familial history.

Unjustly dispossessed though he may be, Dr. Bradley nevertheless subjects himself each morning to the lung-lacerating exhalations of Nagasaki Bay—and I can't quite yet imagine why, as I spend my own morning doing the same. Even from clear up here, it's a smelly toilet, one part dioxin to two parts methyl mercury chloride—thanks to dear old "Unker" Tom, who "singlehandedly industrialized this once gorgeous country, turning it into the toxic wasteland it currently is," according to the scorched-earth essay, "Bloodsucker of Nagasaki" (excerpted from the seventh chapter of the present volume and published in Identity Theory Magazine), written by this dead prick's great-great-great-whatever nephew, which you'd better read if you think pride of propinquity had anything to do with these clashing relatives winding up in the same town.

On the other hand, if you're looking for the answer to my perennial question, i.e., what in God's name is our man doing here?—let's just say it's a bit early for jumping to the conclusion that mere coincidence has drawn both terrible Toms together in space, if not time. Tom the Younger might not make much of a Nagasaki Martyr, but he could be seen as a Nagasaki Penitent. That hypothesis would clear up part of our perplexity. What might have fetched him here is—well, we could call it an intense awareness of the Scottish Samurai's military-industrial exploits, and a certain unhappy identification on Dr. Bradley's part with his voracious ancestor. As so often happens with insurmountable points of shame, this could have been inverted into a matter of pride. If so, I suspect another atom bomb will be needed to knock this Moses off his Horeb. (Pyongyang's working on that.)

Until the next flash of eye-melting light, he will remain here, steadfast, spinning on this turd-colored jello mold, toward whatever expiatory end that may serve—something sort of piously ritualistic, I suppose, like non-orgasmic self-flagellation. Not yet comprehending the exact nature of the atonement our outsized Nagasaki Penitent essays here, we might nevertheless assume, on a provisional basis, the following: that as long as Japan's dwindling economic and deoxyribonucleic momentum continues to falter on, he won't forsake his self-appointed post, not until every trace of his Unker's hard work and discipline and self-motivation and entrepreneurial industriousness and venturesomely capitalistic go-getterism has fallen to pieces; not until Dr. Bradley's religio-magical spinning has somehow sent the Kirin Chemical Beer Works, the mines, the railways, the slip-docks, Mitsubishi Heavy Industries, and Glover Garden itself, all straight to the murky bottom of the bay. And, considering the headlong speed at which Nipponese "civilization" is declining, these and other submersions will certainly happen, with or without the aid of religion or magic, well within the stingiest actuarial estimate of what's left of Tom Bradley's life, including years deducted for obesity and excessive height (although he should get at least two decades' worth of points for cardiovascular fitness).

And, in that halcyon time to come, "...this muggy waste, un-Glovered at last, will revert to the fishing village it was before my tribal curse descended: a place where the natives can once again develop personalities (will they be able to remember how?); where they can get out the old martyr-impaling spears and have a weenie roast, TEFL trash as the main course, and just forget about forcing themselves to pretend to encompass the impossible task of learning my beautiful language (masticating it to ugly shit in the effort); where they can have time and leisure and silence to play with their children, and chat with them in their own inchoate but, I suppose, adequate idiom; and make more children, at least to the extent their exhausted bloodlines permit; and sleep eight hours a day, and work no more than that, with a two-day weekend at least; and stop their screaming and their crass imitation American-style boosterism and huckstering—" (the latter so poignantly depicted in the essay, "The Nagasaki Literary Scene," now on offer for syndication at Featurewell.com; second electronic and all other rights available—editors act now) "—and heal the hole inside them."

Then, and only then, our man's amends will be made, hereditary debt worked off, and Tom Bradley can die, alone, spent, in peace, in the dark, draped over tricky bars, etc., etc., okay, fine, I got it. Apocalyptic this and Sacrificial Lamb that.

As a second, less obvious, not to say mawkish, alternative—since we're talking ex-cathedra anyway—we also might classify his morning constitutional among the Works of Mercy, though not strictly "corporeal" in the catechistic sense. To clarify this proposition, let's consult the man himself—I mean his words, spoken live. Let's squat awhile longer among the tricky bars and listen to what he gasps and rants as he jogs.

For posterity's sake, he happens to hold, in a hand huge, glowing and white as any pagan's chryselephantine hallucination, a Sony micro-cassette tape recorder, which he employs to play himself back every few phrases. One is reminded of Frau Forster's older brother, filling a notebook with aphorisms and constant emendations thereof, while wandering along the brisk Alpine foothills. But our philosopher has reached his summit, and is doing a liturgical dance, having changed the linear hiker's notebook for a whirling mechanism on which to spool and unspool mantras received and given. Here is a prayer wheel far trimmer and more serviceable than the Nepalese-style clunker, about the size of a carny thrill-ride, being swished about by Miss Queerbait Tangerine-Flake Buddha next door. When its reverse button is pushed, Dr. Bradley's compact appliance makes the sounds of words inhaled and taken back, difficult to distinguish from the circularly breathed chirps and tweets of Sakyamuni's feathery booger across the gorge.

I can eavesdrop most effectively on what he replays when he's tracing my particular arc of the grand cycle on his gigantic all-weather radial tire-soled sandals, retreads sloughed in arcs from still other wheels, satellites within orbits in various states of decay. Here are the first, and almost the last, words I have ever heard my interview subject say (he sounds even more like Orson Welles in the flesh than on RealPlayer):

"The dragon's mustache mirrors mine. A commissioned portrait of the one I inherited, it originally occupied the upper lip of my blood Unker, my spitting image, the Bloodsucker, who founded, along with countless other dark satanic mills on the brim of our bay, the so-called brewery that excretes the piss that fills the cans upon which the golden-mustachioed dragon struts, less avatar than advert.

"One mark of his death-dodging pride is this transplantation of his facial hair onto the flying snake's muzzle, thus claiming and bruiting abroad for himself the status of adept, or magus—he put the Naga in -saki. This is not implausible if we assume he took the left path. Look around you. His prideful works were more than human, yet less than a generation after their completion from the ground up, they were cast down, with the requisite confounding of tongues—hence the TEFL trash infestation. His stomping grounds were consumed in flames of retributive Nemesis.

"All the political damage he did, more than 10,000 normal men's worth, did not satisfy him. It wasn't enough that he riled up the pithecoid samurai; not sufficient that he put the nibbling Mongoose Family on the throne, resulting in all of Greater East Asia being flooded in blood. I'm sure he found wreaking mischief among these easy marks about as challenging as shaking insects in a Mason jar to see if they'll fight. But I notice he didn't feel quite up to attempting such incitement among vigorous occidental tribes and nations. Then again, on a literary level, neither does his nephew, the habitual East Asian expatriate, who, likewise unable to make his mark in the real world, hides out on the wrong side of the International Date Line, instead of engaging his own civilization head-on..."

(Tom Bradley's fans, demurring at such self-effacement, disarming though it may be, will point out that the first two mighty volumes of *The Sam Edwine Pentateuch* are set squarely nowhere else than America, and have engaged some of the best heads of that civilization. No less a personage than Stanley Elkin found *Acting Alone* to have "an incredible energy level," and R.V. Cassill said, "The contemporaries of Michelangelo found it useful to employ the term 'terribilita' to characterize some of the expressions of his genius, and I will quote it here to sum up the shocking impact of this work as a whole. I read it in a state of fascination, admiration, awe, anxiety, and outrage." Stephen Goodwin opined that he'd be "be hard pressed to think of any writer who has Bradley's stamina, his range, his learning, his felicity," and the great Gordon Weaver spoke of the "flawless surface of [Tom Bradley's] stylistic facility," and his "ability to walk the edge of a tone that is simultaneously irreverent and profoundly serious." It's clear that Bradley's tower reaches at least as high as Glover's. But its staircase spirals in the opposite direction, and will bring down no heavenly wrath and destruction. Quite the reverse. As for confounding of tongues, the books themselves lay any such linguistic anxiety to rest.)

The good doctor continues:

"Like sorcerer-Pope Sixtus V recapitulating himself with pathological rapidity as the fearsome Ahkoond of Swat, sidestepping what should have been six or seven thousand years in the devachanic antechamber, my vampire Unker jumped the normal metensomatotic rails to have another crack at what he calls life, but what I call festering. He required a second gross container for his gluttonous spirit, but couldn't fasten his soul-fangs on a lineal descendant. His only son, also Tom (Madame Butterfly's unsuccessfully aborted and ill-reared bastard), strangled the family dogs and hanged his septuagenarian self just because an atom bomb was dropped on him, the pussy. A good illustration of the ill-advisability of miscegenation with the exhausted races, and—"

Its reverse button pushed by what I can only imagine to be a forearm-sized thumb, the Sony micro-cassette recorder makes a peremptory chirp—

"Don't say 'miscegenation,' you moron. And 'pussy'? Have you completely given up on ever getting back to America? Shit. Where was I? Oh yeah—

"Tom Glover craves to take further and bigger bites out of this lugubrious landscape. But a big enough bite was taken thirty-four years after his first death. That's my opinion, and I deserve to be consulted—"

Our author suddenly switches his battery-operated mechanism to the other hand, clenches it tighter against his mustache and, in a whisper never intended for my profane ears, says, "After all, it's my carcass up for grabs."

At least that's what I think he said. Before he can hear me cry, "Huh? What—?" our fallen local aristocrat swings around again on the occult circle which he has woven thrice into the volcanic mush underfoot, and passes me by a third time—and you know how any times it must happen in fairy tales and dirty jokes. He makes more revelations into the Sony's microphone—

"It was Old Man Glover's death, and he duly died it, and he's trying to cheat it through me. But he has made a fatal mistake: he chose a body half-compounded of unmitigated Bradley, Jack Mormon renegade-style, whose nature is to cooperate with nobody and nothing. If the Glovemeister was half as clever as the Nipponese make him out to be, he'd have lit upon a less congenitally perverse set of inlaws. We Bradleys told the bloody desert dictator Brigham Young to get fucked, right up in his face. Did Unker Tom think I'd hesitate to tell him the same in deference to my mom's maiden name? It's good for opening bank accounts, but that doesn't make it the password to my temple of the Holy Spirit."

(If I, Cye Johan, were the type of scribbling academic hack to insert footnotes, I might grab this opportune moment to distract you, and me, from the frankly distressing glimpse we've just gotten into our author's, shall we say, state of mind. I would provide a little solid, non-metaphysical historical background here, just to assure us of our footing, if not his. I'd take us back to the dry, ghost-free, wide-open spaces of the Far West, and point out that Dr. Bradley's agnatic line paid the full price, plus tax, for telling Brigham Young to "get fucked, right up in his face." I'd refer you to the masterful autobiographical essay, "Suspensions of Disbelief," yet another example of our man's death-dealing nonfiction to be highlighted in Arts & Letters Daily. Its arguments organized in paragraphs crystalline and inevitable as Eighteenth-Century counterpoint, this essay, like all his others, would stand up as evidence of our author's sanity in any court of law. So much for forensic psychology.

(For more on his paternal ancestors' courageous flippancy toward the Mormon cult, see, passim, the aforementioned Genesis of our Pentateuch, *Killing Bryce*, which, according to the promo copy, "shows the disintegration of a family of Jack Mormons who get scattered across two continents like bits of rock salt sprayed from the muzzle of a shotgun." No fewer than seven well-shaped novels intertwine in this 300,000-word epic, bouncing off one another, each told from inside a different character's mind, seven centers of consciousness generating their own idioms and idiosyncratic styles, prompting rumors of seven distinct corporeal authors having passed the manuscript to and fro—or, indeed, gossip about a certain benign schizophrenia on the author's part.

(Based on personal experience, of this very morning in fact, I subscribe to the latter suspicion, with reservations regarding the qualifier. And can you blame me? I mean, this big crazy fuck thinks a dead Scotchman is crawling around inside him—and judging from his dimensions, I'd say there's room for at least six more. I should have stayed home—Osaka, in my hideous TEFL-trash case—and just done a normal book review, full of nice, easy sentences like this: "For all its bulk and problematical etiology, *Killing Bryce*'s greatest virtue is its tight structure. There are few technical feats in fiction that come anywhere near. By comparison, *War and Peace* deserves Henry James' dismissive epithet, 'primitive.'" Back to text.)

Dr. Bradley is saying, "...and not only do I defy the mustachioed dragon, but I am allowing, no, teasing, inviting and encouraging the avuncular eidolon to pursue me, till it gets exhausted and stumbles off the track that I have stomped so deliberately close to this raggedy rim, and falls off the cliff to join the swinish legions at the bottom of the bay he poisoned. I'm determined to have been neither driven nor lured here to continue Tom Glover's career of insatiable rapacity. Rather than be the beneficiary of astral nepotism, I choose to occupy his place on my own terms..."

The voice now swells to even greater than normal Orson

Wellesian stentoriousness, frightening the ravens overhead—

"For I am the Human Exhaust Fan, the Great Whirling Air Exchange System of Boom Town II."

(Well, that's one way to encourage yourself to do your aerobics every day. His resting pulse rate's probably the same as his age: extremely low fifties. A tree's going to have to fall on this guy and stun him first, then Pyongyang can have a crack at him. Or maybe the "exhaust fan" is just another of the fart jokes with which he's inordinately fond of puffing up his widely anthologized "flash fiction"—a form whose extreme concision isn't normally associated with puffing or padding. But such is the ludic virtuosity of the master: he can conjure a universe in twenty-five words, and fritter away the remaining seventy-five teasing us like a feather up a nostril. I'm sure that's what this Uncle Soul-Vampire business is about. He's just tickling me, waiting for me to sneeze and reveal my peeking presence, so he can roar, "Gotcha!" and make me shit my pants. Big laffs.)

Tom Bradley has taken possession of this aerie, a natural fortress commanding coastal access to a downtown no less mountainous than its suburbs. From up here he enjoys an air traffic controller's-eye-view of the inlets and outlets carved by immemorial lava among the maze of volcanic hills upon which Boom Town II is built. (History's stupider choice for a nuclear strike, Nagasaki makes Rome look like Topeka.) He is in a position to help unravel these tousled braids of topography on behalf of whomever or whatever might be wandering down there in a state of disorientation.

As if in commemoration of the morning when they broiled under a much brighter sun, the snaking inner-city gorges still, in certain slants of dawn's early light, seem to flow with gamma particles and molten humans in their myriads. It's said that sudden murder of particular violence and treachery can knock astral monads off the Circle of Necessity's treadmill, resulting in unquiet dead, doomed for a certain term to walk the night, and so forth. In this case, the certain term has lasted nearly sixty years. The poor Nagasaki-jin, like their brethren the Hiroshimites before them, were sucker-punched, black-jacked, cudgeled on the noggin harder than anybody since the sage Aurva gave the fire missile to King Sagara in the *Vishnu Purana*. Their hard-won coats of matter annihilated instantaneously, stripped and disorganized so suddenly, the atomic dead got lost in the labyrinth. For about three human generations, these pulverized pilgrims have been buffeted around the gutters and alleyways, not even allowed to linger on pools that stand in drains, unable to curl once, nor yet so much as halfway, around their houses to sleep, as the latter are no less vaporous than they. With the post-war proliferation of motor vehicles, they're sucked without stint into the radiators and shat out the exhaust manifolds of numberless speeding Mazdas and Toyotas, often pureed through several internal combustion systems in rapid succession, so suicidal are the tailgating tendencies of their postmodern townsmen. They've been smutched and rendered insensate by constant adulteration with unburnt diesel fuel and other airborne hydrocarbon solids.

Tape machine chirping, our author skirts the bit of rim, opposite the bay, that overlooks Ground Zero, nestled snugly between a reductive Palatine and a bathetic Esquiline. Right about now, during the hours just before, during and after dawn, the road traffic down there is sparse as it gets in this insomniac land, and a cleansing geothermal mist begins briefly to gather and rise. The air isn't quite so thickly streaked with static electric-blue bolts of frantic, hopeless nervous energy generated by a post-war citizenry exhausted as Mexicans, but not allowed to relax and snooze away their last few gasps as a race. At this time of day, Dr. Bradley's golden hours, the nuked souls come the closest they ever get to being alive, in the sense of possessing some rudimentary approximation of will, and at least a hint of self-locomotive power, like amoebas in a dilute acid bath with only two thirds of their flagella rendered immotile. They're susceptible to being summoned, or seduced in certain depraved cases. Swirling and shrieking like tiny songbirds with their pinfeathers singed off, they're more likely to hear and respond to Dr. Bradley's voice on the micro-tape, his words played backwards, which is inhalation. The recorder, held near his face, chirps and beckons the semi-senseless beings up the hill to the neighborhood of his nostrils, like a muezzin luring the faithful to the twin portals of the sanctuary of his respiratory system and the microcosm it constitutes.

The doctor snorts astral monads. He aspirates them in their singularity, as uncompounded atoms. And at some point during the process of metabolic gas exchange that takes place in our genius' serviceable alveoli, they can latch onto waste molecules of carbon dioxide excreted from his own mortal coil.

Each night and morning, as far as I am able to gather, he goes round and round, rescuing defunct Nips in this heterodox manner. Just as I briefly intuited a bit earlier in this essay, he does indeed seem to be "working off some kind of tribal karmic sludge"—that portion left behind by Unker Tom, who's responsible for bringing down the greatest disservice yet done to any other town but one in the post-Mahabharatic age: he founded Mitsubishi Heavy Industries, the target of America's famous Big Boy.

The doctor allows his Unker's victims a period of devachanic rest, immeasurably long from their point of view, but only lasting a half-lap on this track, as manifested on our phenomenological plane. The particulate wretches are blessed with an apparent sempiternity inside Tom Bradley to compose themselves, to gather up as much useful consciousness as possible, along with whatever matter he can spare them, with which to seed their new embodiments. I fear he's allowing his infinitesimal nurslings to erode the delicate lining of his bronchial tubes. Physicians, who tend to be rationalists even in Japan these latter days, would say our jogger guarantees himself a world-class case of emphysema by stubbornly insisting on doing his morning workout not in a civic gymnasium with a proper air-filtration system, but outdoors, where there's pollution—thanks, again, to the Glovemeister. But amends are being made, as the victims are coddled, recruited, not to say transmogrified (just yet), by way of an occult ritual to which I am not privy, prayer wheel whirled, charms mumbled.

Bizarre conditions call for freakish measures; a man of normal dimensions couldn't do this chore. Poison Tom Glover supplied his own antidote in his enormous Celtic genes, which his distantly descended nephew has inherited and supplemented with equine Anglo-Saxon Bradleyness, and religious observation of this cardiovascular regimen, exhibiting self-discipline uncharacteristic of a scion of fallen aristocracy, which would tend to support his vocation's genuineness.

He expels the hopeful, naked little beings on a jet-blast as cyclonic as his triple-sized lungs and trampoline-taut diaphragm can blow. He launches them on sturdy vehicles of carbon dioxide as far out into Nagasaki Bay as he superhumanly can, to give them a boost, over and beyond the lethal Styx of the avuncular docks and out into the open sea, where they might come to rest and start fresh among the corals and jellyfish and polyps.

I almost rise up from my tricky bars in protest against this sudden dip into debased exoteric superstition (there is no phylic regression in proper esoteric Buddhism)—"But," says Dr. Bradley, as though he wants me to stay put for the time being, "look whose shadow I'm working in." He gestures to saggy Sakyamuni, as if his Sony micro-cassette recorder had an eye as well as an ear and a larynx, and all three were hooked up to various orifices in my head.

It's only the Nagasaki-jin incinerated during that vast epoch which transpired within the second minute after the eleventh hour of the morning of August ninth, 1945, that concern him: somewhere between thirty-nine and seventy-five thousand of them, depending on which of several estimates you buy. Dr. Edwine has chosen to err on the side of generosity, and has pledged himself to service the full load. He accepts no responsibility for casualties after the fact, collateral damage, so to speak, such as his own dog-strangling cousin Tom (a favorite Christian name in this clan). Radiation sickness, liver cancer, the suicidal despair of the vanquished, etc., allow you ample time to pack and get tickets, and if you wind up an astral vagabond, it's your own god-damned fault.

As for those immediate blast victims too solidly mired in desire when alive, therefore incapable, in death, of riding on gaseous wings across the bay with their former fellow townsmen—gentry such as Nagasaki's wartime military bureaucrats, Nanking rapists on R and R, methamphetamine-maddened twelve-year-old kamikaze trainees bivouacked at the local airstrip, and General Tojo's Thought Police, who were kicking down paper doors and burning books right up to the moment of detonation; not to mention the various sundry civilian undesirables whom you'll find living and dying under a glutinous layer of demerit in all places and times: small businessmen, thugs, monastics, naughty toddlers, physicians of most specialties, people associated in any way with those sewers of lowbrow invidiousness called junior colleges, neighborhood gossips, mediocre artists, smokers, masturbators, malcontent rickshaw boys, just to name a few—these are the ones whose spirits, due to extra layers of ethical avoirdupois, are too coarse for aspiration and osmosis. They get stuck in Tom Bradley's sinus passages.

It depends on how misanthropic you are, or pretend to be, what percentage of the 39-75,000 holocaustees you're ready to envision lodged among his nostril hairs and upper mucous membranes. They, and not Utah cloddishness, are the reason why Dr. Bradley is constantly snorting back letting fly. Lukewarm, they are spewed out as loogs and lungers.

No sooner do these moral inferiors with their weighty load of sin splat on the ground than, in a puff of steam, they rise to possess the bodies of low, loathsome and noxious life forms, like mongooses and bosozokus. They proceed to waste an incarnation terrorizing the suburbanites and staid burghers with their night cries. And that explains the noises which made me so nervous on the way up here. It was these discombobulated fuckers who finally got fitted with coats of skin to replace those melted off their skeletons by "Harry Truman's gift of Hell"—to borrow a phrase from our author's profoundly moving contribution to the otherwise cutesy-pootsy McSweeney's Journal.

But even teen bikers' obnoxiousness is not without limits. Eventually (never soon enough to suit most sentient beings in the neighborhood), they grow tired of buzzing the stomach cancer hospice in the wee hours. In deep disgust with themselves, they begin to yearn for annihilation. This is more like the bottom of an endocrine cycle than a moral insight. They end, according to procedure established by New Testament precedent, skittering down to dissolve and rid themselves in the noxious Kama Loka called scenic Nagasaki Bay, overlooked by lovely Glover Garden. No wonder the derriere garde of what I took for bozo stragglers looked imperfectly materialized. Their name is legion, like the two thousand swine in the synoptic gospels, which ran violently down a steep place and were "choked in the sea" (not drowned, but choked: the Gloverian water is so foul there's no time for a proper drowning before the throat revolts unto death with brainstem-ripping seizures and gags).

Has Tom Bradley gone insane, or is he just working on a new novel? I suppose the two alternatives are not mutually exclusive. He's the unchainable lunatic who cries at night and cuts himself with stones among the tombs. He is exorcising Boom Town II, of course, but himself as well. Someday soon a skittering snarl at the bay's greasy brink will be heard to have a definite Scotch brogue to it. It will be followed by a particularly furious gagging and choking, and an ample splash, as of a morbidly obese and splenetic quadruped, and my author will no longer be so noticeably insane.

In the meantime, Tom Bradley, who might appear upon superficial reading to be a misanthropic, sarcastic, mean old fuck, turns out to be pure and self-sacrificing. He's worked out a way to do his Bodhisattvic bit without getting too personally involved and taking on the nurture of fully embodied disciples, which, if his reputation as a teacher has any foundation in fact, would be anathema to his very DNA—and don't think for a moment this renders my current suppliant position any less untenable than it already is. (See his Salon.com articles on the vexed question of pedagogy, "Turning Japanese" and "Bathtub Revolutionary," both published in the days before that magazine's contemptible degeneration.)

But why would he break precedent and use Rikki Tikkis and teen bikers as disposal agents instead of pigs, as Our Lord did in the country of the Gadarenes? I suspect it's in fond consideration of the wild boar-meat restaurant downtown whose kitchen he's been known to shut down singlehandedly after a series of especially taxing, peckish-making jogs up here, when he needs to take on extra protein to reline the double matrix inside his ribcage. Embosomed with the portly man's womanish dugs, he's like that ambiguous entity who "...over the bent World broods with warm breast and with ah! bright wings." He's feeling broody over what's incubating in the dark, damp womb of his loving lungs.

(Note to my American readers: if you want to find out how you, too, can learn to manage those guilt feelings associated with the atomic devastation of the Land of Zen and sukiyaki and Pokey Mon and small-boned, sexually promiscuous young women with baby-mouse voices, now's the time to consume the good doctor's nthposition essay, "My Public Ministry Among the Heathen," also featured Arts & Letters Daily, which blogs the absolute cream of the intellectual web, Monday through Saturday.)

And he rants something frightening which I have been told never to repeat as long as I live, especially if I want to live a long time. While embarrassed to admit the warning came via dream, I'm nevertheless skeptical, or maybe self-destructive, enough to throw you a hint. It's about another invisible fluttering intelligence of a different sort altogether, the kind you'd never want anywhere near your lungs under the best of circumstances. Not formerly human at all, it's to be counted among the sprites which were here first, hovering over the sea foam before Nippon itself coagulated from a few blobs of tectonic lava—or so, at least, an uncharacteristic and unaccountable burst of intuition leads me to extrapolate from what I hear being magnetized onto Dr. Bradley's micro-tape.

Philo the Jew must have been right: the air is indeed full of spirits. There seems to be a scarcely imaginable number of varieties and ranks and orders—undines, sylphs, gnomes, you name it. The unseen universe resembles nothing so much as one of those promotional scuba diving videos which the Hashemite Kingdom of Jordan's Tourism Ministry shoots at the Gulf of Aqaba. Dr. Bradley rants about one particular species, which are intelligent as trained sea mammals, or pretty nearly, and are eager to run errands and perform chores for any powerful human personality, as humanity is the condition that they, like no small number of the so-called angels and gods themselves, aspire to.

Our novelist appears to believe that, through the agency of one of these inhalable phocidae, he has bestowed a whopping dose of terminal lung cancer on some unhappy local slob. He excoriates, or maybe congratulates, himself for having sent an especially plump and ravenous specimen to lodge and fasten like a coal miner or bull crab in the unnamed victim's bronchia and set about the task, apparently spiritual, but by no means intellectually taxing, of chomping down normal epithelial cells and shitting out malignant ones. In most cases no such effect could be achieved by any other means than the sort of left-handed black occultism that would be karmically fatal to anyone who employed it on purpose. But Dr. Bradley assures himself (along with any unseen listeners) that his role in this slow, smelly murder resembles an air traffic controller's more than a sorcerer's. The demon has been summoned in blameless unconsciousness on our man's part. He offers his own strictly maintained ignorance of formal conjury as proof of his innocence.

To claim the ability of analyzing in detail one's own unconscious mind's machinations without the benefit of several pricey decades on a trained alienist's couch would be paradoxical, not to say self-deceptive, in anyone but a major novelist. The latter rare category of human possesses that overdeveloped sense of self-objectivity which makes such an operation possible. Nobody else's head is so detachable from his heart. In this way the Dostoevskis, Nabokovs and Bradleys of this world enjoy a position of great privilege: they're capable of crime without culpability.

He provides neither name nor demographics for whoever's being murdered from the inside out in such a remote and unactionable manner, and I can't imagine who it would be. The only sort of person who inspires that kind of hate, at least in my experience, is a boss. But who could be the boss of this man? I pity anyone with the temerity to set himself up as such. A tumor would be the easiest way out of that predicament. I quake to consider what politicians, hypocrites, ignoramuses and Latter-Day Saints have suffered in his essays and books—and nearly die, myself, when I try to imagine all that fury focused on a single human lung. The age-old mystery of spontaneous human combustion might just have been solved.

In spite of the blasphemous, not to say homicidal and psychotic, tenor of what's erupting from this behemoth stranger's mouth, I am very nearly persuaded at this moment to climb down from my tricky bars and register my presence, come what may. I'm motivated less by the desire to preserve this problematic personality for posterity in an unpublishable interview than by certain hissings and gnawing sounds that have started up in the wild poinsettias behind me. The hellions are saying offputting things in their broad bestial vocabulary.

I still don't know if he's seen me or not. I hope not, because it would place a strong negative construction on his next action, which is to hawk up a stringy, glossy, eggnog-colored loogy and aim it right for my left eye. I duck, hear a plop in the poinsettias, followed by a sizzle and hiss, as of a small release of steam, then a rustle, then—

"Rik-tikk-tikki-tikki-tchk..."

The horror skitters up my spine: that awful sensation we sometimes feel when truffle-tusks are rooting between our buttocks for kundalini esculents. I grab my ass and, whooping like a goose, scamper out into the path of the bus. I freeze in the headlights glaring from the top of his face. The first twelve-

and-a-third of the thirty-three words, total, that I, Cye Johan, interviewer, authorial profiler, literary stalker-groupie, will ever, for as long as I live, speak to my idol are as follows:

"Denis and Tran featured my review of *The Curved Jewels* in Arts and Letters D—"

He grabs me. Can you imagine how childish it makes you feel to be looking into a face big as your whole head plus your neck and torso all the way down to the belly button and back again? It's like being shot back to early elementary school days and collared by Dad, who's about to kick the damnation out of you, just on general principles.

He drags me to the cliff edge, terrifying this simple scribbler not so much with the prospect of being flung off (nor of loosening the wild banana rot underfoot and bringing down, under our combined weight—three-fourths of which is easily his—this whole side of the jello mold called Horeb East), as by the not-so-quasi-homoerotic surrender that the touch of his hand on my elbow elicits. Honestly, I had no idea his work had affected me in such a deep way.

He gives me a look unaccompanied by words, but explicit as if he'd shouted straight into the side of my head, "How much of that did you hear?"

Instead of replying to the question, all I can think of to do with my mouth is to ask another—the very one, in fact, that the natives put to me every day of my own expatriated life, to which my reply must always be a sheepish affirmative. Under the present circumstances, it's the stupidest question of all history, whose answer, an emphatic negative, will already be known by anyone even briefly exposed to the slightest breath of this man's reputation (and that's a considerable number: of the approximately one million items his name googles, without quotation marks, Tom Bradley the novelist is always the first two, and usually the third and fourth, before Tom Bradley the Mayor, Tom Bradley the baseball player, Tom Bradley the International Terminal, Tom Bradley the Civic Center, Tom Bradley the dead Negro sharecropper's son, Tom Bradley the Kiwi kiddy book writer, et al. Add any literary term or obscenity and he's got the first two or three whole pages covered).

In the face of such utter distinguishedness, I hear myself simper, through a rickshaw boy's buck teeth, gutturalizing around an Adam's apple protuberant as the prow on a mackerel boat, "A-a-a-ah, so, Bladderly-san, you speakie za Chappy-knees, yes-no?"

His reply, delivered without pause or consideration, sounds recited by rote and is addressed more to himself than any mere intruder whose full material existence he hasn't bothered to ascertain (indeed, he looks through me, like Prospero through Ariel, as though idly entertaining the possibility that I'm one of his carcinogenic sprites reporting for duty):

"I mouth a half-dozen phonemes," he says, "but couldn't tell you how they build a sentence. I've heard rumors that they tend to postpone the predicate, as our Teutonic brethren do."

Those two sentences comprise the totality of what this century's Dr. Johnson has ever said to his Boswell. The only words he has enunciated when conscious of being in my earshot are layered into a perfectly balanced brace of gemlike periods, both rounded and complete. Have they been pre-crafted and rehearsed? For the benefit of what audience? Or do major novelists think and speak extempore in these polished terms? Can I claim them as my exclusive acquisitions?

Here, in any case, is the sole exile I've met on these islands who can say more than three of his native words in a row without dropping in a Japism—including, I am humiliated to admit, me.

I've long suspected my racial, national and tribal identity of being more or less shorn; but now my eyes are opened to my true deracinated condition as never before, just by sustaining a single absentminded glance from this banished Utahn. He has not trodden New World soil for nearly a quarter of a century, and probably never will again in this particular existence, yet remains more American than I could be if I went straight back home tomorrow and started eating dirt with both fists. I feel diminished and darkened, and made to squint. I'm a full-blooded Asiatic by comparison. Damned here for barely two years so far, I've already allowed much more of the locality to seep into my skull and infect my soul than has Tom Bradley, destined to be cremated here.

Now would be the time, not to excuse, but perhaps to attempt to explain poor little Cye Johan's presence in this miserable country. Yes, here's the opportunity to expose this scribbler and finally disburden his load of shame onto your lap: his domesticated pet barbarian condition, his status as collaborator and traitor in this particular fizzled-out culture war. Little Cye's got himself a full-time job as token Caucasoid in an Osaka junior college, complete with automatic tenure, thanks to his mastery of Yamato groveling techniques. He's been shrugging and bowing and cringing so long that his spine has sunken into itself, his body become short. At an animalistic level, he loathes himself because more than one of his native students have managed to outstrip him vertically—and they lord their superior centimeters over him with about as much mercy as you'd expect from the descendants of the folks whom China scorned as "island dwarves" for forty centuries: "...the climax of two generations of adequate nutrition under American auspices," to quote little Cye's favorite NBA-sized author, "these kids are about, finally, to achieve their full genetic potential." Cye is here to witness and meekly applaud, from below, the physiological fulfillment of the race, which comes, ironically, on the eve of its self-extinction.

While waiting for that to happen, Cye-baby has married a Jappess because, as that big, tall, fictional racist bully, Sam Edwine, would cruelly say, he can't handle fully-developed women. Maybe Cye's just a faggot who got scared away from civilization by AIDS and hightailed it to a place where, with no manly charms, skills, or even impulses, he can have his pick of any number of non-male (hence more likely to be HIV-free) fuck-buddies, unencumbered with breasts, hips, body hair, or personalities, who, bent over and viewed from behind, cannot be distinguished from pliant boys. And his catamite wife, his butt-boy spouse, comes equipped with J-kids, and a J-house financed with low-interest J-loan (throw in a lengthy barrage of pure bourgeois J-money talk here, that couldn't contrast more sickeningly with everything noble and Bradleyan above and below). Cye's got J-legal residency, which brings the promise of a comfy J-pension and, when the time comes, a J-death, with J spilling out his ears and J oozing from his pores in the form of more cringing body language. Even his final throes will be sheepish and apologetic: watch my big white outlander's nose turn strangely blue as I gasp my last.

It's easy to see why, immediately after allowing me my precious lifetime budget of exactly thirty Bradley words, our author dismisses the ludicrous likes of me from his awareness. He continues his stomp as though just the two of us have never privately shared an awakening peak, among the world's very first on this particular day in literary history. It is clear that I've ceased to enjoy even the attenuated existence I had while his attention was semi-fixed on me. Now I might as well never have been born, except to write this whatever-it's-going-to-be. I'm left with nothing but boundless vacant space, that vacuum wake which vast people leave behind them. When someone of this significance turns his back on you, Limbo gapes. In despair, I run after Sam (make that Tom) like a baby boy dogging big Daddy on legs of inferior length, trying to buck himself up and choke out further syllables of baby-talk.

Without bothering to turn around, the doctor waves that orange-shaggy arm across the cliff and down the slope, toward his Unker's toilet bay. He's too—what shall I call it, kind?—to say it outright; but I get the drift. I had no more business climbing up here than the callow youth in *Zanoni* had poking his nose into Mejnour's forbidden chamber (almost fatally—his soul was nearly eaten alive), where he saw—

"...shapes, somewhat resembling in outline those of the human form, gliding slowly and with regular revolutions through the cloud. They appeared bloodless; their bodies were transparent, and contracted or expanded like the folds of a serpent..."

Like Clarence Glyndon, I don't belong on the high places. So Tom Bradley, the serpent's nephew, ambiguously throws or magicks me back down to my proper milieu.

* * * *

I found myself in a strange condition, mostly blind, feeling two-thirds drunk, though not necessarily with alcohol or any other compound in the repertoire of modern chemists. It wasn't easy to know where I was. Besides the green vinyl stool wedged between my hams, what clued me that I'd been deposited in some kind of tavern was this drinking song, rendered by various coarse and vulgar falsettos, squawking more or less to the tune of Mary Wells' 1964 Motown smash-hit, "My Guy":

I'll cling to my guy like shit to a blanket.
If he proffers up his prong, I will briskly wank it...

Though my eyes couldn't yet quite make out the vocalizers,

there was something familiar about their senseless intonations, every line ending with a question mark, no vowels but schwas. Most of them were not really pledging fealty to my guy, or anyone else's, but were just mumbling and following along without comprehension, having gotten the words phonetically, because their intellects were ill-equipped to negotiate grammatical constructions at the level of sophistication favored by the major Motown lyricists of yesteryear.

It was comforting to know that I'd not been precipitated to some even more emphatically nether realm, such as the methyl mercury hell of Nagasaki Bay, but had landed in familiar territory—Home Sweet Home, in fact. Father knows best. He had expelled me back to the hand-job hostess bar by the seawall, where I could swill and grunt with my peers, and share the meager contents of my undersized skull in simple declarative monosyllables tempered with lots of vocalized pauses. Dr. Bradley was making a statement: "These TEFL trash, and not the natives you daily fellate, are your folk."

Leading the chorus was someone familiar-sounding: none other than the storefront language school manager, our ever-coughing Englishman, who seemed still to be in the middle of the same parasitic lap dance which I've depicted him receiving in the very first section of this succinct book review of mine. His face remained concealed behind that slip of Manila flesh both darling and decrepit, belonging, at least rightfully, to the tiny prepubescent Filipina sex-slave, who had her own racial demerit to work off. It would have been better for the sad child if she'd squatted, instead, on Ground Zero fifty-eight years ago. At least now she'd have the attention of a heavy breather who could do her some spiritual good.

This manuscript was being passed from hand to semi-literate hand without my having given anyone permission to see the thing—which, furthermore, Coleridge- and Burroughswise, I had no recollection of writing in the first place.

"What kind of author profile is this?" I heard the Limey bark. "Give us his daily behavior, the details of his wage-earning life, if any. Quotidian panem, that sort of thing. You haven't shown him eating or drinking something—we like that, don't we, boys?"

"Um, yeah, you bet, boss?"

"For, like, sure, Nigel?"

"What kind of journalist is this Cye Johan?" coughed the boss (I should have known his name would be Nigel). "Too good for reality?" Then he bothered to glance at me long enough to ascertain that I was among the so-called living, and added, into my face, "You might do us the favor of mentioning, for example, certain well-known bits of common knowledge. Such as, did you know, this bloke lives in a bleeding car?" When I failed to react, Nigel decided to feign the sort of breathless, titillated confidentiality which constitutes the main contribution of his countrymen to America's current journalistic scene. He shifted to one of those stage whispers that give you tinnitis at fifty paces, and said, "Not only that, my dear, but he—"

As my eyes and head slowly cleared, I listened to him go on and on, hacking up blackish lungers the while, which the Filipina dabbed away with a wet cocktail napkin and a strange air of smug satisfaction. He enumerated the kind of snickering and no doubt true things which I did not want, and you won't be able, to hear. Maybe it's just the air of authority which a Brit accent, any Brit accent, lends to the spoken word—but my heart began with sore reluctance to acknowledge these lurid weaknesses in my ideal man of letters. I saw streaks of more than human frailty in him, such as a certain obsessive-compulsive morbidity which should have been obvious at the time, but was by no means evident to my starry eyes on the mountain, where Dr. Bradley was in his demigodly mode. Soon enough, on my green vinyl barstool, under Nigel's barrage, I began to blush, to think that suggestible Cye had almost allowed himself to be convinced that damned souls could be recycled, if not redeemed, through someone's respiratory system.

Between bringing up hefty clumps of Southampton alveoli, Nigel said, "You silly bitch." For good measure, he added, with the kind of offhanded but utter scorn that can be registered only by people who've been living smashed together, nuts to butts, for thousands of years, "What a ridiculous idea. Snorting astral monads, indeed. Not even the sky-clad Jains imagine that."

He gave his lap-slave a kind of eyebrow-cock, as a cue that she was to laugh derisively. Though on duty, she disobeyed, and chose instead to stare at me carefully as possible through the smoke and the red particulate mist that hung around her master in place of a less unwholesome aura.

Nigel did air one bit of gossip which I chose to acknowledge here, because it has already given me one nice transition between paragraphs and promises to yield numerous more in the future. Just as I predicted in my Exquisite Corpse rave about *The Curved Jewels*, Tom Bradley evidently did, a while back, wind up getting into a fight with a bunch of Yakuza hireling-thugs. They were allegedly sicced on him by Hirohito-worshiping extreme rightists outraged over his portrayal of that dead god's grandson's penis as resembling "something you wouldn't want to step on at low tide" (as referenced above), and they got lucky enough to kill him, almost. It's not clear how many of them he sent to Kama Loka. The local "imperial" university's med school (which is supposed to be his last known place of employment; he's said to have taught conversational skills to their freshman dentistry majors—but I declare that idle bullshit) took him in, patched him up, and he woke up in the very vivisection chamber made famous on the front page of tombradley.org.

Some say that shock is what made him wind up weird as he is today—but I hesitate to ascribe such feelings of delicacy or squeamishness to my man. If he'd been born at the time, the good doctor could have witnessed firsthand the removal of our Gary Cooper-look-alike bomber pilots' living lungs, followed by the eating of their livers, sushi-style, at festive banquets under the proud Rising-Sun banner, and gotten off with half as many bad dreams as I'll take from this one-day visit to Gloverland.

Nigel happened to agree with me on this point. He ascribed Dr. Bradley's current eccentricity to another sort of trauma entirely. Winding himself up for the sort of actual sentence production that enthralled his American employees as surely as a line of spit glistening on a concrete floor hypnotizes broody hens, he declared, "Your man has been driven mad by neglect. Poor old bugger is a walking rebuke to the Yank literary establishment, is what he is. What's with your powers-that-be over there? At least our powers-that-be gave Auberon and Martin a fighting chance to rise up from obscurity. That such an artist should have to live in a place like this, among sods like us, eking out a living in one of the most degrading ways imaginable—fuck me, isn't that what drove your own Ezra Pound crazy? Seeing the best minds of his particular generation waste their vitality behind the cunting Berlitz podium? No wonder he scampers about in the night air, all frantic, the sad, windy cunt. He'll catch his death of pneu—"

The last word was cut off by the expected pathological symptom. I took advantage of Nigel's incapacitation to speak up and express my sincere doubt that Dr. Bradley ever lived by teaching, contrary to the legends, the gossip, the novels, the essays, the promo copy, and everything else on and off the record. And the TEFL trash backed me up, bravely contradicting their boss (on whose lap the Filipina baby was now dozing like a puppy just come in from being injured in the gutter):

"Are you, like, kidding, Nigel?"

"The big dude a instructor? In a classroom?"

"He couldn't, you know, get work? Not with all the Japanbasher, um, stuff he has wrote?"

Nigel exploded: "He did these paltry shits a huge favor writing about them. He's the all-American high school quarterback with the golden heart, who danced a slow one at the prom with the wallflower wog who don't talkie za Amellican so goot. But is she grateful, the slag? I should think not. He's been unofficially declared an enemy of the state. I'm surprised he hasn't been deported or accidented away by some hit and run tail-gater. I've heard that his visa hasn't been renewed. He's rotted here longer than most of you wankers have sucked air, and is still on a one-year renewal. He's enduring exile within exile."

The lap dancer awakened from her junkie nod-off, and, in distressingly good English, said, "Our Sweet old Tommy's just like a restless ghost. He's got unfinished business that he can't get done, but tries over and over again, anyway. He shunts and shuffles from one Boom Town to the other and back again."

"Know what?" said her master. "Nobody cares what you think. Roll us a joint, you silly cow." At the first glimpse of cigarette papers, Nigel commenced depositing a blackish-red film of tracheal tissue on the walls and beers and people all around.

"It's Hiroshima he's published novels about, not us," murmured the Filipina in a defiant little voice as she licked a gummed edge. "But I think he was just looking for Nagasaki in Hiroshima."

The extent to which I was willing to disclose what I had

learned to these profane ears was only to say, "He has a particular connection to this town."

I've seen something impossible of attainment for the usual matter-mired pilgrim, and am in danger of winding up sad as Kevin Klein's Bottom the Weaver on the morning after, but without the considerable consolation of Michelle Pfeiffer's scent and angel hairs lingering and clinging about my person in a golden fairy mist. I do have a few bristles which sloughed off onto me at the moment of contact, beastly-coarse, but seraph-hued, which I am saving in a lid baggie to show any of you, if you're ever in Osaka between now and, say, 2050, and remember to look me up. It won't be too hard to find me in the ghost town. I'll be the one burrowed in like a fox among Jerusalem's rubble.

Meanwhile, confident that the voices of this hole in the seawall will never be heard outside its confines, I, Cye Johan, who am turning out to be Dr. Bradley's full-blown biographer, hereby, for all eternity, suppress all but one more of Nigel's whispered factoids about my subject. I've got no problems with him "living in a bleeding car," because my imagination could never place the creator of Sam Edwine between four stationary walls, anyway. So I will now, before your very eyes, cause Tom Bradley to live on wheels, just as the Limey said.

As a matter of fact, I have just decided to recollect that I did pass a ratty van on my way up the good doctor's mountain, somewhere between the mongooses and the bosozokus. I noticed it because it was covered in dents and scratches—still rarities, for the time being, even in nose-diving Nippon. Maybe he's sticking around just so he can play the trend-setter when these anal-retentives are forced by their own penury to transport their humiliated selves in rusty jalopies.

Sunken lopsidedly into its suspensions, this old van, to whose existence I am prepared to swear in the presence of a notary public, was clearly accustomed to bearing a heavy load on the drivers' side, but, perhaps sadly, none on the other. Like me, does he have an anorexically skinny wife? And scrawny kids? How can I be said to have profiled and interviewed a man when the most fundamental questions are left up in the air? Religious perusals of his works, print and electronic, yield exactly counterbalancing contradictory suspicions. I'm not even sure if the big fellow is a hetero. I could have asked Nigel, but was unable, as the word "profanation" loomed before my mind's eye like a red sign nailed to a cinder-brick wall.

I like this idea better and better the more I think about it. Living in a car is quite an accomplishment. It shows a practical-minded resourcefulness that you wouldn't expect in a literary figure, especially in this overpoliced state. Not that Japanese police do any crime solving to speak of, just peeping, aided by "neighborhood association" housewives—which leads to the question of where he could stop and sleep. I'll work on that. Maybe I will create the greatest of all Japanese implausibilities: an unpopulated stretch of land large enough to park a motor vehicle upon without paying dearly for the privilege.

And, having accomplished that, I will wedge our novelist in his van, probably stretching him out on the diagonal. I'll let him rest from his labors, and snore as far into the broad day-light as his big dark heart desires. Then I'll skulk back to my origami house, raw-fish wife and disemboweling job.

He learned me his language. Should I curse him for it?

TOM BRADLEY taught British and American literature to Chinese graduate students in the years leading up to the Tiananmen Square massacre. He was politely invited to leave China after burning a batch of student essays about the democracy movement rather than surrendering them to "the leaders." He wound up teaching conversational skills to freshman dentistry majors in the Japanese "imperial university" where they used to vivisect our bomber pilots and serve their livers raw at festive banquets. But his writing somehow sustains him.

Various of Tom's novels have been nominated for The Editor's Book Award and The New York University Bobst Prize, and one was a finalist in The AWP Award Series in the Novel.

Reviews, excerpts, links to his online publications, plus a couple hours of recorded readings, are at http://tombradley.org

SPUYTEN DUYVIL
Meeting Eyes Bindery
Triton